THE PERFECT VICTIM

"Castillo has a winner! I couldn't stop turning the pages!"
—Kat Martin, *New York Times* bestselling
author of *The Fire Inside*

"*The Perfect Victim* is a gripping page-turner. Peopled with fascinating characters and intricately plotted . . . compelling suspense that never lets up. A first-class reading experience!"
—Katherine Sutcliffe,
bestselling author of *Darkling I Listen*

"Intense action . . . sizzling sex . . . a thrilling climax . . . The reader is carried along on the ride."
—Lynn Erickson, author of *On Thin Ice*

"Linda Castillo delivers a powerhouse punch."
—Merline Lovelace

"An exciting thriller . . . action-packed [and] powerful . . . A strong tale that fans of suspense will love."
—*Midwest Book Review*

"Realistic dialogue, beautifully vivid descriptions, and an intricate plot add up to a chilling, fast-paced, riveting read."
—*Library Journal*

"Linda Castillo takes readers on a dear and treacherous journey. The perfect blend of suspense and sensuality . . . Masterful, heartwarming, and heart-stopping . . . an author to watch."
—*Romantic Times*

"Action, chills, and a scintillating romance."
—*The Romance Readers Connection*

The
Shadow
SIDE

Linda Castillo

B

BERKLEY SENSATION, NEW YORK

THE SHADOW SIDE

A Berkley Sensation Book / published by arrangement with the author

PRINTING HISTORY
Berkley Sensation edition / July 2003

Copyright © 2003 by Linda Castillo
Cover design by Pyrographx
Text design by Julie Rogers

ISBN: 0-425-19102-8

A BERKLEY SENSATION™ BOOK
Berkley Sensation Books are published by The Berkley Publishing Group, a division of Penguin Group (USA) Inc., 375 Hudson Street, New York, New York 10014.
BERKLEY SENSATION and the "B" design are trademarks belonging to Penguin Group (USA) Inc.

PRINTED IN THE UNITED STATES OF AMERICA

10 9 8 7 6 5 4 3 2 1

I have a lot of people to thank for helping to make this book a reality, either for moral support and encouragement or for lending an amateur their expertise. First and foremost, I'd like to thank my husband, Ernest, for his unending patience and support—I love you always. To my sister Debbie, who let me drag her to the cemetery in that little town just off the interstate. To my fabulous editor, Kim Waltemyer, for having the vision to make this story a reality—and a very talented red pen. To my agent, Jennifer Jackson, for having faith in my ability to tell the story—and for that really cool afternoon we spent in New York City. To Kathy Baker, the best bookseller in the business—thanks for always going above and beyond. To D.B. for answering my crazy questions and guiding me through the intricacies of a fascinating industry. To Sergeant Frank McElligott with the Plano, Texas, Police Department for patiently answering all my police procedure questions and never asking me why I was so interested in murder. Any and all errors included herein are mine, either from my own lack of understanding or my taking creative license. Finally, to my sisters in crime Cathy, Jen, and Vickie: thanks for sharing the dream—I love you guys.

"Thy soul shall find itself alone
'Mid dark thoughts of the gray tombstone—
Not one, of all the crowd, to pry
Into thine hour of secrecy."

—*Edgar Allan Poe,*
"Spirits of the Dead"

prologue

BLOOD RAN LIKE TEARS OVER THE PALAZZO TILE, trickling thick and dark down the walkway and into the cracks of the sidewalk. Rivulets gleamed black and wet in the stark glare of the porch light. The smell of violent death hung heavy in the air, like the zing of ozone after a lightning strike.

She lay on her back, alive, watching him through eyes glazed with shock. Eyes that had gone calm with blood loss and the acceptance of her impending death. Even in the throes of dying, she was lovely. Her robe had fallen open just enough for him to see the curve of her breast. The same breast he'd touched gently and lovingly countless times in the last four years. The hem of her robe rode high on her legs, exposing the silky flesh of her thighs.

The image of her lying there helpless and dying shouldn't have aroused him, but it did.

He stood silent and still beneath the light, shaking with rage, and watched her life drain away. He'd never seen so much blood, hadn't known a human body could bleed so much. The sight of it fascinated him, rousing something dark inside him, horrified him until he thought he would vomit.

God in heaven, what had he done?

He looked down at the gun in his hand, shocked yet strangely comforted by its deadly weight. Heart pounding, he opened his mouth and set the muzzle between his teeth. His hands shook, the cold steel rattling against his incisors. The barrel tasted of old gun oil and powder and the pungent tang of his own fear. He would join her now. They would be together in death as they had been in life. Together. Forever.

Closing his eyes, he squeezed the trigger.

And the world shattered.

chapter

1

ADAM BOEDECKER WOKE AS HE HAD NEARLY EVERY morning for the last three years—with a headbanger of a headache and the final vestiges of a nightmare clinging to him like a leech. He closed his eyes against the pounding in his head only to realize the sound was emanating from the living room. Someone was knocking on the door. Glancing at the clock next to the bed, he cursed. Who the hell was hammering on his door at four o'clock in the morning?

Not bothering with the light, he rose gingerly and set his bare feet on the floor. Two seconds of dizziness and then his head cleared. Every morning he was faced with the same moment of truth. And he uttered a silent but heartfelt thanks that the dizziness passed quickly. There had been too many mornings in the last three years when it hadn't.

Grabbing his sweatpants from the foot of the bed, he stepped into them and walked shirtless to the living room. At the door, he flipped on the porch light and looked through the peephole. A jab of alarm speared his gut when he saw a uniformed police officer and a disheveled-looking detective standing on his porch, their expressions grim. Adam recognized the detective from his days at the precinct. Ned O'Brien, homicide. The patrol officer beside him was young enough to be his son and looked more like a high school football star than a cop.

Adam didn't want to ponder why two of Chicago's finest were standing on his front porch at four o'clock in the morning. He opened the door.

"Detective Sergeant Boedecker." O'Brien stuck out his hand. "Adam. Sorry to bother you so early this morning."

Adam stared hard at the detective as he accepted the handshake, and felt a sinking sensation in his stomach. The other man stared back, his cop's eyes telling Adam the news wasn't good. O'Brien had that look about him. A look Adam had possessed too many times himself not to recognize it as a precursor to tragedy.

"This is Officer Miller." The detective motioned to the patrol officer.

Numbly, Adam shook the younger man's hand. "What's this about?"

"Lieutenant Henderson asked us to stop by and talk to you personally. I'm afraid we've got some bad news."

Adam braced, shoring up the scattered remnants of defenses that were too battered to do him much good. "What happened?"

"Your brother has been involved in a shooting."

"Michael? Jesus. Are you sure?" Adam couldn't seem to get his brain around the idea. A shooting involving his older brother didn't make sense. Michael had always been the good one. The successful one. The brother who'd devoted his life to keeping his nose clean.

The detective nodded.

"How bad?" Adam asked.

The patrol officer looked over his shoulder at the street beyond, fiddled with a nonexistent speck on his jacket. The detective grimaced, glanced down at his shoes. "I'm sorry, Sergeant, but he's dead."

Pain jolted Adam like the shock from a stun gun. He didn't believe it; his mind couldn't absorb the meaning of the words. Michael couldn't be dead. Not his only brother. Certainly not by an act of violence.

"Are you sure?" he heard himself say, realized with a keen sense of irony that was the first thing everyone asked when someone they loved was killed.

The detective jerked his head once, but his eyes said it all. There was no mistake.

Denial welled like blood on a wound. A dozen questions droned in his head, but Adam didn't trust his voice to speak. Because the two men were cops, they understood and gave him a moment to pull himself together.

"Jesus Christ." Raising his hand, he put it against the jamb and leaned, his mind reeling. "When?"

"We got the call a couple of hours ago. Neighbor heard shots, went around to the back patio, saw . . . blood. Patrolman swung by and called it in."

Blood. Christ. Adam closed his eyes, let out the breath he'd been holding. "How did it happen? Robbery? Home invasion? What?"

The two cops exchanged looks. Adam had been a cop long enough to know that look, too. And he knew the news of his brother's death wasn't the worst of what he would hear before all was said and done.

"Is there someone we can call for you, Sergeant?" the detective asked quietly. "Family member? Girlfriend?"

"The only thing I need is for you to tell me what the hell happened."

"Uh, we don't know the details."

That was the standard line cops used when they knew damn good and well what had happened—and didn't want to discuss it. Adam had used it a time or two himself over the years. It irked the hell out of him that they were using it on him now.

"I can handle it," he heard himself say.

"Sure you can, Sergeant. I didn't mean to imply otherwise."

The detective's politeness annoyed him. Adam didn't want polite. Not when the questions were punching through his brain with increasing ferocity. He wanted answers. And he damn well wanted them now.

"Were you at the scene?" he asked.

"You and I both know this isn't the time to get into the specifics," the detective said.

"There isn't ever a good time to talk about murder when it hits close to home."

Detective O'Brien didn't have anything to say about that.

Adam stared at him, incredulous that a fellow officer was going to stonewall him. "Cut the bullshit, Detective. Goddamn it, I'm a cop. I want to know what the fuck happened."

"You know I can't speculate—"

"I'm not asking you to speculate. Just tell me what you know."

"All I know is that a patrolman found two bodies. Both deceased from gunshot wounds. That's all we know at this point."

Two bodies. The words struck him like a jab to the solar plexus. That meant Michael's wife, Julie, had been killed as well. Adam had met her only a few times, but he'd liked her. Julie was a dark-eyed beauty with a pretty smile and quick wit. He wondered if the cops knew she'd been pregnant.

"Who do you want us to call for you, Sergeant?" the detective asked again.

Adam shifted away from the door, looked at his hands, realized they were visibly shaking. "Have you notified NOK?" he asked.

"The female's parents live in Miami. We're working on getting in touch with them."

"If you need phone numbers . . ."

"We've got them."

"What about . . . my mother, Nancy Boedecker?" A woman he hadn't seen in nearly six months, even though she lived less than an hour away in the suburb of Fox River Grove. "Has she been told?"

"We've got two detectives en route. That okay with you? If you'd rather be the one to break—"

"No. That's good. She'll need someone." Someone who

could look into her eyes and tell her the son she'd loved most was gone forever.

"You going to be all right, Sergeant? Do you want one of us to stay with you until someone gets here?"

Adam ignored the question. In the last three years, he'd seen to it that there wasn't anyone to call. Not for him. Certainly not now. "Did this happen at Michael's house?" he asked.

"Yes, 3553 Holland. Up in the Gold Coast area."

"Who's the primary?"

The detective looked uncomfortable. "Sergeant Deaton."

Scrubbing a hand over his face, Adam muttered a curse. Just when he was certain the situation couldn't get any worse, it did—exponentially. His ex-partner was the last person he wanted to deal with. It was bad enough losing his brother. But facing off with a man who'd betrayed him in the worst possible way a man could be betrayed promised to make this hellish day even worse. Adam had had a lot of bad days in the last three years. He figured one more heaped atop a few hundred others wasn't going to make much difference now.

ADAM KNEW BETTER THAN TO SHOW UP AT THE crime scene. By doing so, he was breaking a long list of departmental regulations that dealt with a police officer's personal involvement in a case. On the other hand, he'd never put much weight in rules. There were some things a man needed to do, rules be damned. Finding out how and why his brother had died was one of those things, even if he knew that bitch, fate, wasn't going to make it easy.

But while the part of him that was a cop—that would always be a cop—knew coming here was a mistake, the part of him that was a brother couldn't stay away. It didn't matter that he hadn't been on active duty for three years. Half the cops here wouldn't even remember him. The other half would watch him very, very carefully.

Slamming the door of his Tahoe, Adam turned up the

collar of his trench coat against the driving sleet and headed for the flashing lights. Michael and Julie's town house was located in an upscale section of Chicago that catered to the upwardly mobile crowd Adam had never quite fit into. The normally quiet area was lit up like a football stadium. Police cars blocked both ends of the street, diverting through traffic even though there wasn't much at this ungodly hour. Uniformed cops swarmed within the maze of cars, their breath spewing white vapor into the cold air as they spoke into their police radios. Curious neighbors in designer robes stood on their front porches and watched the scene unfold with the same fervor as if they were watching an episode of *NYPD Blue*. The Crime Scene Investigation Unit van was parked curbside directly in front of the town house, its engine rumbling, the smell of diesel fuel filling the air. Next to it, the medical examiner's van eased away from the curb and pulled on to the street.

Adam tried not to think about the two bodies inside the vehicle. The two vital people whose lives had been cut short by violence. He couldn't think of them on a personal level. Not when his emotions were scraped raw and guilt sat like a boulder in the pit of his stomach. He needed to get through the next few hours first. He had to find out what happened before he let himself feel, before he let the grief overwhelm him.

Adam walked up the sidewalk toward the front door. Yellow crime scene tape stretched around the narrow porch, the ends flapping in the bitter wind coming off Lake Michigan a few miles to the east. A frazzled-looking female patrol officer had been assigned the crime scene perimeter, and she didn't look happy about it. Adam didn't envy her the duty, but he wasn't going to make her job any easier. She shot him an annoyed look when he reached for the tape and ducked under it.

"I'm sorry, sir, this is a secure area. Step away from the tape."

"It's Detective Sergeant Boedecker." He flashed his badge and a nasty smile. "I've got a free pass." Ignoring her sour expression, he crossed the porch. She snapped something at him behind his back, but he didn't turn around, and he didn't stop.

The front door stood open. Adam paused at the doorway a moment, trying to get his bearings, and watched the crime scene techs work. He could feel a headache building at his temples like a thunderhead gaining momentum and promising a violent release. The worst of the shaking had subsided, but his hands weren't yet steady. He didn't want to face Chad Deaton like this, aching inside and not sure how he was going to handle any of it, but Adam didn't think his emotional state was going to improve in the next five minutes, so he put the thought out of his head and concentrated on getting through this one minute at a time.

He entered the foyer. The crime scene team had spread out in the living room and begun the tedious task of gathering evidence. A young female tech videotaped the scene with a camera small enough to fit in her palm. An African-American man wearing tiny round glasses knelt and plucked minute particles from the carpeted floor with tweezers and placed the evidence in plastic bags.

Adam scanned the living room, the familiarity of it striking a chord within him. The big-screen TV Michael had bought Julie for Christmas last year stood silent and dark. The coffee table where Michael had liked to put his feet when the Bears played on Sunday afternoons held a coffee cup and the morning edition of the *Tribune*. Adam tried to remember the last time he'd been here, realized he couldn't. How long had it been? One month? Two? How many times in the last year had Michael called him with an invitation? How many times had Adam not even bothered to return his call?

Grief encroached, an invading army pushing forward and gaining momentum. He tried to slap it back, put it in a compartment for later, but the emotion was snarling and sharp and ripped into him like a rabid beast.

Shoving his hands in the pockets of his trench coat, Adam stepped into the living room and tried to look at the scene through the eyes of the cop he'd once been. But it had been three years since he'd worked a crime scene, and the mind-set eluded him. Simply vanished. As if it had never existed, as if he'd never been a decorated homicide detective with one of the highest solve rates on the force. Three years was a long time to be away from the job. He felt like an intruder, a foreigner.

He didn't feel like a cop anymore.

"Adam."

He jolted at the sound of his name, turned to see Detective Chad Deaton stride toward him, his face set. Unlike Adam, the other man hadn't changed much in the three years since they'd worked together. He still looked more like a movie star than a veteran homicide detective. Back when they'd been partners, they'd gotten a good laugh out of his good looks and penchant for Italian suits sand leggy blondes. Neither of them was laughing tonight.

Chad wore a troubled expression that was half surprise, half annoyance, and a custom-made suit that was badly wrinkled and smelled of coffee and cigarettes.

"You look like you've been up all night, Chad. What do you have?" Adam asked.

"What are you doing here?" Deaton stopped less than a foot away, his gaze level. "You shouldn't be here."

"This involves me."

"You know better than to show up here."

"It's nice to see you again, too, Chad. How's tricks?"

Deaton scowled at him. "Go home, Adam."

"How's my wife?"

"Damn it, Adam. This isn't the time or place—"

"Sorry. Ex-wife. Give her my best, will you?"

Rubbing his hand across his mouth, Deaton cursed. "Why the hell aren't you with your mother and sister, for chrissake? They need you a hell of a lot more than I do."

"Because I'm a better cop than I am a son or brother." Adam looked past him, toward the kitchen where another detective stared at them, shaking his head. "This is where I need to be."

"I'm sorry about Michael."

Adam winced. The last thing he wanted was this man's sympathy. "I need to be in on this."

"You know I can't allow that." Deaton grimaced. "For

too many reasons to count, not the least of which is that you're the deceased's brother, for God's sake."

"Tell me what happened."

Deaton sighed unhappily. Adam figured the other man would rather be anywhere than where he was at this moment. Adam would have drawn some satisfaction from that knowledge if the feeling hadn't been so goddamn mutual. He and Chad Deaton went back a lot of years. They'd once been friends. Fifteen years earlier they'd gone through the academy together. They'd partnered up in some of Chicago's toughest neighborhoods for the better part of six years. They'd passed the sergeant's exam together, gotten their detective shields within a year of each other. Deaton had been Adam's best man when he got married. Deaton had been with Adam the night of the shooting. The night a fifteen-year-old kid with crack in his veins and a grudge against cops had stuck a Saturday night special against Adam's head and pulled the trigger.

"Let's take a walk."

Deaton tried to take his arm, but Adam shook it off. "Fuck that."

"Don't make this any more difficult than it already is, Adam. You may think I'm a son of a bitch, but you know I'll do right by Michael."

As much as Adam disliked Deaton, he knew the other man was a good cop. But the knowledge didn't take his temper down.

"Let's go." Deaton started for the door.

Knowing a confrontation would be counterproductive at this point, not certain if he was up to it in the first place, Adam fell in to step beside him. They walked in silence down the sidewalk toward the street.

The crowd had thinned. The curious neighbors had gone back inside to their down comforters and flannel sheets. Only the crime scene van, a couple of police cars, and a television news van remained. The sky was still dark, but dawn was only an hour away. The sleet had stopped, but a bone-chilling wind had kicked up off the lake and Adam felt the cold all the way to his marrow.

They stopped at the curb. Adam looked back at the

town house, felt another punch of shock as the finality of what had happened sank in a little deeper. Two people he'd loved were dead, their lives stolen by a senseless act of violence. The side of him that was a cop ached to be part of the investigation, to find the person responsible. The side of him that was a brother cried out with the pain of his loss and the shadowy need for revenge.

He looked at Deaton, felt another emotion unfurl, an uncomfortable awareness he had absolutely no desire to deal with. Adam's ego had taken a beating over the last three years. He might not be a cop anymore, but he was damn well still a man. Enough of a man to think about the woman who was keeping Chad's bed warm while he was out on this godforsaken night.

Jesus Christ. What a mess.

Deaton reached into the pocket of his trench, pulled out a pack of cigarettes, and lit up. He offered one to Adam, but he declined. A man in his condition chose his vices wisely. Smoking wasn't one of them.

"Tell me what happened," Adam said after a moment.

When Deaton didn't answer, Adam shot him a hard look. "You owe me, goddamn it."

"I don't owe you a thing," the other man snapped. "I could have busted your balls back there, but I didn't."

"You didn't bust my balls because you owe me."

Deaton looked toward the town house, took a drag off the cigarette. "It's ugly, Adam. You're not going to like it."

"My brother is dead. I already don't like it."

Taking another drag off the cigarette, Deaton tossed it to the ground and crushed it with the toe of his wing tip. "Christ, it's cold out here. Let's go sit in my car."

Deaton's unmarked Crown Victoria was parked curbside. The two men crossed the street. Deaton slid behind the wheel and started the engine. Adam took the passenger seat. He wondered why Deaton wouldn't look at him, felt the hairs on his nape prickle.

"It looks like a murder-suicide."

Adam felt the words like a sharp instrument twisting just behind his breastbone. Denial tangled with grief. He stared at Deaton, looking for a lie, praying for a lie. "That's not possible," he heard himself say.

"You asked. That's my preliminary finding."

"Your preliminary finding is wrong. Michael wouldn't . . . For chrissake, he wasn't in that frame of mind." God, he sounded just like the dozens of faceless, nameless civilians he'd devastated with terrible news in the course of his career.

"We'll check ballistics and prints, but it's cut-and-dried. I saw the bodies. I've seen enough to know what happened. He cut her. He shot her. Then he shot himself."

Holy Christ. "There's got to be a mistake. . . ."

"There's no mistake. I'm sorry. Damn it, you asked. I'm telling you the way it is."

Adam looked out the window toward the town house. Grief was a lead weight on his chest. He didn't believe the brother he'd grown up with would murder his wife, then take his own life. Not the Michael who'd believed Adam's career to be too violent. Not the Michael who'd reached out to Adam and seen him through some of the darkest days of rehab.

"Did you find any brass?" he asked.

"We dug one slug out of the wall. Sent it to the lab for ballistics." Deaton turned up the heater. "It's not going to change anything."

"I want in on the investigation."

"That's not going to happen. You're not even on the active roster, for God's sake."

"So I'll get back on the roster."

Deaton made a sound that was half exasperation, half laugh. "I hate to remind you of this, buddy, but you're on long-term disability."

"I'm ready for full duty. I've been ready for weeks."

"That's not my call. You do what you have to do, but you're *not* going to work this case."

"Henderson wants me back. He's been trying to reach me."

"Yeah, and from what I've heard, you haven't bothered to return his calls."

"I've been busy." Adam rolled his shoulder, wondering

about the rumor mill. "I've got physical therapy two days—"

"Cut the bullshit. You've been avoiding coming back because you don't want a desk job. Ruffles your ego."

For a moment, Adam wanted to point out that what ruffled his ego was when Deaton had slept with his wife while he'd been in the hospital recuperating from a devastating brain injury. But Adam figured they both had enough on their plates at the moment without getting into ancient history. He didn't want Shelly back, but it never ceased to infuriate him that the two people he'd trusted most had been carrying on while he'd been fighting for his life.

"I want in on this," he repeated.

Deaton cut the engine. "Go home, Adam. I would imagine your mother could use a shoulder to cry on right now. Go home to your mother and sister. They need you. I sure as hell don't."

chapter
2

ONE OF THESE DAYS, ELIZABETH BARNES WAS GOING
to live someplace warm. Someplace with balmy breezes
and palm trees and sandy beaches. A place where the
water was crystal blue year round, and the fishermen
didn't have to chop a hole in the ice to fish in January.
Someplace where the temperature never got below sixty
degrees, and the locals had never seen the likes of sleet
or snow or wind chill.

Someday.

Balancing a box of doughnuts with one hand, Eli set
down her overstuffed briefcase with the other, dug her
security card out of her purse, and swiped it through the
card reader. The tiny green light flickered, and the lock
clicked. Scooping up her briefcase, she shoved open the
door with her hip and walked into the darkened lobby of
Roth Pharmaceuticals.

It was Friday and not yet seven A.M., so the building
was still relatively quiet. Recessed lighting cast a soft
glow on walls painted a drab institutional blue. Framed
oil paintings by amateur artists from the University of
Michigan's art department adorned the lobby walls with

abstracts and stills. The carpet muted the sound of her pumps as she crossed to the receptionist's desk.

Most of the scientists had already raided the coffee station and retreated to their respective offices or laboratories to immerse themselves in the dynamics of nucleic acids, the validity of teratogenic testing or, perhaps, a quick game of FreeCell before starting their day. They tended to be a reserved bunch and more than a little predictable in their daily routines and work habits. The more rowdy administrative staffers didn't arrive until eight. While Eli fell solidly within the first group as far as her profession went, she'd never quite managed the reserved part.

Stopping at the receptionist's desk to retrieve her messages, she looked down at the check-in sheet where all employees were required to sign in each morning and noticed that her direct supervisor, Dr. Walter Sanchez, director of research and development, had already arrived. Fleetingly, she wondered why he'd come in so early when he normally didn't arrive until nine.

Next to the sign-in sheet, some good-humored soul had typed a verse titled "The Office Prayer," which read: *Grant me the serenity to accept the things I cannot change, the courage to change the things I cannot accept, and the wisdom to hide the bodies of those people I had to kill today because they pissed me off. Also, help me to be careful of the toes I step on today, as they may be connected to the ass that I may have to kiss tomorrow.*

Eli laughed outright and added her nickname, which she pronounced with a long "i," to the sign-in sheet and a smiley face next to the verse. She was halfway down the hall before she glanced at her stack of messages. The one on top was from none other than Roth Pharmaceuticals' founder and owner, Peter Roth, and stopped her dead in her tracks.

Congratulations.

Her heart began to pound as the possibilities simmered at the back of her brain. Eli forced herself to take a calming breath. She was *not* going to jump to conclusions over a cryptic message. She knew better than to get her hopes up. As far as she knew, Peter was congratulating her on that lime green Volkswagen she'd driven off the show-room floor last week.

Still, after ten years of sixty-hour work weeks, of putting her heart and soul and every ounce of knowledge and energy she possessed into a single-minded goal, could it be that one of her longtime dreams was about to come true?

The possibility staggered her.

Winning the Distinguished Woman of Science Award by the American Institute of Scientific Research was a goal she'd held dear to her heart since attending the awards ceremony at the University of Michigan nearly fifteen years ago. The experience had moved her profoundly and left a lasting impression on her young mind.

Eli had always known she would devote her life to pharmaceutical science. As a teenager, she'd seen first-hand the ravages of disease. She'd seen more suffering and death by the time she was twenty years old than most people saw in a lifetime. The images branded into her brain had left an indelible mark on her soul and scars on her heart that she would carry with her the rest of her life. Taking to the front lines in the battle against disease was the only way she could fight back.

Shaking off the memories, Eli continued down the corridor toward her office. In spite of her practical nature, she couldn't curb the swift kick of excitement or the ensuing swell of pride at the thought of the award. Closing her eyes briefly, she held the message against her chest and fought back an uncharacteristic rise of emotion. The giddy laugh that followed wasn't a dignified sound—not for a scientist, anyway—but there was no stifling it.

She wondered if Walter knew what the message was all about. The thought of sharing this with her best friend and mentor made her laugh outright again. Without Walter, none of it would have been possible.

Eli had been fresh out of the University of Michigan when Dr. Sanchez had hired her as his assistant. She'd had no experience, no related internship or credentials, and a bad case of first-interview jitters. But Walter had seen through the inexperience and nerves and hired her on the spot. Months later, when she finally mustered the courage to ask him why, he'd simply replied: "Because you have passion."

In the years since, Walter had generously shared his wisdom, experience, and undying love of pharmaceutical science. Hungry for knowledge and equally driven, Eli soaked it up like a sponge. She earned her Ph.D. in biology. And, under Walter's intense tutelage, she learned more in ten years than many scientists amassed in a lifetime.

Not bad for a farm girl from Indiana.

On reaching her office, she set her briefcase on the floor, fought the key from her purse, unlocked the door, and shoved it open with her hip. The familiar smells of recirculated air, paper dust, and yesterday's toner greeted her like an old friend. The office was a closet-sized room with a spindly ficus tree and a small window that looked out over the parking lot. Not glamorous by any means, but to Eli it was her castle.

Flipping on the light, she tossed her briefcase onto the visitor's chair adjacent her desk. Out of habit, she reached for the CD player atop her credenza and pressed the power button, and the gossamer notes of Bach drifted from the speakers.

"I see you brought bagels."

She spun at the sound of Walter's voice, the box in question slipping from her hand and landing on the carpeted floor at her feet with a thud. A dozen emotions churned in her chest when she saw him standing just inside her office door in his customary lab coat and baggy trousers. Walter Sanchez might have a poker face when it came to gin rummy, but one look into his bespectacled blue eyes and she knew. She *knew*.

For a moment she couldn't move, didn't trust her legs to cross the distance between them, her voice to speak. Then she was rushing toward him. Vaguely, she saw his arms open. She heard laughter, realized it had come from her. She went to him, put her arms around him, and squeezed hard.

"Doughnuts," she whispered.

"What?"

"Doughnuts. Not bagels."

"Oh. Good." He hugged her back fiercely. "I brought the champagne."

"French?"

"Of course."

Laughing, she hugged him harder and blinked back the burn of tears. "I got the award, didn't I?"

"You did it," he replied.

She'd never heard his voice quiver before. Not Walter Sanchez, the coolheaded scientist who relied on fact and objectivity to guide him through a life that had been as fascinating and diverse as hers was ordinary. But his voice trembled like a plucked violin string at the mention of the prestigious Distinguished Woman of Science Award.

"Pinch me," she said.

"Male superiors get into serious trouble these days for pinching female subordinates."

She smacked him good-naturedly on the shoulder.

After a moment, Walter cleared his throat and eased away from her just enough to look at her over the tops of his bifocals. His white goatee was freshly trimmed this morning. His breath smelled of the imported mints he kept in the pocket of his lab coat. As usual, he wore a tad too much Old Spice aftershave.

He set the bottle of champagne on her desk with a hand that wasn't quite steady. "I gather that was you who was giggling like a schoolgirl in the hall a moment ago."

"Guilty." She wiped at her eyes. "I can't believe it."

"Believe it, Eli. You deserve to be recognized for your work and dedication. You've earned it." He gazed steadily at her, a grandfather admiring a grandchild who was secretly his favorite. "Not bad for a kid who has yet to see her thirty-second birthday, wouldn't you agree?"

"The Distinguished Woman of Science Award." Her voice broke on the last word. "I never dreamed—"

"Ah, yes, you did. You dreamed. That's one of the first things I saw in you, Eli. You know how to dream, and you know how to dream big."

He was right. She'd always been full of dreams. The

dreams of the lonely little girl she'd been growing up in a small town in Indiana had been silly, frivolous. But the dreams she'd forged as a young woman had grown into goals. Goals she'd made great personal sacrifices to achieve. Eli had dreamed of this moment for so long, now that it had come, the meaning was almost too enormous to absorb.

"The world is a better place because of Valazine." Walter's rheumy eyes looked larger than they really were as he contemplated her through the thick lenses of his wire-rimmed glasses. "Your mother would have been proud of you, Eli."

The words moved her so profoundly that for a moment she feared the tears she'd been holding at bay since reading Peter Roth's message were going to break free and she was going to end up embarrassing herself.

"Thank you," she said.

Walter put his hands on each side of her face, drew her to him, and kissed the top of her head. "I'm incredibly proud of you, too."

Needing a moment to rein in her emotions, Eli turned toward the fallen box of doughnuts and picked it up. "If I'd known we were going to be celebrating, I would have brought something a little more appropriate."

"Ah, Friday doughnuts. What could be more appropriate for a celebration of this magnitude?"

"Caviar. Truffles . . ."

"Just between you and me, I prefer apple fritters over caviar any day." Taking the box from her, Walter set it on her desk, then proceeded to uncork the bottle of champagne.

"Shall we wait for Thomas?" she asked, referring to Dr. Thomas Bornheimer, the clinical research associate who'd been an inherent part of the R & D team from the beginning. "I'm sure the rest of the team will want to be in on the celebration."

The cork shot out of the bottle and struck the acoustic-tile ceiling. Smiling, Walter pulled two plastic champagne glasses from his lab coat, set them on the desk, and poured. He handed one of the glasses to Eli. "We'll have

lunch with Dr. Bornheimer and the rest of the team later."
He raised his glass. "Let's just you and I enjoy this toast
privately, shall we?"

Smiling, Eli clinked her glass to his. "To Valazine."

"Next, the Nobel Prize in Medicine. Cheers."

They drank the champagne in companionable silence,
smiling at each other on occasion, basking in a moment
Eli had worked toward for ten long years.

"This is going to be a busy week," he said after a moment.

"Parties. Dinners."

"Lectures and interviews."

"I imagine Peter is in his office, working on a press
release, at this very moment."

At the thought of the press release, another wave of
excitement jolted Eli. "When news of ROT-535 hits the
media—"

"Ah, one miracle at a time, my dear." Finishing his
champagne, Walter set the glass on her desk, then turned
to her. "I've achieved everything I've ever dreamed of
and more," he said. "This award for you is the icing on
the cake. I couldn't have asked for a more talented and
dedicated protégé."

Eli watched him, hearing something she couldn't quite
pinpoint in his tone, and felt a nagging sensation in her
chest. "Valazine is just the beginning," she said.

"Ah, your youth is showing, Eli. You're inexhaustible."

"I'm lucky if I can keep up with you."

"I'm seventy-four years old." At her so-what? expression, he cocked a brow. "The Energizer bunny I am not."

"You're seventy-four years *young*, Walter, and you
have more energy than anyone I've ever met, including
me."

"My memory is going—"

"You have a better memory than most of the interns
around here."

"I'm sure their lack of retention has more to do with
alcohol consumption than age or IQ." Smiling in his
grandfatherly way, he approached Eli and set his hands
on her shoulders.

She stared at him, knowing what he was going to say next and dreading it with every fiber of her heart. "Don't tell me you're still planning on retiring?"

He nodded. "I'm sorry, but yes."

It took every ounce of discipline she possessed not to try to talk him out of it. She knew that would have been selfish of her; they'd had this conversation before. Walter had worked hard on Valazine and its new and improved cousin, ROT-535, the clinical trials of which were scheduled to begin in a few months. She was well aware that the workload, the brutal hours, and the accompanying stress had taken a heavy toll on him.

"I know that look," he said gently.

"I always look this way when I'm biting my tongue."

He chuckled. "I'm tired, Eli."

The sad thing was, she *knew* he was tired. She'd seen the haggard look in his eyes. The fatigue etched into every time-worn line on his face. Hell, *she* was tired, and he was more than forty years older. The truth of the matter was he deserved to retire on this high note in his career. It was selfish of her to want him to stay simply because she enjoyed working with him. Because she owed everything to him. Because she loved him.

"You'd give up all this?" she said, making a sweeping motion that encompassed her cramped office and keyhole window, "for bridge and dominos?"

"Bridge and dominos is life on the edge for an old curmudgeon like me."

She was about to dispute that, but the serious glint in his eyes stopped her. "You're really going to do it this time, aren't you?"

"I'll be moving to Orlando next month. I've got a daughter there. Two grandchildren I haven't seen since they were babies."

"I'm . . . happy for you."

"Ah, my dear, you're a very bad liar, but I'd be terribly disappointed if you weren't."

"I'm that transparent, huh?"

Walter nodded. "I didn't want to bring the matter of my retirement up this morning, but Peter is going to announce it at the press conference. I didn't want you to find out that way."

"Thank you." She looked down to where her hands were twisted together. "I don't know what to say. I didn't realize you even had grandchildren."

"I divorced many years ago. I was much too devoted to my work, and I'm afraid I didn't make a very good husband." He shrugged. "I'm going to take my grandsons fishing."

"You hate to fish."

Walter chuckled good-naturedly. "You're missing my point." He caught her gaze, held it. "You know, a career makes for a cold bedfellow when your bones are as old as mine."

She frowned, knowing what was coming next. "You're not going to give me the old you-should-get-married-and-have-children lecture, are you?"

"I was working up to it."

"Don't. I'm happy. You know that."

"You're a workaholic, Eli. Admit it. If you didn't work here sixty hours a week, you wouldn't know what to do with yourself."

The need to defend the way she lived her life jumped through her, but she bit back a sharp retort. This wasn't the first time Walter had broached the subject. And it wasn't the first time Eli had disputed it. Of course, he didn't know about her complete inability to communicate with anyone who couldn't comfortably discuss pharmacoepidemiology or norepinephrine and serotonin reuptake.

"For your information," she began, "if I wasn't a so-called workaholic, as you so aptly put it, I wouldn't be standing here with you, discussing my Distinguished Woman of Science Award."

"Touché." He went to the desk and dug an apple fritter from the box. "And you dress too frumpily."

Eli resisted the urge to look down at her suit, trying hard not to be offended. "I'm a scientist. I'm supposed to dress frumpily."

"You've been hanging out with too many crotchety old men."

"Maybe I like crotchety old men."

"You're an attractive young woman. You should be going to fancy restaurants with attractive young men. You should be letting them woo you."

She put her hands on her hips, trying to look angry, unable to manage it because her personal life—or lack thereof—was the one area of her life she didn't quite have a handle on. "The only thing attractive young men woo is my patience."

He sighed. "Eli . . ."

"I have plenty of time for family . . . later." Not for the first time she wished she could make him understand that her one and only love would always be her work.

"Don't make the same mistake I did," he said.

Uncomfortable with the subject, not wanting to spoil the moment with an argument, she reached for an apple fritter. "It's going to be hard to find another colleague who likes Bach *and* doughnuts."

"Tough prerequisites, indeed."

They leaned against her desk, listening to Bach's *La Stahl* and eating apple fritters. Eli knew she was going to have to accept his retirement and go on with the research and development of ROT-535 without him. But, God, she was going to miss him.

"You *will* be at the awards ceremony, though, won't you?" she asked after a moment.

"I wouldn't miss it for the world."

chapter
3

FORTY-EIGHT HOURS PASSED BEFORE ADAM WAS able to get inside Michael's condo without running into a cop. The irony of the situation didn't elude him as he used the key Michael had given him and went in through the front door like he had every right in the world to be there.

Of course, he didn't.

The holster containing his police-issue Glock nudged his ribs reassuringly. His badge was clipped prominently to his belt. But Adam wasn't a cop anymore. Hell, he hadn't even been a decent brother. He had no lawful right to breech the crime scene of an ongoing investigation. In fact, he was about to commit a serious offense that could cost him more than his badge.

But Adam knew the badge was only a technicality these days. He also knew if he didn't get in touch with Lieutenant Stuart Henderson soon, his long-term disability was going to become a hell of a lot more permanent. The only reason he hadn't been fired yet was because it wasn't good PR for the department to fire a decorated detective who'd been shot in the line of duty. People hated it when a hero got the shaft—even if the hero had it coming.

Regardless of the shaky state of his career, Adam wasn't going to sit on the sidelines while the department investigated his brother's death as a murder-suicide. He wasn't going to let the media sharks destroy what was left of Michael's reputation. Adam might still be suffering the aftereffects of a traumatic brain injury, but his judgment wasn't so flawed that he believed Michael was a killer. He was willing to stake what was left of his career on it.

Closing the door behind him, he flipped the dead bolt and faced the dimly lit living room. The town house had the lifeless feel of a place that had been long vacant. Julie had kept a neat home, but magazines and books now lay in disarray on the floor. The knickknacks in the curio cabinet had been shoved aside and never put back. The sofa cushions had been removed and stacked haphazardly on the floor. It hit Adam then that he would never again walk in to this room and see Michael slouched on the sofa in his baseball cap. Adam's memory flashed to his brother sitting there, grinning like a fool because he'd just found out he was going to be a father. . . .

"Jesus, Mike." He scrubbed his hand over his face and walked into the kitchen. There wasn't enough light, so he risked turning on the overheads. Silver fingerprint powder mottled the tile countertops, the back door, and the front of the refrigerator. He wondered if the techs had lifted any prints. Careful not to touch anything, he walked through the kitchen and looked through the French door. A privacy fence surrounded the palazzo-tile patio. A walkway banked by winterized flower beds led to a gate and, Adam guessed, to the carport beyond. The chalk outline of two bodies glowed yellow beneath the glare of the porch light. Slipping latex gloves from the rear pocket of his jeans, he put them on and opened the door.

The night was bitterly cold. Even though it had been more than forty-eight hours since Julie's and Michael's deaths, the smell of blood hung in the air. An unpleasant metallic odor that made him want to hold his breath. The cops had tried to hose the blood off, but the water had frozen shiny and red between the tiles.

Adam stared at the stains, wondering if someone could

have come in through the back door and forced both Michael and Julie to the patio and then killed them. But why would an intruder kill them outside when he would have more privacy and make less noise indoors? Why had Julie been stabbed when the intruder had evidently been also armed with a gun? She'd had more than a dozen knife wounds. Those kinds of injuries were more consistent with a crime of passion than robbery.

He studied the frozen stains. Something dark and uncomfortable niggled at the back of his mind. "What the hell happened here?" he said aloud.

The police seemed relatively certain nothing had been taken. Deaton had sent a handgun and a butcher knife to the lab. Adam wondered if Michael had owned the gun. He wondered if Michael's fingerprints would be the only ones found.

Putting the chalk outlines to memory, he turned his attention to the rear gate. No lock. He clucked his tongue at the lack of security and strode to the gate, opened it, and peered out at the carport area and alley beyond. The lighting was poor, which would make good cover for a perp looking to score some quick cash from a rich yuppie.

Adam closed the gate and took a few steps toward the town house, noticing for the first time the blood spatter on the siding. The shooter who'd taken out Julie had been facing the town house. He looked down, found he was standing within the outline of Michael's body.

Cursing, he rubbed his left temple. The headache had receded to a dull throb that was barely discernable now, but Adam knew from experience that it could explode quickly and without warning. Because of the constant threat of migraines, he didn't go out much, but Michael's death was going to change that. This case was going to change his life because he wasn't going to let it go. Not until he knew the truth.

Kneeling at the French door, he studied the lock. Expensive brass knob and locking mechanism. Cheap bolt lock. Neither showed any signs of tampering. Security had been sacrificed for beauty. Adam grimaced. How very like Michael. He'd never been suspicious and had invariably trusted fate to be kind to him. He'd always seen the good side of people. Unlike Adam, who'd learned to trust no one, particularly fate, and to expect the worst from people, especially if he loved them.

Rising, he went back inside, closed the door and locked it behind him, then walked through the kitchen toward the bedroom. Most people kept their valuables in the bedroom. Jewelry. Money. Purses. Even if the perp had come in hoping to steal something as large as the TV or DVD player, if Michael had surprised him or put up a fight, the perp may have changed his mind and settled for something easy to carry.

The blinds were pulled and the bedroom was dark, so Adam chanced turning on the lamp beside the bed. The comforter was rumpled. A small spot of blood contrasted darkly against the pale green and lavender fabric. A section had been cut out, and he imagined the crime scene techs had taken a sample to the lab to be analyzed. Adam wondered whose blood it was and how it had gotten on the bed.

Retracing his steps, he walked into the hall and flipped on the light. A red stain marred the wall. Another single drop marked the floor at the kitchen threshold. A red smear blemished the front of the refrigerator. Combined, the trail of blood told him Julie had probably been stabbed in the bedroom, then somehow made it to the back porch. Jesus.

Back in the bedroom, he went to the dresser, where a bottle of men's cologne sat next to a silk tie, a cell phone, and the antique watch that had once been their grandfather's. As much as he didn't want to believe it, Adam knew a thief, no matter how stupid or rushed, would never pass up a watch like that.

Picking up the cell phone, he hit the redial button, saw Michael's home number come up on the display. Had Michael's last call been to let Julie know he was on his way home from the office? Adam set the phone down on the dresser, then opened the top drawer and rifled through boxer shorts, socks, and T-shirts. He looked through each drawer, then switched over to the night tables, only to find the usual junk people kept next to their beds. Paperback books, magazines, nail polish, and hand cream.

Growing frustrated, he went into the bathroom and flipped the light switch. Stark fluorescent light rained down on him. He looked in the mirror, saw a man with black, short-cropped hair with a hint of gray at each temple. He stared at his reflection a moment, startled by the severe features and dark, troubled eyes. He thought he looked older than his thirty-eight years, realized most of the aging had taken place in the last three.

He tried to imagine Michael looking into the very same mirror. Michael had been older by two years. Responsible. Levelheaded. Successful.

All the things Adam was not.

Closing his eyes, he tried to get inside his brother's head. An investment banker. Early to the office. Home late. A lot of responsibility. Power lunches. Dinner parties.

Adam couldn't do it, couldn't find the mind-set. As close as they'd once been, his brother had become a stranger in the last several years. Not because of anything Michael had or had not done, but because Adam had alienated him and just about everyone who'd once been close to him.

Staving off the press of guilt, he turned from the mirror and opened the first drawer. Julie's makeup. The sight of her ordinary things, things she'd painstakingly shopped for and bought, sent a pang through his gut. He hadn't known her well, hadn't allowed himself to get close to her, but he'd known she was a decent person. Michael had loved her. She hadn't deserved to get shot down like an animal.

Adam left the bathroom. Aware that his heart rate was up and that his hands weren't quite steady, he surveyed the bedroom, spotted the walk-in closet, and opened the door. The faint scents of cedar and cologne met him when he stepped inside. Julie's clothes hung neatly on the left, Michael's button-down shirts, suits, and Dockers on the right. Starting at the end of the rack, he began going through pockets, looking inside shoes and opening boxes and envelopes, checking for anything that might give him the answers he so desperately needed.

He was nearly finished when he came across a cylindrical-shaped object inside the breast pocket of one of Michael's suit jackets. Reaching inside, Adam pulled out a brown prescription bottle. Curious, he squinted down at the label, saw that the prescription was, indeed, for Michael. *Valazine. Take two tablets in the A.M. and two tablets in the P.M. with a full glass of water.* A smaller label warned that the medication may cause drowsiness.

Adam wasn't sure, but he thought Valazine was an antidepressant drug. What the hell was Michael doing with an antidepressant? Had he been depressed? Had he been despondent enough to murder his young wife and their unborn child, then turn the gun on himself? His gut told him no. Michael wasn't a violent man; Adam knew that in his heart. But as much as he didn't want to admit it, the evidence told a different story. Holding the prescription bottle in his hand, he realized the seed of doubt had taken root. The possibilities made him queasy.

The sound of the doorbell jolted him from his reverie. Cursing under his breath, he twisted the lid off the prescription bottle and shook out two pills. Removing an envelope from his trench coat, he dropped the pills inside, folded the envelope, and shoved it into his pocket.

The doorbell blasted again. Frowning, Adam replaced the bottle and left the bedroom, turning off lights as he went. At the front door, he checked the peephole. Uncertainty quivered in his gut. Chad Deaton, flanked by two uniformed patrol officers, stood on the front porch, looking none too happy to be out on a call in subzero weather at one o'clock in the morning.

Well, this was just dandy as hell.

Fishing the envelope out of his pocket, Adam stuffed it in the waistband of his jeans and opened the door.

Deaton glared at him. "Why aren't I surprised to find you here?"

"Maybe because this is my brother's house and I have every right to be here."

"This is a crime scene."

"I was just leaving." Adam reached into his trench for his gloves and keys.

"Like hell. Keep your hands where I can see them."

Adam raised his hands. "Hey, no problem."

"What the hell are you doing here?"

"I was driving by. Thought I saw someone inside."

"Why didn't you call the cops?"

"Because I am the goddamn cops."

The two patrol officers moved forward, but Adam held his ground, refusing to move aside. "Call off your dogs, Deaton," he warned.

Amusement glinted in Deaton's eyes. "Cuff him and make sure he didn't take anything from the scene."

Anger snapped through Adam, even though he'd expected this. "Fuck you."

"Don't make this any more difficult than it already is, Adam."

"Wouldn't dream of it." Temper pumping, Adam let one of the uniformed officers take his arm and guide him out to the front yard. With a great deal more respect than would have been used with a suspect, the officer pulled Adam's arms behind him and snapped on the cuffs.

"Nice job," Adam murmured.

"Thanks, Sergeant." The young officer shot him an uncomfortable look, then proceeded to pat him down, stopping cold upon finding the Glock.

Uh-oh.

"Sergeant Deaton." The officer upholstered Adam's weapon, then held it up with two fingers for Deaton to see.

"Jesus." Shaking his head, Deaton pinched the bridge of his nose. "Give it to me." He took the gun from the officer, released the clip, and dropped both into the pocket of his trench. He glared at Adam. "You stupid son of a bitch."

"Same goes."

"I might be a son of a bitch, but I'm not stupid enough to break into a crime scene and tamper with evidence."

"I didn't break in."

Deaton glared at him, then addressed the officer again.
"Take whatever key he used to get in."

"Yes, sir."

"It's on my key ring," Adam said to the officer. He
wouldn't be needing the key again. "Left pocket of my
trench."

The officer retrieved the key, then removed it from the
ring.

Adam looked at his ex-partner. "Do I need a lawyer,
Chad?"

"Do you want to make this official?" Deaton snapped.

When Adam only continued to stare, the other man
heaved a sigh. "Uncuff him," he said to the patrol officer.
"I'll take care of it from here."

Nodding once, the officer unlocked and removed the
cuffs.

Adam rubbed his wrists. "I hope you didn't enjoy that
as much as I think you did."

"If you pull a crazy stunt like this again, I'll bust your
ass." Deaton turned to the officers, thanked them for as-
sisting, and advised them not to file a report on this stop.

Adam waited until the two uniformed men had retreated
to their cruiser before speaking. "I want my side arm
back."

"Go tell the lieutenant. I don't want to hear it."

"Henderson likes me, Chad."

"Henderson thinks you're fucked in the head. So do I."

Adam didn't mention that he'd thought the very same
thing himself a time or two in the last three years. "I
appreciate your vote of confidence."

"I'm serious, Adam. Next time you get in my way, I'll
make damn sure you're off the force for good."

"It's not like I need your help with that."

"This is the last time I'm going to warn you."

"Next time I'll be more careful."

"You do that."

Silence built long enough for Adam to notice the bite
of wind coming through his trench. "What have you got
so far?" he asked.

Deaton scowled. "I've got two bodies in a case that's

about to be ruled a murder-suicide, then closed."

"You and I have been around long enough to know things aren't always the way they seem."

"Most times they are. Unless someone isn't ready to accept reality."

Adam swallowed the queasiness that tried to work its way up his throat. "Or unless some cop isn't willing to dig."

"It's over. Let it go."

Not for the first time, doubt twisted brutally inside Adam. That was the worst part about the head injury, he realized. Not trusting his own mind, his own emotions, the gut instinct that had once made him such a good cop.

"So, are you going to arrest me, or can I go?" Adam asked after a moment.

"Why don't you do yourself a favor and work on getting your shit together instead of beating your brains out on a case that's cut-and-dried and only going to screw up your already screwed-up career?"

"Advice from a friend, Chad?"

"Advice from a cop who's going to bust you next time."

"You and I both know you feel a little too guilty to do anything like that."

Even in the dim light coming off the sodium-vapor streetlamp, Adam saw the other man's face redden. "The wife part, not the shooting," Adam clarified. "I mean, it was my idea to go through that door first, wasn't it?"

"Fuck you, Boedecker."

Adam smiled. "Too late, Chad. Fate already did that." Turning on his heel, he started toward his Tahoe parked down the block and left Deaton staring after him.

ADAM HAD HAD HIS ASS CHEWED ENOUGH TIMES BY Lieutenant Stuart Henderson to know when the man was pissed. Noticing the color riding high in his cheeks, the pinched mouth, and the you're-dead-meat expression, Adam figured he'd be lucky to walk out with his badge.

He sat in the visitor's chair across from the lieutenant's

desk and watched the rain slip down the window, wishing
he was anyplace but where he was. Today was the first
time he'd been at the precinct since he'd been shot, and
he was more than a little uncomfortable. Some of the old-
timers who remembered that night gave him a wide berth.
The rookies who'd heard the stories—some true, some
not—all but saluted. The officers he'd worked with and
once called friends shook his hand and slapped him on
the back. But Adam saw the unspoken questions in their
eyes. He couldn't blame them. Cops just didn't know how
to react to a guy who'd had to learn the alphabet *after*
receiving his detective shield.

Shifting uneasily in the chair, he waited none-too-
patiently while Henderson finished his phone conversation. He shouldn't have been surprised by the lieutenant's
call at eight o'clock that morning, but he'd definitely been
caught off guard. In between the shouted curses, Adam
had understood enough of the one-sided conversation to
know he'd better show up. Henderson wasn't known for
subtlety.

Henderson hung up the phone and leaned back in his
high-back leather chair. "I guess you know why you're
here."

"I don't think it's to receive my award of valor."

Frowning, Henderson rose and walked over to the carafe on a side table near the window and dumped coffee
into a paper cup. "Coffee?" he asked.

"I'm cutting back."

"Right." Henderson went back to his desk and sat
down. "How are you feeling these days, Adam?"

"Are you asking as my superior who wants me to come
back to work, Lieutenant? Or as a friend who's concerned
about me because I got shot in the head and haven't been
right since?"

Henderson winced. "That's not goddamn funny."

Adam said nothing.

"I've been trying to reach you for two weeks. You
haven't been answering the phone or returning my messages."

For the dozenth time, Adam berated himself for answering his phone that morning. "I'll have to talk to my answering service about that."

Shaking his head, Henderson opened the manila folder in front of him. Adam saw his name and badge number on the folder, and a quiver of unease ran the length of him.

"I want you to come in for a physical," Henderson said after a moment. "A week from today. I've already set it up."

"Don't tell me you want to put me back on the street?"

"That will depend on what the doc says. You look fine to me. Your mouth seems to be up to par, anyway. If you're not fit for active duty, there are other positions available."

"I'm not up to desk work, Stuart. You know that."

"I'm not asking you if you're up to desk work, Sergeant. I'm telling you to come in for a physical. You've been on disability for three years. It's time to shit or get off the pot."

Blowing out a sigh, Adam watched the rain hit the window. It was mixed with sleet now and likely to change over to snow by afternoon. He figured he'd rather be running around naked in the cold than sitting here, waiting for his lieutenant to figure out what the hell to do with him. If life were only that cooperative.

"If you want back on the active roster, I suggest you adjust your attitude. A lot of fine police officers work behind a desk. There's no reason why you can't do it, too."

"I've worked the street for twelve years. That's what I want. You know that. We've had this conversation before."

"And your attitude pisses me off every time."

"That's good to know, Stu, but—"

"I want you to come in for a psych evaluation, too."

Adam had known that one was coming, but hearing the words spoken aloud made them even more brutal. Made him feel like maybe the other man thought he wasn't going to pass. Having often wondered the very same thing himself, he'd avoided putting himself to the test. "I guess that's what this meeting is all about, isn't it?"

"A psych evaluation is required after a police officer is involved in a shooting." Stuart cut him a hard look. "I know you've had a tough time of it. I'm not stupid, Adam. I know what happened."

Translated, Henderson was telling him he knew about Deaton and Shelly. Well, that was cozy as hell.

"This isn't personal," Henderson continued. "It's a department rule. Get the physical. Get the psych. And don't fuck it up."

"I'll do my best."

Henderson caught the sarcasm and shook his head. "For such a good detective, you can be amazingly stupid."

"Thanks."

"Deaton told me you showed up at your brother's condo last night."

"I was wondering when you were going to get around to that."

"He chose not to write it up."

"Well, that was big of him." *Especially since the bastard slept with my wife while I was in rehab learning to tie my shoes.*

The unspoken words hung in the air like a bad smell. Adam saw them in the other man's eyes, felt the brutal kick of anger in his blood.

"That little excursion last night could have cost you your badge."

"That'd be a hell of a note. How would the Chicago PD get along without me?"

Closing his eyes, Henderson visibly struggled for patience. "Pull yourself together, Adam. Get your physical. Come in for your psych. I'll see what I can do about putting you back on the street."

Adam heard the words, saw the attempt at sincerity, but he'd been around the block enough times to know when someone was blowing smoke. Henderson was blowing smoke like a chimney.

"I guess now would be a good time to tell you that Deaton missed something important at the scene." Adam knew that was the last thing the other man wanted to hear.

But he also knew Henderson was too good a cop to ignore it.

"You're not on that case, damn it. Stay out of it."

Adam rolled his shoulder, looked down at the floor, waited.

Stuart tapped his pen against his desktop. "Well, what did you find?"

"There was a prescription bottle with some pills in the right pocket of a man's tweed jacket in the bedroom closet, right side. Have Deaton send one of his uniforms over there. You might want to have it analyzed, see what's in it."

"Like you haven't already done that."

"Just trying to follow protocol, Lieutenant."

Henderson laughed, but it came out like a snarl. "Yeah, and I'm taking yoga classes."

Adam smiled, but he didn't feel anything even remotely close to humor.

"I don't want you and Deaton getting into a pissing contest over this case."

"With all due respect, we already have and Deaton has evidently outpissed me."

Grimacing, Henderson opened the desk drawer, pulled out Adam's Glock, and set it on the blotter between them. "Just get the physical, okay?"

Adam reached for the pistol, checked the clip and safety, then rose. "Anything else?"

"If it's not too difficult, stay the hell out of trouble."

"So what you got for me, Rosie?" Shaking the snow from his trench coat, Adam entered the cramped front office of Signal Laboratories two blocks from the precinct and addressed the Chinese man behind the counter.

Rosie Fam looked up from his work and smiled. "You going to owe me a lotta money, Boedecker, because I know you don't want this getting back to the department."

"Don't worry about the money, Rosie. Disability pays well."

"I could blackmail you, you know."

Adam smiled. "But you won't because you know I'd have to kill you."

Pulling a manila folder from a slot in the wall, Rosie walked over to the counter and handed it to Adam. "You ain't going to be able to make heads or tails of this, so I'll summarize for you. The pill you brought in is an MAOI inhibitor. An antidepressant called Valazine."

"You sure?"

"What do you mean am I sure? I stayed up all night last night doing the testing. Of course I'm sure."

Adam reached for the file, opened it, and scanned the first page. Rosie was right. He couldn't make heads or tails of the compounds broken down on the lab report. But he could damn well read the information at the bottom of the page. Valazine. Researched, developed, and marketed by Roth Pharmaceuticals, Ann Arbor, Michigan.

Adam reached for his wallet. "How much?"

Turning his nose up at the sight of the wallet, Rosie waved him away. "Your money's no good here, Boedecker."

"You can't bill this back to the department, Rosie."

"Yeah, I know. You're doing this on your own time."

"Just between you and me."

"Yeah, yeah, you already told me that."

"So what's the problem?"

"There's this old Chinese proverb."

"You have a Chinese proverb for everything. I think you just make them up."

"This Chinese proverb pertain to you, Boedecker. It say, never take money from a man with a hole in his head."

Adam laughed outright. "I'll try to remember that."

IN THE DIM LIGHT CAST BY THE BANKER'S LAMP IN his study, Adam stared at the computer monitor and read the article for the second time.

Sixteen-year-old Eric Rickerson, a junior at
Lewiston High School in Bartonville, Tennes-

see, went on a shooting spree Friday, killing
two of his classmates and wounding six others. Witnesses claim Rickerson burst into his
afternoon history class with a semiautomatic
pistol and began calling out names, shooting
each individual whose name he called. The
carnage continued for four minutes. By the
time it was over, two people lay dead. Six
others lay wounded, two critically, including
the teacher, fifty-four-year-old Sally Treece.

Rolling the mouse to the print button at the top of the
screen, Adam added the article to the growing stack in
the print tray.

A beating with a fatality in Gainesville, Florida. A
mother accused of murdering her two children in Dallas.
A factory worker who went berserk in Pittsburgh, killing
a coworker. Violent crimes committed by seemingly ordinary people with no criminal record and no history of
violent behavior. To someone not looking for a connection, the crimes would appear unrelated.

It had taken nearly a week, but Adam had found a connection. A tenuous one, but a connection nonetheless.

Using the mouse, he went back to the search engine
and typed in *Valazine*. The search produced over two-
hundred matches, the first linking him to the website of
Roth Pharmaceuticals in Ann Arbor, Michigan, the second
to a press release that had appeared in the *Ann Arbor
News*. He clicked on the second result and read:

Dr. Elizabeth Barnes, a scientist at Roth
Pharmaceuticals, a small, privately held pharmaceutical firm based in Ann Arbor, Michigan, has been awarded the prestigious
Distinguished Woman of Science Award by
the American Institute of Scientific Research
for her contribution in the research and development of a new generation of antipsy-
chotic and antidepressive drugs. Valazine,
which went on the market early last year, has

improved the lives of millions suffering from
treatment-resistant forms of depression and bipolar disorder, and from some forms of
schizophrenia. The thirty-one-year-old laure-
ate, a clinical research manager, will be honored with a dinner at The Dahlmann Campus
Inn.

The grandfather clock in the living room chimed three
times. Adam clicked the print button, then leaned back
and rubbed his eyes. He'd been at it since midnight and
could no longer ignore the headache ebbing and flowing
behind his brows. Shutting down the computer, he rose
and walked into the living room. The fire he'd started
earlier had burned down to embers but was still throwing
off some heat. He paused next to the hearth and brooded.

Seven unexplained murders in five states in less than a
year. Not unusual considering population and crime rates.
On the surface, there was nothing to connect any of the
killings. Except for a drug that had been on the market
for less than a year—a drug that had just gotten a young
scientist nominated for one of the highest honors in the
industry. And a pharmaceutical company that was poised
to make billions.

Adam had broken every rule in the book, but in the six
days since Michael's death he'd discovered more than a
dozen cases where an individual who'd been prescribed
Valazine had committed some type of violent act. Individuals with clean records and no history of violent behavior. He knew the angle was questionable—maybe
even desperate—but he'd been a cop for too many years
to believe in coincidence. He might not trust his instincts,
but Adam knew Michael wasn't a killer. No amount of
evidence would ever change that.

Lieutenant Henderson wasn't going to like it when he
found out Adam had been using his police credentials to
garner information from medical examiners and homicide
detectives across the country. But Adam couldn't ignore
his instincts on this—even if he didn't trust them. For the
first time in a long time he felt as if he were on to some-

thing; he felt it in his gut, like a bad case of food poisoning leaching into his system. The question was, how could he prove it without the resources of the PD? When his credibility was already on shaky ground?

Watching the embers in the fire hiss and glow, Adam rubbed his temples and contemplated his options. He wasn't going to walk away from this, even though he knew it was the smart thing to do. He couldn't, even knowing that launching his own investigation would probably spell the end of his career.

"What happened that night, Mikey?" he whispered. "What did you do?"

Outside, the wind whipped snow against the windowpanes. Dark possibilities and a growing suspicion percolated in his brain. And Adam knew with a growing sense of dread that he wasn't going to make that physical tomorrow.

chapter
4

ELI HAD JUST SETTLED DOWN IN FRONT OF HER COM-
puter with a cup of coffee and an unfinished draft of the
phase I protocol of the clinical trials for ROT-535 when
her phone buzzed. Never taking her eyes from the monitor, she pressed the intercom button.

"Dr. Barnes, Detective Adam Boedecker is here to see
you."

Detective Boedecker? Her concentration broken, Eli
gave the phone call her full attention. Grappling for her
engagement calendar, she paged quickly through it but
found no entry. "Does he have an appointment?"

"No, but he says he only wants a few minutes of your
time."

"Did he say what it was about?"

She heard the receptionist speak to the visitor, then the
receptionist came back on the line. "He says it's official
business, and he'd like to speak with you privately if you
have a few minutes."

Official business? With a detective? Torn between the
need to find out why a police detective wanted to talk to
her and her enthusiasm for the task at hand, Eli looked

longingly at her computer screen, then minimized the file. "All right. Send him in."

She was in the process of closing the report in front of her when a knock sounded. She looked up to see a tall man with dark, short-cropped hair and piercing brown eyes standing at the door, watching her intently.

Eli stared at him, taken aback by the image he presented, her only thought that he didn't look like a cop. Cops were safe. This man looked anything but safe. He had the rough-around-the-edges look of a man who'd seen a lot of things, and she could tell by the haunted look in his eyes that not all of those things had been good. He wasn't a handsome man. The planes of his face were too angular, his features imperfectly arranged. But it was a fascinating face nonetheless. The kind of face that told stories about a person. Stories she somehow knew would disturb her. Stories she probably couldn't imagine.

His jawline was rigid, his cheeks were hollowed, and the narrow slash of his nose led to a harsh mouth that was pressed into an unfriendly line. His eyes were the color of ebony beneath heavy, arched brows. Eyes that looked . . . battered. A keen intelligence shone there, but it was more street-smart than bookish, and Eli knew instinctively that her magna cum laude wouldn't be an advantage.

A black trench coat opened to reveal a nicely cut charcoal suit and conservative tie that were at odds with his rugged face. He was leanly built but seemed to fill the entire room even though he hadn't yet set foot inside. The word *dangerous* floated through her mind, but she quickly shooed it away. The man was a cop her intellect told her, not a mafioso.

But on a more fundamental level she couldn't ignore the rise of alarm that crept up her spine when he stepped into the room. His features were sharp, direct, his gaze focused entirely on her with an intensity that made her heart roll into an uneven staccato. Even though he was cleanly shaven, his five o'clock shadow gave him a menacing appearance that made her think twice about her decision to see him without an appointment—or a security guard standing by.

"Dr. Elizabeth Barnes?"

At the sound of his baritone voice, she rose abruptly, knocking her knee hard against her desk. "Please, call me Eli. How can I help you?"

"I'm Detective Boedecker." Glancing in the general direction of where she'd bumped her knee, he tugged a badge from his suit jacket and flipped it open. "Chicago PD."

She smiled and raised her hands. "I didn't do it."

"Homicide."

An awkward moment ensued when he didn't smile. Eli felt her face heat, surmised a sense of humor wasn't his strong point. "Sorry, I was . . . just kidding."

His smile looked like a poorly executed afterthought— or maybe he just had a bad case of indigestion. Moving forward, he extended his hand. "If you have a few minutes, I'd like to ask you some questions."

"Yes, of course." Rounding her desk, she reciprocated the handshake without hesitation. His hand was large and encompassed hers completely. The contact jolted her solidly, like a mild electrical shock that jumped from his hand to hers and ran the length of her body like a power surge.

His gaze bore into her as he took her measure. "Your hands are cold," he said.

"Wh-what?" Taken aback by the odd remark, she looked down at their still-clasped hands. "Oh, well, they're always cold. You know what they say."

"What's that?"

She resisted the urge to squirm beneath his scrutiny. "Cold hands, warm heart," she said, feeling like an idiot.

His expression didn't change. "I understand you were recently awarded the Distinguished Woman of Science Award."

The statement shouldn't have caught her off guard; she'd been asked about the honor dozens of times in the last week. But for the life of her, she couldn't seem to rally her brain to come up with an appropriate response. "Um . . . yes, I was."

"That's quite an achievement."

In the back of her mind, Eli noted that he hadn't congratulated her. "I'm . . . very pleased." She tried to tug her hand from his but he held it firmly, all the while skewering her with those disconcerting eyes.

Finally he released her hand. She resisted the urge to wipe her damp palm on her skirt. "It isn't every day a detective pays me a visit. What's this all about?"

"Just some routine questions, if you don't mind."

"Questions about what?"

When he merely stood there, watching her, Eli stepped back, wondering why she felt so off-kilter. "Would you like to sit down? Coffee? Hey, I've got some doughnuts left over from this morning."

His eyes sharpened, reminding her of black diamonds expertly cut—and as cold as ice. "No thanks."

She'd meant the offer as a joke—the doughnut part, anyway—but he either didn't have a sense of humor or didn't appreciate cops-and-doughnuts jokes.

He took the visitor's chair. She watched him out of the corner of her eye as she went back around her desk and sat down. He moved with the ease of an athlete, but that easy facade was tempered by a wariness that told her he wasn't as relaxed as he wanted her to believe.

Starkly aware of the tension that had entered the room with him, she closed the legal pad in front of her, using that moment to collect her thoughts. "Ann Arbor is a long way from Chicago," she began.

"I'm working on a case," he said. "In Chicago. I need some information."

"What kind of information?"

He withdrew a small notebook from the pocket of his trench coat. "How about if we start by getting some preliminary questions out of the way?"

"All right." She said the words, but she was still baffled as to how she could possibly help him.

"I understand you're a clinical research manager. Can you tell me exactly what you do?"

"I write protocol for and administer clinical drug trials." When he continued to stare at her, she continued. "I oversee the trials, gather the raw data, condense it into reports, and disseminate it to the director of R and D. I'm also the liaison between Roth Pharmaceuticals and the FDA."

"Did you oversee the drug trials for Valazine?"

A tiny alarm began to wail in the back of her brain at the mention of Valazine. "Valazine has been my main focus for the last ten years."

"Who, besides you, was involved in the clinical trials?"

"Dr. Walter Sanchez, who is the director of R and D, and Dr. Thomas Bornheimer, the clinical research associate. There were also the medical personnel at the clinic where the trials were administered, of course, as well as the test subjects."

"How many people was the drug tested on?"

"More than three thousand subjects participated in the trials."

"So, three thousand people took Valazine?"

"Not all of them. Some test subjects were given a placebo. These are controlled trials. Phase two and three were placebo controlled and double blinded."

"I see."

She didn't think he did—the clinical drug trial process was extremely complex—but this was his show so she didn't elaborate.

"Who's in charge of noting any side effects?" he asked.

The alarm in her head augmented. "The doctors at the clinic administer a detailed questionnaire to all the test subjects on a biweekly basis. The subjects, in turn, list any and all symptoms they may be experiencing. The medical personnel also conduct personal interviews with each subject individually. The doctor records all information and passes it on to Dr. Bornheimer and me."

"Do you see the raw data or do the doctors at the clinic compile a report?"

"I see the raw data as well as a summarization that has been signed by the physician in charge." Eli was growing increasingly uncomfortable with the detective's line of questioning. What was he after? And why had he sought her when Roth had a public relations director who was geared for questions of this sort?

"Can you tell me what this is all about, Detective?"

"I'm just gathering information at this point, trying to figure out how this works so I can finish up my report." He lifted his lip, and Eli wondered if that was his idea of a smile. "Routine."

"We have an in-house PR director—"

"I know you're busy, Dr. Barnes, but this will only take a few more minutes if you could just bear with me."

"I'd be happy to call her if—"

"You're doing fine." He didn't give her a chance to interrupt again and asked his next question quickly and forcefully. "Have there been any complaints with regard to Valazine?"

"What do you mean by complaints?"

He shrugged nonchalantly. "Adverse reactions. That sort of thing."

Eli felt a chill at the base of her spine, and suddenly she knew there was nothing nonchalant about anything this man had said or done since stepping in to her office. He was after something. Something specific that he didn't want to have to come right out and ask. And she wasn't merely helping him compile information for his so-called report; she was being interrogated. "The Food and Drug Administration has a database containing all adverse event information."

"There's another detective working that angle with the FDA, and he's drowning in red tape. I thought I'd take a shortcut and come directly to the source."

"What exactly are you looking for?" she asked.

"For starters, I'd like to have a look at the clinical studies."

"Why?"

"I'm looking for adverse reactions."

"The adverse reactions are listed on our website and in the pamphlets of every pharmacy that carries the drug. If you like, I can—"

"I'd like to see the raw data, actually."

"You won't be able to understand—"

"We cops can be pretty resourceful when we put our minds to it." When she only continued to stare at him, he leaned forward and whispered conspiratorially. "I got an A in biology."

It took her a moment to realize he was being sarcastic. Probably because he thought she'd been talking down to him or evading his questions—which she hadn't. Still, she felt the need for caution. "Confidentiality may be an issue here, Detective Boedecker. I'll have to clear it with Dr. Sanchez. That could take some time."

"I can wait."

Eli took a deep breath. "Dr. Sanchez is already gone for the day."

"What about his boss?"

"That would be Mr. Roth, and I don't think—"

"I can go see Mr. Roth, if you prefer."

"Actually, Detective Boedecker, I think it would be best if you let me discuss this with Dr. Sanchez in the morning. I can call you at your office tomorrow and ship the reports to you."

"While you're at it, I'd like to contact some of the clinical trial participants."

"I'm afraid that's not possible."

"Why not?"

"Again, there are confidentiality issues. Surely you understand that because of the nature of the medication most of these people don't wish to have their illnesses made public."

"I can assure you, Dr. Barnes, that I would be the only person in the department to see the names."

"Even I don't have access to those names. I identify the subjects by number only."

He scrubbed a hand over his jaw, and Eli could hear the scrape of his whiskers. "How soon can I get the adverse event data?"

"Well, some of the files have already gone to archive. I can put a rush on it, have it delivered here, make copies of what you might need. Maybe a week?"

"I was hoping to have it by this afternoon."

"I'm afraid that's impossible."

"That's unfortunate." Rising from the chair, he stepped up to the desk, flattened his hands against the blotter, and leaned closer.

Eli had to lean back in her chair to maintain a comfortable distance between them. She wasn't intimidated easily, but something about this man rattled her nerves.

"Maybe you'd prefer, Dr. Barnes, if I procured a search warrant from the Washtenaw County prosecuting attorney's office and had an army of sheriff's deputies pay you a visit and tear your neat little office apart."

"Don't you dare threaten me—"

"That's not a threat. I'm just warning you what could happen if you decide you're too busy to cooperate with the police."

Eli told herself it was temper that had her heart skittering wildly in her chest. But her fight or flight instinct was winding into high gear and it took every bit of discipline she possessed to meet his gaze. The logical side of her knew she wasn't in imminent danger; he was a police officer, for Pete's sake. But the knowledge didn't stop the uneasiness from slinking through her.

"You do whatever you feel is necessary, Detective," she snapped, "but that's not going to get you the information you need any more quickly."

"You sure about that? I've always been under the impression that you get things faster if you don't ask nicely."

"That may be true, but I don't respond well to threats." Eli swallowed hard. "And if you don't get your hands off my desk, I'm going to call security and have you removed from my office."

He straightened, and Eli thought she saw a measure of surprise in his expression, felt a flash of satisfaction that she'd stood her ground.

Her satisfaction was short-lived.

Tugging a brown clasp envelope from his pocket, he removed several sheets of paper. She jumped when he slapped them down on the desk in front of her.

"Maybe you'll change your mind after you read these," he said.

Shocked by his audacity, not knowing what else to do,

she looked down at the papers. On top was a copy of a newspaper article. She scanned the title. LEWISTON HIGH SCHOOL STUDENT GOES ON SHOOTING RAMPAGE.

Aware that her heart was racing out of control, she looked up at him. "I don't see what—"

"Read the damn thing."

A word highlighted in yellow in the center of the page caught her attention. *Valazine.* She skimmed the article, felt the hairs on her nape prickle. *Sixteen-year-old Eric Rickerson had been prescribed Valazine for depression just ten weeks earlier....*

Before she could read farther, he flipped to the next page. The headline jumped out at her. FACTORY WORKER MURDERS COWORKER, KILLS SELF. The article was short, but once again, near the bottom of the page, the word *Valazine* was highlighted in bright, damning yellow.

"What's your point?" Eli heard herself ask.

"I think my point is obvious."

Tearing her eyes away from the article, she risked a glance up at him. "I don't know what you're trying to prove, but I don't appreciate your tactics and I won't stand for it."

"I don't give a damn what you think of my tactics," he growled. "People are dying and you're giving me corporate doublespeak."

"Those are terrible crimes, but—"

"Seven people are dead. In every instance, the perp had been prescribed Valazine. How do you explain that?"

"Virtually every individual who is prescribed Valazine is emotionally troubled in some way," she said.

" 'Emotionally troubled,' as you so aptly put it, isn't synonymous with violent, is it?"

"Well, no, of course not. But if you look at the statistics and measure that with per capita population—"

"Those people weren't violent prior to taking Valazine."

"Detective Boedecker, I appreciate where you're coming from, but this is not proof of anything and I will not perpetuate your misguided theory by telling you what you want to hear. While these murders are horrible tragedies, they're also coincidental."

"Pretty consistent coincidences, don't you think?"

"What I think is that you should leave." Eli could tell he was angry. His eyes had gone black. His jaws were clamped tight. He was breathing heavily. But she was angry, too, and she didn't like the way he was talking to her. Scooting her chair back to a safer distance, she rose. "I'd like you to leave," she repeated.

He stood his ground, eyes level with hers, his jaw flexing. "I need your help."

Her hand trembled when she went for the phone on her desk. Before she could punch in the numbers, he reached out and put his hand firmly on hers. "Don't," he said. "Please."

His hand was warm and large and incongruently gentle over hers. Eli stared at the long, blunt-tipped fingers. The urge to jerk her hand away was strong, but she resisted. She was keenly aware of his closeness, and that he was furious. She could feel the anger coming off him, see it in the way his nostrils flared. The way his eyes glittered.

As if realizing he'd crossed a line, he removed his hand from hers and stepped back. Eli's knees went weak with relief. Swallowing hard, she punched in three numbers. Roth's chief executive officer Kevin Chambers answered on the second ring.

"Kevin, this is Eli. I need you to come to my office immediately."

"Hey, Eli, what's up?"

"Just come to my office. Right now."

"Uh . . . okay." She'd heard the tension in her voice, knew he'd heard it, too. His tone grew concerned. "Hey, is everything all right?"

Resisting the urge to snap at him, she hung up without answering and returned her attention to the detective.

He was standing a few feet from her desk with his hands on his hips, scowling at her. "Calling for backup?"

"You can't come into my office and start making wild accusations based on a few newspaper stories and then lose your temper when I don't agree with you."

"I don't have any patience for people who don't co-operate with the police."

"I don't have any patience for public servants who overstep their authority."

He made a sound of annoyance. "People are dying, damn it."

"Not because of Valazine."

"You didn't look so sure about that a moment ago."

"I'm not going to discuss this with you."

"It's your conscience."

Eli felt herself shaking inside. She told herself it was anger that had her so rattled. But she knew that wasn't all there was to it. The man was unsettling in a way that didn't have anything to do with her temper.

"I'll get proof," he said in a low, dangerous tone. "When I do, you can bet I'll be back."

"Be sure to call first. I'll have security waiting."

Something dark played behind his eyes, making his smile all the more ominous. Leaning forward, he tapped his finger against the stack of articles. "You can keep these," he snarled. "My card's on top."

"What's going on here?"

Eli look up to see Kevin Chambers at her office door, looking like an overprotective older brother whose sister had just been cuffed by the neighborhood bully. His sandy hair was mussed. His tie hung askew. And his usually unflappable corporate demeanor had transformed into one of self-righteous indignation.

Ignoring Kevin, the detective turned anger-bright eyes on her. "Give me a call when the body count gets too high for you."

Kevin had to step swiftly aside to keep from getting mowed over as Boedecker pushed by him and left the room.

"*Body count?* Who was *that*?"

Eli's heart settled back into her chest. "That, believe it or not, was a police detective."

"A *detective*?" He made a sound of disgust. "If looks could kill, I'd be in a hundred pieces right now. Since when does the police department hire thugs?"

"I'm glad I'm not the only one who got that impression."

"Scary guy." Shaking his head, he looked over his shoulder toward the hall. "What on earth did he want with you?"

"He said he's working on a case." Quickly she summarized the conversation.

"That's ridiculous!" Kevin said.

"I think so, too." She blew out a calming breath. "Thanks for coming by. He was making me . . . uneasy."

His chest puffed out a little. Straightening his tie, he shot her a speculative look. "Are you okay? You look a little shaken up."

"Fine. He just . . . caught me by surprise."

She picked up the articles on her desk and handed them to him. "He left these."

Kevin's expression tightened as he skimmed the first article. "Just because he's a cop doesn't mean he can walk in here and start making unfounded accusations based on a few articles. We ought to file a complaint or something."

Eli nodded. "I can do that. He's with the Chicago police. I'll give them a call and file a complaint."

"Good." Leaning toward her, Kevin tossed the articles into the trash container next to her desk. "I wonder why he didn't go through the PR department."

"He didn't seem like a proper channels kind of guy. And I suppose he wanted to interrogate the mad scientist responsible for putting the world at risk."

Kevin snorted.

Eli resisted the urge to look down at the articles. She wasn't sure why, but she wanted to read them. If she'd learned anything in the course of her education, it was that one could never have too much information.

"Come on, Eli. You're not taking this guy seriously, are you?"

The words snapped her gaze to his. "Of course not. It's just that . . . those kinds of accusations could look very bad for Roth from a PR standpoint. Especially if the accusations come from a credible source. Maybe this is something we should look into, even if it's a coincidence."

His brow furrowed. "Are you talking about adverse events?"

"That would be a start." At Kevin's worried expression, she added, "If only for ammunition in case we need it."

"We both know how complex the clinical trial process is. And we both know how hard it would be for a layperson to understand all the intricacies of R and D when it comes to pharmaceutical drugs. Face it, we make good bad guys these days. The media loves to hate us." He sank down into the chair opposite her desk. "The people who take Valazine are depressed. Some are emotionally disturbed. Some are even unbalanced. A layperson can't waltz in here and blame bizarre or violent behavior on the drug those people are taking."

"I understand that, and I agree."

"Maybe we ought to get legal involved," he said.

"At least give them a heads up."

His expression softened as he regarded her with sky blue eyes. "You're not worried about this, are you?"

She shrugged, not sure exactly what was still troubling her. "Not worried, just . . . concerned."

"Eli . . ."

"I conducted the trials."

"Come on! You're a freak about accuracy. The trials you conducted on Valazine were thorough, extensive, and detailed. You had top-notch staffing at the clinic. You had Walter's experience to draw upon and Dr. Bornheimer's expertise. There's no way serious adverse events could have gone unnoticed. There were too many checks and balances." He glanced down at her trash can. "This cop is barking up the wrong tree in a very big way. Don't let it get to you."

"Seven people are dead, Kevin."

"It's a sad fact, but seriously depressed people do desperate things sometimes."

She knew he was right. Eli was good at what she did. Valazine was her greatest work. Since going on the market a year ago, the drug had helped hundreds of thousands deal with the debilitating effects of depression, bipolar disorder, or schizophrenia. She wasn't sure exactly what was bothering her. All she knew was that a terrible accusation had been made, and the scientist inside her needed to disprove it.

On a more personal level, she knew all too well what a seriously depressed individual was capable of.

"You've got that look in your eye," he said.

"I always look that way when someone gets my back up. I'll call Chicago PD and file a complaint."

"Good. I'm sure nothing will come of this, but just to be safe, I'll apprise legal of the situation." He rose and began to fiddle with his tie.

Eli waited, wondering if there was something else on his mind.

He glanced down at his watch and frowned, tapped on it with his index finger. "Jeez, it's late."

"Six o'clock already."

"Well, uh, I was wondering, if you're not doing anything later . . ." He cleared his throat, shifting his weight from one foot to the other. "I've been wanting to try that new Thai restaurant over on Rush Street. You know, the one with the dragon mural on the marquee. . . ."

"Oh, well . . . hmmm." Surprise and discomfort made her fumble for words. It wasn't that she didn't like Kevin. She did. He was handsome and intelligent and successful. They had a lot in common; he was one of the few people she knew who was as dedicated to his work as she was. She supposed that was part of the problem; her work was her life and she didn't have any room in it for much else, especially a relationship with a coworker. While she respected him on a professional level, she had absolutely no inclination to make their relationship personal. Eli might be a whiz at writing protocol, but she sucked at relationships.

"Ah, I can't tonight, Kevin." She knew it was a cop-out, but she'd never been adept at this sort of thing. Eli could talk for hours about pharmacodynamics, but mention anything that even remotely sounded like a date and she just froze up inside.

"Hey, no problem," he said quickly.

"I'm sorry."

His Adam's apple bobbed when he swallowed. "No big deal. I just thought . . . a friendly dinner. Hey, maybe another time."

"I really, um, don't . . . you know, date much." Mercy, she was really bad at this.

"I understand. Me, too." He laughed and some of the tension eased. "It's a tough world out there."

"Downright frenetic." She offered a smile, feeling a little guilty for turning him down. He was a good man and a decent person. She wasn't sure why she'd rather have a root canal than go out with him. "I'll see you tomorrow?"

"Sure." He walked toward the door, looking a little lost. "Don't work too late."

"I won't. Good night."

Eli sat unmoving for a few minutes, feeling like a fool, hoping she hadn't hurt Kevin's feelings. She didn't want this to affect their relationship. Even more she hoped he wouldn't ask again. He might be a smart man, but she'd been around long enough to know even smart men did dumb things once their hormones got involved.

Damn it. What was wrong with her? Why couldn't she be like other women and enjoy an occasional date? It wasn't like going out with a man was rocket science, after all.

Glancing down at the paperwork in front of her, Eli sighed. She had a ton of work to do on the phase I trials for ROT-535, Valazine's new and improved cousin. But between Detective Boedecker's troubling visit and Kevin's invitation to dinner, she was feeling distracted and unsettled.

Having learned long ago that it was best to head trouble off before it turned into a problem, she reached for the phone and dialed Chicago information, got the number for the police department, then made the call.

"I'd like to file a complaint against one of your detectives," she said.

"Hold, please."

Eli leaned back in her chair and rubbed at the sore spot at her temple where a headache had broken through.

"Internal affairs. How can I help you?" came a deep male voice.

"I want to file a complaint against one of your detectives."

"Can I have your name, address, and phone number, please?"

Impatiently, Eli rattled off the information.

"What's the detective's name, ma'am?"

"Adam Boedecker."

A pause ensued. Eli could hear computer keys clicking on the other end of the line. "Are you certain City of Chicago is the right police department? Perhaps he's with one of the suburban jurisdictions."

"No, he's with Chicago PD. At least that's what he told me."

"Ma'am, we don't a detective on the roster by that name."

Surprise rippled through her. "Are you sure? I met with him just—"

"Do you know what division he's in?"

"I believe he's in homicide."

"Hold, please."

Groaning inwardly at being put on hold again, Eli reached into her desk drawer, pulled out an aspirin bottle, tapped out two pills, and downed them with the last of her coffee.

"Homicide. Deaton," a curt male voice uttered.

Surprised that she'd at least landed in the right department, Eli leaned forward in her chair. "I'd like to file a complaint against Detective Adam Boedecker."

The ensuing silence stretched so long that Eli thought she'd been disconnected. "Hello? Are you there?"

"Yeah, I'm here."

She heard the rustle of his hand being pressed over the receiver and the muffled utterance of a few choice words. "Are you the person I need to talk to?" she asked.

"Uh, yes, ma'am."

"The person I just talked to said they didn't have a

detective by that name. Is Adam Boedecker with your department?"

Another long silence. "To the best of my knowledge he is."

Odd answer, she thought, but trudged onward. "In that case I'd like to lodge a complaint. I want to let the person in charge know he came into my place of work and harassed me about a case he's working on. He was rude and unreasonable. In fact, the company I work for will consider legal action if he shows up again."

"Where are you located?"

"Ann Arbor, Michigan."

"Jesus."

"What?"

"I said . . . hell. What company do you work for?"

"Roth Pharmaceuticals."

A sigh hissed on the other end of the line. "Ma'am, look, if this is about that thing with his brother . . ."

His brother? Eli's mind worked that over for a moment. "Actually, he didn't mention anything about his brother."

Another pause.

"Are you still there?" she asked.

"Yeah. Look, he's . . . sort of working on a case."

"Sort of?"

"Well . . ."

"Is Roth Pharmaceuticals under some kind of investigation?"

"Uh, no, not really . . ."

"Not really?" she echoed, growing increasingly annoyed. "I don't understand. Why is one of your detectives coming to my office and interrogating me about the company I work for if the company is not under investigation?"

"He's . . . pursuing some . . . leads on a case."

"What case? What leads?"

"I'm not at liberty to discuss the particulars with you, ma'am."

Eli suddenly got the sudden distinct impression that the man on the other end of the line was covering someone's ass—namely Adam Boedecker's. "If you won't answer my questions truthfully, Officer Deaton—"

"Detective Deaton."

"Whatever. If you won't help me, I'll find someone who will."

"Look, all I can tell you is that Boedecker is a good cop. He's . . . following up on some leads. He's doing it on his own time."

The truth dawned on her then, and she found it even more infuriating. "Are you telling me this so-called investigation isn't authorized by the Chicago Police Department?"

Another long silence ensued, then he asked, "Can you tell me exactly what happened?"

Quickly, she relayed what had transpired earlier. "He was clearly trying to intimidate me, Detective Deaton. To the best of my knowledge, I'm not a suspect in a crime and I don't appreciate being treated as such. I certainly don't appreciate being lied to."

"Ah, well . . . Detective Boedecker tends to be a little vigorous."

"He's making some very serious allegations. I can't let that stand."

"Look, if you want to lodge a formal complaint, I can have someone fax you over a form, or if you have access to a computer, I can send it as an attachment in an e-mail."

"An e-mail would be fine."

"I'll, uh, be sure to have a talk with Detective Boedecker."

"I'm sure you'll be doing everyone who comes in contact with him a huge favor."

"Right." He hesitated. "Anything else, ma'am?"

"Keep him away from me, and keep him away from Roth Pharmaceuticals or we're going to sue him personally as well as the Chicago PD." Eli disconnected, everything the detective had said playing in her mind.

If this is about that thing with his brother . . .

Turning to her computer, she called up a search engine and typed in *Boedecker*. The search returned eighteen

matches. Eli clicked on the first one, felt her blood run
cold when she read the header: GOLD COAST INVESTMENT
BANKER KILLS WIFE, TURNS GUN ON SELF.

A shiver swept through her as she scanned the *Chicago
Tribune* article dated just under two weeks earlier.

> The bloodied bodies of forty-year-old Michael
> Boedecker, a successful investment banker,
> and his wife, Julie, a graphic artist, were dis-
> covered in their Gold Coast condo early
> Thursday morning by a neighbor. Their deaths
> have been ruled a murder-suicide by the Cook
> County coroner. Michael Boedecker had been
> employed at the high-powered, North Michi-
> gan Avenue securities firm of Goldstein,
> Smith & Associates for the last twelve years.
> News of the investment banker's death
> shocked coworkers. . . .

Eli could barely believe what she was reading. This
wasn't just a case to Adam Boedecker, she realized, but
a crusade to justify his brother's death. Quickly, she
scanned the article, found herself relieved when Valazine
wasn't mentioned. She printed the page, then clicked on
the next story. Dread congealed in her chest when, a third
of the way down the page, the journalist reported that six
weeks earlier, Michael Boedecker had been prescribed
Valazine.

Two hours later a ream of paper lay in her print tray.
Indeed, Michael Boedecker wasn't the only person who'd
been prescribed Valazine and committed suicide. But he
had been depressed. Was it the depression that had driven
him to murder and suicide? Or was something more ominous in the works, as Adam Boedecker had suggested?

Scooting her chair back, she leaned down to retrieve
her briefcase and spotted the corner of one of the articles
he'd left, sticking out of her trash can. On impulse, she
reached over and pulled them out.

LEWISTON HIGH SCHOOL STUDENT GOES ON SHOOTING
RAMPAGE.

The headline chilled her. Gooseflesh rose on her arms. A fist of dread slowly unfurled in the pit of her stomach as she stuffed the articles into her briefcase. She wasn't going to take this too seriously, she assured herself. There was no way any of this could be directly attributed to Valazine. Still, she thought, it wouldn't hurt to read the articles, would it?

chapter
5

ADAM FIGURED HE WAS GETTING PRETTY GOOD AT screwing things up. He'd sure as hell blown his big chance to talk to Dr. Elizabeth Barnes. He'd known better than to come on like some hotheaded rookie. What the hell was the matter with him, losing his temper like that when he should have been finessing her? It wasn't like he'd had the option of hauling her downtown if she didn't cooperate. Not only was he out of his jurisdiction, but neither the Ann Arbor police department nor the Chicago PD had sanctioned what he was doing. They didn't even *know* about it.

But Adam knew all too well why he'd blown it, and he hated the reason almost as much as he feared it. Not being one hundred percent in control of his emotions—in this case his temper—was an aspect of his traumatic brain injury. His volatility scared the hell out of him. He'd gotten exponentially better in the last three years. He could function normally for the most part; he even considered himself a productive citizen most days.

But most days wasn't good enough. Not for him personally. Certainly not if he wanted to be a cop again. Too many times in the last three years he'd found his emotions spiraling out of control over something that shouldn't have set him off. Times like today when he'd lost his temper over something he should have taken in stride. Then again, maybe he'd just lost patience with the human race.

The headache wasn't making things any easier. Pain always put him in a bad mood. Judging from the spots dancing in his peripheral vision, it was probably going to get a lot worse before it got any better.

Muttering a curse, Adam stopped at a traffic light and watched the wipers beat sleet off the windshield of his Tahoe. He wished he hadn't blown it with Barnes. Damn it, he needed to talk to her. He needed her help. Maybe if he stuck around, gave her some time to cool off—gave himself time to cool off—he could approach her again. Maybe even do a little begging for good measure.

The thought made him grimace. He hated dealing with academic types. Most of them thought they were smarter than God but hadn't a clue what it was like in the real world. Still, when he thought about the way she'd held her ground, he found a grudging respect for her. She might look like a piece of fluff, but she wasn't. Adam appreciated that despite the situation.

She wasn't what he'd expected. He'd anticipated gray hair, bottle-cap glasses, and a white lab coat over a matronly figure. She'd tossed those preconceived notions right out the window. While she wasn't exactly beautiful, she was . . . striking. She might even have been pretty if she'd put a little effort into it. Let that dark brown hair down a notch or two. Lose the glasses. But despite the little square glasses perched on the end of her nose, he'd noticed her eyes. They were large and intelligent and fringed with long, dark lashes. Adam had never been drawn to the bookish type, but there was something subtly appealing about her. She had a small-town look about her along with a hint of hard-won sophistication that didn't come naturally. Clear, pretty eyes and the flawless skin of a child. Her lips were too full for her face, but it was a flaw that appealed rather than detracted. He hadn't been able to see much of her beneath that unflattering suit, but he could tell by the way the fabric swept over her that she had some very nice curves.

The image of the way she'd looked sitting behind that big desk sent a pleasant flutter low in his gut. He knew it was counterproductive to think of her in any way except as a possible source of information, especially if his suspicions about Valazine were correct. But a man could look. Even a cop could look. As long as he didn't touch.

After turning left onto Washtenaw, he headed toward the interstate. She wasn't the only one who needed a cooling-off period. He would drive back to his home in Palatine tonight and give her a call in a few days. He'd come up with a plan. Do some rethinking. Find another way to approach this.

But he would be back, he vowed. Next time, he would stay until he found what he was looking for.

ELI PUT OFF READING THE ARTICLES FOR AS LONG AS she could. She fixed dinner, balanced her checkbook, and started a load of laundry. Every time she passed by the door of her study, she paused, found her gaze drawn to her briefcase on the floor next to her desk. By nine P.M. the last of the laundry was folded. If it had been any later, she might have gone to bed. But Eli never went to bed before ten o'clock. And as the grandfather clock struck once, announcing the half hour, she found herself sitting at her desk in the study, pulling the articles from her briefcase, cursing herself for not leaving them in the trash can where Kevin had put them.

The first article shocked her. The crime was savage and seemingly unprovoked. By the time she finished reading it, her palms were clammy. The next article was worse. Two innocent children murdered by a woman who didn't even have so much as a parking ticket on her record. A woman who'd been diagnosed with bipolar disorder and prescribed Valazine just twelve weeks earlier. By the time Eli finished the last article, her hands were shaking.

She understood how a layperson could draw incorrect

assumptions. Everyone needed something tangible to blame when tragedy struck. A fall guy. Some faceless enemy to lash out at. Eli understood the psychology of grief, had been through it too many times herself not to empathize. But she also knew that depressed individuals sometimes reacted destructively. And that sometimes there was no one to blame but the one who was gone.

She thought of her mother and felt the familiar sweep of sadness. For an instant, the grief transported her back to the farmhouse in Jasper, Indiana. She was fifteen years old. Running through the kitchen, sliding on the linoleum. Blood on her hands. Terror in her heart. A scream buried in her throat . . .

"Jesus." Setting the articles on her desktop, Eli lowered her face into her hands. It had been a long time since she'd thought about her mother, about the terrible things she'd seen in that pretty, old farmhouse all those years ago.

Beautiful, laughing, troubled Patricia Barnes. The talented pianist whose mind was a torture chamber. The wife and mother who'd been unable to cope with the pressures of life. The depressed woman who'd seen death as her only means of escape.

Shoving thoughts of her mother aside, Eli glanced at the brass clock on the mantel. Nearly ten o'clock. Logic told her to toss the articles in the trash and forget about them. Her emotions told her to call Walter and tell him about Detective Boedecker's allegations. What could it hurt to confide in her mentor? It wasn't like she believed Valazine was suspect. She'd spent ten arduous years bringing the drug to market: three years working for Walter in an R & D capacity. Two years writing protocol for the clinical drug trials. Five more years administering the four phases of the trials. Time and time again the benefits of the drug had greatly outweighed the side effects, which were minimal. The FDA had agreed and approved the drug in less than a year. Violent or bizarre behavior had not been reported by a single study participant.

"So what are you so worried about?" she said aloud,

her voice sounding tense and perplexed in the silence of her study.

Knowing Walter would ease her troubled mind, she snatched up the phone and dialed his number from memory. He answered on the second ring.

"Hi, Walter. I'm sorry to bother you so late," she began.

"No need to apologize. I was just putting some finishing touches on a sundae I'm about to devour."

"Sounds serious."

"Hot fudge is about as serious as it gets." A thoughtful silence ensued. "You sound distracted."

"I am. I mean, a little."

"Is everything all right?"

"Yes, everything's fine. I just . . . Do you mind if I come over?"

"Eli, you're beginning to concern me. Are you sure—"

"I swear. Everything's fine." She looked down at the articles. "I just . . . need to talk to you."

"All right." He paused. "Want a sundae?"

"With almonds?"

"Of course."

"See you in ten minutes."

WALTER LIVED OFF OF GREEN ROAD IN A TWO-story colonial near Sugarbrush Park. Eli pulled her Volkswagen into the driveway and parked next to his Volvo. Grabbing her briefcase, she opened the door and stepped into the blustery wind. She was still wearing the suit dress she'd worn to work, and the wind snaked around her legs like icy fingers.

Halfway to the house she realized Walter hadn't turned the porch light on for her. Odd, she thought, but figured he'd probably gotten busy with their sundaes and forgotten. She reached the door and rang the bell, shivering when a gust of wind cut through her coat.

"Come on, Walter," she said, opening the storm door and knocking. "Sometime before hypothermia sets in."

After the third knock, Eli was perplexed. From where

she stood, she could see the large front window. The drapes were drawn, but the light was on in the living room. Where the heck was Walter?

She knocked one last time, then left the porch. From the sidewalk, she noted that the second level was dark, so she ruled out his being upstairs and not hearing the bell. Staving off concern, she left the sidewalk and braved the snow to cut through the side yard to the rear of the house. The kitchen light was on. Peering through the French door, Eli used her ignition key to tap on the glass. When the noise didn't produce Walter, she reached for the knob. To her surprise the door was unlocked.

"Walter?" She stepped inside, grateful to be out of the cold. "Hey, I'm here for my sundae."

A half gallon of vanilla ice cream and two bowls sat on the counter. A Mozart concerto purred from the stereo in the living room.

"Hellooo?" Shaking the snow from her coat, she hung it on the back of a bar stool, then wiped her feet on the welcome mat inside the door. "Walter?" Puzzled by his absence, she walked into the living room. The gas logs in the stone fireplace burned happily. A Tom Clancy novel lay facedown on the sofa. "Walter? Hey? Is everything okay?"

Eli told herself the uneasiness creeping into her brain was an overreaction. She didn't have any reason to be uneasy. More than likely, he'd gone over to his neighbor's house for chocolate syrup. Telling herself everything was fine, she strolled back into the kitchen. The half gallon of ice cream was melting fast, so she replaced the lid and put it in the freezer. Taking a stool at the bar, she removed the articles from her briefcase and started to read. But the silence weighed heavily on her concentration. She couldn't stop thinking about how odd it was that he'd simply left.

Dropping the article on the countertop, she walked into the laundry room and opened the door leading to the garage. Finding both areas unoccupied, she crossed back through the kitchen and living room and headed toward the stairs. In the foyer, she peered up the stairs at the darkened landing. Surely if he was up there, he would have turned on the light, wouldn't he? Unless, God forbid, he'd fallen or had a stroke, a worried little voice said. Walter was in terrific physical condition, but he was elderly.

She flipped the hall light switch, but nothing happened. "Of course," she muttered, and started up the stairs. "Walter? Hey, are you up there?"

She was halfway up when she heard the music. Not the classical they both preferred, but a rock and roll serenade of a steel guitar and a lilting male voice. Walter detested rock and roll. Baffled and growing increasingly concerned, she took the steps two at a time to the top. Three bedrooms opened to the hall. The fourth door—to Walter's room—was closed. Jogging the short distance to the door, Eli rapped on it. "Walter?"

She heard the tremor in her voice and she knew her concern for him had crossed over into fear. Fear that something had happened to her friend. A dozen terrible scenarios raced through her mind as she reached for the knob and twisted. The door swung open. Darkness and cold and an unpleasant odor greeted her. The too-loud music blared beautiful and terrible at once from the radio she knew was next to the bed. Eli grappled for the wall switch, flipped it.

Light flooded the room. Walter lay faceup on the bed, his mouth slack, his eyes open and staring. The sight of blood soaking through the sheet stunned her, and she rushed to him. "Oh, *God*. Walter!"

Leaning over him, she pressed a trembling finger to his throat. But there was no pulse. His flesh was warm, but he wasn't breathing.

"Hang on," she whispered. "Oh, God, Walter, hang on." She'd left her cell phone in her purse. It was in the kitchen, on the bar. Looking wildly around, she spotted a phone next to the bed, snatched it up, and punched 911.

"I need an ambulance!" she shouted to the voice on the other end. "At 226 Briarwood! Please hurry! A man's unconscious. He's elderly. He's bleeding! I don't know what happened to him."

"Is he breathing, ma'am?"

"I don't think so." She looked down at Walter's pallid complexion. "I'm going to try CPR."

Without waiting for a reply, she dropped the phone and removed the pillow from beneath Walter's head. Sliding her hand beneath his neck, she tilted his head back—only to notice blood at the corner of his mouth. "Walter . . ."

Eli jerked the sheet down to expose his chest. Shock froze her in place as the amount of blood registered in her brain. She heard a buzzing sound in her ears. She stared, unable to move until the stench of death sent her stumbling back.

Dimly, she was aware of the voice coming from the dangling phone. The 911 operator, she realized. Eli knew she should pick up the phone and let the operator know what had happened, but panic overrode logic. A strangled sound tore from her throat. Nausea sent bile into her mouth. She took another step back. Her hand clipped the lamp shade, sent the light tumbling to the floor. The ceramic base shattered, plummeting the room into darkness.

Walter was dead.

She couldn't believe it. Couldn't accept that there was nothing she could do for him. Her mind refused to accept the reality that he was gone, refused to absorb the finality of it.

A sound escaped her. She smothered it with a hand to her mouth. She knew running was a cowardly thing to do. But the smell of blood sickened her. The horror of death overwhelmed her. Spinning, she staggered toward the door. Her legs took her down the hall at breakneck speed. She descended the stairs and stumbled onto the landing. Her shoulder slammed hard into the banister when she turned the corner, but she righted herself without noticing the pain. Then her hands were on the front door. Mewling sounds seeped from her throat. She felt wild inside as her fingers clawed at the chain. She had to get out of there or she was going to be sick. She needed air. Cold, clean air. Her fingers fumbled with the bolt lock. She'd been in the house a hundred times but couldn't remember which way to turn it.

The door finally opened. Eli slammed her palm against the latch of the storm door. It swung wide. She heard glass break, but she didn't stop. Her legs took her across the porch and down the steps.

She wanted to scream but couldn't get enough oxygen into her lungs. "Help me! Somebody!" But the words were breathless and thin. Nobody could hear her. Just like before. All those years ago when she'd been fifteen. She hadn't been able to scream then, either. She hadn't been able to help her mother. Even after all these years, after all the education and hard work, she was still helpless. Helpless and terrified and paralyzed by the horrors of death.

On the sidewalk, Eli fell to her knees and vomited. Her hands plunged into the snow. Her body shuddered. Vaguely, she became aware of the snow against her palms. Icy concrete against her knees. The slick of cold sweat at the back of her neck.

Raising her head, she looked over her shoulder at the front door. She couldn't believe Walter was gone. Couldn't believe such a vibrant person could just cease to exist. Couldn't imagine her life without him.

She squeezed her eyes closed against the pain. "No!" she cried, and let her tears fall unchecked into the snow.

chapter
6

THE FIRST POLICE CAR ARRIVED WITHIN FIVE minutes, followed by an ambulance and a fire engine shortly thereafter. Eli stood on the sidewalk in front of Walter's house, shivering with cold and grief and shock, watching the chaos unfold. Two more police cars arrived, followed by the medical examiner's van. Within half an hour of her initial call to 911, the entire cul-de-sac was filled with law enforcement vehicles and a cacophony of flashing lights. Idling on the perimeter of the action, a Channel Five news van's engine spewed exhaust into the cold, still air.

"Ms. Barnes, I'm Detective Lindquist."

Eli turned to see a man in a trench coat approach her. She guessed him to be in his mid-fifties. Completely bald, with dark brows and a salt-and-pepper mustache, he wore a long tan coat and a black muffler wrapped haphazardly around his thick neck. He had hound-dog eyes and drooping jowls. But Eli wasn't fooled by the benign face. The man might have hound-dog eyes, but they were the eyes of a hound that could be nasty when stirred to anger.

"I'd like to ask you a few questions," he said. "Can you come with me, please?"

"Is he . . . Is he . . . ?" Unable to complete the sentence, she let the words trail off.

"I'm afraid he's dead, ma'am."

"I can't believe it." She looked over at the house. She'd been hoping for a miracle, praying for a miracle she knew wouldn't come. "I can't believe he's gone."

"I'm sorry. I know this must be a shock." Taking her arm gently, the detective guided her toward an unmarked car parked curbside. "It's a little bit warmer in my car."

Though she was shivering violently, Eli barely felt the cold. She was aware of it, but the shock of finding Walter made physical discomforts seem insignificant. Still, she knew the temperature was hovering somewhere in the teens. She hadn't worn a hat and her hair was already wet from the falling snow.

"How long will this take?" she asked. "I've . . . got to let some people know what happened." They would be terrible calls, she thought, but Peter Roth and Kevin Chambers would want to be informed as soon as possible. Briefly, she wondered who would contact his family. His daughter in Florida. The grandsons he would never take fishing. She didn't know their names, didn't have any phone numbers or even addresses.

What a terrible, terrible tragedy.

"This will only take a few minutes," Lindquist said.

"He was murdered, wasn't he?" she asked.

"He was shot. Doesn't look self-inflicted."

The words hit her like a fist to the solar plexus. "He was such a good, decent man. Why would someone do something so heinous?"

"That's what I intend to find out." He opened the passenger-side door for her. "Have a seat and I'll take your statement, okay?"

Eli slid into the car. Lindquist crossed to the driver's side, then got in beside her. He started the engine and turned on the heater. The police radio crackled, but he lowered the volume, then pulled a notepad from his coat.

"I want you to tell me everything that happened tonight," he said.

She looked at him, found those hound-dog eyes watching her closely. Too closely. "I've already told the patrol officer everything."

"I apologize if it seems like we're duplicating our efforts, but I've been assigned this case. If I'm going to find out who murdered Dr. Sanchez, I need to know exactly what happened."

Murdered.

The word sent a bone-deep chill through her. Disbelief and grief and a hundred other emotions tangled inside her, clogging her throat, tightening around her chest until she could barely draw a breath.

"Dr. Barnes? Are you—"

"I'm okay."

"If you need a minute . . ."

"No. Let's just get this over with." Starting with the phone call she'd made to Walter, she told the detective everything. She wasn't sure how she managed it, but she relayed every detail she could think of, right down to the sundaes. It was almost as if she were having an out-of-body experience. Her voice produced words and strung them together while she slowly came apart inside. She steeled herself against the horror when she told him about finding Walter. By the time she finished, her voice was hoarse and she was shaking all over.

"How did you know Dr. Sanchez?" he asked.

"We're colleagues. We work together at Roth Pharmaceuticals."

"Nice place." He smiled at her. "My son was an intern there a couple years back during his summer break from U of M."

"Mr. Roth hires a number of interns every summer." How could they even be having such a normal conversation when Walter was lying in his bed with a hole in his chest? "It's a good program."

He looked down at his notebook. "Were you and Dr. Sanchez friends?"

"Yes."

"Anything closer than that?"

"No."

"What were you doing here tonight?"

"I wanted to discuss something with him."

"Work related?"

"Yes."

"A problem? What?"

"We worked on an R and D project together and—"

"What project?"

"A drug. Valazine. It's been on the market now for—"

"Oh, yeah, they run that touchy-feely commercial with the two golden retrievers. Antidepressant, right?"

"That is generally how it's used."

He scribbled something in the notepad. "Go on."

"I wanted his opinion on some information I'd been given earlier in the day. Walter had been out of town and had arrived back just this evening after hours."

"It was something you couldn't discuss over the phone?"

"Well, I called him, and he suggested I come by." Remembering the sundaes, Eli felt the burn of tears behind her eyes. "We were going to have ice cream."

"So you called him?" he pressed.

She nodded.

"What time was that?"

"About . . ." She looked at her watch. "Almost ten."

"That late, huh?"

"Ten o'clock isn't that late, Detective."

He scribbled in the notepad. "Anything else you can think of that might be important?"

Eli shook her head. "Not that I can think of."

Watching her carefully, Detective Lindquist closed the notepad. "I'd appreciate it if you didn't take any trips or vacations in the next few days."

She stared at him.

"Just routine," he clarified. "I'll probably need to ask you some more questions. It would make things a lot easier if you're available and I don't have to run you down."

"Oh. Of course." She looked down at her hands. "For

a moment I thought maybe you thought I—"

"You've been very helpful. This is all just routine procedure, okay?"

She wished cops would stop telling her that. None of this was routine for her.

"Thanks again, Dr. Barnes. I'll be in touch." He handed her a card. "If you think of anything else, call me as soon as possible."

Needing to get out of the confines of the car, out from beneath his probing, suspicious eyes, she reached for the handle and opened the door. She knew she wasn't in any condition to drive but wanted badly to go home. By the time she reached her car she felt light-headed and nauseous. Grief was like a fist in her chest, twisting every organ into knots. For an instant, she considered calling Kevin Chambers, but she quickly squashed the idea. The kind of pain churning inside her wasn't something she wanted to share.

Somehow she got the car door open and the engine started. Checking her rearview mirror once, she backed from the driveway. Out of the corner of her eye, she saw Lindquist standing in the cul-de-sac, talking to a uniformed police officer, but his eyes were on her as she put the car in gear and pulled into the street.

The drive across town was a blur of snow and traffic lights and headlights. The CD player was on, but she barely heard the music. Ten minutes later, she parked in her driveway. She hardly felt the cold as she made her way up the walkway and to the front door. She dropped her keys twice before getting the door open. By the time she walked into the foyer, she was sobbing. Wrenching sobs that shook her all the way down to her belly. She dropped her briefcase next to the door. In the living room, she lost one of her pumps, but she didn't stop walking. Tears blinded her as she started up the stairs. On the landing she went to her knees. Bending at the waist, she braced one hand against the step, hugged herself with the other as the brutal punch of pain shocked her system.

Walter was dead. She would never hear his voice again. Never hear his laughter. She would never see him smile or look into his eyes and see wry humor light up his face. Already she needed him. Already she wanted him back. The unfairness of having his friendship stolen from her by a senseless act of violence left her feeling empty and alone and incredibly violated.

Worse, she knew there was nothing she could do about any of it for the time being except hurt.

RAIN FELL IN SHEETS, POUNDING THE COLD EARTH into mud and sending a rise of fog into the frigid morning air. Eli stood beneath the canopy and watched the water cascade down. Beyond, the priest's voice rose over the din of rain. He was a rotund man with solemn eyes that spoke of strong character and an even stronger faith. He stood at the podium with the Bible cradled in his hands and recited the twenty-third psalm from memory.

"The Lord is my shepherd, I shall not want . . ."

Even though the temperature was barely above freezing, people had come. Eli had known they would, bad weather or no. Everyone had loved Walter.

Kevin Chambers stood to her right, staring straight ahead, his jaw set. Peter Roth and his wife, Karen, stood to her left. A few rows over, Thomas Bornheimer and several of the administrative staffers from Roth paid their last respects. Even Detective Lindquist had come. He stood just inside the canopy at the rear, holding his hat and watching everyone with those mean hound-dog eyes. Eli wondered if he was here to pay his respects—or to scope for suspects.

"Yea though I walk in the valley of the shadow of death, I will fear no evil for thou art with me . . ."

Eli listened to the psalm, trying to take comfort in the words, trying hard to believe that Walter was in a better place. She'd spent the last four days struggling to come to terms with the reality of his death. That he was gone forever. Senselessly murdered in his own home. Her best friend. Her mentor. A man she'd loved like a father for the last ten years.

A hand on her arm jerked her from her reverie. Eli

looked over at Kevin Chambers, saw the concern in his eyes, and realized she'd been staring off into space.

"You okay?" he asked softly.

Automatically, she nodded and gave him a smile she hoped looked real. "Fine."

"It's going to be all right," he said.

He was still watching her when she looked away. Eli wasn't good at sharing grief. In her mind, grief was a private thing. A personal journey one took alone. Even as a teen, when her mother had died and the world had come crashing down, she had preferred to deal with it alone. As an adult, she knew keeping emotions bottled up wasn't necessarily a smart thing to do. But emotions were seldom logical or timely, so she'd just have to deal with them the best way she could.

When the priest finished reciting the psalm, Peter Roth walked up to the podium, cleared his throat, and began the eulogy. Eli could hear one of the administrative assistants crying. Karen Roth blew her nose. Even Kevin reached up and wiped his eyes a couple of times.

Eli hadn't been able to cry since that first terrible night. Maybe because she'd cried herself out. Maybe because she knew from experience that tears never really helped. Or maybe because right alongside the grief there was a cauldron of anger boiling in her chest. Anger at the person responsible for her friend's death.

She wanted justice. For Walter. For the daughter in Florida he'd left behind. For the two grandsons he would never take fishing. Maybe even for herself.

Peter Roth delivered the eulogy with the eloquence of a Shakespearean actor. His insights and anecdotes rang true even to Eli, who'd known Walter better than anyone, and elicited a few chuckles when he touched upon some of the lighter moments of Walter's twenty-nine-year career at Roth. The words lulled Eli into a state of quiet melancholy. She watched Peter work his audience. She listened to the rain, felt the snake of cold air against her legs. The tempo of the rain slowed and hardened, and Eli realized it had changed to sleet. She could hear it striking the canopy and bouncing off like tiny frozen peas. As

Peter's voice droned on, she found herself looking out over the rows of headstones, the naked trees, and the clumps of winter-dead grass and piles of snow.

Surprise rippled through her when she spotted a familiar figure walking toward the tent. A tall man with long, purposeful strides. His trench was open despite the chill and she could see that he was wearing a black suit beneath. She recognized him immediately as the Chicago detective who'd stopped by her office four days ago. The cop who'd brought in a handful of articles and made some very serious allegations against Roth Pharmaceuticals. She searched her memory for his name. Adam Boedecker. She knew why he'd come and felt a stir of anger that he would breach this solemn occasion to further his misinformed agenda.

She watched him approach, aware that he'd spotted her and was heading toward her. She stared back, telling herself she wasn't unsettled by his presence. She had no reason to be uneasy. Still, she was keenly aware of her heart beating a hard tattoo against her ribs.

He stopped several yards away just inside the tent and shook the water and sleet from his coat.

"Excuse me," she said to Kevin, then turned and started toward the detective.

Boedecker watched her, his expression inscrutable. Gooseflesh raised on her arms when he scanned the length of her with those cop's eyes of his. Hard eyes, she thought. Unemotional. Cold. The calculating eyes of a predator. She held his gaze, but the directness of it unnerved her.

She stopped a few feet away from him. "You've got some nerve coming here."

He wasn't wearing a hat, and his face and black hair were damp. The shoulders of his trench were wet and dotted with tiny sleet pellets. "I want to talk to you."

"I have nothing to say to you."

"You know, Doc, a little cooperation would go a long way—"

"I'm not going to cooperate with you. You have no right to be here. How dare you intrude? At a funeral, for

God's sake." Despite her resolve to remain calm, her voice had risen, drawing the looks of several people.

"Calm down," he said.

"I am calm, goddamn it."

"You don't want to make a scene," he said quietly.

"You're damn right I don't, so I suggest you take your half-baked agenda and leave."

"Look, I drove all the way from Chicago to see you. I'm not here to cause problems. I need a few minutes of your time."

Anger and adrenaline made her heart pound. "You should have called. I would have told you not to waste your gas."

"Dr. Barnes, if you don't help me, I'll have no recourse but to go to the media."

"Roth has nothing to fear from the media. Neither do I."

A smile twisted one side of his mouth, but there was no humor in his eyes. They were cold, and they chilled her. "I think eight dead bodies is something the media will be very interested in."

She wanted to laugh, just to piss him off. But her throat was so tight she couldn't manage it. Instead she stared at him, willing her heart to slow.

"Believe me, you don't want that to happen," he said.

"I didn't want a lot of things to happen."

He glanced over at the casket. "If you help me, we might find your friend's killer."

Fresh anger rose in a flood. "Don't you dare try to use Walter's death to gain my cooperation," she said.

His expression didn't change. "Be reasonable, Dr. Barnes. Talk to me. An hour of your time. That's all I'm asking."

Shaking with fury, Eli looked over at the podium and struggled to pull herself together. She seldom lost control of her emotions, but she supposed the grief of the last four days had pushed her to her limit. She took a deep breath, blew it out slowly. In her peripheral vision, she saw Kevin watching her, watching *them*, and realized they had the attention of several Roth employees. She turned back to Boedecker. "I'll give you ten minutes, but not now."

"When?"

"Tomorrow. At my office. I'll have the PR director there to answer your questions."

"Just you."

"No." Giving him a final, scathing look, she turned and started toward her place at the front. She felt his eyes on her as she walked, but she didn't turn around, didn't look at him.

"What the hell is he doing here?" Kevin asked when she sat down beside him.

"Nothing. I told him to leave."

Kevin looked over at her. "Jesus, Eli, you're shaking."

"I'm fine."

She pretended to listen to Peter Roth as he closed the eulogy, but all the while her mind whirled. The articles she'd read the other day had named seven dead. Boedecker had said eight. She told herself that the number didn't mean anything, but it didn't keep dread from curdling in her stomach like sour milk.

Boedecker's theory was far-fetched at best. She didn't believe a word of it. Still, she knew it was something she was going to have to deal with. She was going to have to deal with him. As much as she wanted to believe otherwise, she knew he wasn't the kind of man who went away when asked.

When she turned and looked over her shoulder, the detective from Chicago was gone and the sleet had turned to snow.

IT WAS NEARLY THREE P.M. WHEN ELI UNLOCKED the front door of her house and dragged herself inside. The funeral had exhausted her, both physically and emotionally. After the service, Peter Roth and his wife had hosted a get-together for Roth employees at their home near the university. Eli hadn't been able to get out of it, so she'd driven across town and watched her coworkers

•

devour hors d'oeuvres, drink imported beer, and try not to talk about why they were really there.

In the plush opulence of Karen and Peter Roth's formal dining room, Peter had announced that Roth Pharmaceuticals would be offering a ten-thousand-dollar reward for information leading to the arrest and conviction of the person or persons responsible for Walter Sanchez's murder. Eli thought it was a generous offer, but she wondered how much of it had to do with his friendship with Walter, and how much had to do with public relations.

Now, some three hours later, she wanted nothing more than to sink into a hot bath and forget about everything for a few precious minutes. Of course, fate had other ideas.

She'd barely set her purse down when the doorbell rang. She started, wondering if Kevin had decided to pay her a visit even after she'd asked him not to. A rise of annoyance made her sigh. Why couldn't he understand that she needed to be alone? That she needed to deal with this in her own way and in her own time?

Angry, she strode to the door and looked out the peephole to see Detective Boedecker standing on the porch. Trepidation congealed in her chest at the thought of facing off with him when she felt so fragile inside. He didn't play nice and didn't follow the rules, and she simply wasn't up to those kinds of tactics this afternoon.

For a moment she considered not answering the door. But she knew that even if she managed to avoid him now, he would be back later. He wasn't the kind of man who would give up easily. No, she thought, Adam Boedecker was like a shark that had scented blood. It would be best to get this over with.

Taking a calming breath, she opened the door as far as the security chain would allow. "Meeting here isn't what I agreed to."

He gazed steadily at her, his face expressionless. "I know this is a bad time, but it won't wait."

"I'm not going to let you in."

She started to close the door, but he smoothly stopped her by sliding his foot between the door and the jamb.

"With all due respect, Dr. Barnes, I can't let you do that. It will only take a few minutes."

"Actually, Detective Boedecker, this won't take any time at all because I'm not going to talk to you. And if you don't get your goddamn foot out of the door, I'm going to call the police and have you arrested."

His expression didn't change. "If you want to find out who murdered Sanchez, I think you'd better listen to what I have to say."

She felt herself recoil. She tried not to let the reaction show, but it was involuntary and she knew the detective didn't miss it. Being the predator he was, he moved in for the kill.

"Sanchez had agreed to talk to me." he added.

The statement struck her like a boxer's punch. The meaning behind the words made the hairs at her nape prickle. "I don't believe you."

"If I'd gotten to him sooner, he might not be lying in the ground right now."

Stepping back, Eli leaned heavily against the console table in the foyer and pressed her hand against her stomach. Walter hadn't mentioned anything about the detective having contacted him. Surely he would have mentioned it, wouldn't he?

"Dr. Barnes?"

She straightened, then looked at him through the partially open door, her heart pounding.

He stared back at her with those dark, emotionless eyes. "I have nothing to gain by lying to you," he said. "Please, just hear me out."

Something in his voice chipped away at her resolve. An odd mix of urgency and sincerity that belied his cold demeanor. Sighing, she disengaged the security chain and opened the door.

He stepped into the foyer with a swirl of cold air and a hint of expensive aftershave. "Thank you."

Unprepared for the effect of his presence, she took a step back. "Don't thank me. I didn't let you in out of the kindness of my heart. I did it because I suspect it's the only way I'm going to get rid of you."

"Fair enough."

Hugging herself against a sudden chill, she turned away and walked into the living room. "I can't believe you'd come here at a time like this."

"Times like this are the times most people need a cop."

"I don't need a cop."

"Sanchez sure as hell could have used one."

For the first time Eli noticed he was no longer wearing the suit he'd donned for the funeral but a pair of navy slacks and a white button-down shirt beneath the trench coat. He should have looked casual, but there was nothing even remotely casual about this man. He had an agenda. He was determined to see it through no matter how many toes he stepped on. And she was pretty sure her toes were the first in line.

"Did you read the articles I gave you the other day?" he asked.

"I read them." When he only continued to stare at her, she added, "The media likes to sensationalize. Pharmaceutical companies make good bad guys," she said, borrowing Kevin's phrase.

"Add Sanchez's murder to the mix, and what do you have?"

The realization of what he was getting at shook her. She gaped at him, aghast. "Detective Lindquist told me Walter's death is being investigated as a robbery. I have no reason to believe otherwise, and neither do you."

"Sanchez had agreed to talk to me. Someone killed him before he could."

Stunned by the implications, sick with dread, she took a step closer. "Surely, you don't think . . . You can't possibly think . . ."

"I think someone at Roth put an unsafe drug on the market," he said. "A drug that turns people into walking time bombs."

"That's utterly ridiculous—"

"I think someone at Roth Pharmaceuticals knows about this side effect. In fact, I'll bet they went to great lengths to hide that information from the FDA." His eyes never left hers. "I'll also bet Sanchez knew about it or found out about it after the fact."

"Even if such a thing were possible—and I don't believe for a moment that Valazine is flawed in any way— there were a lot of people involved with the research and development of Valazine. Even more involved with the clinical trial process. One person could not pull off something like that."

"Even so, you know it's a possibility," he said.

"What I know, Detective, is that you went to a great deal of trouble and mistakenly believe you've uncovered a deep, dark corporate secret when in reality you've done nothing more than unearth a few terrible and bizarre coincidences that have absolutely nothing to do with what happened to Walter."

"I don't believe in coincidence. When it comes to murder, neither should you."

"Look, I appreciate what you're trying to do," she said tiredly. "From a scientific standpoint, I can even appreciate where you're coming from. But I oversaw the clinical trials for Valazine. I know you're wrong. There were no such adverse events as the ones that were alluded to in those articles."

"Prove it to me." He said the words without impertinence. "Prove me wrong. That's all I'm asking."

Eli took a deep breath. She didn't believe what he was telling her. Not about Valazine. Certainly not that Walter's death was in any way related to his work at Roth. "Look, Detective, this really isn't a good time. Give me a few days—"

"I understand this is an upsetting time for you, but this won't wait."

She didn't want him to know just how upsetting this was or how close she and Walter had been, so she refrained from telling him. She instinctively knew he was the kind of man who would take any sign of weakness and use it against her to get what he wanted.

"Dr. Barnes, Walter Sanchez isn't the only one who's died. There are other people grieving. Wives and children. Entire families—"

"Detective—"

"With all due respect, Dr. Barnes, I don't have time to twiddle my thumbs while you recover from your shock and grief."

There weren't many people Eli truly disliked. But in that moment, she detested this coldhearted man. "Don't you dare talk to me like that."

"Look, I'm sorry for your loss—"

"Don't patronize me, either. You're not very good at it."

He clamped his jaws shut, but his gaze didn't falter. For an instant Eli thought he was going to turn around and leave. He proved her wrong by starting toward her.

It was hard to do, but she held her ground. "Walter's death has nothing to do with your . . . theory." But uncertainty warred with anger as he neared. She struggled to hang on to her anger, knowing it was safer than the alternative. But when he stepped close and invaded her personal space, she didn't have a choice but to retreat. She hated giving up ground. She knew it was somehow symbolic with regard to power and strength and the pecking order being set between them. Evidently, he wasn't the kind of man to miss out on any opportunity to gain the upper hand.

He was so close she could smell mint on his breath. Anger glittered in the depths of his eyes, radiated from him like heat. "You think you know what grief is?" he asked. "How are you going to feel when you realize you played a role in the deaths of dozens—possibly hundreds—of innocent people across the United States, Canada, Mexico, and Europe? Brothers and sisters. Teenagers. Parents. Friends. Neighbors. Grandparents. How's that going to sit in your craw, Doctor?"

Anger snapped through her like the flick of a bullwhip. "This interview is over."

"I'm not finished with you."

She stared at him, speechless, her heart beating out of control. "My trials were not flawed," she said.

"Or maybe you're just protecting your interests."

"Go to hell."

His lips drew back in a snarl. "Let me clue you in on something, sweetheart. I'm not going to let this go. Not ever. I'm like a pit bull with an obsessive-compulsive personality. I've got my teeth in this deep, and if it's the last thing I do, I'm going to prove your little pet project is killing people. I'm going to do it with or without your help. I'm going to hound you, Doctor. And I'm going to make your life a living hell until I get what I want."

"Don't threaten me," she said with a calm she didn't feel.

"If you really cared about Sanchez—"

"Don't you *dare* bring my feelings for Walter in to this."

"Someone put a bullet in his chest. Don't you want to know who did it? Don't you want to know why, for chrissake?"

"Of course I do!" Only when her back bumped against the wall did she realize she'd long since relinquished her ground—all of it—and now she was trapped.

"The Ann Arbor police will find out who killed Walter." Struggling to keep a grip on her composure, she crossed her arms protectively in front of her, no longer caring what her body language told him. "In the interim, I will not indulge your fantasies, Detective. I stand by my work. You can make all the accusations and threats you want."

"Promises, honey, not threats. And rest assured I always make good on my promises."

Brushing past him, she headed toward the phone in the kitchen. "I'm calling the police." But her legs were shaking so badly she feared her knees might buckle before she reached it. She heard him behind her, but she didn't stop. Snatching up the phone, she raised her hand to punch the numbers only to see his broad hand come down and disconnect the line.

Eli wasn't easily intimidated, and she didn't scare at the drop of a hat. She'd had to fight dozens of battles in the course of her career. She'd waged war against highly-educated, driven, ruthless men and women with money, career, ego, or any combination of the three at stake. Because she believed in her work—because she believed in herself—she'd always been able to hold her own with even the most vocal of her counterparts.

This morning, however, grief had shattered her defenses and left her feeling fragile, her emotions raw and dangerously close to the surface.

"Get out," she said in a trembling voice.

"I'm not the enemy," he said.

For the first time she realized her breaths were coming short and fast. That her chest was tight and her voice was wedged in her throat. Oh, God, she was going to cry!

Appalled and humiliated that she would lose control in front of this heartless cop, she tried to turn away. A strong arm blocked her way. She stared at the obstruction, incredulous that she'd gotten through four days without breaking down, and her emotions had chosen this moment to betray her.

"Look, you may not like the way I operate," he said. "I don't blame you. I'm not the most likable guy. You may not like me personally, but goddamn it, I need some answers."

"You, Detective, are your largest impediment to getting what you want." Eli swiped at the traitorous tears scalding her cheeks. She wanted to shout at him to leave her alone—at least until she could get a handle on her emotions—but she didn't trust her voice.

"So I've been told," he muttered.

Closing her eyes, she rallied for control. But it wasn't enough. The tears burst their banks with a ferocity that left her shaking and weak. Mortified, she lowered her face into her hands and tried not to think about the predator watching her.

chapter
7

ADAM WATCHED HER COME APART WITH THE COOL indifference of a man who'd seen too many emotional displays to be affected by one now. He'd known he was pushing her. One look into her eyes and he'd known she wasn't going to be able to take much. Of course, being the bastard he was, he'd pushed anyway.

He should have been pleased. After all, this was what he wanted, wasn't it? To break her down. Make her vulnerable. Reduce her to tears so he could do a quick Jekyll-and-Hyde and approach her as the good cop. A nice guy she could spill her guts to. He shouldn't have felt like a coldhearted bastard for making her cry, but he did.

Sighing, Adam scrubbed a hand over his jaw and watched her shoulders shake. This was where he was supposed to do the 180-degree pirouette and apologize for being so hard on her. Tell her how tough this case has been. Not only for him, but for the families involved. This was the moment when he was supposed to show empathy and understanding. Get her to trust him. Comfort her. Touch her lightly on the shoulder to reassure her and let her know he was on her side.

Oddly, he couldn't bring himself to do any of those things. He told himself it was because he was out of practice. After all, it had been a while since he'd worked a witness. But as much as he didn't want to admit it, he knew his reluctance to interact with her on a personal level had more to do with the way he was reacting to her than his own shortcomings. The fact that she was attractive—and that he'd noticed—threatened to complicate an already complex situation.

Adam had always dealt with women the same way he dealt with men. Pretty eyes and curves had never made any difference when it came to getting what he wanted. Chad Deaton had called him an equal opportunity bastard.

Only Elizabeth Barnes wasn't some shady witness or two-bit hustler. She was an upstanding citizen with a respectable profession and a highly regarded place in the community. She wasn't accustomed to law enforcement tactics—or the last-ditch efforts of a bad-tempered, burned-out cop facing professional ruin.

Shoving his hands into his pockets, he watched her struggle to pull herself together, telling himself the tears weren't getting to him. He'd seen his share in fourteen years on the force, not to mention in the course of his own troubled marriage. He couldn't count the number of times tears had been used by some hard-up female hustler hoping to pluck his heartstrings. They'd soon learned he didn't have heartstrings to pluck.

Eli's glossy brown hair fell forward into her face. Her scent was clean and crisp and incredibly soft. She wore a black dress that buttoned up the front and came down to just below her knees. It wasn't tight, but he could make out her shape. Slender shoulders. Narrow waist. Generous hips. The black wool was a stark contrast to her pale features. Her shoes were patent leather with clunky heels that made her calves look too thin. But Adam thought she filled out that dress just fine.

He stared at her, stunned that he was standing there, ogling her. It had been a long time since he'd noticed those kinds of details about a woman. Even longer since he'd actually wondered what it might be like to do something about it.

He cleared his throat. "Dr. Barnes?"

Turning away from him, she walked to the sink and took a glass out of the cupboard. He stared at her back, refusing to let his gaze dip lower. Without speaking, she filled the glass with water, drank it down, then turned to him. "This is not a good time for you to be here."

"I know. I'm sorry. But it can't be helped."

"Walter and I were close," she said. "Losing him like that . . ." Her voice trailed off.

"I'm sorry." When she only continued to stare at him, he shifted, uncomfortable, and added, "I mean that. It's tough losing someone."

She leaned against the counter. Her face was pale within the frame of brown hair. She looked like she hadn't slept. Another twinge of guilt nipped at him, but he quickly shoved it back. He didn't have time to feel guilty for the way he'd treated her.

"For the record, Detective, I disagree with your theory about Valazine. But I suspect that in order to get you off my back, I'm going to have to play along."

"Fair enough."

She walked into the living room and settled into the loveseat. Adam followed and sat opposite her.

"What do you want to know?" She fingered the glasses that hung on a tiny chain around her neck, then slipped them on. The frames were too heavy for her face. But even bloodshot from crying, her eyes were amazing, he noticed. Not brown. Not hazel. Tawny, like a cat's and very pretty.

"I'm working a homicide," he began. "A murder-suicide committed by a man with no history of violence and no police record. He was successful. Had a loving family. He was happily married." Adam paused. "The crime was . . . brutal. His wife was pregnant. He stabbed her. He shot her. Then he put the pistol in his mouth and shot himself."

He knew just where to strike for maximum shock value,

and it worked. A shudder ran the length of her, then she exhaled a long breath. "God, that's horrible."

"The autopsy showed he had Valazine in his bloodstream. There was a prescription bottle and some pills found at his residence. He didn't leave a note. No explanation. I have two dead bodies. But I don't have a motive. I'm trying to find out why it happened."

"We're talking about your brother, aren't we?" she asked.

He glanced away, uncomfortable that the conversation had become personal, then nodded.

"Was he depressed?" she asked.

"I was able to find out that he had been to a shrink. I don't know for certain if he was formally diagnosed. Is there any other reason why Valazine would be prescribed?"

"Was he schizophrenic?"

"No."

"You're attributing his violent behavior to the drug as opposed to his depression?"

"I didn't realize depression turned people into murderers."

"It doesn't, generally speaking. But serious depression can bring on thoughts of death or sometimes even a preoccupation with death. Serious depression can certainly impede one's judgment. It can cause destructive behavior. Sometimes enough to commit suicide."

"Murder seems extreme."

"I agree."

"I'm trying to find out if it's feasible for the drug to be suspect."

"Of more than three thousand test subjects, not one of them reported violent or bizarre behavior as a side effect of the medication they were taking."

"None of them? Are you certain?"

"I saw the test results myself. I wrote the protocol and the final report. Yes, I am absolutely certain."

The words rang in his ears with dreadful finality. That wasn't the answer he wanted to hear. Damn it, it wasn't the answer he *needed* to hear. To believe his brother could have flipped out, murdered Julie and their unborn child, and then turned the gun on himself was unthinkable.

Adam didn't believe it. He wouldn't.

"Have you spoken to his psychiatrist?" she asked.

"The shrink stonewalled me. Doctor-patient confidentiality bullshit."

She didn't look very sympathetic. "If your brother was prescribed Valazine by a psychiatrist, more than likely he was depressed. Perhaps even bipolar or schizophrenic. Valazine was developed specifically for forms of depression that are difficult to treat. Unfortunately, some emotionally troubled individuals act destructively."

"I don't believe that's what happened in this instance."

"I think he took the drug and wigged out," he said.

"I think you're wrong. The incidents cited in those articles are coincidental. There's no way a side effect such as what you've outlined could have been missed."

Adam turned the information over in his brain. "Is there any way someone could have covered up side effects?"

"That might happen in the movies, Detective, but not in real life."

"Why not?"

"Well, for one thing, there are too many people involved in the clinical trials and then in the approval process. There are dozens of check-and-balance systems in place that are designed solely to prevent any one individual from handling that kind of information alone."

"So, hypothetically speaking," he began, "in order to pull something like this off, it would have to be a group effort?"

She nodded.

"So it's not impossible."

"Not impossible, but extremely unlikely. You keep forgetting that I was very much involved with the trials themselves. I dealt with the medical personnel at the clinic. I saw the patient interview transcripts. I wrote reports based on those transcripts. There's no way information like that could have gotten past me."

"Is there any way I can get my hands on the paperwork dealing with the clinical trials?"

"I don't have the authority to give you that information. All the scientists at Roth sign confidentiality agreements. I'm afraid you'll have to go through the proper channels."

"I'll keep this strictly confidential. You've got my word."

She shook her head. "I can't."

He wasn't sure why he believed she was telling the truth about the drug, but he did. She was too serious. Too sincere. Too passionate about what she did. On the other hand, maybe his willingness to believe her had something to do with those pretty eyes. "Tell me about the side effects that *were* reported."

"If you're looking for adverse event data, all adverse events are on file with the FDA. All of that data is made public as specified by the Freedom of Information Act. It's on the website."

"What about post-marketing complaints?"

"They would be filed with the FDA's MedWatch program."

"Would Roth be notified as well?"

"Yes."

"Have you been notified of any adverse reactions citing irrational or bizarre behavior?"

"No."

She pressed her lips together and Adam noticed a dimple on her left cheek. He wondered if she had dimples when she smiled.

"There's not a drug on the market that is without side effects," she said. "All drugs, particularly prescription drugs, have adverse reactions and must be prescribed very carefully by medical professionals."

"What are the most common side effects of Valazine?"

"Well, the most common is orthostatic hypotension—"

"Ortho—" He let out a self-deprecating laugh. "Ah, in English."

"Abnormally low blood pressure upon standing."

"Got it." Removing his notepad, he jotted it down phonetically. "What else?"

"Sedation. Palpitations, nausea, dizziness, insomnia, constipation, tachycardia—"

"Tachycardia?"

"Racing heart."

He scribbled. "What else?"

"There's also agitation, peripheral edema, sexual dysfunction."

"Sounds like you're talking about a disease instead of the medicine used to treat one."

"Depression can be debilitating for some individuals. Treatment-resistant forms of depression and schizophrenia can most certainly lead to suicide. The adverse reactions I mentioned are usually quite mild compared to the depression some of these people suffer. Most of the symptoms I listed appear in less than four percent of the tested population."

"That's a small percentage."

"Valazine is an amazing drug. It's safe. And I stand by my work."

"You mentioned agitation as one of the side effects."

"Yes."

"How do you measure agitation?"

"Participants rated the level of agitation on a range of one to five. Most of the affected test subjects reported a feeling of restlessness or general impatience." She looked at him over the top of her glasses. "Again, this was experienced by only a fraction of the tested population."

"What about paranoia?"

"No."

"Bizarre behavior?"

"No." She leaned back in her chair and studied him.

Adam knew he was treading on thin ice. He wasn't here on official business. If she checked up on him, he could find himself in very hot water. But whether he was doing this as a cop—or a brother—he couldn't let it go. He smelled a rat with regard to Valazine, and his predator's instinct was in full alert.

"What else?" he pressed.

"What you don't appear to be hearing, Detective, is that Valazine is safe. It has been tested extensively, has given countless people their lives back, and more than likely has prevented a number of suicides. The drug does not cause violent behavior."

"Unless someone kept the information from coming to light."

"You're very determined, aren't you?"

"As determined as you are to protect your territory."

"I assure you, this has nothing to do with territoriality."

"Or maybe someone is just covering their ass."

"Are you finished?"

He scowled at her. "I want to contact the people who took part in the trials."

"You asked about that once before and my answer is still unequivocally the same. Absolutely not."

"I'm not asking, Dr. Barnes. If you don't help me, I'll find another way."

She rose from her place on the loveseat. "You'll have to find another way, Detective. Or is that still your title these days?"

Adam tried to hide his surprise, but it jolted him with the force of a small electrical shock.

"I did some detective work of my own, in case you're wondering how I discovered your little secret," she said. "I know you're not on active duty. Would you mind terribly explaining that to me?"

That she knew he wasn't on the active roster told him she'd called the precinct. He should have anticipated that, but he hadn't. Damn her. "Not bad for a civilian."

"We research scientists can be pretty resourceful when we put our minds to it."

Adam hadn't expected a confrontation. Not from this scientist with her weird glasses and practical shoes. Now he was faced with the uncomfortable task of setting the record straight before it spiraled out of control. "I'm a cop. I'm on leave. That's all you need to know."

"Why are you on leave?"

"Because I got shot, goddamn it."

Her eyes widened with surprise. "Oh." She looked away. Adam tried not to notice when her fingers fumbled with the heart-shaped locket between her breasts. "I didn't know. I'm sorry."

He almost smiled at genuineness of her shock and the polite way she dropped the subject. He found himself unduly relieved she had the good manners not to question him further. "Who did you talk to at the precinct?" he asked. "Internal affairs? Who?"

"About a dozen people, actually, but I finally ended up with a Sergeant Deaton."

His temper coiled, a snake preparing to strike. "Deaton gave you an earful, did he?"

She tilted her head quizzically. "Actually, he told me you were a good cop."

That stopped Adam cold. He stared at her, not sure what to think, not sure what to say next. In the back of his mind, he wondered what else Deaton had told her. If he'd given her the details of the shooting, told her about the seriousness of Adam's injuries, talked about the months he'd been unable to speak or stand or even feed himself. He wondered if Deaton had tried to discredit him. If he'd reported her call to IA. He wondered if Deaton had mentioned that most of the other cops at the precinct thought Adam had already taken a leap off the deep end. That his career had been dying a slow and painful death over the last three years. He wondered if Deaton had been the one to tell her about Michael.

"So did your conversation with Deaton satisfy your scientific curiosity?" he asked.

"Most of it." She looked down at her hands. "He told me about your brother. I'm sorry."

Adam felt himself recoil. He tried to curb the reaction, but didn't succeed and could only hope she didn't notice.

"I didn't mean to upset you," she said.

"You didn't," he snapped. But the mention of Michael had thrown him.

He rose from the sofa, feeling deflated because he was no closer to getting any solid information than he had been when he'd left Chicago some six hours ago.

"I think we're finished here," she said.

Adam looked up, watched her walk to the foyer. She had nice legs, he mused, even if her calves were a little skinny. He made eye contact with her a moment later only to realize she'd caught him checking her out.

"Is there anything I can say or do that will convince you I'm right about this?" he asked.

She thought about it for a moment. "Prove that someone falsified records. Find a formal complaint filed with the FDA. Of course, a controlled trial with those kinds of results would do the job, but that's not going to happen."

She opened the door.

Adam paused in the doorway, turned to meet her gaze. "Thanks for talking to me."

Her smile lacked enthusiasm. "It's not like you gave me a choice."

"I hope you were straight with me."

"I have no reason to lie."

"Some people like to see cops ram their heads into brick walls."

"In your case, I'm afraid I'd have to sympathize with the wall."

Adam smiled. "Point taken."

She glanced at her watch. That was his cue to leave. Oddly, he wasn't in any hurry to get out of there. But he'd run out of questions and his witness had long since run out of patience.

"Let me know if you think of anything else, Dr. Barnes, even if you think it might not be important."

"Of course."

He wanted to say something else, but by the time he realized what it was, she'd closed the door in his face.

"Be careful," he whispered, and started for the Tahoe.

THE MONDAY MORNING EXECUTIVE-TEAM MEETING at Roth Pharmaceuticals was a solemn affair. In the formal conference room furnished with rosewood furniture, plush ergonomic chairs, and state-of-the-art audiovisual equipment, the team members took their seats around the large oval conference table.

Peter Roth settled into his chair at the head of the table. Next to him, Kevin Chambers sipped his coffee and scribbled notes on a legal pad. Dr. Thomas Bornheimer, the youngest member of Roth's executive team, slouched in his high-back chair and stared into his Yogi Bear coffee mug, looking as if he'd just lost his best friend.

There were two other people present who normally didn't attend the Monday morning meetings. Eli recognized the woman as Ruth Monroe, a consultant with the public relations firm Mr. Roth used on occasion. The man was Clyde Cummings, the new security director Peter Roth had hired just last month. Eli wondered why Peter had seen fit to summon them to the meeting.

She left her place at the door and entered the room with her leather day planner in hand, taking her place opposite Peter. The chair next to her was profoundly vacant, and she felt Walter's absence like a stake in her heart.

Kevin looked up from his coffee and smiled faintly at her. Eli returned the smile, but it felt plastic on her face. There wasn't a whole lot to smile about this morning.

Peter cleared his throat. "I appreciate each of you coming in so early on this cold Monday morning. I know last week was a tough week." He paused, his eyes scanning the silent listeners. "I extend my deepest sympathy to each of you. I know some of you were very close to Walter." His gaze paused on Eli. "All of us liked and respected Dr. Sanchez, and he will be missed greatly by me and, I'm sure, the rest of you.

"While this is a sad time for Roth Pharmaceuticals, Dr. Sanchez's passing also presents certain challenges we must work hard to overcome and some more serious problems we must work hard to avoid." He glanced over at the two new meeting attendees sitting at the table. "I've invited our security director, Clyde Cummings, as well as Ruth Monroe of Levinson Public Relations to our executive-team meeting this morning. Clyde is an ex–state trooper and will be working with the Ann Arbor PD to keep us apprised of how the case is progressing. As most of you know, pharmaceutical companies face some unique PR problems, and Dr. Sanchez's murder may complicate the delicate balance we've worked hard to achieve. My only request at this point is that each of you refrains from talking to the media with regard to Dr. Sanchez. Ms. Monroe will handle all contact with the media to avoid anything we say being taken out of context. Are there any questions?"

When no one answered, Peter nodded to the security director.

Clyde Cummings's corporate blue suit stretched taut over his muscled shoulders. His hair was cut military short and he wore a grim expression that seemed permanently etched into his face. "As you all know, Dr. Walter Sanchez was murdered last week in his home near Sugarbrush Park. I've been in contact with Detective Martin Lindquist, and as of last evening, there are no suspects. The motive does not appear to be robbery, as was first believed. The police have interviewed several Roth employees. If they need to talk with any of you in the future, I will notify you."

Eli was still grappling with the fact that the police no longer believed Walter's death was due to an attempted robbery when Cummings continued. "Mr. Roth has very generously increased the reward to twenty thousand for information leading to the arrest and conviction of the person or persons responsible for Dr. Sanchez's murder. I have a meeting scheduled with Detective Lindquist at four o'clock this afternoon. The investigation is ongoing at this time. I'll keep Mr. Roth apprised of any and all developments."

He looked over at Roth. Roth nodded, then his gaze went to Ruth Monroe.

Monroe flashed a smile that was a little too bright for the subject of murder. "Levinson Public Relations plans to maintain a very low profile during the ongoing police investigation. I will be on call twenty-four hours a day for the next few weeks in case something comes up with the media. While Dr. Sanchez's death is not in any way related to Roth Pharmaceuticals, there are precautions we will need to take to prevent any PR problems from arising. Mr. Roth and the rest of you have worked very hard at community relations in an industry that sometimes is not portrayed in a favorable light by the media. I intend to ensure your hard work has not been in vain."

She shuffled the index cards in front of her. "Mr. Roth and I are working on a plan to put together a scholarship fund for Dr. Sanchez's two grandsons who live in Orlando, Florida. Right now we're looking at financing two scholarships to the college of each boy's choice. I have been in contact with Dr. Sanchez's daughter, Marie, and she appreciates very much what Mr. Roth is doing for her sons." She looked around the room. "I reiterate what Mr. Cummings said earlier about the media. Please direct any and all inquiries from the media to my office. If I'm not there, you can page me." She passed a stack of business cards to Cummings, who took one and passed it on to the next person. "Even if you think a media inquiry is just routine, please let me know."

Eli thought about her meeting with Adam Boedecker and wondered if she should bring it up. If Dr. Sanchez's death was high enough on the potential-problem scale to warrant a PR consultant, a homicide detective making noise about clinical trials and undisclosed adverse events would be off the charts.

But some inner warning stopped her. It wasn't that she didn't trust the other members of the executive team. She did. Implicitly. But in light of the accusations that had been made against Roth, she figured it would be best to run her concerns by Thomas or Kevin first. If they felt the situation warranted action, then she would take it directly to Peter Roth.

chapter
8

"HEY, YOU."

Eli looked up from her computer to see Dr. Thomas Bornheimer enter her office. Pleasure fluttered through her, and for the first time all day her smile felt genuine. "Hey yourself."

"If you're busy, I can come back."

"I'm never too busy for you." She minimized the file she'd been working on and gave him her full attention. He was wearing the required button-down shirt and tie plus his usual faded jeans despite Peter Roth's efforts to get him into khakis. Two tiny gold rings glinted at his left earlobe. Thin and blond, Thomas looked more like a college student than a clinical research associate who, at the ripe age of twenty-nine, had already been with the firm for eight years. Like her, he had been hired by Walter fresh out of the University of Michigan. He was the youngest member of the executive team—and one of the most talented scientists she'd ever known. He was intelligent, gifted, and, like Eli, driven. She liked him as a person and admired him as a scientist and enjoyed working with him.

"I like the goatee," she said.

"Really?" Looking a little embarrassed, he scrubbed his fingers across the new growth of hair on his chin. "I thought it might make me look . . . you know, older."

"It does. A little, I mean."

"Peter asked me this morning to shave it."

"That's his job. You drive him nuts."

"He's going to fire me one of these days."

"He's bluffing. You're much too talented to lose. Some other firm would snatch you up in a second." Smiling, she removed her glasses. "I think it's the blue jeans and button-down theme you have going that gets to Peter. He's very corporate, you know. He wants you to conform."

Thomas grinned. "Never." Shoving his hands in his pockets, he looked around her small office, then at her. "Mind if I sit down and bug you awhile?"

"Not at all. Have a seat."

She felt a ripple of concern for him as he took the visitor's chair opposite her desk, and for the first time she realized she wasn't the only person grieving for Walter. Thomas had been close to him. She'd seen him several times in the last few days, and each time he'd been walking around looking like a lost pup.

"You holding up okay?" she asked.

"Yeah. How about you?"

"All right, I think."

"It must have been tough, uh . . . finding him like you did."

Eli picked a mechanical pencil off her desktop and stowed it in a drawer. "It was . . . awful."

"I'm sorry, I didn't mean to—"

She raised her hand. "It's okay," she said. "You don't have to walk on eggshells around me. I mean, we're both trying to deal with it. It's a good thing to talk, you know?"

"Yeah, I guess." Leaning forward, he put his elbows on his knees. "Jeez, I can't believe the old man's gone. He was . . . larger than life. I mean, shit, if Walter can die, it could happen to anyone."

"It's hard to believe he's gone."

"That's what I've been thinking about all day. I can't seem to get it out of my head, Eli. The way he died . . ."

"I know. It's hard to come to terms with something like that," she offered. "It takes time."

"Things just aren't going to be the same around here without him." Silence reigned for a full minute, then Thomas chuckled. Eli looked up to find him grinning sheepishly at her. "Remember that time Walter spoke at the U of M graduation ceremony two years ago?" he said.

The memory brought a smile to her face. "How could I forget?"

"He spoke for twenty-two minutes and didn't notice the six-inch train of Charmin sticking out the back of his pants."

"Good thing the television news crew didn't catch that rear angle."

"You and I were backstage, laughing our asses off."

She laughed now, realized it felt good to remember the better times. "It was a good speech," she said.

"The Charmin made it better."

Eli giggled.

"The old man was a good sport about it when we told him."

She sighed. "God, Thomas, I miss him."

"Yeah, me, too. I hope the cops find who did it."

She was about to agree when Kevin Chambers poked his head into her office. "Eli, what are you still doing here? I thought you'd cut out early today."

She suppressed a quick rise of annoyance. Kevin hadn't even acknowledged Thomas, hadn't even noticed him sitting there. "I'm trying to finish up some work on the protocol for ROT-535," she said.

"You're ahead of schedule on that. It can wait, can't it?"

She looked over at Thomas. "Thomas and I were just talking about Walter."

Kevin glanced at the young man slumped in the chair as if seeing him for the first time. "How's it going, Bornheimer?"

"Hey, dude." When Kevin turned his attention back to Eli, Thomas rolled his eyes.

Kevin pulled out the second visitor's chair and sat. "You doing okay?" he asked Eli.

"I'm fine."

She wasn't fine. She was heartbroken about Walter, tired from not getting any sleep the night before, and deeply troubled by the thoughts pounding through her head courtesy of a certain detective from Chicago. Ever since her meeting with Adam Boedecker last week, she hadn't been able to get his accusations off her mind.

"I just heard that Peter has upped the reward to twenty-five thousand," Kevin said. "He paid for the funeral, too." When neither Thomas nor Eli responded, he added, "To help the family, you know."

And to put a feather in Roth's PR cap, she thought. "That's very generous of Peter."

"Yeah," Thomas chimed in, "real charitable."

Kevin didn't seem to notice the subtle sarcasm, but Eli did and shot Thomas a cut-it-out look. Now wasn't the time for squabbling. It was, however, a good opportunity for her to confide in the two men about Detective Boedecker's accusations. She'd debated all morning whether to talk to Peter Roth directly. He'd taken the decision away from her by being in meetings all day. But the accusations were eating at her, and she wanted the opinions of her peers.

"Kevin, do you remember the detective from Chicago who came to see me in my office last week?" she asked.

Thomas started to rise, but Eli raised her hand. "This involves you, too, Thomas. Would you mind staying for a couple of minutes? I'd like your opinion on something."

"Sure." Shrugging, he sat back down.

"Yeah, that scary guy that looked like a hit man," Kevin said. "He was at the funeral, too. Criminy, I can't believe that guy was a cop. Chicago PD must be hard up."

"He came to my house after the funeral," she said.

Kevin's brows snapped together. "What on earth for?"

Quickly, Eli summarized her meeting with the detective, leaving out the part about his brother and that she'd broken down and cried. The minutes when she'd lost it and he'd just stood there like a stone statue and watched.

Reaching for her briefcase, she pulled out copies of the articles Boedecker had given her and passed them to the two men. Silence pressed down on her as they read.

Thomas looked up first. "A bunch of psychos wig out and this cop tries to lay the blame on Valazine? That's a stretch."

Kevin shook the papers in his hand. "This is ridiculous and outrageous." He tossed the articles onto her desk. "That cop doesn't have a clue what he's talking about. He's not a scientist or a doctor, for God's sake. He's making some serious allegations without one iota of proof. That's slander. Roth doesn't need garbage like this floating around." He frowned at Eli. "Have you talked to Peter about this?"

"I was going to, but he's been in meetings all day. I didn't think it was appropriate to introduce this kind of information at the executive team meeting this morning with Ruth Monroe and Clyde Cummings there."

"Good call," said Thomas.

Eli looked from Thomas to Kevin. "None of these allegations is founded," she said. "It's all speculation. Frankly, I wasn't even sure how seriously to take them. But this detective seems very . . . determined."

"I'm glad you told me," Kevin said. "I'll apprise Peter of the situation myself. He'll probably want to get legal involved. We'll have our lawyers take care of Boedecker."

"He threatened to go to the media," she said.

"A lawsuit ought to stop him," Thomas put in.

"Do you think these allegations are something we should look in to?" she asked. "I mean, just to be safe?"

Kevin narrowed his eyes. "What are you saying?"

"I mean, should we have another look at our study material? Maybe review the adverse reaction raw data? Just so we're armed in case something . . . unexpected comes up."

"Based on a few sensational articles and some moron with a badge?" Kevin asked. "I don't think that's cause for a knee-jerk reaction."

"The FDA will let us know if they receive any complaints," Thomas added. "They're very diligent about that, Eli. You know that. As of now, they have not done so."

"I know, but what if . . ." Eli let her words trail off, not sure how to finish the sentence. They were talking about her lifework. Walter's lifework. A drug that had helped thousands deal with the ravages of depression and bipolar disorder. She didn't want to see a breakthrough medication vilified by an overzealous media for no other reasons than a couple of bizarre coincidences and one man's personal crusade.

Kevin leaned forward in his chair. "These articles might look to a layperson like they hold water, Eli. But you and I know differently. We know there are hundreds of thousands of people taking Valazine. We know that not one test subject reacted violently to the drug. We also know that if there had been any complaints of this sort, the FDA would be breathing down our necks so hard we'd get windburn."

"For once, I agree with Corporate Kevin," Thomas added.

She regarded both men, choosing her next words carefully. "I'm going to play devil's advocate for a moment, and only because I want your professional opinions. I can't help but wonder if, because of the very nature of the disorder for which Valazine is prescribed, it could be that we . . . overlooked something important."

Thomas shook his head. "If I hadn't been involved with the study, I might say it's possible. But I know how diligent we were. All of us. There's no way in hell we missed anything, Eli."

Kevin looked downright indignant. "Absolutely not. And I think it would be a total waste of time and resources to rerun any phase of those trials."

"So you don't think we should look in to this?" she asked.

"No," Kevin said.

"Agreed," Thomas concurred.

"You'll talk to Peter?" she asked Kevin.

"He needs to know. And I'm sure he'll want me to take

the matter to legal." He tapped on the articles with his fingers. "We can't have some loose cannon running around spewing unfounded accusations that could not only tarnish the image of a promising new drug but do irrevocable damage to Roth's reputation."

Thomas nodded. "It freaks me out a little to agree with Kevin twice in the same day, but I do. Guess I'm going for a record." He cut the other man a wry smile.

Frowning, Kevin folded his set of articles in half. "Eli, this is the kind of misinformation that causes the public to panic. Pharmaceutical companies make terrific bad guys. According to Joe Public, we have secret government contracts. We kill bunnies just for the fun of it. We dump biological hazards into rivers and lakes. We keep drugs from cancer patients and the elderly because we like playing God. And we're making billions at the cost of those who are seriously ill or dying. The bottom line is this, Eli: People love to hate pharmaceutical companies. You know that. This cop from Chicago is simply too damn lazy to solve whatever crime he's working on and needs a scapegoat."

Of all the words that came to mind when she thought of Adam Boedecker, *lazy* was not one of them. She looked at Thomas. "Thomas?"

"I think it would be unwise to consider the information relayed in these articles too seriously at this point. There's virtually no medical evidence to back up any of the allegations."

Eli had known the two men would concur. The fact of the matter was she agreed, too. Still, Detective Adam Boedecker had planted a fragment of doubt in the back of her brain. That minute fragment had somehow managed to take root. She would never be able to live with herself if she found out a drug she had spent her life putting on the market had a severe side effect that had indirectly caused dozens, maybe even hundreds, of deaths. The thought made her shudder.

*   *   *

ELI SAT ALONE IN HER OFFICE, STARING OUT AT the parking lot. Darkness had fallen, and the single sodium-vapor streetlamp cast yellow light over the few remaining vehicles. She glanced at her watch, surprised to see that it was nearly nine P.M.

She should have packed up her briefcase and called it a day hours ago. She was tired to the bone. Worse, she couldn't stop thinking about the allegations Adam Boedecker had made. What if he'd somehow stumbled upon an insidious side effect that caused previously nonviolent people to become violent? While her scientist's mind assured her that that was not the case, the possibility refused to leave her alone.

Spinning back to her computer, she logged in to Roth's network and called up the summary report she and Walter had compiled from the raw data garnered during the clinical trials on Valazine nearly eighteen months earlier. Once the report was retrieved, she paged down to the final labeling section and began to skim headings. "Clinical Pharmacology." "Indications and Usage." "Contraindications." "Warnings." She wasn't sure exactly what she was looking for. Anything that indicated, even indirectly, that bizarre or violent behavior had been experienced by any of the study participants during the trials.

She left the final labeling section and clicked on another file that contained the summarization of adverse findings.

Adverse Findings Observed in Short-Term, Placebo-Controlled Trials with Valazine.

In a placebo-controlled study of depressed patients, 10% (23/235) of Valazine patients discontinued due to an adverse event.

	Valazine (n=235)	Placebo (n=235)
Nausea	5.3%	0.4%
Asthenia	2.7%	0.6%
Dizziness	1.9%	0.7%
Somnolence	1.6%	0.1%

Eli closed the file and paged down to the "Discontin-ued/Study Deletions" page and read. Of the twenty-three individuals who dropped out of the study, most had done so because of problems with nausea. Nowhere had any individual listed that their depression had worsened or they had experienced any bizarre, violent, or unexpected behavior.

At the bottom of the page, she noticed a side notation that one individual, an eighteen-year-old male, had been removed from the study due to death. Patient number 3259. Her heart kicked hard in her chest when she realized this was the first time she'd seen the information. For some reason, it hadn't been included in the reports sub-mitted to her by the clinic doctor, and therefore she hadn't included it in the report she'd submitted to Kevin Cham-bers and Peter Roth. Heart pounding, she read on and quickly realized patient 3259's death had been caused by a motor vehicle accident. Under different circumstances, she would have assumed the death was unrelated to the study. Tonight, with an increasing uneasiness churning in her stomach, she knew she didn't have a choice but to check it out.

Finding the name of a study participant was going to be tricky business, considering that all participants' names were kept strictly confidential. At the two clinics where the trials were administered, each participant was issued a number at the beginning of the study. In the course of the trial, all Roth personnel dealt strictly with patient num-bers. The only people who knew the names of the study participants were the medical professionals at the clinic where the actual study was administered. In the case of patient 3259, the clinic was Manicon Laboratories in Yp-silanti, Michigan, half an hour away.

Eli had worked with the head physician, Dr. Gordon Rudnick, on a number of clinical trials. They'd attended a few conferences together over the years. He was more of an acquaintance than a friend, but her conscience wouldn't let her put this aside. She wanted the details of patient 3259's death. Even if it wasn't related to the study, she should have been told. The details should have appeared in the report sent to her by the clinic.

Eli didn't like breaking the rules. The last thing she wanted to do was put a colleague on the spot. But she couldn't ignore this.

Knowing it was a long shot, she pulled up her contact information database on her computer and typed in Dr. Rudnick's name. Both his office and home numbers appeared on her screen. She picked up the phone and punched in his home number.

He answered on the first ring. "Hello?"

"Dr. Rudnick?"

"Yes?"

"This is Elizabeth Barnes."

"Oh, hi, Eli. Is everything all right?"

She glanced down at her watch, saw it was after ten o'clock. "I didn't realize it was so late. I'm sorry to bother you at home . . ."

"Ah, no problem. Unfortunately, I'm an insomniac. You're still at the office?"

"Well, yes," she said a little sheepishly.

"Walter always said you were something of a workaholic." He lowered his voice. "I was very sorry to hear about his passing."

"Thank you." Eli closed her eyes against the quick swipe of pain. "I'm wondering if you can tell me where I can get some information."

"I'm a walking encyclopedia. Shoot."

"This is regarding the Valazine trials we did a couple of years ago."

"Sure, I remember. Excellent study. Congratulations on the Distinguished Woman of Science Award."

"Thanks." She chose her next words carefully. "I'm looking for information on a test subject."

"What kind of information?" His voice had turned cautious.

She hesitated, held her breath. "A name."

"Ah, Eli, you know I'm not supposed to—"

"Gordon, I understand the rules. But I thought maybe we could overlook the confidentiality issue since this particular subject is . . . passed away."

"Um, well . . . we've got that privacy policy, you know?"

Hating that she'd put him in a tough position, she took a deep breath and trudged onward. "There was an eighteen-year-old male who died in a car accident in the course of the study. I'm compiling a report on the drop-out rate for Kevin Chambers and I need more information on this individual." She disliked lying to him, disliked even more asking him to break confidentiality rules. But if there was a shred of truth in Adam Boedecker's accusations, she needed to know.

"Well, if it were anyone but you asking, Eli, I'd give them an unequivocal no."

"I know you would. Gordon, you know I wouldn't ask if it weren't important."

"Walter always said you were persistent."

Her throat tightened at the mention of Walter, but she quickly shoved the emotion back. Oh, how she wished he were here now to guide her through this. "I'm sorry to put you in an uncomfortable position."

He sighed. "How soon do you need it?"

"Yesterday?"

He laughed. "Tomorrow morning will have to do."

"I appreciate it Gordon. Thank you."

"Give my best to Kevin and Peter, will you?"

"Sure will."

Eli was still holding the phone when he disconnected. Turning in her chair, she looked out the window at the parking lot below, and wondered what she'd just set into motion.

chapter
9

ELI KNEW BETTER THAN TO SHOW UP AT ROTH Pharmaceutical's off-site archive storage warehouse at eleven o'clock at night. It wasn't as if she expected to find a glaring error she'd made some eighteen months ago. She wasn't exactly sure *what* she was looking for. Perhaps correspondence between Manicon Laboratories and Roth Pharmaceuticals that would explain why information on the death of patient 3259 hadn't been included in the study.

She knew it was a long shot, but her scientist's curiosity had been roused. Her scientist's ego ruffled. Boedecker's accusations threatened not only the reputation of Roth Pharmaceuticals but her professional reputation as well. More important, and something she held far more dear to her heart, her personal integrity was being questioned. Right or wrong—and no matter how painful—she wouldn't stop digging until she was certain there was absolutely no way she or anyone on her team had missed adverse events with regard to the Valazine clinical trials.

Eli prided herself on the meticulousness of her work. That she could have overlooked something so important disturbed her deeply. If she didn't find anything tonight, at least she could assure herself that she hadn't made a mistake. Chances were, the information about patient 3259's death had never been given to her by the clinic. Once she proved that to herself, she'd be on her way home and calling herself a fool for letting Boedecker—and her conscience—cajole her into coming here in the dead of night to dig around in some dusty old files.

"I'm an idiot," she muttered as she pulled the Volkswagen up to the gate. "It's twelve degrees outside, and I'm going to rummage through record-storage boxes for God only knows what. Wonderful." Lowering the window, she leaned out and punched the security code into the numerical keypad. The iron gate swung open with a grate of steel against steel and she pulled in to the lot.

She parked the Volkswagen adjacent to storage building number 2 and shut down the engine. The place was deserted. Not surprising considering the hour and the temperature. Most sane people were at home watching the news or already in bed. Picking up her gloves from the passenger seat, she opened the car door and got out.

The wind greeted her with a biting slap of cold. A halo glowed around the three-quarter moon in the western sky. Around her, it was so utterly quiet she could hear the branches of the trees that grew along the creek behind the warehouse clicking together in the wind.

"And if you had an ounce of sense you'd get back in the car and drive home," she muttered.

But Eli knew there was no way she could let this go now that she knew at least one person had died in the course of the study. Common sense told her that patient 3259's death had absolutely nothing to do with Valazine. But she needed an explanation. She needed to know in her heart she was right. She needed black-and-white proof. Because the alternative was too terrible to contemplate.

Huddled against the cold, her low-heeled pumps clicking smartly on the asphalt, she crossed the lot to the building and used her key to open the door. Inside, the warehouse was cavernous and dark as a cave. She flipped a switch, and overhead lights illuminated heavy-duty floor-to-ceiling shelving units stacked with hundreds of corrugated boxes. A number written in bold red marker identified each box.

Eli stared at the endless rows, feeling a little over-whelmed by the task ahead of her, then dug through her purse for the manifest containing the box numbers she needed. She found box numbers 587 through 591 in nu-merical order halfway down the fourth row. Luckily, they weren't too high for her to reach. Stepping up on the edge of the lowest shelf, she wrestled the box from its perch and let it drop to the concrete floor with a *thunk*!

Crossing box 587 from her list, she knelt next to it, opened the top, and skimmed the folder tabs inside. She found early protocol drafts and correspondence between herself and Gordon Rudnick at Manicon Laboratories. In-ternal memorandums. Dozens of forms required by the Food and Drug Administration. Meeting minutes. Tucked inside her correspondence file, she even found a birthday card from Walter. Smiling, she opened the card, felt the heat of sudden tears behind her eyes. Inside, Walter had roughly quoted Henry David Thoreau: "Go confidently in the direction of your dreams." That had been on her thir-tieth birthday a year and a half ago.

Pressing the card to her chest, feeling foolish at her sentimentality, Eli blinked back the tears, then slipped the card into her purse. Glancing at her watch, she realized if she didn't pick up the pace, searching the files was going to take her all night. Quickly, she closed the box, heaved it back onto the shelf, and pulled down the next one. After crossing it off her list, she opened the top and began pag-ing through the manila folders. FDA correspondence. Study-related invoices. More meeting minutes. Manicon Laboratories correspondence. Trinity Laboratories. Her fingers paused on the brown expanding folder labeled "Potential Study Participant Profiles." She pulled the folder and opened it.

Each application was identified with a number as op-posed to a name. Flipping quickly through the numbers, she found patient number 3259 and read his information.

Eighteen-year-old male. Caucasian. Full-time college student enrolled in the liberal arts program at the University
of Michigan. Diagnosed with bipolar disorder at the age
of fifteen. Did not respond to Prozac. Tendency to take
medication erratically. Some alcohol use. Some binge
drinking. Smoked cigarettes on occasion. Parents divorced. Mother worked at the world headquarters of a
major pizza company based in Ann Arbor.

Realizing she may have enough information to find this
individual's name without having to rely on Dr. Rudnick,
she folded the profile, tucked it into her purse, and went
to the next file. Her knees were cramped, her fingers aching and stiff from the cold, but she didn't stop. She paged
through another correspondence file and then the fully executed contract with Trinity Laboratories before closing
the box and hefting it back onto the shelf. Three more
boxes, then she could go.

She was in the process of hustling the third box from
its nest when she found herself plunged into total darkness. Straightening abruptly, she bumped her head on the
shelf above her. "Ouch. Crap." Aware that her heart was
pounding, she listened to the silence, blind, trying to decide what to do next.

She couldn't recall if the warehouse was manned after
hours. She hadn't seen any cars parked in the lot. Willing
her heart to slow, she reached out and touched the shelf
in front of her. Looking up, she realized a Plexiglas sky-
light overhead let in a small amount of natural light from
the moon and the streetlamp outside. Not enough light to
illuminate details, but as her eyes adjusted to the darkness,
she realized it would be enough to keep her from breaking
her neck on the way out.

A noise to her right, in the general direction of the door,
snapped her head around. "Hello?" she called out. "Is
someone there?"

The silence was even more profound without the buzzing of the lights. She could hear the wind whistling around
the building, a ghost lost in the dark and cold.

"Would you please turn the lights back on?" she hollered. Then, when no one answered, she added, "Some-time today, if you don't mind."

Feeling her way down the aisle toward the door, she bumped her knee on a box that was protruding from the shelf. "Damn it," she muttered. Irritated and feeling fool-ish for being so jumpy, she shoved the box back. "This was a really stupid idea, O distinguished woman of sci-ence."

She'd reached the end of the aisle when the sound of a door slamming stopped her dead in her tracks. For the first time, she knew for certain that she wasn't alone, and a jolt of adrenaline streaked through her. She tried to stay calm by telling herself that an employee or security officer had happened by, seen the lights on, and assumed some-one had forgotten to turn them off.

But if that was the case, why didn't he respond when I called out?

Eli ordered herself to stay calm. Surely there was a logical explanation. She just didn't know what the hell it was at the moment. She stood there, straining to see in the darkness, trying in vain to slow her breathing and ignore the burn of adrenaline in her gut. She'd taken one step out of the aisle toward the door when the sound of footsteps sent her slinking back.

Someone was coming toward her.

Fear trembled through her. Aware that she was breathing heavily, she put her hand over her mouth. Her heart was beating so hard it nearly drowned out the sound of the footsteps. She stared into the darkness, eyes wide, senses honed. Something shifted in the shadows to her right. She squinted, spotted the silhouette of a man less than a dozen feet away.

He was just standing there, silent and still, making ab-solutely no attempt to communicate with her. If he was an employee or security officer, why hadn't he called out to her? Even if she wasn't supposed to be there so late, wouldn't an employee be concerned about a trespasser?

Eli eased more deeply into the shadows of the aisle, watching him through the gaps between the boxes stacked on the shelves. He stood motionless for what seemed like an eternity. All the while, her heart hammered like a piston against her ribs.

Suddenly a flashlight beam cut through the darkness. The beam played wildly on the boxes just a few feet away. Eli ducked. If he shone the light on the floor, he would see her feet. . . .

Searching desperately for a shelf space not filled by a box and staying as quiet as possible, never taking her eyes from the beam, Eli backed down the aisle. She'd nearly reached the end of the row when she felt an empty place on the shelf. Silently, she put her foot up on the heavy-duty particleboard shelf and ducked into the space.

An instant later, the beam cut through the darkness right where she'd been standing. Shaking with fear and adrenaline, she squeezed her eyes shut and concentrated on controlling her breathing. If she didn't calm down, she was going to give away her location.

Two deep breaths and she opened her eyes. The light swept inches above her head, then moved on to the next row. Eli sank back into the boxes, her mind whirling. What the hell was going on? Was she being paranoid? Or were her instincts to hide right? Was the man a threat? Did he plan to rob her? It wasn't like there was much of value in the warehouse. What could he possibly be looking for?

Remembering her cell phone, Eli dipped her hand into her purse only to realize she'd left the phone in her car. Damn. Damn. *Damn!*

Craning her neck to see over the top of the box next to her, she spotted the flashlight beam on the other side of the warehouse, fifteen yards away, no longer blocking her path to the door. Indecision hammered at her. The urge to run was strong, but she held back. Could she make it to the door and slip out before he noticed? Or would he catch her before she reached it?

Anxiety coiled like a spring in her chest. Knowing it was now or never, she eased off her pumps, dropped them into her purse, then set her feet on the floor. The concrete was icy cold. Slowly, she crept from her hiding place. Never taking her eyes from the bobbing beam of the flashlight, she jogged to the end of the row, then sprinted toward the door. She'd gone only a few yards when her hip slammed into the edge of a box jutting from a shelf. The sound of the box hitting the floor thundered through the warehouse like a gunshot.

In her peripheral vision, she saw the flashlight beam jerk toward her. Terror gripped her when she heard footsteps behind her. Hard soles against concrete. Oh, God! Oh, *God*! He was coming after her!

She ran blindly, whipping around a shelving unit and streaking toward the door. Boxes and shelves whizzed by. The beam of the flashlight played over her, transforming shadows into a hundred menacing forms.

The footsteps grew louder, but she didn't look back. Grasping the steel support of a shelf, she rounded another corner, her nylon-clad feet nearly slipping out from under her on the slick concrete. But she maintained her balance and flung herself toward the door at a reckless speed.

"Get away from me!" she screamed.

Murky light bled through the single diamond-shaped window on the door. She raced toward it, praying it wasn't locked. Arms outstretched, she slammed into the door hard with both hands. The door didn't budge. She twisted the knob. A moment later the door swung wide and banged against the side of the building. Cold air and gray light rushed over her. Gulping in the frigid air, Eli sprinted across the asphalt toward her car. She could hear her keys jingling in her purse. Never breaking stride, she reached inside and fumbled for them. Just when she was certain she wasn't going to find them in time, her fingers closed around her key chain.

She reached the car a moment later. Flinging open the door, she thrust herself behind the wheel. Her palm hit the door locks. She stabbed the key into the ignition. Movement at the edge of her vision jerked her head around. A scream tore from her throat when she saw the black-clad figure loom outside her door. An instant later her window shattered. Glass pelted her. Disbelief swamped her. This couldn't be happening. She screamed when a hand reached in and snaked around her throat. "Let go of me!"

"Shut up, bitch, and listen," he said a guttural voice.

She fumbled with the ignition key, but he jerked her back against the headrest, his hand gripping her throat. "Hold still," he warned.

Suddenly, she couldn't breathe. Panic assailed her when she realized he was going to choke her. She fought him, tried to break his grip, but he shook her hard. The jolts were so forceful, she felt herself gagging. His strength stunned her. For an instant, she thought he might drag her through the window. Then he loosened his grip. Eli sucked in a breath. Then a gloved hand fisted in her hair and shoved her face toward the jagged edge of the broken glass at the window's base.

"Be still or I'll fuckin' cut you to pieces!"

The ugly threat shocked her brain. Eli gripped his wrist with her left hand, but she wasn't strong enough to keep him from pressing her cheek against the jagged glass. She could feel the sharp prick of it against her cheekbone, then the burn as it cut her.

"Give me that fuckin' purse."

She handed it to him. "Take it."

He snatched it from her hand. "I'm only gonna tell you this once, bitch, so listen up." When she didn't respond, he jostled her. "You listening?"

"Yes," she said in a strangled voice.

"Let sleeping dogs lie." He loosened his grip on her hair. "You got that?"

She didn't wait for an explanation. Twisting the ignition key, she slammed the car into reverse and floored the accelerator.

"What the fuck!"

The car shot backward, the momentum shoving her against the steering wheel. Out of the corner of her eye, she saw the man lunge away. Cutting the wheel hard to the right, she punched the gas. A sickening thud sounded when the left fender slammed into him. He went down. Banging the car into drive, she pressed down on the accelerator. The car shot forward. Glancing in her rearview mirror, she saw the man lying motionless.

"Ohmigod. Ohmigod." At the gate, she stopped the car. Her hands were shaking so badly, she could barely punch in the exit code. The gate opened. Her tires screeched as she turned on to the street.

Disbelief and horror engulfed her as she realized what had just happened. She felt the warmth of blood on her cheek, the pain of a cut. She couldn't get the sound of his voice out of her mind.

Let sleeping dogs lie.

If not for the cut on her face, she could almost convince herself nothing had happened. Faceless intruders with cryptic messages in dark warehouses didn't have a place in Eli's wonderfully dull life. She was a scientist, for God's sake. Things like this weren't supposed to happen.

By the time she turned off of Green Road, she was shaking so badly she had to pull over. At a twenty-four-hour service station, she halted her Volkswagen, picked up her cell phone, and dialed 911.

IT WAS JUST AFTER THREE A.M. WHEN ELI PARKED her Volkswagen in the garage and let herself into the house. After surviving the proverbial night from hell, she was so glad to be home she nearly cried at the sight of her laundry room, the smells of fabric softener and detergent, and the sight of her folded bath towels stacked neatly on the dryer.

After dialing 911 she'd driven directly to the Ann Arbor police department. The sergeant on duty had immediately dispatched a patrol car to the warehouse, but by the time the officers arrived, the man was gone. Even the warehouse door was locked the officer had reported. Almost as if no one had ever been there.

She'd given her statement to a sleepy-eyed detective who looked like he'd been on the graveyard shift a few decades too long. He yawned so many times while she was talking to him that she eventually started yawning herself. He fussed over the cut on her cheek, but the broken safety glass hadn't cut her deeply enough to require stitches, so she declined a visit to the emergency room. The detective listed the incident as a purse snatching and simple assault in his report. As Eli sat in the steel chair next to his desk, trying in vain to keep her legs from shaking, she quickly learned that while the events of this terrible night were routine for the Ann Arbor police they would haunt her for a very long time to come.

Locking the dead bolt behind her, Eli crossed through the laundry room toward the kitchen. At the pantry, she toed off the "inmate slippers" the police had given her— since her shoes had been in her stolen purse—then headed directly for the kitchen. Draping her coat over a bar stool, she went to the sink, filled the teakettle with water, and set it over a burner.

Up until she'd left the police department, she'd been able to hold off on analyzing what had happened. But the moment she was alone, the questions began to pummel her. Had it been a random purse snatching, as the police believed? Or was there something more ominous in the works? What had the man meant when he'd warned her to let sleeping dogs lie? That wasn't something muggers normally said to their victims, was it?

The most glaring question of all nagged at her like a bad tooth. A niggling pain that wouldn't go away no matter how badly she wanted it to. Did what happened at the warehouse have anything to do with her work at Roth?

She told herself she was merely reacting to the nonsense brought to her by Adam Boedecker. That was the only reason her mind kept going back to Valazine. But for the first time in her professional career, Eli doubted the integrity of her work—a fact that twisted her insides into knots. At some point between the time Detective Adam Boedecker had left those articles in her office and the moment she'd learned that clinical trial participant number 3259 had died in the course of the study, a kernel of doubt had taken root.

After brewing a cup of tea, she walked into her bedroom and stripped out of her suit and badly torn hose. She walked naked to the shower, adjusted the water, and

stepped under the hot spray. Water stung the cut on her
cheek. She closed her eyes against the pain only to see
the man's face, hear his snarled words, feel his hands
around her throat, choking off her oxygen.

Let sleeping dogs lie.

A chill barreled through her despite the pound of hot
water. Refusing to think of his words now, she scrubbed
herself ruthlessly from head to toe and stepped out of the
shower. After slathering on a generous amount of moisturizer, she slipped into flannel pajamas and a thick robe,
carried the tepid tea into her study, and switched on the
computer. Going directly to a search engine, she typed in:
"Dynamo Pizza" + fatal + "car accident" and hit enter.

The search returned ten results. She scanned the head-
lines, then clicked on the third result, an article from the
Ann Arbor News dated twenty months ago:

> An eighteen-year-old University of Michi-
> gan student was killed instantly Friday night
> when his vehicle slammed into a concrete em-
> bankment just off of Highway 23. Several wit-
> nesses, including a Michigan state highway
> patrol officer, stated the vehicle, driven by
> Lonny Brock of Ypsilanti, was traveling at
> well over one hundred miles per hour and had
> been swerving in and out of traffic for several
> miles.
>
> The MHP told reporters on Monday that
> there were no skid marks. "It appears Mr.
> Brock was traveling at a high rate of speed
> and lost control of his vehicle." Preliminary
> findings indicate Mr. Brock's brakes may
> have failed. The accident is still under inves-
> tigation by the MHP.
>
> Mr. Brock is survived by his mother, Irene,
> an administrative assistant at Dynamo Pizza
> headquarters in Ann Arbor.

Eli printed the article, then went back to the search
engine. Her hands trembled slightly when she typed in:

Lonny Brock. This time, the search engine returned more than two dozen hits. The first article was titled VEHICULAR SUICIDE: A NEW TREND IN SUICIDE? Eli clicked on the header and read the article.

> Eighteen-year-old Lonny Brock wasn't unlike other University of Michigan students his age. He partied on Friday and Saturday nights with his fraternity brothers down at the Blue Tattoo bar on Rush Street. He listened to alternative rock groups like 3 Doors Down, Everclear, and Hole. He had a steady girlfriend and took her to the movies on the weekend. He hated algebra. He loved pizza. His passion was for football and his 1971 Mustang Fastback. But on Friday evening, Lonny Brock ended his life by driving his beloved car into a concrete embankment in a horrific accident that killed him instantly.
>
> The MHP stated there were no skid marks, indicating the car's brakes may have failed. It was just another tragic car accident—a young life cut short by too much speed and not enough experience—until the day Lonny Brock's girlfriend produced an e-mail she'd received from Lonny the day before the accident. An e-mail the police later described as a suicide note. Two days later, the Washtenaw County medical examiner ruled Lonny Brock's death a suicide. The victim of a dangerous new trend in teen suicides called vehicular suicide . . .

Rolling her chair back from the computer, Eli pressed her hand against her stomach. She felt gut punched—and sick to her soul. This was exactly the kind of information she'd been searching for. This was exactly the kind of information she hadn't wanted to find.

As much as she didn't want it to be true, Eli knew in her heart that Lonny Brock was patient 3259. No one had made the connection between Lonny and Valazine. But Eli knew in her heart the possibility was there, that it needed to be explored.

The only question that remained was whether or not she intended to do anything about it.

chapter
10

FOR THE FIRST TIME IN TEN YEARS ELI CALLED IN sick. She spoke with Peter Roth's administrative assistant at eight A.M., simply telling her she was feeling under the weather and would be working from home.

She spent twenty minutes in front of her mirror, trying to cover the damage done to her face the night before. The cut on her cheek had bloomed into a bruise overnight and stretched from cheekbone to jawline. Staring into her bathroom mirror, pale and sleep-deprived and bruised, she thought she looked more like a not-so-talented stunt woman than a respected scientist.

She hadn't slept, but it wasn't for lack of trying. Every time she'd closed her eyes she saw the dark silhouette of the man who'd attacked her, heard his muffled threats, felt the bite of the glass against her face, the pressure of his hands against her throat. She'd be seeing him for a long time to come.

But Eli knew what had happened the night before was the least of her worries. As she moved about the kitchen making coffee and toast, she knew the call from Gordon Rudnick was what she feared most. She knew it would probably alter the course of her career. Maybe even her life.

She'd just poured her first cup of coffee when the phone jangled. Taking a deep breath, she picked up the phone. "Hello?"

"Eli, hi, this is Gordon."

She closed her eyes. "Hi, Gordon."

"I tried to catch you at the office, but Dr. Bornheimer told me you were sick. I hope it's nothing too serious."

"No, uh, just a little . . . flu, I think."

"Something nasty has been going around. You sound . . . stopped up."

"Oh, um, I am, just a little."

"Well, I'm catching a flight to New York and wanted to pass on that information we discussed yesterday."

Guilt nipped at her conscience for asking him to break such a staunch rule. She could tell by his stiff tone that he was uncomfortable with her request. Still, there was no way she could tell him what she suspected until she had indisputable proof. And she knew that would probably take some time. "I apologize if my request put you on the spot, Gordon."

"Hey, I've known you since your first day at Roth, Eli. I know I can trust you not to let this go any further."

"You've got my word."

"The name is Lonny Brock."

The name shook her so profoundly, she had to lean against the counter. "Are you sure?"

"I pulled the app today and looked at it myself."

"Okay. Uh, thanks, Gordon. I owe you big time."

"I might just take you up on that someday."

Eli wished him a good flight, then hung up. Her mind whirling, she stared down at her coffee. Guilt and a kind of quiet, maddening horror slipped through her. Lonny Brock. Vehicular suicide. Why hadn't she known about it?

Gordon's call had taken her one step closer to seeing a tangible connection between violent behavior and Valazine. The scientist inside her knew that connection was blurred by the many variables of the depressed mind. She hadn't totally accepted the idea that the drug she'd spent the last ten years developing and testing was solely responsible for the deaths of the people in the articles. But the connection was now an undeniable possibility. A possibility she needed to investigate.

But how had her detailed clinical trials overlooked such a significant adverse event? Why hadn't Lonny Brock's death been listed as a suicide when his death had, indeed, been ruled as such by the Washtenaw County medical examiner? Had she missed it? Had someone else missed it? Or had the information been withheld from her?

The possibilities chilled her.

Lowering her face into her hands, she closed her eyes and rubbed her temples. Guilt sat on her shoulders like a boulder. Eli had never shirked responsibility in her life. She accepted blame when it was due her. It hurt, but she accepted her share of the blame for this now.

She'd been instrumental in getting Valazine approved by the FDA. She was the liaison between the Food and Drug Administration and Roth Pharmaceuticals. It had been *her* responsibility to make sure all adverse events were reported accurately.

Why hadn't she known about Lonny Brock?

She couldn't bring herself to believe anyone from the team would purposefully conceal adverse event data from the FDA. Not Thomas Bornheimer, the brilliant young clinical research associate with a bright future ahead of him. Not Gordon Rudnick, a respected medical doctor. Certainly not Walter Sanchez. Kevin Chambers and, in a lesser capacity, Peter Roth had also worked on the project, but not nearly to the extent that the scientists had. It was unthinkable to consider the possibility that one of her coworkers could be responsible for such a heinous dereliction of duty.

The seed of doubt had taken root and grown into something massive and ugly. The implications were too far-reaching for her to handle alone. As much as she didn't want to involve another person—or sabotage her career or risk tainting a promising new drug—she was savvy enough to know when she was in over her head.

This was one of those times.

Dreading what she had to do next, she reached for the phone.

ADAM PARKED THE TAHOE CURBSIDE, SHUT DOWN the engine, and studied the house as if seeing it for the first time. Elizabeth Barnes lived on a quiet, tree-lined street in an upscale neighborhood less than a mile from Roth Pharmaceuticals. The location was expensive, convenient, and upwardly mobile in a very big way. Pale blue siding, a wide front porch, and black shutters adorned the two-story colonial. Snow clung to the branches of a stately spruce guarding the tastefully landscaped yard. Someone had shoveled and salted the sidewalk in front of the house. Elizabeth Barnes lived well. He wondered if she lived within her means.

Slipping on his gloves, he got out of the truck and started toward the house. The tang of burning pine hung heavy in the air. Smoke curled from the chimney of the house next door. The icy wind slapped at his face and whipped his trench coat against his legs. Steel gray clouds roiling in the western sky threatened something frozen and nasty.

He wasn't sure what to expect from this meeting. She'd sounded shaken when she asked him to meet her. When he'd asked for an explanation, she'd refused to discuss it over the phone. That had gotten his attention.

It had taken some hard driving but he'd made the two-hundred-mile trip from Palatine to Ann Arbor in just under three hours. A state trooper had pulled him over outside of Kalamazoo, but Adam had done some fast talking and managed to wheedle his way out of a speeding ticket. Good thing cops were tight.

He crossed the porch and rang the bell. Wind chimes tinkled off to his right. It was a pleasant sound that reminded him of a time when his own home had been more to him than just a place to sleep and shower and eat. A time when he'd still been human enough to take pride in such mundane things. It seemed like a lifetime ago.

He was about to make use of the brass knocker when the door opened. Elizabeth Barnes stood in the doorway looking at him. In one quick sweep, his eyes took a picture of her. Brown hair pulled back from a face that was drawn with tension and a little too pale. Dark eyes fringed with worry. She wore a pair of black wool slacks and a cream-colored sweater. He felt himself do a double take on seeing the nasty looking cut on her cheek. The sight of the purpling bruise sent a low-grade twist of male outrage through him. He'd been a cop too long to believe a woman got marked up like that without the help of some dirtbag. He wondered who'd seen fit to mess up her pretty face.

"Dr. Barnes," he said. "I got here as soon as I could."

"Thank you for coming."

While he should have been assessing the situation and formulating questions, he found his eyes skimming down the front of her instead. He told himself he was merely gauging her frame of mind, but he was honest enough with himself to admit he was a lot more intrigued by the way she filled out that sweater.

Tearing his eyes away from the gold heart dangling between the swell of her breasts, he scowled at her. "What happened to your face?"

A minute jolt ran the length of her, then she raised her hand to her cheek. "I was . . . mugged last night."

"Mugged?"

She nodded.

"Are you hurt?"

"No." She laughed, uncomfortable. "I mean, aside from my face. It looks worse than what it is."

Adam stared at her, his cop's instincts telling him something wasn't right with the picture. She looked nervous, but he didn't think she was lying about getting mugged. The only other possibility that came to mind was the timing. It seemed pretty damn coincidental that she would get mugged right after he'd shown up at her office, asking questions about Valazine. Adam had stopped believing in coincidences at about the same time he'd stopped believing in the tooth fairy.

"Did they catch the guy?" he asked.

"No." She stepped aside. "Come in."

Adam entered the foyer. Warmth and the smell of fresh coffee and of something else that was subtle and sweet greeted him. "It's cold as hell out there."

"Welcome to Ann Arbor in January."

Plucking off his gloves, he stuffed them into the pocket of his trench. She was wearing those weird little black glasses again. The kind with square frames that were heavy and dark and hid her eyes. He wondered why she preferred to cover her pretty eyes with glasses when perfect vision could be had with the zap of a laser.

"Let me get your coat," she said.

He shrugged out of the trench.

"The weatherman is calling for snow." Her hand trembled slightly when she reached for the coat. "As if we haven't already had enough."

Adam watched her closely, taking in her carefully controlled motions, the rigid set of her shoulders. She was wound tight as a spring, he realized. "Bad year for snow. We've had our share in Chicago, too."

"I hope you don't hit bad weather on your way home—"

"Dr. Barnes, you didn't ask me to drive two hundred miles to talk about the weather, did you?"

"No." Turning away from him, she opened a closet and hung his trench. "Would you like some coffee?"

"Sure. Black."

"Make yourself comfortable." She motioned toward the living room. "I'll be right back."

Shoving his hands into his pockets, he watched her disappear into the kitchen. When she was out of sight, he crossed the hall and strolled into the living room. The room was spacious and tastefully decorated. A hint of untidiness made the room look lived-in and cozy. A few too many throw pillows littered the sofa, and an afghan was tossed haphazardly over the arm of a chair. Her taste in furniture ran from dark antiques to the clean lines of contemporary. A butter-soft leather sofa lined the wall to his right. A distressed antique coffee table separated the sofa from twin brown jacquard chairs. A sizable collection of books filled the floor-to-ceiling bookcases on either side of the fireplace, mostly popular fiction with a few classics thrown in.

A thick text lay facedown next to the hearth. Adam leaned over and read the title on the spine. *Pharmaco-economic Issues and the Treatment of Major Depressive Disorders.* Jesus.

He was sitting on the sofa when she returned a moment later with a tray containing two cups of coffee. Taking the chair across from him, she set the tray on the table between them. "You're probably wondering why I asked you to come here when the last two times we spoke I nearly threw you out."

"The question did cross my mind."

"Before I explain, let's get one thing straight."

He arched a brow. "By all means."

"I'm not convinced Valazine is responsible for the deaths mentioned in those articles you gave me."

"I guess that's why you called me, huh?"

Her eyes were large and earnest in the pale frame of her face. It was a fragile face, he realized, and instantly regretted his sarcasm. It had been a long time since he'd dealt with anything even remotely fragile. Well, aside from his own state of mind.

"But you know it's a possibility, don't you?" he asked quietly.

She nodded. "I've seen enough to be concerned. I'd like to investigate further if only to prove you wrong."

"For everyone's sake, I hope you can," he said dryly.

"I'm a scientist, Detective Boedecker. I rely on facts and indisputable proof before I make a judgment. I'm not afraid of information or ideas no matter how wild or unconventional. I am, however, wary of prejudices and preconceived notions."

"I'll do my best to keep all my prejudices and preconceived notions out of this."

"And no matter what happens, I want you to know ethics always come first."

"Whose ethics are we talking about?"

"Mine."

Impressed despite himself, he took a sip of coffee, watching her over the rim. She stared back at him, her eyes conveying something deeper than concern, something more profound than simple fear. The cut on her cheek bothered him. He hated seeing it. Hated even more knowing that it had been intentionally done. The cop in him wanted details about the mugging, but his instincts told him to hold back for now and listen. If he wasn't mistaken, Dr. Barnes had something to get off her chest.

Impatient, he scrubbed his hand over his chin. "So talk to me."

"After you left yesterday, I reviewed the summary report on Valazine. That's the final report Dr. Sanchez, Thomas Bornheimer, and I worked on some eighteen months ago and submitted to Kevin Chambers and Peter Roth. It's basically an informational summary of all the clinical studies." She sighed. "I'm not even really sure what I was looking for. Anything unusual or out of place, I suppose." She laced her fingers together and rested them in her lap. "I stumbled onto some information about one of the study participants. Patient 3259. A young man who died in the course of the trial."

Adam's interest flared. "Go on."

"I didn't remember losing a study participant due to death. Something like that is highly unusual. A death event would have and should have been documented in the study. Only it wasn't. That concerned me, so last night I drove over to the archive storage warehouse and went through the boxes until I found his profile. Even though I didn't have a name, I learned enough from his profile to discern his identity."

"Nice detective work. How did he die?"

"The Washtenaw County medical examiner ruled his death a suicide."

"Let me get this straight. You had a study participant commit suicide during a clinical trial for an antidepressant drug, and you people didn't see fit to note that little detail in your goddamn study?"

"It wasn't that simple," she defended herself.

"Why not?"

"He committed what's known as vehicular suicide."

"Was he taking Valazine?"

"It was a double-blind study. I have no way of knowing if he was taking the drug or the placebo."

"If we wanted to find out, how would we go about it?"

"The only people who have that information are the medical personnel at the clinic. Without a court order or a subpoena, I'm afraid we won't be able to determine whether he was taking Valazine or not."

"Or an exhumation order." Adam tasted frustration at the back of his throat. "These confidentiality regulations are convenient as hell."

She drank some of her coffee. "Valazine is my project, Detective Boedecker. I've been on the project from the start. Any and all responsibility for adverse events falls on my shoulders."

"Well, that's noble of you, Dr. Barnes, but it's a day late and a dollar short for patient 3259 and at least eight others."

"I'm going to dispute that until I have proof," she cut in. "I called you because I want to know how you came to believe Valazine is responsible for those deaths. I need to know everything you know. Who you talked to. Where you got your information. I need copies of autopsy reports and any other official documentation you might have. I need to know how you came to draw the conclusions you have."

Adam studied her, trying to reconcile himself to her sudden change of heart—that she now wanted information from him and that she looked determined as hell to get it. "I'll share information with regard to the case with you on one condition," he said.

"What condition?"

"You give me access to any and all data I need to complete my investigation."

"I'm afraid I can't do that. I signed a confidentiality agreement with Roth."

"Lady, that confidentiality agreement was null and void the day the first body showed up."

"We don't know for certain—"

"Those are my terms."

She fidgeted, looking at him over the tops of her glasses. "You're being unreasonable. It could take me months to reconstruct what you already have."

"Life is unreasonable. I'm an unreasonable man. Take it or leave it."

Adam saw the war raging inside her. The one among loyalty to her company, whatever personal ethics drove her, and the need to get to the bottom of eight or more suspicious deaths.

"All right," she said after a moment.

Adam stared hard at her, looking for a lie, expecting a lie. And for the second time that day, Elizabeth Barnes surprised him because he saw none. "Now that we've got that out of the way, why don't you tell me what really happened last night?"

She fidgeted again, then her gaze dropped to her coffee cup. He didn't miss the quivering of her hand as she lifted the mug to her lips and sipped. "The cops said—"

"You already told me what the cops said. I want to know what happened."

He listened intently as she told him about her trip to the warehouse the night before. An odd protectiveness rose up inside him when she told him about the man breaking her car window and purposefully grating the side of her face against the broken glass. She was small-framed. Adam knew it wouldn't have taken much for some muscle-bound idiot to seriously injure her—or worse.

The son of a bitch.

"That wasn't very smart, going to a warehouse all by yourself," he said.

"There's a security gate, and the warehouse is under lock and key."

"I can see all that security had a big impact on the perp." He scowled, trying not to think of all the other things that could have happened. "You don't think it was a mugging, do you?"

Her gaze snapped to his. In its depths, Adam saw knowledge and dread and the same suspicion he felt creeping into the back of his own mind. And he finally understood why she'd wanted to meet with him.

"No," she said after a moment.

"Did he say anything to you?"

"He told me to let sleeping dogs lie."

"Odd thing for a mugger to say, isn't it?"

"I thought so, too."

"We both know this wasn't a mugging, don't we, Dr. Barnes? That's why I'm here, isn't it?"

She stared at him with those dark, serious eyes. "Yes."

Adam didn't like the way this was shaping up. Her personal safety was one problem he hadn't counted on. He found it ironic as hell that he would be thrust into the role of protector for a woman who could very well be embroiled in this mess up to those pretty eyes of hers. The idea was almost laughable. Adam could barely keep his own ass out of a sling these days, let alone someone else's.

"I'd wager the farm that what happened to you at the warehouse last night is related to your work at Roth," he said. "I strongly suspect that's why Sanchez was murdered, too."

The color leached from her cheeks so quickly that for a moment Adam thought she was going to keel over. It impressed him that she maintained eye contact. That she didn't cry. It impressed him even more that she didn't try to deny it.

"You don't pull any punches, do you?" she asked.

"Personality flaw."

"You seem to have a lot of those."

Adam frowned at her. "Who have you told about my suspicions?"

She thought about it for a moment. "Kevin Chambers. Thomas Bornheimer. Peter Roth knows because Kevin talked to him."

"In other words all the players know."

She nodded.

Downing the remainder of his coffee, Adam rose.

"Where are you going?"

He walked into the foyer without answering, aware that she was trailing him. At the closet, he opened the door and pulled out his trench. He turned and just about ran into her. He reached out to steady her and caught a whiff of her scent. She smelled like vanilla ice cream, only a lot sweeter and a hell of a lot more grown up. Uneasy pleasure fluttered low in his gut. Acutely aware that he was touching her, he released her and stepped back.

"I left my briefcase in the trunk," he said.

She looked relieved. "So you're going to work with me?"

If she hadn't been staring at him so seriously, if the subject hadn't been so grave, he might have laughed. "We're going to share information."

"I want your word that you won't shut me out."

"Same goes."

"Deal." She stuck out her hand.

Adam looked down at it, then grasped it firmly.

"I need your word that you'll keep this confidential," she said.

"I'll keep this confidential until the time comes to take down the bad guy." He spoke the words, formed the thoughts in his mind, but his attention was on the soft warmth of her hand within his.

"All I want out of this is the truth," she said.

He thought about Michael, about the agony he must have endured in the last hours of his life. "I hope you can handle the truth."

chapter
11

ELI WASN'T USED TO HAVING A MAN IN HER HOUSE. The only male visitors she'd had in the two years since she'd bought the place were her father when he'd made a rare trip from the farm, Walter for an occasional dinner, and Kevin Chambers once or twice when he'd either picked her up or dropped her after a business meeting or dinner. Safe men, she thought. Family. Friends. Business associates.

Adam Boedecker wasn't any of those things, and he definitely wasn't safe.

Sitting at her dining room table, he looked as out of place as a rogue wolf in a kennel. Absently sipping his coffee, he brooded over the document he was reading. The man had brooding down to an art form, she thought. If the crease between his brows got any deeper, he was going to need stitches.

Realizing she was staring, Eli left the kitchen and entered her study. There, she fished the summary report from her briefcase, snapped the laptop from its docking station, then walked down the hall into the dining room.

He looked up when she set the 224-page report on the table in front of him.

"That's the final official report on Valazine that went to Peter Roth and Kevin Chambers a little over eighteen months ago," she said.

"What does it contain?"

"Everything you always wanted to know about Valazine."

"Are adverse reactions listed?"

"Yes, broken down by specific reaction and again by the ratio of study participants who experienced the reaction versus the total number of participants." She opened her laptop. "I think we need to come up with a game plan."

"The game plan is for you to give me all the information you've got on this drug and let me do my job."

"You've got my cooperation as long as that cooperation works both ways."

Using her wireless connection, Eli logged on to Roth's network, then maneuvered into the finalized summary report section. There was so much information that she wasn't sure where to begin. Printing summary reports was probably as good a place as any.

"Who at Roth stood to make a financial gain with the success of Valazine?" Adam asked after a moment.

Eli looked up from her laptop. "Money or stock?"

"Either. Both."

"Roth will be going public next year."

"So who's going to get rich?"

She thought about it for a moment. "Kevin Chambers. Certainly Peter Roth. Everyone on the executive team in research and development."

"Who's on the executive team?"

"Myself. Kevin Chambers. Peter Roth. Thomas Bornheimer." She looked down at her laptop. "Walter Sanchez."

"Anyone else?"

"No."

"How much money are we talking about?"

Taking her fingers from the keyboard, she skimmed her

hands along her arms. "Valazine was a breakthrough medication. We did something no one else has ever done by
offering a drug that stops depression at its source with
minimal side effects. We've got investors. The drug has
paid off big-time as far as sales. Plus, there will be bo-
nuses based on profits and sales and market share. Not to
mention stock when the company goes public."

"How much?"

"Depending on the criteria I just mentioned, a single
bonus could be upwards of a million dollars."

"That takes care of motive." He set down the report,
rested his hand on it. "What else?"

She thought of her Distinguished Woman of Science
Award and realized it no longer seemed as huge an
achievement as it once had. "Recognition. Grants.
Awards. We're probably in the running for a nomination
for the Nobel Prize in Medicine."

"Who had control of the information fed to the FDA?"

"Me. Thomas Bornheimer to a degree. Walter Sanchez."

His eyes sharpened on hers. "How so? What's the information flow?"

"I rely on a number of sources, mainly Thomas Bornheimer. He's the clinical research associate. He deals with
the doctors and other medical personnel at the clinics administering the trials. I deal with them also, but to a lesser
degree."

"How many clinics were involved?"

"We used two for the Valazine trials."

"How many medical personnel?"

"Two or three doctors per clinic. A dozen nurses and
technicians per clinic."

"That's a lot of sources." He scrubbed a hand over his
jaw.

Eli heard the scrape of beard against his palm and
looked away, uncomfortable with the intimacy of the
sound. She shouldn't be noticing things like that.

"I want you to provide me with all the paper on Valazine," he said.

"That's a lot of paper."

"I want final reports and backup documentation on those reports. If they're not in plain English, then I'll want you to translate them for me."

"I'm printing from the network now."

"I'll need source information, too. The raw data. Something to back everything up."

"The raw data is in storage."

"I thought you brought it here."

"I'd put only a few papers in my purse. The mugger took it."

He scowled. "We need the raw data."

"The rest of it is still in the warehouse."

Finishing the last of his coffee, he rose. "Let's go."

"It's after hours." Eli looked at her watch to find it was after six P.M. The afternoon had blown by and they'd gotten through only a few reports. A look out the front window told her the weatherman hadn't lied when he predicted snow.

"Is that a problem?" he asked.

"As long as you don't mind the muggers."

One side of his mouth hiked into a smile, but it was humorless and cold and Eli realized she wouldn't ever want to cross this man. Even if he was a cop.

"Running into me would be very unfortunate for the mugger," he said.

Eli believed him.

THE SNOW WAS COMING DOWN HARD WHEN ADAM pulled his Tahoe up to the security gate of Huron Archival and Record Storage. A barely visible sign boasted a temperature- and humidity-controlled environment. He sure as hell hoped so.

"What's the code?" he asked.

"Press 1300 star, then enter."

He punched in the numbers, and the gate grated open. Eli guided him over to the corrugated steel building farthest from the gate, and he parked the Tahoe across from the entrance. She jumped when he reached over and tugged his .40 Glock and shoulder holster from the glove box.

"Expecting a shootout?" she asked.

"I like to be prepared." Sending her a dark look across the cab, he got out of the truck, crossed in front of it, and opened the door for her. "I suggest you get used to the gun."

She looked away as he fastened the holster and shoved the Glock into its leather nest. "How many boxes are we talking about?" he asked.

"Five."

"They should fit in the truck. We'll take them back to your place and go through them there."

"Okay."

They walked side by side to the door, their footsteps quiet in the snow. Not for the first time, Adam noticed her scent on the wind. The sweet essence of vanilla inspired childhood memories of sweet cream melting on his tongue—and not-so-innocent thoughts of how the prim Dr. Barnes might taste if he had the mind to kiss her. She might wear practical shoes and librarian eye glasses, but it was the not-so-practical side of her that kept snagging his attention.

His response to her surprised him. She wasn't exactly the kind of woman that usually appealed to him. He'd always preferred blue-eyed blondes who wore tight jeans and had a weakness for cops. . . .

Adam wasn't even sure why he was thinking about her in terms of how sexy she was. The last thing he needed in his life was a woman. While the sexual aspect of a relationship appealed, he wasn't sure he was up to the task. Every facet of his life had changed since the shooting, since the fiasco with Shelly and Chad. Adam had made an amazing recovery—both mentally and physically—but the lingering effects of the traumatic brain injury had taken a heavy toll on his confidence. Not only as a cop, but as a man. The fact of the matter was he hadn't been with a woman since the shooting. Hadn't even gone out on a date. Not that any sane woman would have him.

Three years was a long time for a man, and it seemed like a lifetime since he'd felt that deep stir of male interest. He told himself it was just his body's way of telling him he was healing. That it was time to move forward and forget the past. The shooting. The indelible wounds Shelly's betrayal with his best friend had left on his pride. He didn't want there to be anything more to it. Damn it, he didn't.

At the entrance, Eli removed a key chain from her purse and opened the door. Adam stepped inside first, senses alert, the Glock pressing reassuringly against his ribs. The smells of mildew and paper dust hung heavy in the air. Next to him, Eli flipped on the overhead lights, then motioned toward the endless floor-to-ceiling rows of identical corrugated boxes.

"I always feel like a spy when I come here," she said.

He looked over at her, amused. "You are, tonight."

She looked around, huddling more deeply in her coat. "I know this is silly, but I feel like I'm betraying the people I work for."

"You're doing the right thing."

"I don't think we're going to find anything."

Adam didn't answer. He followed her past a dozen rows stacked twenty feet high with boxes. "They don't mind you poking around after hours?" he asked.

"I have a high-level security clearance." She jingled the keys. "I've been with the company a long time. I'm in solid."

He'd once thought the same thing about himself and the Chicago PD, but didn't mention it. She didn't need to know he was just a phone call away from becoming an ex-cop.

Several rows in, she turned left and they walked down a narrow aisle. The shelves on either side were laden with hundreds of record storage boxes, each labeled with a different number. Adam was about to comment on the cold when she halted abruptly.

"What is it?" he asked, barely avoiding running into her.

Staring at the boxes, she walked quickly down the aisle,

then turned to face him. "The boxes are gone."

"The five boxes you left here last night?"

"Yes."

"Maybe the warehouse people moved them."

"No." She craned her head and looked up at the boxes above them. "The surrounding box numbers are the same." She turned to him, her brows knitting. "Someone took them."

Adam tried not to notice how dark her brows were against her pale skin. Or that he had the sudden and irrational urge to smooth out the line that had formed between them with his thumb. Like that would go over real well. "Who has access?"

"All executive team members. Some of the administrative assistants. The office manager. The mail person."

"In other words everyone."

She sighed, nodded. "Damn it."

"Are you sure this is where you were last night?" he asked. "You said it was dark. You were scared—"

"Of course I'm sure."

Adam looked around, felt the hairs at his nape prickle. In an unconscious gesture, he put his hand on the leather sheath where the Glock rested.

"I guess this would qualify as one of those coincidences you cops don't believe in," she said.

"Ranks right up there with the tooth fairy." Pulling the Glock from his holster, he checked the clip, then started down the aisle.

ELI'S HEART JUMPED IN HER CHEST WHEN SHE SAW him tug the pistol from beneath his coat. "What are you going to do, start shooting boxes?"

Casting her a dark look over his shoulder, he continued down the aisle. "Stay close to me."

"What are you doing?"

"The official term for it is taking a look around."

"God, you're a smart-ass." She looked uneasily over her shoulder, taking in the myriad shadows and countless hiding places within the cavernous warehouse.

"Is there a record of who comes and goes?" he asked.

"I don't know, but I could—"

Her last word was cut off abruptly when the warehouse suddenly went black. She stopped dead in her tracks, a sense of déjà vu engulfing her. "Oh, no."

"Quiet."

She gasped when a strong hand closed around her shoulder. "Shhh. Easy," he whispered. "Just take it easy. It's probably nothing."

"I thought you didn't believe in coincidences."

That he didn't answer chilled her. She stood still and listened. She could hear him breathing. The darkness seemed to heighten her sense of smell and she was keenly aware of the scent of his aftershave surrounding her.

"You doing okay?" he whispered.

"No. This is exactly what happened last night."

"Yeah, well, if the bozo who took your purse tries something stupid with me, he's going to get some lead for his trouble."

Eli didn't doubt he would make good on that statement if push came to shove. Adam Boedecker would make a formidable foe to anyone who crossed him.

"Let's get out of here." He turned her, and they started toward the door.

"It wasn't this dark last night."

"Cloudy," he said. "You're not scared of the dark, are you?"

"Only when I'm trapped in a warehouse with a maniac."

"We're not trapped," he said. "And the only maniac running around is me." She heard a click and then a thin ribbon of light illuminated his face. "Better?"

A flashlight, she realized, relieved. "You came prepared."

"I'm a cop. It's kind of like being a Boy Scout only we're not so nice."

Her only thought was that he didn't look like a cop with that gun in his hand and those dark, troubled eyes.

"Let's go see what happened to the lights." Shining the beam ahead of him, he quickened his pace.

Because the fear was fresh inside her, Eli let him take the lead. "Maybe the bad weather took out the power," she said.

"Maybe."

The sound of the front door slamming shut stopped them. Raising his arm, Adam put his fingers to his lips to silence any questions. He shut off the flashlight, plunging them into inky darkness.

Eli had never been afraid of the dark. But it was frightening not being able to see. And knowing someone was there and unwilling to show themselves. "Someone is in here with us," she whispered.

"Shhh. Listen."

The quiet was so complete she could hear the patter of snow against the tin roof overhead. "I don't hear anything," she said.

"That's because you're talking."

She jolted when the sound of shattering glass broke the silence. Adam backed up a step, and Eli felt the solid warmth of his body brush against her. "Easy," he whispered.

She couldn't tell if the low roar in her ears was her own racing heart or something else.

"Shit."

"What?" Craning her head to see around him, she glanced between the shelves and spotted the flickering yellow light beyond. "I see a light," she said.

Another curse burned through the air, only this time Adam's voice was colored with fury. "Not a light. Fire. Son of a bitch."

Adrenaline careened through her midsection. She breathed in, discerned the pungent odor of smoke. "Oh, my God."

"Stay here," he snapped.

"But, I—"

"Don't argue. And, damn it, don't move. I'll be right back." With that he left her.

The fire cast just enough light for her to see him sprint to the end of the row and turn right toward the front entrance; then she lost sight of him. She could hear the fire now, a low hum in her ears as it devoured cardboard and paper. Alone, she was keenly aware of the darkness around her, the fear hammering through her. The urge to run was strong, but there was a part of her that trusted Adam to return and get them safely out.

Two muffled pops scattered her thoughts. At first she thought some sort of container—a bottle or aerosol can— had burst. Then she realized what she'd just heard were gunshots. Either Adam had just fired his gun, or someone was shooting at him.

A colder, harder fear gripped her. "Adam!"

She ran to the end of the aisle, where orange smoke hovered like a veil. She could see now, and at first attributed it to the fact that her eyes had adjusted to the darkness. But one look at the fire, and she realized she could see because the warehouse was no longer dark. The fire was like a raging beast, twenty feet high, twice as wide— and burning like an inferno between where she stood and the front entrance.

"Adam!"

Yellow flames licked the steel beams overhead. Eli stared, mesmerized by the terrifying beauty of it.

She yelped when a strong hand wrapped around her forearm. Forming a fist with her right hand, she spun. Her legs went weak when she realized Adam had come up behind her. "I heard gunshots," she said.

"Yeah, well, here's a news flash for you: He missed. I think I might have winged him, but I'm not sure."

The next thing she knew she was being dragged down the aisle. "Are you telling me someone shot at you? I mean, like, *shot* at you?"

"I don't mean he took my goddamn picture."

A tidal wave of disbelief tumbled over her. Things like this didn't happen in her happily boring life. A shootout in a dark warehouse in the middle of a raging fire was too much to absorb. She felt as if she'd stepped onto the set of some low-budget shoot-'em-up movie.

"But that's . . ." Her words trailed off when she realized he was taking her in the opposite direction from where they'd come in. She dug in her heels. "This is the wrong way."

"The fire's blocking the door. We're going out the back way."

"I don't know that there *is* a back way."

"There is. The loading dock." He tugged on her hand and forced her to follow him. "You want the bad news?"

A sound of hysteria bubbled up, but she swallowed it before it could escape. "I thought maybe that was the gunshots part."

"This place is full of paper. It's going to go up like a goddamn tinderbox."

"But what about overhead sprinklers?"

"They should have come on by now." He muttered a curse. "You got a phone on you?"

"It's in my car."

"Well, that's handy as hell."

"Where's yours?"

"In the truck. Shit."

The smoke was getting thicker and burned her nostrils. The flames roared like a hot, raging sea. Eli was sweating beneath her coat, but she wasn't sure if it was because of the heat or the stealthy fingers of panic crawling over her.

"How are we going to get out?" she asked.

"We'll try the doors in the back."

Because she didn't have a better idea, because her mind was stuttering drunkenly, Eli allowed him to lead her toward the rear. The roar of the flames deafened her. Yellow light flickered between the shelves like a thousand candles. Above, the flames reflected eerily off the steel-beamed ceiling.

"This way."

Eli looked down. Fingers of smoke curled in the beam of Adam's flashlight. She wanted to point that out to him, but fear had her throat in a vise. She risked a look at him. A sheen of sweat coated his face, but his expression was determined and focused. He was gripping her wrist so tightly, her hand was numb.

The fire pursued them. Orange-gray smoke billowed

between the boxes on the shelves. Visibility dwindled. She could feel the heat of the flames at the back of her head. The stench of the smoke choked her and stung her eyes.

Adam released her hand a moment later. Eli glanced behind her and her heart stopped. Just a few yards away, a wall of yellow flames engulfed an entire row of shelving.

They reached the rear of the warehouse. "We're going to be fine," he said. "Put your sweater over your nose and mouth. It'll help with the smoke."

Eli looked down at her sweater, raised the hem to her face, and cupped it over her nose and mouth. It didn't help, but she didn't complain.

"Better?" he asked.

She nodded.

"Good girl. Stay put." Sprinting over to the door, Adam tried the knob, then used his shoulder against it. "Hey!" he shouted, and slapped both hands against the metal. "*Hey!* Fire!"

Eli tried hard to gather her thoughts, looked wildly around for something, anything, with which to force open the door. Hope jumped through her when she spotted the old-fashioned rotary phone mounted on a steel support beam a few feet away. She streaked over to it and snatched it up only to be met with a dead line.

"Damn it!" Dropping the phone, she stumbled back. The relentless heat pushed her toward the wall. Only when she reached the wall and turned did she realize visibility had dropped to a few feet. She could no longer see Adam. That frightened her, made her feel alone. She ordered herself to stay calm, told herself the fire department would arrive soon. But the panic was like a wild animal inside her, straining against its leash, crazed to break free.

For the first time, she considered the possibility that they were going to die. The thought petrified her, spurred the panic slithering inside her. "Adam!" she choked, and stumbled toward where she'd last seen him. "Adam!"

"Over here!"

Relief swamped her at the sound of his voice. She

started toward it, staggered blindly through the smoke. She spotted movement near an overhead door that led to the loading dock and felt her way along the wall. "Adam! Where are you?"

She heard the sharp edge of panic in her voice and knew the beast inside her had broken free of its shackles and was running wildly through her. "Help us! Please! Somebody *help*!"

Heat billowed outward from the fire, scorching her face, burning her throat like hot lava. Choking, she bent at the waist and tried to spit, but her mouth was desert dry.

Smoke rushed over her, a stinking, hot breath from hell. It blocked her vision and sucked the oxygen from her lungs. Panic squeezed her, sent a burst of adrenaline through her body, but when she drew in air, the rancid smoke seared her lungs like a branding iron shoved down her throat.

"Get down on the floor!"

She spotted Adam an instant before she felt his hands on her shoulders. "Oh, God! Adam! Oh, God!"

"Get *down*!" But he was already grasping the back of her neck, shoving her down. Eli stumbled, went down to her hands and knees, not sure if she'd collapsed or if he'd pushed her.

An instant later, he had her by the hand and she was being dragged toward the overhead door, her slacks sliding easily over the concrete floor. "There's air coming through where these doors are," he shouted.

Eli wanted to answer, wanted to get to her feet, but the smoke was making her dizzy and nauseous. "Adam—"

"Easy." A strong hand gripped the back of her neck, turning her face toward a small crack where cold, clean air rushed in to greet her.

"Take a breath," he said.

She tried, but couldn't stop coughing.

"Stay here. Keep low. I'll be right back."

She reached for him, but he was gone. Squeezing her eyes shut, she gulped air, let it cool her raw throat. Behind her the fire roared like an enraged giant. The knowledge that they would both perish within minutes if they didn't get out sat like a lead weight in her chest.

"Help us!" she cried into the gap. *"Please!"*

Four pops sounded off to her right. She looked in the direction of the sound. Through the thick haze of smoke, Adam leveled the pistol at the lock on the nearest overhead door. "Adam!"

Barely sparing her a glance, he rammed the door with his shoulder. Once. Twice. Another pop sounded. A flash. She could hear him coughing. . . .

Eli crawled toward him. "Adam!"

An instant later, a slash of light cut through the darkness and billowing smoke. Clean, cold air rolled over her, and she gulped it like water. The overhead door, she realized. He'd somehow managed to force it off its track.

Sobbing with relief, choking on the smoke, Eli crawled toward the opening. "Adam!"

"Stay back!"

Through the haze, she saw him land a solid kick to the door. The sheet metal creased, but held. He kicked again. The door peeled away from the track. The burst of fresh air stunned her. Eli tried to get to her feet, but the dizziness stole her equilibrium and she stumbled, went back down to her knees. Then strong arms were lifting her, carrying her toward the light.

"I keep telling you to stay put and you keep moving," he growled.

"I've never been very good at following orders," she choked.

"Remind me to yell at you later."

As he carried her out of the building, she looked back at the warehouse. Black smoke gushed from the broken door, billowing into the night sky, swirling like a fiery tornado. She wanted to speak, to thank the man who had carried her to safety, but her throat was on fire. Her face and hands were tingling. She sucked in a breath, felt her lungs seize, and she broke into coughing all over again.

"Easy does it, Doc."

His voice barely registered as she fought to pull oxygen into her lungs. When the worst of the coughing had passed, she risked a look at him. Dark, concerned eyes met hers, softening the hard lines of his face. Black soot ringed his nostrils. A dark smudge creased his forehead just above his left eyebrow. In the back of her mind she wondered if she looked as bad as he did, but couldn't muster the energy to care.

"Shallow, easy breaths, okay? Not too deep."

Only then did she realize he was still holding her. He'd carried her a short distance from the building, but hadn't yet set her down. Logic told her to protest, but his body felt like warm steel against hers. Powerful. Solid. Safe. She tried not to notice the way his arms seemed to swallow her whole. Or the way he was looking down at her with those dark, dangerous eyes.

"I'm okay," she said after a moment. "You can put me down."

Gently, he set her on her feet. At first Eli wasn't sure if her legs would support her, but she somehow managed to stay upright. "That was close," she said.

"Too close." The muscles in his jaw worked as he looked over his shoulder toward the building. "You okay? I need to call this in."

The shakes hit her at about the same time the disbelief did. Both were so powerful, she had to brace a hand against the chain-link fence to maintain her balance. "How did that happen?" she asked. "I mean, someone just tried to kill us. If you hadn't gotten that door open—"

"I did, though," he snapped. "It's over."

"We could have been killed."

"We're all right. That's what counts. That's what you need to think about."

Eli knew he was right. She knew better than to dwell on what might have been. But the reality of what had nearly happened shook her all the way to her foundation.

She turned and looked back at the warehouse. Yellow flames licked the night sky. Smoke belched ugly and black. Snow swirled crazily, like handfuls of confetti tossed for a ticker-tape parade. The sight was surreal. She felt detached from it, as if she had somehow left her body and was watching the scene play out from a place that was safe and warm and far less dangerous.

She couldn't believe someone had just tried to kill them.

"Come on, Doc." Taking her hand, Adam led her toward the parking area. "Don't get shocky on me. I don't do hospitals."

Too numb to speak, Eli followed, concentrating hard on putting one foot in front of the other. At the Tahoe, Adam leaned her against the fender, retrieved his cell phone, and punched in numbers. She listened as he slipped into cop mode and reported the fire. His demeanor changed. He used cop lingo with the dispatcher. He even made a joke. Eli watched him, felt her respect for him solidify. She bet he was a good cop.

Adam Boedecker might be on leave from the department, but he was definitely still a cop through and through, she thought. The realization should have been a comforting one considering someone had just tried to murder them. But something else had happened in the minutes they'd been trapped inside that warehouse together. Something vague and disconcerting that she couldn't quite pinpoint. Something that was niggling the back of her mind like a pebble in her shoe.

As she stood hugging herself against the cold, listening to Adam talk to the dispatcher, she realized what it was. This tough-talking, uncompromising, foul-mouthed detective had saved her life. Worse, in those few short minutes when he'd held her in his arms, she'd reacted to him in a way that had nothing to do with his being a cop.

The realization made her start shaking all over again.

"Fire department will be here in a few minutes."

Eli looked up to find him standing just a couple feet away. He'd removed his trench coat and was putting it around her shoulders. "I'm okay," she began, but he cut her off.

"Don't argue. You took in some smoke, and it's plenty cold out here."

She let him wrap the trench around her shoulders. It didn't help with the shaking, but she didn't point that out.

He stepped back and for a moment they leaned against the truck and watched the flames.

"You saved my life," she said after a pause.

"Come on, Doc. I saved my own ass and you just happened to be there."

Blinking back the images of the fire, trying not to think about what could have happened, what almost happened, she looked at him. "If you hadn't told me to get down on the ground, if you hadn't come looking for me—"

"Do us both a favor and don't go there. All right?"

Before he looked away, she thought she saw something she hadn't seen before in his eyes. Emotion, she realized. Hard-edged and raw, but it made him a little bit more human.

The wail of sirens rose in the distance.

"Do you have any idea who might have done this?" he asked.

The question shouldn't have surprised her, but it did. Until now, it hadn't even entered her mind that she might actually know the person responsible. "No. I can't imagine anyone I know doing something like this."

Her lungs seized and she started coughing. Adam put his hand on her back and tapped gently. "You need to get yourself checked out," he said.

Not up to an argument, she looked down at her ruined clothes. The smell of smoke clung to her. It was a smell she would never forget as long as she lived.

"We can't tell the police what we suspect," he said.

Shocked, she glanced over at him. "This has moved beyond corporate secrets. Someone tried to kill us, for God's sake. The police need to know."

"If you tell Lindquist what we were doing here tonight, you'd better be prepared to tell him what we suspect with regard to Valazine and deal with the consequences."

"I don't want to go public with this yet," she said. "But we can't lie to the police."

"You can't have it both ways."

The sirens grew louder. Eli had the feeling she was about to make a profound decision—one that would affect her for the rest of her life. She glanced over at the warehouse where the fire raged. Even fifty feet away, she could feel the heat from it.

"What's it going to be, Doc?"

She hated being in this position. Logic told her to tell the police everything. Yet she knew she couldn't go public with her suspicions. Not until she was absolutely certain. To do so prematurely would not only taint a promising new drug, but irrevocably damage Roth's reputation.

The first fire truck stopped at the rear of the complex next to the chain-link fence. She watched one of the firefighters jump from the truck and proceeded to cut through the fencing with a huge cable cutter. Another firefighter peeled open the fence so the truck could pass through.

"Don't mention Valazine," Adam said as the truck rolled toward the warehouse. "Tell them we were here to pick up some old records. Tell them I'm a friend visiting you from Chicago."

"Damn it, Adam—"

"It's the only way," he said. "Despite what you might believe, the cops aren't stupid." When she only continued to stare at him, he added, "Eli, we'll eventually tell them everything. But we need some time to put this thing together. If they find out too soon—before we have all the facts—it'll blow the top off of everything we're doing and we'll lose any chance of proving our case."

She watched two firefighters and a paramedic approach, dread and indecision hammering at her.

"What's it going to be?" Adam pressed.

Sighing, she jerked her head once. But she'd never been more unsure of anything in her life. And she couldn't ignore the little voice telling her she was making a mistake. A mistake that would probably end up costing her a lot more than just her career.

chapter

12

ELI COULDN'T BELIEVE SHE'D WITHHELD INFORMA-
tion from the police. All her life she'd followed the rules.
Even as a teenager, she'd listened to her father. She'd
gotten straight A's in high school. She'd made the dean's
list her first year at U of M. She didn't even speed!

She wasn't prone to idiotic behavior or lapses in judgment. Not until recently, anyway. Of course, she didn't
have a whole lot of experience to draw upon when it came
to dealing with rogue cops, corporate fraud, or murder.

The drive from the warehouse to her home was fraught
with tension. Eli was too angry to speak and evidently
Adam Boedecker didn't see fit to fill the long, uncomfortable silence with small talk. Like that was a surprise.

He parked on the street, and she got out without speaking and made a beeline for the front door. After stomping
the snow from her shoes in the foyer, she went directly
to the closet. But one whiff of her coat and she carried it
out to the laundry room and tossed it into a garbage bag,
hoping it didn't stink up the rest of the house before she
could make a trip to the cleaners.

Adam was standing in the foyer when she returned.

He'd removed his trench and draped it over his arm. She didn't offer to take his coat when she passed him and started for the kitchen.

"You got something on your mind?" he asked, following her.

Glaring at him over her shoulder, she moved to the coffeepot and concentrated on pouring water and dumping dark roast into the filter basket. "Your perceptivity astounds me. No wonder you're a detective."

"It's obvious you're angry about something. Why don't you clue me in?" Adam said from his place at the bar.

Shoving the carafe under the drip, she turned to him. "How do you expect Lindquist to figure out who set that fire tonight when he doesn't have all the facts?"

"The fire marshal can work the physical evidence."

"Lindquist knows we're hiding something from him. I think it's in our own best interest to cooperate."

"It's in our own best interest not to take this public until we have proof."

"I don't like hiding information from the police," she said.

"Deal with it," he said mildly.

"Maybe I'll deal with it by calling Lindquist and telling him everything I know."

"You do that and we'll never know who's responsible for putting a dangerous drug on the market."

"Why not?"

"Because once the cat is out of the bag, it's going to be a free-for-all. You'll give everyone involved time to cover their ass. Even if the drug gets jerked off the shelf, you'll probably never know who was responsible for messing with those trials. They'll say it was an unforeseen side effect and get off scot-free." A cruel smile twisted one side of his mouth. "Unless, of course, someone needs a fall guy and points a finger at you. You were the one in charge of the trials, weren't you, Doctor?"

Eli forced a laugh, but she wasn't amused. In fact, his words sent an icy finger of dread scraping up her spine. "That won't happen," she said.

"Why not?"

"Because I followed protocol. Because I documented everything along the way, and there are a dozen or more checks and balances in place to keep any number of things from happening." Because she didn't want him to see the uncertainty she knew was on her face, she turned away and got two cups out of the cupboard. "You shouldn't have told Lindquist we're . . . involved."

"I couldn't think of any other reason why a cop on disability from Chicago would be in Ann Arbor with a woman at an archive storage warehouse after hours, could you?"

"He didn't believe you," she said halfheartedly.

"I'm sure the killing looks you were sending me helped."

Eli picked up the carafe and poured two cups of coffee. "So what do we do now?"

"Do you think Chambers or Bornheimer are capable of setting that fire?"

The question made her feel queasy. "No," she said. "I've known both of them for quite some time. There's no way either of them could do something like that."

"What about hired help?"

"You mean if one of them hired a . . . thug to do it for them?"

Adam nodded. "It's not like it hasn't been done before."

Eli thought about it, then shook her head. "I just can't see either of them doing something like that. I mean, these guys are scientists. They wouldn't even know where to *find* a thug, let alone hire one."

"The fire wasn't a coincidence," Adam said.

She wanted to argue, wanted to believe the fire had nothing to do with Roth or Valazine, but the words curdled on her tongue. "My God, who would do something like that?"

"Someone with a lot at stake."

"Adam, the police could help us."

"Oh, for chrissake," he said crossly. "Will you drop the police issue?"

"Okay, I'll drop it," she snapped back. "But I want to

know one thing before I get into this any deeper. I want to know why you're working on this alone. I want to know why this isn't an official investigation. Why the Chicago PD and the FBI and FDA aren't behind you on this."

He studied her, saying nothing. She could tell by the look in his eyes that she'd pissed him off. Frankly, she didn't care. She'd almost been killed tonight. She deserved to know everything, including whatever it was he was hiding from her.

"Why don't you trust the police?" she asked.

He laughed, but it was a humorless sound. "Look, Eli, this case has huge ramifications. Think about it. I need some kind of proof before I waltz in and tell my lieutenant that a multibillion dollar company is killing people with a drug gone haywire. If I take them what I've got now—which basically amounts to a couple dozen newspaper articles, a few inconclusive autopsy reports, and a somewhat suspicious warehouse fire—the lieutenant will have a heart attack laughing his ass off."

"I don't agree with you."

"Now there's a surprise."

"This is too big for two people to deal with."

"I'm a cop. I'm experienced—"

"Look what happened tonight, Adam! We were nearly killed. We lost some files that can never be replaced. Things could have turned out much worse."

"We're fine," he said. "We'll just have to stay on our toes. In a few days, things will start coming together. We've just got to work the case. Look at everything, then look at it again. Damn it, I need your help. Don't bail on me now."

He talked a good point. But Eli couldn't help but think a vital piece of the puzzle was missing. Something he wasn't telling her. Things just weren't adding up. She understood his motivation if, indeed, his brother had been taking Valazine. But she couldn't comprehend his lack of faith in his own department.

"Is this really about your brother, Adam?" she asked. "Or is it about something else?"

He scowled at her.

She pressed on. "Or maybe this has to do with your needing to prove something. To the department. To yourself, maybe."

If she hadn't been watching him closely, she wouldn't have noticed the flash in his dark eyes. He might be good at hiding his feelings, but Eli was well schooled in reading people. And if she wasn't mistaken, she'd just touched a raw nerve with a cattle prod.

"You think this is about my needing to prove something?" One minute he was standing at the bar separating the kitchen from the dining room, the next he was right next to her with his fingers clamped around her biceps, forcing her over to the dining room table.

"Get your hands off me," she snapped.

"I'll show you what this is all about, goddamn it." Grimacing, he reached down and removed a battered manila folder from his briefcase. Eli jumped when he slapped the folder down on the table before her.

"Look at it," he snarled.

Eli knew it was something she didn't want to see, so she kept her eyes on his. "Your strong-arm tactics don't frighten me."

"Look at it!"

She forced herself to look at the open file in front of her. The color images struck her brain with the force of a baseball bat. She saw pasty flesh and torn clothing and the shocking red of blood. She saw a man lying on his back in a wide, dark pool of it. The top portion of his head had been blown away. What was left of his face was little more than a jagged mass of flesh and bone and brain tissue.

"Oh, God. Jesus . . ." She tried to turn away, but he wouldn't allow it.

"There's more." Using his free hand, he flipped to the next photo.

Unnerved, shaking, and growing angry, she glanced down at the photo. A woman with dark hair lay sprawled on glossy tile. The robe she was wearing rode high on her thighs. Blood spatter covered the white flesh of her legs.

Eli stared, sickened yet unable to tear her gaze away from the horrific sight. The woman's eyes were wide and glazed with death. Her mouth gaped open, the tongue protruding grotesquely.

Eli closed her eyes against the carnage. "That's enough."

"That mess was my brother and his wife. She was pregnant. He couldn't wait to become a father."

She tried to turn away, but he shook her. "He was taking Valazine, Dr. Barnes, and this is what happened to him. Take a good long look. Remember it next time you're not quite sure of my motivations."

Cruelly, he flipped to the next photo. A young man in blue jeans and what was left of a white T-shirt was slumped against the wall, his organs and life blood draining from a terrible slash that cut from sternum to navel.

"This is what my quest for the truth is all about," Adam said quietly. "It's about violence and murder and some ruthless son of a bitch letting it happen because he wants to retire before he's too goddamn old to enjoy himself. It's about some corporate sociopath who wants his name in some goddamn book that no one will ever read."

Eli closed her eyes to shut out the terrible images. Bile rose in her throat. "I've seen enough."

Adam released her.

She stumbled back, shocked and furious that he would do this to her. "You had no right to do that."

"Neither did the person responsible. Don't forget that."

Eli had seen death before. Had witnessed several autopsies in the course of her education. She'd seen the ravages of disease and aging and natural death. She'd seen the shocking results of violent death. She would never forget the images branded into her young mind the day she found her mother's body. Yet the police photos in that file went beyond violent and made her entire psyche recoil with horror and revulsion.

"If you're trying to shock me, you've succeeded," she said in a voice she barely recognized. "Is that what you wanted?"

"What I want is your cooperation."

Leaning heavily against the bar, she willed away the nausea and concentrated on getting fresh air into her lungs.

Adam walked into the kitchen, leaving the file on the table, and turned his back to her. "Each victim either was murdered by someone who had been prescribed Valazine or had been taking the drug themselves and committed suicide after committing murder. I've got autopsy reports. Copies of prescriptions and lab reports. The evidence might be circumstantial, but it's compelling as hell."

Eli squeezed her eyes shut for an instant, willing her mind not to replay the images. "Don't ever do that to me again," she said after a moment. "I'll help you with this. I said I would and I intend to keep my word. But don't ever treat me like that again."

chapter

13

ADAM FELT LIKE A BASTARD FOR DOING THAT TO her. A real son of a bitch. Then again he'd never claimed to be a nice guy. He figured it was better for her to learn that now as opposed to later because he had a sinking feeling they were going to be working on this nasty case for a while. Better she know what kind of man she was dealing with right off the bat. The kind of man who wasn't afraid to fight dirty or use any means at his disposal to get what he wanted. He certainly wasn't above intimidating her.

Still, it bothered him that she'd gone milk white when he'd dragged out the police photos and forced her to look at them. He wasn't proud of what he'd done, even if it had been effective. He was even less proud of the fact that he'd acted out of anger. Not that it took much to set him off these days. The shrink he'd seen during rehab had warned him that his hair-trigger temper was only one of a myriad unpleasant aftereffects of the traumatic brain injury. Adam had learned to deal with it for the most part. But there were times—too many times—when he felt out of control. Times when he'd flown off the handle for no good reason, times when he'd blown his stack in situations he should have been able to handle. He could have handled this one better.

He turned and looked at Eli. Shame cut him when he saw that she was rubbing her arms where he'd grabbed her. Appalled that he'd touched a woman in anger—that he'd touched *her* in anger—he strode to the window that looked out over the backyard. Big flakes of wet snow floated from the night sky, clinging to the naked branches of the trees, weighing down the boughs of the evergreens at the rear of the property.

"I'm sorry," he said after a moment. "I shouldn't have done that."

When she said nothing, he turned to her. "You're right. I have some things going on in my life. But what I'm doing is about my brother." Feeling more in control, he took a step toward her. "At least it started out that way."

She held her ground at the bar, her eyes wary. "And now?"

"We both know this involves more people than just my brother."

She considered his words for a moment without comment, then asked, "Why isn't your police department behind you?"

That was the question he didn't want to answer, he realized. The question that caused him the most angst. It was bad enough that he had a personal stake in the case, that his personal involvement made him less than objective. But it was infinitely worse knowing he no longer had any credibility when it came to his own department.

"I'm on leave," he said.

"Because you were shot in the line of duty, right? You told me."

He nodded, hoping she didn't ask for more.

"The two incidents are unrelated?" she asked. "I mean, your brother's death and your being shot?"

"I was on disability when Michael . . . when Michael died." He felt his lips twist into what he hoped passed for a smile. "Want to see my scar?"

She didn't smile back at him. "How long have you been on disability?"

Adam didn't want to get into the dynamics of a traumatic brain injury or the devastation it had wreaked on his professional and personal life. He rolled his shoulder, considered his options, decided on a compromise. "A few months." He didn't want her to know it had been three agonizing years since he'd been a cop. Since he'd worked a case—or even trusted his own mind. "I've been using my time off to work this case."

"But you have resources at the department. I mean, if this were an official investigation, you would have access to those resources, wouldn't you? You would have the power to get warrants and—"

"I have someone inside the department helping me."

She looked surprised at that. "Oh, well, I suppose that's a help."

"Interrogation over?"

"I meant what I said earlier," she said.

"I was out of line," he said. "It won't happen again."

Tense silence filled the kitchen. Needing something to do, Adam walked over to the dining room table and began gathering the photographs. He reeked of smoke from the fire. His throat hurt. He tasted ash on his tongue. Remembering the reports he wanted to go through, he turned toward Eli just in time to see her walk over to the sink. She'd taken off her shoes at some point. Her feet were slender and pretty. Adam watched her rinse their mugs, his eyes skimming over the curves of her breasts, and wondered what she looked like beneath that sweater.

"Would you like some more coffee? I can make another pot."

He almost jolted at the sound of her voice. He'd been staring at her. Sheepishly, he looked down at his ruined clothes. "I could use a shower," he said.

"Oh, well . . . if you want to use my guest bathroom, I don't mind." She looked down at her own clothes. "I need one, too."

"I thought we might try to get through that report tonight," he said, not sure why he suddenly felt so awkward.

"That is, unless you'd rather do it tomorrow."

"No, I'd rather get it over with." She set their clean mugs in the drainer. "The guest bath is upstairs. Towels are in the linen closet just inside the door. Let me show you."

Adam followed her through the living room and up the stairs. He tried not to notice the way those slacks hugged her ass, but he gave up when she bent to pick up a cast-iron door stop. Elizabeth Barnes had one of the nicest asses he'd ever laid eyes on.

"I just want to get some of this smoke off me," he said.

"No problem. I'm going to duck into the other shower," she said. "I'll be out in ten minutes."

"We can go through the summary report," he said from the bathroom doorway.

"Right." She set out towels then turned, seemed surprised to see him standing so close. "Sorry."

Even over the stink of smoke that clung to his clothes, he could smell her sweet vanilla scent. Pleasure flared with unexpected force, and he realized with some surprise that he wanted to touch her. His expression must have conveyed his thoughts because her eyes widened. He couldn't tell if her reaction was caution or fear, but he reached out anyway. She tried to step away, but there wasn't enough room and she ended up bumping the back of her head against the door.

"Ouch," he said, and wiped the smudge of soot from her chin with the pad of his thumb. When she only stared at him, he said, "Soot."

"Oh, um . . . well." Color tinged her cheeks.

Adam smiled, charmed. It had been a long time since he'd seen a woman blush.

Never taking her eyes from him, she eased past him. "Excuse me," she said, and hurried down the hall without looking back.

He stood in the doorway and watched her walk away, wondering what the hell he was doing.

*   *   *

TWENTY MINUTES LATER, ADAM SAT AT THE DIN-
ing room table and skimmed through the first dozen or so
pages of the summary report. The shower had taken off
the soot, but he'd had to put on the same clothes so he
still smelled of smoke. He was just going to have to live
with it until he got back to the hotel and into a change of
clothes.

Annoyed because he was distracted, he looked down at
the report and tried to concentrate. It wasn't helping that
the report was written in hard-core scientific jargon. It
grated on his patience that he was going to have to rely
on her to translate.

A noise from the living room alerted him to her approach. He looked up to see Eli walk into the kitchen,
glance over at him, then head directly to the coffeemaker.

"Do you want some more coffee?" she asked.

Adam was so engaged in watching her cross the room
that it took him a moment to realize she'd asked a question.

"Black," he managed.

She frowned at him, pulled two mugs from the drainer,
and poured. Adam looked down at the report, saw the blur
of words, then looked over at her. She'd changed into a
pair of jeans and a faded U of M sweatshirt. He couldn't
see much of her beneath the oversize shirt, but those jeans
hugged every lush curve of her rear end like paint on a
canvas. A masterpiece, he thought, and attraction swirled
hotly, then settled low in his gut. Damn it, one day soon
he was going to have to get laid. Maybe when this mess
was over, he'd find someone. A woman who didn't have
too many expectations or wear her heart on her sleeve or
mind spending time with a mean-tempered ex-cop.

"Here you go."

He hadn't realized she'd walked up to the table. He
jolted slightly, then watched her set the cup and saucer in
front of him. "Have a seat," he said.

Cradling her own cup between her hands, she pulled
out a chair opposite him. Adam let his eyes do another
quick sweep, felt that same uncomfortable stir, and forced
his gaze back to the report.

"I see you're reading the summary report," she said.

"Trying to, anyway." He looked across the table at her. She was still wearing her glasses, but the lack of makeup made her look younger and less sophisticated. Her hair was damp and curling on the ends. Adam could smell her just-showered scent and found himself breathing in deeply, wanting to fill his lungs with her. . . .

Uneasy with the direction of his thoughts, he looked down at the report.

"I was thinking about the fire," she began. "The five archive boxes contained most of the records I'd accumulated over the last six or seven years. We lost quite a bit of information."

"Don't you have backup on microfiche or something?"

"We stopped using microfiche several years ago. I might be able to find some of the preliminary data on microfiche. Some of the information is probably on disk. But we'll never be able to re-create the majority of the documentation."

Adam digested that for a moment. "Who at Roth knew what information those boxes contained?"

"Almost everyone. There's an archive database available on the network. When someone needs a box, they can do a search for contents, find the box number and—"

"What do you mean by 'search for contents'?"

"For example, if someone is looking for phase one clinical trial participant-screening applications, they could do a search for 'Valazine phase one clinical trial participant-screening applications.' All they would have to do is type in some key words, and the database would return all the box numbers with a match or partial matches in the description."

"Okay," he said. "What was in the boxes?"

"Correspondence. Reports. Summaries. Meeting minutes. Participant applications."

"Let's talk about the names of the trial participants."

"Applications, not names. Names are not available to anyone at Roth. We identify participants by number only."

"I've been working this over in my mind, Eli. Everything goes back to those names."

"Why?"

"Because I think that when we compare the raw data to your reports, they're not going to match. We need to talk to the study participants."

"Adam, I'm still not one hundred percent certain—"

"How do I get those names?" he cut in.

She sighed. "The only people who have access to participants' names are the medical personnel at the clinics where the trials were administered."

"Which clinics?"

"Phases one and two of the trials were administered at Folkhum Laboratories. Phases three through four were at Manicon Labs."

"Here in Ann Arbor?"

"Folkhum has since closed. We still deal with Manicon. They're located in Ypsilanti."

Adam took a swallow of coffee. He thought about the report in front of him, about the confidentiality problem with the participants' names. He thought about Michael and asked himself how far he was willing to go to get what he needed.

"I need to get into that lab," he said after a moment.

"Without some type of legal inducement, they won't willingly share that information with you."

"Maybe there's another way."

Wariness sharpened her gaze. "What are you suggesting?"

"I'm not suggesting anything." Amused, he smiled. "Don't worry, I'm not going to ask you to do anything illegal."

"Good, because even if you were to have such a stupid idea, I wouldn't want to hear about it."

"Come on. I'm a cop. I don't do B and Es." But in the back of his mind, he found himself wondering how far he was willing to go. He wondered if a traumatic brain injury would be a good defense angle if he got caught doing something kooky—like breaking into a medical clinic and stealing confidential patient information.

"Maybe if you went through the channels, you could get a search warrant for Manicon," she suggested.

Adam had considered that. He might have followed through if he wasn't so worried about passing that psyche exam. "A judge would never go for it," he said, not wanting to get into his small credibility problem.

The doorbell buzzed, and she jumped.

"Expecting company?" he asked.

"No." Glancing uneasily at him, she rose and started toward the foyer. "Not at this hour."

Adam looked at his watch. Almost ten o'clock P.M. Curious, he followed her to the door and waited as she stood on her tiptoes and looked out the peephole. "It's Kevin Chambers," she whispered, and spun.

Adam tried to get out of her way, but he wasn't expecting her to move so quickly. She plowed headlong into him hard enough to make him grunt. The contact of her body against his went through him like a shock wave, starting at the point of contact and echoing through his body. He felt the soft brush of female curves, discerned her sweet scent over the smell of smoke that still clung to him. Surprised by the power of his reaction, he stepped back.

"Oh, I didn't . . . see you." She grimaced at the door. "This is going to be awkward."

Not for the first time, Adam wondered about her relationship with Chambers. "Is it normal for him to visit so late?" he asked, but his mind was still working over the way she'd felt pressed up against him.

She shook her head. "Security probably called him about the fire. He's probably here to make sure I'm all right. He's a little . . . overprotective."

"Territorial?" he asked.

"Not that way." She looked pained. "What do I tell him?"

Adam thought about that for a moment. Chambers was on his list of suspects. "Tell him I came by to pick up some information. Canned stuff, if he asked. Annual reports or whatever you can think of. I'll tell him I'm finished here and will be driving back to Chicago tonight and closing out my report later in the week."

"Okay." She raised her hand to the knob.

"Eli, after I leave . . . I want you to watch him carefully—"

"He's not involved in any of this," she interjected. "Kevin is a straight arrow. He wouldn't—"

"Look, I don't care what kind of relationship you have with Chambers, okay? All I'm telling you is to watch him."

"We're not involved. I mean it, Adam. We're friends. That's it."

"Okay, that's fine. Still, I want you to be careful. Keep my card handy; it's got my cell phone number on it. Stay aware. Lock your doors."

Waving him off, Eli took a big breath, then swung open the door. "Kevin, hi. I wasn't expecting you."

Kevin Chambers entered without invitation, his cobalt eyes consuming Eli in a single fell swoop. "Clyde Cummings called me about the fire. I couldn't believe it when he told me you were there especially after what happened last night. Jesus, Eli, are you all right?"

"I'm okay," she said.

Adam stomped an uncomfortable wave of territoriality when Chambers took her by the shoulders, turned her to face him, and looked her over. His cashmere overcoat, color-coordinated scarf, and kidskin gloves reeked of money and breeding and success—all the things that would appeal to a woman like Eli. All the things Adam seemed to be in short supply of lately.

"I'm okay, Kevin, really," she said.

Chambers's eyes swept to Adam, then questioningly back to Eli. "I didn't realize you had company."

"You've met Detective Boedecker," she said. "He was just leaving."

Chambers sized him up, stuck out his hand. "You're a detective from Chicago, right?"

Adam shook the man's hand, aware of the overtight grip. Game for a little male tit for tat, he squeezed back. "That's right."

"Is this an official call?" Chambers released his hand.

"I was just getting some information from Dr. Barnes to finish up my report."

Adam watched the other man's eyes sweep past him toward the dining room where the two coffee mugs sat on the table. Inwardly, Adam smiled. It appeared the illustrious Kevin Chambers was, indeed, territorial when it came to Dr. Barnes. Interesting.

"Eli told me about your visit the other day," Chambers said. "I couldn't disagree with you more."

"Sometimes these things lead to nowhere," Adam replied amicably. "Dr. Barnes has been very helpful."

He turned to Eli. She looked flustered and uncomfortable. Adam extended his hand, prepared for the quick jump of heat when she shook his hand. Giving her a small smile, he winked. "Thank you for your time. I won't bother you again."

"You're welcome."

He let himself out through the door, then stood on the porch until he heard the bolt lock click. He didn't like leaving her alone with Chambers. He told himself it was because he hadn't yet eliminated Chambers from his list of suspects. But that didn't explain why he was so damn annoyed.

"Shit," he muttered, and started down the sidewalk. Maybe he'd hang out in the neighborhood awhile. Just to keep an eye on things until Chambers left, he assured himself.

But Adam knew that wasn't the reason why he was so hesitant to leave. Or why he was so damn annoyed. And he couldn't help but wonder how he would feel sitting outside in the cold, watching all the lights go off inside and knowing she was in bed with that smug little son of a bitch.

Adam squashed the thought ruthlessly. What was he doing torturing himself with stupid scenarios like that? For God's sake, he didn't have any kind of claim on her. Their relationship was strictly one of his needing information, her having it, and not a single goddamn thing more.

"Yeah, buddy, and you're going to have to get laid soon," he growled, and wrenched open the door of the Tahoe.

The snow had stopped at some point, but the wind had picked up and cut like a blade. Smoky tendrils of snow whispered across the sidewalk and street to pile into drifts against the curbs. Criminy, he was sick of snow.

Adam started the engine and looked at the house. Yellow light shone in the living room windows. He found his eyes checking the upstairs windows, and he told himself he wasn't relieved when he found them dark. Snatching up his cell phone, he dialed Chad Deaton's home number from memory. Deaton answered on the second ring.

"It's Adam."

A beat of silence. "Ah, the man about to go into permanent retirement. Hope your 401(k) is healthy."

"I need a couple of favors."

"You need a hell of a lot more than that, buddy."

"I need background checks on some people."

Deaton cursed. "Don't tell me—it's a conspiracy, right? Everyone's out to get you and you're the only one who knows what's going on. I saw the movie."

"You could be right."

"I was being facetious."

"You were being an asshole."

"I don't know why I'm going along with this."

"It's that guilt thing, Chad. You know, you and my wife. My going through the door first that night in the warehouse. Bad medicine, you know?"

"Fuck you, Boedecker. I don't feel guilty about a goddamn thing. I feel sorry for you because you had a couple of bad breaks and now you're a sorry son of a bitch."

Watching the snow whisper along the sidewalk, Adam smiled. "Sounds like you have some anger issues to work through, Chad."

"Give me the goddamn names."

Adam rattled off the names of the top five players at Roth, including Dr. Elizabeth Barnes.

"Henderson has been trying to reach you."

"I'm going to call him next."

"He's got the flu, but I'm sure he'll appreciate you dragging his fat ass out of bed."

"What does he want?"

"You missed your psych. What the hell do you think he wants?"

"I think he wants my ass on a platter."

"You've put him in a bad position, Adam."

"He can handle it."

"I guess the real question is how your career will fare."

Rubbing his temples, Adam looked down at his briefcase, where he could see the bound spine of the final summary report on Valazine. If the headache didn't get any worse, he just might be able to get through it tonight.

"The Barnes woman called the station complaining about you."

"I know."

"If you're so all fucking knowing, then you know that if she hadn't gotten me, your ass would be in a sling."

"My ass is already in a sling. Thanks for covering for me."

"You're a hardheaded son of a bitch—you know that?"

Adam sighed. "So I've been told."

"You're treading on thin ice, my man. It's going to end up costing you. Your career is fucked. I ain't going down with you. I'll cut you loose before I let that happen."

"I need those backgrounds by tomorrow morning."

The phone went dead. Frowning, Adam disconnected and sighed. He should have felt like a bastard for using guilt to manipulate Deaton. Then again, Adam figured he had it coming. He wondered how much longer he could count on his ex-partner to help him.

He glanced toward Elizabeth Barnes's house. The living room light was still on. He thought of the way those blue jeans had looked snugged against her ass. The faint scent of vanilla that surrounded her like a soft, fragrant cloud. He knew better than to entertain thoughts of her in those terms, but he was cranky and cold and had one hell of a headache.

He wondered if she was sleeping with Chambers.

Chambers would be exactly the kind of man she would
be attracted to. Educated. Wealthy. Successful. He would
appeal to a smart woman like Eli.

Adam would be lying if he told himself she didn't in-
trigue him. She did. A lot more than he wanted to admit.
And a hell of a lot more than was wise.

Putting the Tahoe in gear, he pulled on to the street.
He'd circle around a few times, let the truck warm up,
and then he'd park down the street and camp out for a
few hours. Not so he could be sure Chambers left, he
assured himself.

He just wanted to make sure she stayed safe through
the night.

chapter
14

ELI GATHERED THE TWO COFFEE MUGS LEFT ON THE dining room table and carried them to the kitchen, aware that Kevin was watching her from his perch at the bar.

"You sure you're all right?" he asked.

"For the third time, I'm fine." Running the cups under the tap, she smiled at him. "Just a little shaken up."

"The warehouse was a total loss."

The final minutes she'd spent trapped with Adam flashed through her mind. The roar of the fire. The scorching heat against her face and hands. The choking stench of smoke. The panic exploding in her chest.

Eli shivered.

Kevin was up and striding toward her an instant later. "You're not all right. I can see that you're shaking and pale as a sheet."

"I'm just . . . tired."

"Shhh. It's okay." Reaching for her, he pulled her gently to him. "Come here."

Because she was still shaking inside, Eli let him hold her. She knew Kevin. She was comfortable with him. He

was a good man and there was no way in hell he was
involved in any of this.

"If it hadn't been for Detective Boedecker, I don't think
I would have gotten out," she said.

He eased her to arm's length and cocked his head to
look at her. "What on earth was he doing in that warehouse with you to begin with?"

Eli didn't like lying, but she especially didn't like lying
to her friends. She'd known Kevin for ten years. She
trusted him, damn it—she did. Still, she held back. "He
asked me to meet him. I felt the need to disprove his
theory, so I agreed."

"After hours?"

"I was working late anyway."

"Single-minded bastard." He shook his head. "So he's
been hassling you?"

"No. Not really. Just the one phone call earlier this
evening."

"Eli, you didn't have to put yourself through this. You
could have called me or Ruth Monroe, or even Peter
Roth."

Her heart was pounding. Lies always sounded so . . .
illogical. "I can handle Boedecker. And I just couldn't
stand to see him running around, spewing misinformation
about Roth."

"So, is he satisfied now?"

She nodded. "I took him to the warehouse and showed
him how carefully the study was documented. I explained
to him some of the check-and-balance systems in place.
The number of people involved. We did some random
checks on some of the documentation, and everything
panned out. He looked at some of the reports, made a few
notes, and said he was satisfied." Oh, it was a bad lie.
She'd never been good at it. Would Kevin believe her?

"Well, I still don't understand why he didn't go through
PR."

She shrugged. "Apparently, he's a very difficult man."
At least that much was true.

"I don't like him sniffing around and hassling you like

that. A cop can't just waltz in, make crazy accusations, and demand our cooperation."

"Well, in this case, my cooperation put his theory to rest."

"I'm glad you're okay." His fingers tightened on her shoulders. "Clyde told me the fire is suspicious."

She wondered if Kevin felt her tense.

"It'll take a while for them to figure out the cause." He lowered his hand and rubbed circles between her shoulder blades. "This has been a tough couple of weeks for you. First Walter. Then you get your purse snatched. And now this. You don't need some macho cop hassling you about some bogus investigation. Next time he comes calling, Eli, let me know, okay?"

"Thank you. I mean, for being so concerned. For coming over to check on me."

"Don't thank me." Raising his hand, he brushed the backs of his knuckles against her cheekbone. "I was worried."

Sensing his concern had just crossed over into something much more intimate, Eli tried to ease away, but he didn't release her. "I'm a little tired," she said. "Why don't we call it a night?"

"I'll just . . . go." He made no attempt to move away from her.

A moment too late, Eli saw him lining up for the kiss like a pilot bringing a jet down for a landing. He leaned forward. Judged his distance. Lined up with the target. She turned her head slightly, and he ended up kissing the side of her mouth.

"I like the way you feel against me," he said. "I like the way you smell. Eli . . . you're driving me nuts."

"Kevin, this isn't a good time."

He tilted her head, kissed her again, tried to stick his tongue in her mouth. "You feel so good against me."

"Kevin, I can't." Firmly, she pushed away from him. "I'm sorry."

He stepped back, put his hands on his hips. "No, I'm sorry. I didn't mean to . . . Whew, we keep apologizing to each other."

Eli almost felt sorry for him. He was a decent man. He simply wasn't the man for her. "I'm just not ready to take this step, okay?"

"It's all right."

But she could plainly see that it wasn't all right. His mouth had tightened into a thin line. Even though he tried not to show it, annoyance shone bright and hot in his eyes. God, she was really blowing this.

"I didn't mean to push," he said.

"It's not you," she said quickly. "It's . . . me. I'm just tired. It's been a bad night."

"I know." He smiled. "I'm really glad you're okay."

She knew he meant it, saw clearly the sincerity in his eyes, and felt a twinge of guilt. For lying to him. For not trusting him. For not being attracted to him, when he was much better suited to her than a man like Adam Boedecker.

That she would compare the two men surprised her. She might be attracted to Adam on a physical level, but she was far too smart to fall victim to her hormones. Kevin was kind, successful in his field, and passionate about his work. She'd sensed for months now that he wanted more than a casual friendship. It disturbed her that he left her cold inside. It disturbed her even more that those same nerves jumped to attention every time she got within shouting distance of Adam Boedecker. How could that be? She was an intelligent woman and knew he was everything that should not appeal to her. He was combative and sarcastic, with a dark side that left her more than a little unsettled.

Yet, on another level that didn't have anything to do with intellect or common sense, he appealed to her like no other man ever had. Eli didn't understand it. She wasn't sure she wanted to.

"I've been wondering, Eli . . . I mean, with Walter gone, I was wondering if you'd like me to escort you to the Distinguished Woman of Science Award banquet to-morrow night."

A sharper twinge of guilt pricked her. How could she have forgotten about the Distinguished Woman of Science banquet? The award had been one of her goals since she was fifteen years old.

"I'd like that," she replied.

"Great." He smiled. "See you tomorrow, then." Turning away, he snagged his coat from the closet. "Let me know if that detective hassles you again, all right?"

Eli nodded. "I don't think he'll be back."

He opened the door. She trailed behind him. "Don't forget to lock your door," he said.

She watched him walk down the driveway and get into the sporty little BMW parked at the curb. Once behind the wheel, he waved. She waved back. By the time she closed the door, it wasn't Kevin Chambers she was thinking about, but a dark and brooding detective who wouldn't be so easily dissuaded.

ELI JOLTED WHEN THE PHONE ON HER DESK BUZZED. Completely enmeshed in the anticipated pharmacodynamics of ROT-535, Valazine's new and improved cousin, she answered on the fourth ring with an absent utterance of her name.

"Detective Martin Lindquist is here to see you," the receptionist announced.

Turning away from her computer monitor, she wondered what could be important enough to warrant a personal visit as opposed to a phone call. She wondered if the police had arrested the person responsible for Walter's murder. Or perhaps the detective was here to see her about the warehouse fire the night before.

"Send him in." Eli glanced at her watch, surprised to see it was nearly five o'clock. That gave her only two hours to get home, shower, and dress before Kevin picked her up at seven. She'd been so immersed in her work, she'd lost track of time. Again.

She'd just shut down her computer when the detective appeared at her door, looking like he'd had a very long day. "Detective Lindquist. Hello."

"Dr. Barnes." He didn't smile, and his eyes were keen as he walked over to her desk. "I was hoping to catch you at home, but I got tired of listening to your answering machine. You always work so many hours?"

"Well . . . yes."

"You're not trying to avoid me, are you?"

She looked at him quizzically. "Of course not. In fact, I was hoping you had some news about Walter."

"Mind if I sit down?"

"Please." She wasn't sure why she felt so uneasy. Until now, she'd been relatively comfortable with Lindquist. He'd always been cordial and professional. Today, however, there was something in his demeanor that put her on edge. "How can I help you?"

"I took a statement from you the other day about your relationship with Walter Sanchez."

"Yes, I remember."

"Well, I'm trying to get a few things straight in my head." When she shot him a questioning look, he shrugged. "You know, just for the record."

"What things?" she asked.

"Well, when I talked to you the other day, you told me you and Dr. Sanchez were just friends. Is that correct?"

"Yes. We were very good friends."

"How long have you been friends?"

"About ten years."

"Were you ever intimately involved with him?"

If the situation hadn't been so serious, Eli might have laughed. But she could tell from the look in Lindquist's eyes that he was dead serious. "Of course not."

"You're sure?"

"Detective Lindquist, how could I not be sure?" She didn't bother to try to keep the exasperation from her voice. "Of course I'm sure."

"I've run across some information that leads me to believe you and Dr. Sanchez were more than just friends."

An incredulous laugh choked her. "*What?*"

"Were you ever romantically involved with Dr. Sanchez?"

"No! And I'd appreciate it very much if you'd tell me what this is all about."

"I had a couple of computer techies out at Dr. Sanchez's house today. You know, lab techs going through some of his files and so forth to see if they could find anything that might point us in the right direction."

"I don't see what that has to do with your thinking Walter and I were . . ." She could barely say the word. "Involved."

"When my computer guys went through Sanchez's e-mail program, there were several e-mails on the hard drive that he'd saved from you."

The hairs at Eli's nape prickled. "Walter and I e-mailed often. It was one of the many ways we shared information and communicated. Everyone at Roth uses e-mail—"

"These were not . . . professional e-mails, Dr. Barnes."

Her uneasiness burgeoned into something akin to dread. Her heart did a long, slow roll in her chest. "What are you talking about?"

Reaching into his coat, Lindquist removed several folded papers. "These are copies of a few of the e-mails. I wanted to stop by in person to talk to you about this. Give you a chance to set the record straight if you wanted to."

Eli stared at the papers, speechless, her mind whirling.

"I'm sure you're aware that it's against the law to lie to the police."

"I haven't lied to the police."

"If you come clean now, I'd be willing to overlook—"

"Come *clean*?" Her voice rose. "Come clean about what?"

"Look, Dr. Barnes, I know this kind of situation can be uncomfortable." He leaned forward and spoke in a conspiratorial voice. "I understand that you might be trying to protect your professional reputation. That you might feel the need to protect Dr. Sanchez's reputation, his memory. Those are honorable motives. But if there's anything you didn't tell me in our earlier discussion, I strongly urge you to do so now."

He handed her the papers. Eli accepted them and began to read. Dread solidified and spread like a thick layer of

ice through her body as the words registered in a brain
that didn't want to believe.

> *To my beautiful Eli, whom I love more than life.
> You've given me the happiest years of my life. You
> made me young again. You made me laugh! You
> gave me the gift of love, something I'll hold
> precious until the day I die. I'm sorry I hurt you
> with news of my retirement this morning. I would
> have told you sooner, but I was weak. I knew you
> would be angry, and I simply couldn't stay away
> from you. But now, my love, I must do the right
> thing. I'm leaving for Florida in a few weeks. I
> know you'll thank me someday for ending our
> relationship. I'm an old man whose better days are
> behind him. You are young and passionate, with
> your entire life ahead of you. You deserve someone
> younger. Someone who can give you his whole
> heart. Someone who can give you children and
> marriage and all the things you deserve. I can do
> none of those things. You'll never know how much
> it pains me to end things this way. I hope some day
> you'll be able to forgive me. I'll love you always,
> my darling.*
>   *Forever yours,*
>   *Walt*

Her hands were shaking by the time she put the letter
down and raised her gaze to Detective Lindquist's. "Walter didn't write this," she said levelly.

"Before you say anything else, Dr. Barnes, I'm going
to caution you that it is imperative that you tell me the
truth from here on out."

"He didn't write that," she repeated. "Anyone who
knew Walter—or me—knows our relationship was
wholly platonic."

"I understand your not wanting anyone to know about
this. He was older. He was your boss. You worked
closely—"

"That's not the way it was."

Sighing, Lindquist nodded at the other papers in her hand. "There's more," he said.

Eli glared at him a moment before setting the remaining papers on the desk in front of her so he wouldn't see that her hands were shaking.

Walter,
I can't believe you've given me this ultimatum. After everything we've been through, after everything we've shared, I can't believe you would toss me aside like a used toy. You claim to love me and yet in the next breath you tell me you're leaving Ann Arbor to retire in Florida. I know what love is, believe me, and this twisted relationship of ours is not love. You can't imagine how much you've devastated me. It hurts even more knowing you had this planned all along. I loved you more than anything in the world, I gave you everything I had to give, and this is how you treat me? I'll never forgive you for making me feel like dirt when I would have done anything in the world for you. I would have quit my work here at Roth to be with you. I would have taken a job at one of the universities in Florida. But you took the choice away from me, and I hate you for that. I'll never forgive you for using me, you son of a bitch.
Eli

She looked at Lindquist. "Surely you don't believe I wrote this."

"I don't know what to believe, Dr. Barnes. I was hoping you would clear things up for me."

"I didn't write this. Is that clear enough for you?"

"That's your final answer?"

"That's my only answer because it's the truth."

Leaning forward, he lifted a paperweight from the corner of her desk and studied it. "I understand the awards ceremony for the Distinguished Woman of Science Award is tonight."

The quick subject change threw her for a moment. Eli

wasn't sure where he was going with it, but sudden nausea made her press her hand to her stomach. "Yes, it is," she said.

"That's a once-in-a-lifetime award, isn't it, Dr. Barnes?"

She stared at him.

He stared back. "You worked hard for it, didn't you?"

"What are you getting at?"

"You wouldn't want all that hard work to slip away, would you?" He set the paperweight back on her desk, then leaned closer. "Level with me now, and I'll see what I can do to keep this under wraps."

A blade of panic sliced her when she realized he thought she was lying. That he was threatening her with exposure. She could only imagine what would happen if news of an illicit affair between her and Walter got back to her colleagues at Roth. "I didn't send those e-mails."

"I'm going to subpoena the network backups. Once I do that, this is going public."

"You won't find anything."

"I already have."

"Peter Roth will never believe Walter or I sent those e-mails." She'd intended to snap, but her voice shook on the last word.

"I don't give a damn what Roth believes. I can't ignore these e-mails. And I can't ignore the fact that they dispute what you've told me."

"Maybe you should concentrate on finding out who really sent them."

"Why would someone go to the trouble to send phony e-mails? What possible motive could they have?"

"You're the cop. You figure it out." She thrust the papers at him. "These e-mails are fakes," she said, her voice shaking with anger. "All of them."

"Maybe you should read the rest."

"I don't have to read them to know they're fakes."

"Some are very intimate."

"I didn't write any of them. Neither did Walter."

"Are you telling me someone waltzed into Roth—a secure campus—logged on to the network with your log-in

ID and password, logged on to another computer with Dr. Sanchez's log-in ID and password, and wrote love letters? Come on!"

She wondered if he'd already talked to the technology information systems group at Roth. If he'd been in contact with Clyde Cummings, the security director. Suddenly, she felt as if she'd stepped into a very small room and all four walls were closing in on her. "There's no other explanation."

"How do you explain the ones that came from your home e-mail account?"

Shock gut-punched her. She stared at the detective, aware of the rush of blood through her veins, the quick jump of panic. "I can't explain it," she said after a moment. "All I can tell you is that Walter and I were friends, nothing more. I did not write those e-mails. Nor did I receive any e-mails of that nature from Dr. Sanchez."

"That's your final answer, then."

"That's the truth, and it's the only answer you're going to get." For a fraction of a second Eli considered telling him about her concerns with regard to Valazine. About Adam's certainty that someone within the company had withheld vital adverse event data not only from her, but from the FDA. That these phony e-mails might be somehow related. But the memory of Adam's warning to keep that information under wraps stopped her.

Rising, Lindquist stuffed the copies of the e-mails into his coat pocket. "If you change your mind and decide you want to talk to me, you've got my card."

"I told you the truth. I'm not going to change my mind about anything."

"Your choice."

A terrible realization dawned. "Detective Lindquist."

He stopped at the door and turned to face her.

"You can't possibly think I had something to do with Walter's death."

"I don't think you're guilty of murdering Sanchez. But I think you're guilty of something. It would make this a lot easier on both of us if you just told me what it was."

She stared at him, concentrated on not letting him see her shake. "I'm not guilty of anything," she said.

"We're all guilty of something," he said, and left her office.

chapter
15

ELI WAS STILL SHAKING WHEN SHE PARKED THE
Volkswagen in her driveway and shut down the engine.
Even though it wasn't yet five o'clock, the sky hovered
low and dark, causing the streetlamps to blink on early.
Intermittent snowflakes streaked down on a brisk north
wind. A dusting of snow whispered across the sidewalk
as she made her way to the front door. By the time she
reached the porch, she was thoroughly chilled.

She'd tried Adam's cell phone twice on the drive home
from Roth. Both times she'd gotten voice mail and left
the same message: "Call me as soon as possible. It's important. I think I'm in trouble."

Where the hell was he?

Grabbing the mail along with a small package neatly
wrapped in brown paper, she let herself in through the
front door. She tossed the mail onto the console table,
then worked off her coat and hung it in the closet. From
the hall, she could see her answering machine blinking.
She strode into the study and hit the PLAY button. Lindquist had called at 1:15. He'd called again at 3:30. No
message from Adam. Damn it. Where was he?

She couldn't believe Lindquist suspected her and Walter of having an affair. Her friendship with Walter had been special and rare, and the thought of someone tainting it with ugly lies outraged her. Walter didn't deserve to have his memory dragged through the mud. Her only hope was that Lindquist would find whomever had send those e-mails and would put a stop to further speculation before any damage was done to Walter's memory—or her professional reputation.

She wondered if Lindquist had already talked to Clyde Cummings or Peter Roth about getting e-mail archive information off of Roth's computer network. She needed to speak to Peter about the situation as soon as possible, she realized. Hopefully before Lindquist did.

She considered the pros and cons of confiding in Peter about her suspicions with regard to Valazine. She wanted to; she trusted him and wanted to get it out in the open. But she'd promised Adam she wouldn't. Of course, that was before Lindquist had found those bogus e-mails.

"What a mess," she muttered as she left the study.

Today should have been one of the happiest days of her life. In a few hours she would be receiving the coveted Distinguished Woman of Science Award at the Dahlmann Campus Inn. It was a day she'd dreamed of since she was fifteen years old. A day in which she would be recognized before her peers and honored with one of the most esteemed awards in the industry.

Instead, she was filled with a terrible fear that someone was going to great lengths to ruin her professional reputation, frame her for the murder of her friend and colleague.

Maybe even kill her.

Eli paced the kitchen, trying in vain to settle down so she could think this through rationally. She didn't know enough about the law or police procedure to determine if she was in serious legal trouble. She knew the e-mails were not incriminating in themselves, but if Lindquist thought he was on to something, he wasn't going to stop digging.

She walked back to the study and plugged her laptop

into the docking station. The log-in screen popped up. Cold realization spread through her when she recalled Lindquist telling her that some of the e-mails had come from her home. If someone had gained access to her e-mail account, that meant he had her log-in ID and password. How had he gotten that information? Eli was by no means a computer expert, but she was savvy enough not to share her ID or password.

Vaguely remembering writing something down when she'd upgraded her operating system, she opened the pencil drawer and shoved aside notepads, disks, and a few pens. Sure enough, both her log-in ID and her password were written down on an address label and stuck to the bottom of the drawer.

  ID: ebarnes
  Password: valazine

A chill rumbled through her, and she looked uneasily over her shoulder. Had someone been in her house? Had they ransacked her desk? Or had they gained access to her ID and password elsewhere? Eli was pretty sure she didn't have anything written down at work. Perhaps one of the information systems people at Roth had given out the information.

It wasn't like either her ID or her password were unduly creative. It wouldn't take a determined hacker long to figure them out. And how many times had she logged on to her computer at work with someone standing over her shoulder?

Telling herself she was being foolish, she left the study, crossed through the foyer, and checked the lock on the front door. "Of course it's locked, dummy," she muttered, annoyed with herself for allowing this to spook her. But for the first time since moving in, she found herself wishing for an alarm system.

Restless, she paced to the living room and spotted the package on the console table in the foyer. Crossing to it, she picked it up. Plain brown wrapping. Computer generated label. No return address.

Perplexed, Eli tore open the box and spotted the video-tape inside. Taking the tape over to the VCR, she slipped it into the slot, hit the PLAY button, and turned on the TV.

A laboratory loomed into view. It was a small lab with no windows. Several deep stainless-steel sinks with goose-neck faucets formed an island in the center of the room. A row of small refrigerators lined the wall on the left. Shelves containing glass specimen jars dominated the wall on the right. Eli didn't recognize any of it.

The camera panned, bringing more of the background into view. Several animal cages sat on shelving units at the rear of the room. She could see movement in the cages. The camera zoomed. Lab monkeys, she realized. Rhesus monkeys. Two or three adults, she guessed.

Hoping for narration, she hit the volume on the remote. The audio was scratchy, but she could hear Muzak and the shuffle of shoes against the floor. The sound of water running in one of the sinks. The screech of a monkey.

The camera focused on the monkeys. Suddenly, one of the animals launched itself at the camera, screeching. Eli jumped. "Jesus," she muttered, pressing her hand to her chest.

The pitch of the screeching changed, intensified. Brown fur flashed. She caught a glimpse of intelligent primate eyes. The length of a tail. She squinted, trying to make out what was happening on the screen, but the camera was too close, the animals moving too fast. It took a full minute for her to realize there were actually two monkey's on screen. Two males locked in battle.

The sight raised the hairs on her neck. Her heart began to pound. She'd seen rhesus monkeys fight before—they weren't exactly the most social of the primates—but never like this. The animals tumbled mindlessly in the cage, screeching and hissing like rabid beasts. For the first time she saw blood. A smear of it on the stainless bar. Matted red fur.

"Oh, my God." Disbelieving, she leaned forward, trying to make sense of it. Who was filming this and why? Who had sent it to her?

Abruptly, the animals separated. The larger primate

staggered, then backed into a corner. The smaller monkey circled, reacting in a manner Eli had never before witnessed. She watched, horrified, as the younger monkey savagely attacked the larger one. The wounded primate shrieked. The smaller one pounced, biting and tearing at the larger primate. Eli wanted to turn away, but she couldn't. The scientist inside her demanded an explanation. The more human side of her was too stricken to move.

After a few minutes, the shrieks quieted. The larger primate sagged and was still. A fleck of blood hit the camera lens. Eli stared, aghast at what she'd just witnessed.

An instant later, the smaller monkey spun and lunged at the camera. Eli gasped, but she didn't look away. Intelligent eyes sought the camera. In their depths she saw animal rage and the frenzied excitement of a fresh kill. Revulsion rose inside her when the smaller monkey pounced on the other and began to feast.

ADAM LISTENED TO ELI'S MESSAGES TWICE, NOT missing the high-wire tension in her voice. Something had her spooked. He'd planned on driving over to see her earlier in the afternoon. Unfortunately, his body had had other plans.

The migraine had come on like an eighteen-wheeler barreling out of control down a steep incline. He'd tried to sleep, but the pain and vomiting had kept him up most of the night. By dawn the pain was intolerable. It was all he could do to make it to the drapes and pull them tight and pray his goddamned head didn't explode before he got back to the bed.

At noon, he'd resorted to the injection. Subcutaneous sumatriptan. Six milligrams. A powerful migraine abortive. He hated taking drugs—any kind of drug—but there always came a point when he was willing to do just about anything to stop the pain.

Adam had lost the entire day. He'd spent nineteen mindless hours lying in bed with the lights out and the drapes closed. Nineteen hours writhing in pain because some joker was gleefully jamming an ice pick into his left temple. Nineteen hours of heaving into the waste basket beside the bed and sleeping when the pain would allow it.

Christ, he hated migraines.

Now, as he left his hotel room and headed toward the parking lot, he could still feel the remnants of the headache taunting him. The nausea had receded, but he still wasn't worth a damn. A lot of help he would have been to Eli if she'd gotten into trouble during the night. Yeah, some cop he was.

The migraines were unpredictable, struck without warning, and sometimes put him down for days. They didn't come as often as they once had. In the months following the shooting, he'd had to contend with one or two a week. Now he was down to two or three a month. Adam figured he could live with that. He wondered if the Chicago PD could.

He dialed Chad Deaton as he wound the Tahoe through light traffic and headed toward Eli's house. "How's tricks, Deat?"

"I was wondering when you were going to call and ruin my day."

"Sorry to make you wait. I've been busy."

"Too busy to call Henderson, huh?"

Adam skirted the question. "I was wondering if you got the backgrounds back on my buddies at Roth."

"Back this morning. Pretty unremarkable bunch, actually. No convictions, misdemeanors, or otherwise. Peter Roth filed for bankruptcy back in 1979. Had a few problems with the IRS. Nothing since. Thomas Bornheimer had a DUI arrest while he was at U of M, but some bigshot lawyer got him off on a tech. Sanchez was squeaky clean. Same with Chambers, aside from a few speeding tickets. The most interesting development was on Dr. Barnes."

Adam's interest piqued. "What do you have?"

"I got a hit on her and did a couple of cross checks. It appears Dr. Barnes had a tough time of it as a teen. Parents owned a farm just outside Decatur, Indiana. Her mother committed suicide when our girl was fifteen."

"Huh. Depression?"

"Back then it was called manic depression. Kid found the body."

Adam realized then that Elizabeth Barnes wasn't quite as unblemished as she appeared. Interesting. "Anything else?"

"Just that I've put my ass on the chopping block for you. If Henderson finds out I'm running background checks for you when he doesn't even know where the hell you are, he's going to castrate me."

"Better you than me."

"Call him, Adam. I mean it, or your ass is toast."

"Thanks for the warning, Chad. I'll take it under advisement." Adam disconnected before the other man could say anything more and dropped the phone onto the seat.

Interesting development about Elizabeth Barnes. He knew it probably didn't have any relevance to the case, but someone didn't go through something like that and walk away unscathed. He found it noteworthy that she'd chosen a vocation that would allow her to fight the very disease that had taken her mother. Depression.

It was just after 6:30 P.M. when he parked the Tahoe in front of her house and shut down the engine. A single light burned in the downstairs living room. Another one on the second level. Snow swirled in the glow cast by the streetlight. Adam knew better than to show up unannounced; it would have been a hell of a lot easier to just call her. But she'd sounded spooked, he rationalized. He wanted to check on her to make sure she was all right. That was all.

Yeah. Right.

Pulling up his collar, he got out of the truck and headed toward the front door. On the porch, he rang the bell and told himself he hadn't driven all the way across town in single-digit temperatures just to see her. Damn it, he hadn't.

The door opened a moment later and she peered out at him. Adam had seen plenty of beautiful women in his time, but the sight of this prim scientist wrapped in snug blue satin with her hair piled on top of her head stunned him to silence.

"I've been trying to reach you all day," she said crossly. "Where the hell have you been?"

He tried not to gawk, but the effort was a losing proposition. His gazed slipped down the front of her. He saw curves and satin and velvet flesh. The lady definitely had his attention, and it didn't have a damn thing to do with the case. "I was tied up," he heard himself say.

"Well, now isn't a good time."

"You expecting company?"

"I don't dress like this to do laundry."

"What time is he picking you up?"

"Seven." She frowned as if realizing he'd baited her.

"That gives us twenty minutes."

Crossing her arms in front of her, she frowned. Adam tried not to notice the way the gesture plumped her breasts, so he kept his eyes on hers.

"Are you going to let me in?" he asked.

She hesitated a moment, then opened the door farther and stepped back. "If this wasn't so important, I'd tell you to take a hike," she said.

"I have no doubt you would." Adam walked into the foyer, then checked her out as she closed the door behind him and engaged the bolt lock. The dress swept over intriguing curves and flowed to the floor like a silk waterfall. The cut was conservative, but the thoughts streaking through his mind were anything but. Adam had never been a dress-up kind of guy. He preferred blue jeans and flannel over a tuxedo and cummerbund any day. But the sight of this woman clad in satin made him wonder if he should reconsider.

"Nothing personal, but I'd prefer it if my date doesn't see you here," she said, turning back to him. "He's usually early."

Adam kept his eyes off the dress. "What did you want to talk to me about?"

"This is going to take a few minutes." She started toward the living room. "You may as well come in and sit down."

He followed her to the living room. A fire burned low in the hearth. A cup and saucer sat on the coffee table. On the sofa, a book lay facedown. He read the spine and frowned. *Social Psychology and Physiology of Schizophrenia, Bipolar Disorder, and Depression.* The good doctor definitely read some dry shit.

"I got a visit from Detective Lindquist this afternoon," she said. "He thinks Walter and I were romantically involved."

"Why does he think that?"

"He has copies of e-mails allegedly written and sent by me. Other e-mails he got off of Walter's home computer."

"What did they say?"

He listened intently as she relayed the details of her visit with Lindquist. By the time she'd finished Adam understood why her hands were shaking. Knowing you were an inch away from becoming a suspect in a murder case was enough to shake anyone.

"I didn't write them," she said. "And I wasn't involved with Walter."

Adam sensed the fury simmering just beneath that controlled surface. "I believe you," he said.

That seemed to bolster her, and she smiled weakly. "I'm glad someone does."

"My main concerns at this point are who went to the trouble of writing them and why," he said.

"I've been thinking about it all evening." She paced to the far side of the room, rubbing her hands up and down her arms. "I think someone is trying to frame me for Walter's murder."

Adam mulled over the information, his detective's brain winding into high gear. "Probably. But it's going to take more than a few e-mails to to nail you."

"I told Lindquist I didn't write the e-mails. Adam, he thought I was lying. I could see it in his eyes. When he came to my office today, it was like he was giving me one last chance to tell the truth."

"Lindquist is grasping at straws."

She stopped pacing. "Those e-mails make it sound as if I have a motive. The spurned lover."

"That may be what Lindquist is shooting for, but it's circumstantial and weak and he knows it."

"I was at the scene, damn it. That means I had opportunity."

"You've been hanging out with too many cops."

"Not by choice."

"Look, I'm a cop. I know what he's thinking. Believe me, he might be interested in your relationship with Sanchez, but his instincts are telling him you're not the shooter."

"Maybe he thinks I hired someone."

"Maybe. But probably not. Eli, sometimes a cop digs, and he's not even sure what he's digging for. Sometimes it solves the case. Sometimes he's just spinning his wheels. Lindquist has a pretty good idea he's spinning his wheels."

"What if someone plants a gun in my car or my office or my home?" Her eyes went round. "Would that be enough for Lindquist to—"

"The cops are a lot smarter than most people think."

Abruptly, she walked over to the television with a swish of satin. Adam watched her, trying to keep his mind off the way the material swept over hips he had absolutely no right to be thinking about at a moment like this. For chrissake, she was meeting another guy in a few minutes. As far as he knew it was someone she was sleeping with. How pathetic was he for getting turned on when she was going to rush him out the back door as if he were some kind of teenaged bad idea?

"And I received a package in the mail today," she said.

He looked down at the video tape in her hand, felt a jolt of foreboding. He looked over at her. "Who sent this?"

Eli shrugged." I don't know."

"What's on it? Adam asked.

She reached for the remote control and pushed a button. "See for yourself."

The TV blinked on. Adam watched the tape with interest, considering its significance, wondering why someone had mailed it to Eli.

When it was over, she turned off the TV, rose, and paced to the far end of the living room. "It's . . . chilling."

"Whoever was behind the camera made sure we got a good look at those lab monkeys."

"They're rhesus monkeys," she began. "I don't work with them, so I'm no expert. But I did have a part-time job at a small lab in my first year of college. I took care of the lab animals. Feeding, changing the beddings, and so forth. I love animals, so I've never been able to bring myself to use them in the course of research."

Adam didn't know where she was going with this, but he let her talk. It was obvious the tape had disturbed her a great deal.

She sat down on the sofa and crossed her legs. His gaze slipped down the length of her thighs, and he felt a low-grade stir of lust, an uncomfortable rush of blood to his groin. It had been a long time since a woman had appealed to him so strongly. If the situation hadn't been so damn wrong, he might have liked to do something about it. So much for timing.

"I've never seen that kind of behavior in rhesus monkeys," she said.

"You mean the fighting?"

"I've watched the tape twice, Adam. Those two animals weren't just fighting. The smaller monkey wasn't just biting the larger one. It appeared to be cannibalizing it."

chapter
16

Her own words chilled her. Eli glanced at Adam. He looked tall and dark and forbidding standing in her living room. She should have been unnerved by his presence. Strangely, she wasn't. At some point in the last couple of days, he'd become more ally than enemy. She didn't want to think about what that meant in terms of what she'd come to believe about Valazine.

"What do you think it means?" he asked.

"One theory comes to mind. But, my God, it's frightening."

"Valazine?"

"My guess is that those animals had Valazine in their bloodstream." The need to pace was strong. Eli could feel her nerves snapping. Rising, she crossed the room, turned, then walked back to the VCR and removed the tape.

"Why would someone send a tape like that without an explanation?" Adam asked.

"I don't know."

"Which lab did the animal testing for Valazine?" Adam asked.

"We farmed out that phase of testing to several labs.

Some of them were out of state. I have the information. I'll need to look it up."

A particularly hard gust of wind rattled the window behind her, and she jumped. She could hear the snow pinging against the glass. Even though the house was toasty warm, she felt cold all the way to her bones. She walked back over to Adam. "From a legal standpoint, the tape is inconclusive," she said.

"Maybe."

"There's no way either of us can prove what's on that tape is in any way related to Valazine."

Adam sighed, clearly frustrated. "It proves something to you, though, doesn't it, Eli?"

That was the question she dreaded with every cell in her body. She knew her answer would change everything. She stared at him, aware of her heart beating heavily in her chest, the indecision pulling her in different directions. The tension like a garrote tightening around her throat. Oh, how she hated this. . . . "Yes."

He was standing so close she could smell his after-shave. It was a pleasant, male scent that sent a new awareness zinging through her. "It feels like everything is starting to come apart," she said after a moment.

"Or come together, depending on your perspective."

She started violently when the doorbell rang, then put her hand to her breast. "That's Kevin Chambers," she whispered.

She was as jumpy as a cat, Adam mused. Lindquist definitely had her shaken. He figured his presence wasn't helping matters, but he couldn't bring himself to give a damn. He didn't much care for Kevin Chambers.

"Do you want me to leave through the back door?" he asked.

"Don't be silly. We're adults. I'll just . . . tell him you stopped by on your way back to Chicago to return some paperwork."

Vaguely annoyed, Adam watched her walk to the foyer, smooth her dress, then open the door. Kevin Chambers walked in with a flurry of snow and an artfully wrapped package adorned with a big silver bow. He smiled a toothy smile, his eyes devouring her in a single swoop. "You look terr—"

His smile crashed when he spotted Adam. A look of incredulity filled his face, and he gazed questioningly at Eli. "I didn't realize you had company."

"Detective Boedecker was just leaving," she said quickly.

Knowing he'd stayed long past his welcome, Adam lifted his coat from the chair in the foyer. "I'll forward a copy of that report to your office as soon as it goes through processing, Dr. Barnes," he said.

Chambers started to speak, but Adam cut him off. "Enjoy your evening," he said, and walked into the cold.

TWO HOURS LATER ADAM WAS AT THE HOTEL BAR, brooding over two fingers of watered-down scotch, when his cell phone rang. It was the first alcoholic beverage he'd had in three years, and it was going down surprisingly well. His neurologist's warning that alcohol could trigger a migraine had kept him away from booze for the most part. Adam made an exception tonight.

He answered with an annoyed, "Yeah."

"It's Deaton."

Surprise quivered through him at the sound of his ex-partner's voice. "What's up?"

"I just heard that a factory worker in Dayton, Ohio, offed his entire family, then tried to shoot himself, and ended up blowing his ear off. It's a real fucking mess."

Adam set down his scotch. "Talk to me."

"The shooter was a thirty-two-year-old white male. Scott Milner. Married. Two children, a boy and a girl. Works the assembly line at a factory making oil filters. Second shift. Good attendance. No record. Not even a traffic ticket."

"Sounds like a real upstanding guy."

"Up until he cut his family into little pieces a couple of hours ago."

Adam let the information roll around inside his head for a moment. "History of mental illness?"

"He started seeing a shrink through the employee assistance program about six months ago."

"Interesting."

"I thought so, too."

"What else?"

"It's a bad scene. He cut up his goddamn kids. Tortured his wife, then cut her, too. Did some weird shit to her after she was dead. Sick motherfucker."

"What's this got to do with me?"

"You know what it has to do with you." Deaton paused. "I give you this and we're even, Adam. Goddamn it, I mean it. No more shit. No more game playing. No more fucking with my head over what happened in that goddamn warehouse. I hand this to you, and we're even. Got it?"

"I got it."

A frustrated sigh hissed over the line. Adam wondered if Deaton's conscience was bothering him. Wondered if maybe that conscience had been festering like a big, ugly boil for the last three years.

"The perp had been prescribed Valazine eight weeks ago," Deaton said.

Adam felt a zing in his brain. "I want in on this."

"I already called the primary," Deaton said. "I told him you'd be there."

Adam wondered just how involved the local yahoo would allow him to get. In the back of his mind, he wondered why Deaton would do this for him. Wondered if it had something to do with absolution. "I'll want to talk to the perp."

"That's up to the primary." Deaton sighed. "I told him your interest stemmed from a similar case you're working on here. Don't fuck it up."

Astounded that Deaton had gone out on a limb for him, Adam removed a notepad from the inside pocket of his jacket. "Who's the primary?"

"Troy Wagner. He's a good cop. And a friend. Don't make me sorry I called you."

"Wouldn't dream of it."

"Don't give me that crap. Wagner owes me one, but

he's not going to screw up this case so you can get what
you need from his suspect. The media's going to be all
over this. Don't make it any worse for him, got it?"

"Yeah, I got it."

Deaton disconnected.

Rising, Adam looked at his watch, then glanced out the
window at the parking lot, where snow continued to fall.
If he left now, he could be in Dayton in four hours. Well,
as long as the weather didn't deteriorate.

He wanted to interview the suspect. He wanted a list
of physical symptoms. Find out what the man had experienced in the weeks and days and hours before he'd
flipped out. Adam needed to get inside his head. He
needed the primary to take a blood sample to measure the
level of Valazine in the perp's bloodstream. Adam wanted
the information officially documented.

He knew it was going to be tough getting all those
things when he wasn't even a cop anymore. Deaton's call
had opened some doors, but Adam wasn't qualified to do
a psychiatric evaluation. Put him in an interrogation room
with some dirtbag who'd just hit a liquor store and taken
out the clerk, and Adam would have the guy spilling his
guts in an hour.

This was different. He needed someone with intimate
knowledge of Valazine. The drug's symptoms, both physical and psychological. A person who knew how to interpret those symptoms. A person who knew how they
related to Valazine.

Adam thought about Eli and cursed. She was at some
fancy banquet, about to get some fancy award. There was
no way he was going to persuade her to drive to Dayton
with him. No way in hell.

Shrugging into his coat, he weighed his options. He
could go it alone and risk blowing it. Or he could ask her
to go with him, in which case he might just get what he
needed. Eli was his best bet, he realized. His only bet.
Maybe it was time to find out where Elizabeth Barnes's
loyalties really lay.

*   *   *

ADAM KNEW THAT SHOWING UP AT THE DAHL-
mann Campus Inn where the Distinguished Woman of
Science Awards banquet was being held was a bad idea.
Eli wasn't going to be happy to see him. Kevin Chambers
especially wasn't going to be happy to see him. But Adam
had never been much good at making people happy. Why
start now?

He didn't want to think about all the other reasons he'd
shown up. Reasons that had nothing to do with the case
and everything to do with hormones and chemistry and
the way that dress swept over her body. He knew it was
stupid, but it pissed him off every time he thought about
Chambers standing there in his thousand-dollar tuxedo
and putting his hands all over her.

Damn it, he didn't need this shit.

He illegally parked the Tahoe near the grand portico of
the hotel. A young female parking attendant with platform
boots and an eyebrow ring approached, but Adam flashed
his badge and she backed off. The main doors took him
into a marble-walled lobby with bronze sculptures and a
huge glass and mahogany chess set.

A circular staircase led to the ballrooms on the mez-
zanine level. He took the stairs two at a time to the top.
Two young men looked up from the ticket table when he
walked into the common area outside the ballroom. Adam
glared at the men. Neither of them said a word when he
passed by the table. The band was jazzing up a 1940s
swing tune when he entered the main ballroom.

Inside, couples danced on a huge platform glittering
with a thousand pin lights. A buffet table heaped with
food lined the wall to his right. To his left, another long,
gowned tabled offered up cholesterol and sugar in the
form of fancy little cakes and strawberries dipped in chocolate. Adam guessed there were a thousand people in attendance. He began looking for a slender brunette in a
royal blue dress.

He spotted her ten minutes later at the bar, talking with
an older man who looked like a cross between Boy
George and Colonel Sanders. University type. Aging hip-
pie who'd never seen fit to cut his hair. Eli held a
stemmed glass in her hand. Red wine, he noticed. She

laughed at something the man said. Her head went back slightly, and Adam noticed the slender column of her throat. He saw pale flesh that shimmered silkily in the light. The shadow of cleavage that swept down to generous breasts. A waist he could span with his hands . . .

Never taking his eyes from her, he skirted a table and threaded through a group of silver-haired men. He wasn't sure why he hadn't noticed before just how attractive she was. Maybe he'd been too blinded by who she was and how she fit into the case. Maybe because he knew pursuing her would complicate things. Adam didn't need complications. He was doing well just to make it through the goddamned day.

He assured himself it was just his hormones kicking in after a three-year hiatus. Nothing more complicated than male lust. A common enough affliction, and Adam was mature enough to know it was not to be taken too seriously. Maybe he'd find a woman to go out with when he got back to Chicago. A woman who didn't expect too much in return.

Eli spotted him a moment later. She jolted, then visibly stiffened. Adam reached her and tried not to feel conspicuous in his parka and jeans. "Did you get your award?" he asked.

"Yes." She didn't elaborate. "What on earth are you doing here?"

"I need to talk to you," he said.

"About what?"

Adam gave the man she'd been talking to a hard look. "Excuse us for a moment."

The man's brows shot up, and he looked questioningly at Eli.

"Wait just a—" she began, but Adam cut in.

"It'll only take a moment," he said to the man, then motioned toward the buffet table. "You might check out the crepes."

Huffing his displeasure, the man stalked away.

Eli glared at Adam. "That was rude. What the hell do you think you're doing?"

"Getting rid of the old codger for you."

"That old codger is the head of research and development from the University of Texas Southwestern in Dallas," she hissed. "This had better be good."

"It is." Taking her arm, he guided her to a quiet area in the corner of the ballroom. "I need a favor."

"*Now?*"

"I didn't walk in here because I need it tomorrow."

"Then the answer is no."

"You haven't even heard what it is yet." Spotting Kevin Chambers walking toward them, Adam motioned toward the other side of the room. "Let's walk."

"You're not the kind of man who asks for easy favors."

"How much longer does this thing last?"

"That's irrelevant since you're leaving." She started to walk away but he stopped her by putting his hand on her arm. "How on earth did you get in without an invitation, anyway?"

"I used my charm."

"I hate to burst your bubble, but that wouldn't get you past the parking attendant."

Adam knew he wasn't chalking up any points. But easy persuasion had never been his forte. "Badge works just as well, and takes a hell of a lot less energy."

"Damn it, Adam, what are you *doing*?" She dug in her heels, stopping their forward momentum, and spun to face him.

"I need you to drive down to Dayton with me."

"*Dayton?*"

"Ohio."

"I know where it is, damn it. Why do you want me to go with you?"

"Because there's been another Valazine crime."

She went still. "Someone was killed?"

"Three people. A family. Kids, goddamn it."

"God." Horror flickered in her eyes. She looked down, her brows drawn together. "A suicide?"

"Attempted suicide. The son of a bitch murdered his family but screwed up when it came time to blow his own brains out."

"What do you want me to do?"

"I want you to be there when I talk to him."

She closed her eyes briefly, then pressed her hand to her stomach. "Let's go sit down and discuss—"

"We don't have time to discuss this. We need to leave. Now."

"How can you possibly know this . . . event is because of Valazine?"

"Because the perp was prescribed the drug eight weeks earlier."

"That's not definitive—"

"Goddamn it, Eli, don't give me that shit. You saw the tape. That may not be proof, but three more people are dead. How many more bodies do you need before you wake up?"

She started to turn away, but he reached out and grasped her upper arm. "Don't walk away from me," he growled.

"Let go of me," she said evenly, glancing over her shoulder at the crowd. "You're making a scene."

Letting out a pent-up sigh, he released her. "If you don't believe these murders are happening because of Valazine, then at least prove me wrong." Adam heard desperation in his voice, felt it grip him, worked hard to bank it.

"I'll go with you and do what I can, but it's going to have to wait until in the morning."

"This won't keep until tomorrow."

Alerted by some inner instinct, Adam looked up to see Kevin Chambers standing a few feet away, taking in the entire scene as if he were watching an annoying sitcom.

"What's going on here?" Chambers asked.

"We were just . . ." Eli stammered.

"Having a private conversation," Adam finished. "You're not invited."

"Sounded like an argument to me." Chambers's eyes slipped from Eli to Adam, then back to Eli. "Is he harassing you?"

"Well . . . yes, but—"

"Let me handle this, Eli." Chest puffing out, Chambers

stepped forward and positioned himself squarely between Eli and Adam. "Maybe you should leave."

"Maybe you ought to mind your own goddamn business."

"Kevin, I can handle this," Eli said.

Chambers ignored her, a male animal prepared to fight for his mate, and focused his attention on Adam. "Look, Robocop, this is a private party. You weren't invited, and you have no right to harass this woman, or anyone else for that matter. Leave now or I'm going to call the police."

If it hadn't been for the need to keep this low-key, Adam would have decked him. Surprising himself, he opted for the diplomatic route. "Dr. Barnes *invited* me."

Chambers craned his head around and gaped at Eli. "You *invited* him?"

"I—I . . . well, yes, I did," she said.

Satisfied, Adam lifted his lip, hoped it looked like a smile instead of the snarl it was. "I was just finishing up with a few final questions for my investigation, weren't we, Dr. Barnes?"

"What sort of questions?" Chambers asked.

"I'm not at liberty to discuss the details."

Chambers looked over at Eli and laughed incredulously. "Would you listen to this guy?"

Only then did Adam notice the glassy eyes and red cheeks. It seemed Kevin Chambers had had one too many martinis. Terrific. "You don't want this to escalate," Adam said quietly.

"What I do want is for you to leave Dr. Barnes alone," Chambers said. "She's made it clear she doesn't want you around. Neither do I."

Adam knew he should turn and walk away. Knew he should forget about Elizabeth Barnes and Kevin Chambers and drive down to Dayton and concentrate on the case.

He'd never been much good at walking away.

Chambers started for Adam.

"Don't do this, Kevin." Eli tried to grab his arm.

He shook her off, lunged at Adam, and shoved him

hard. Caught off guard, Adam reeled backward several steps before regaining his balance. "You don't want to fuck with me."

The other man grinned, his confidence bolstered. "You're like a toothache that won't go away, aren't you?" he said.

Clamping his jaws in anger, Adam grabbed the other man by the lapels and slammed him against the wall so hard it shook. "I believe you're drunk and disorderly."

Chambers tried to ram his knee between Adam's legs, but Adam danced aside. "Cut it out, you little prick."

"Get your hands off me!"

Adam jerked him forward, then slammed him against the wall a second time. Chambers head snapped against solid wood. He grasped Adam's wrists, but Adam didn't let go.

"You're going to pay for this," Chambers snarled.

Adam got in his face. "Listen to me. I'm a hell of a lot worse than a toothache. More like biting down on a stick of dynamite, especially if you get on my bad side. You're about one inch from being on my bad side."

Some of the fight went out of Chambers. "Let me go."

Even in the dim light, Adam could see the sheen of sweat on the other man's brow. "I think you've humiliated yourself enough for one night, don't you?"

"You're not a cop. Who the hell are you?"

"Someone you don't want to know." Adam twisted his lapels, pressed his knuckles into the other man's clavicle bones. "I suggest you walk away nice and easy, and we'll forget this ever happened."

"I want you to leave Eli alone."

"I'm afraid I can't do that." Adam drew him from against the wall, swung him around, then shoved him away. "Now get lost."

Chambers stumbled back, his blond hair falling over his forehead. Chest heaving, he brushed his hands over his lapels, then shot an accusing look at Eli.

"Kevin . . ." she began.

He cut her off by raising a hand. "Don't bother," he said, then turned and stalked away.

She started to go after him, but Adam stopped her by gently touching her arm. "Let him go," he said. "He's not going to want you hovering over him right now."

"I don't want to leave things like this." She shook her head, looking miserable. "That wasn't necessary."

"Someone had to convince him to stop being such an uppity prick."

She stared at Chambers's retreating form. "You hurt him."

"The only thing I hurt is his pride." He put his hand on her shoulder, squeezed gently. "We don't have much time, Eli. I need your help. Please. Come to Dayton with me."

She bit her lip. He saw the indecision pulling her in different directions. The need to do the right thing. Loyalty to her company. Loyalty to herself. To her profession. A thin layer of fear.

"Dear God, Adam, I'm afraid of what we might find when we get there," she whispered.

"So am I," he said.

They started for the door at a brisk clip.

chapter
17

THE DRIVE TO DAYTON WAS A STRESSFUL AFFAIR.
The snow made driving difficult and added to the tension
already snapping between Adam and Eli. Several acci-
dents along Interstate 75 slowed traffic to a crawl in
places. Four hours stretched into five. Eli wished she were
anywhere but on her way to talk to a man who'd just
murdered his family.

After leaving the banquet, Adam had taken her home
to change clothes. Eli had thrown on a pair of wool slacks
and a turtleneck, then topped it off with a jacket. If she
was expected to appear in some kind of official capacity,
she supposed she ought to dress the part.

Now, some five hours later, she sat in the passenger
seat of Adam's Tahoe and watched the windshield wipers
wage a losing battle with the snow. She couldn't believe
she'd left the banquet early. Couldn't believe Adam had
roughed up her co-worker. Most of all, she couldn't believe she'd committed herself to helping a man who was
determined to prove her life's work had caused an untold
number of deaths.

The son of a bitch murdered his family.

Adam's words rang in her ears like the retort of a killing shot. Chilling words that had played through her brain
a hundred times in the last five hours. It tore her up inside
to believe Valazine was causing violent behavior in some
of the people it was prescribed to. But she could no longer
deny it, and the realization terrified her. How had she
overlooked such a glaring side effect? How in the name
of God was she going to live with herself?

"Cold?"

Only then did she realize she'd shivered. "I'm fine,"
she said, pulling her coat more snugly around her shoulders.

"You want some coffee?"

"I want to get this over with."

"It's going to be a long night."

She glanced at her watch. Three A.M. "It's already been
a long night."

Pulling his cell from the console, he punched in numbers. Eli listened as he identified himself, made a few
jokes that weren't the least bit funny considering the circumstances, then asked where he could find the suspect
so he could ask him a few questions. He hung up without
thanking whomever was on the other end of the line.

"Where are we going?" she asked.

"St. Elizabeth Hospital. It's downtown by the river. Not
far." He looked over at her. "You up to this?"

"I'm not exactly sure what you want me to do."

"The primary on the case has authorized us ten minutes
with the suspect." He glanced over at her. "Unofficially."

"What does that mean?"

"That means he's going to let us in to talk to the guy,
but he didn't tell the brass."

"Terrific." Eli felt cranky and exhausted. "So what's
my part in this?"

"I'm going to ask him some leading questions about
any symptoms he might have had since he started taking
Valazine. I'm going to ask him to tell us what happened.
I'm going to concentrate on how he was feeling at the
time. How he felt in the days and weeks and months leading up to today."

"You're looking for possible side effects brought on by Valazine."

"I'm looking for the truth." Frowning, he changed lanes and exited the interstate. "I want you to tell me if his symptoms jibe with what you know about Valazine. If he's not clear about something you think is relevant, I want you speak up and ask him to clarify. I want specifics as far as what he was feeling. Paranoia. Rage. Whatever. I want you to help me read between the lines. Help me interpret what he says."

"I've got the picture."

"You know this drug, Eli. You've dealt with it. You administered the clinical trials. Most of this will be familiar to you."

"Most of my study participants didn't just murder their family."

Adam grimaced. "This isn't going to be easy. Not for you. Not for him. He's probably . . . distraught."

Eli wondered if *distraught* was the right word. "How badly is he hurt?"

"Mild concussion. Maybe some hearing loss. He blew off his ear."

She closed her eyes. "How can you possibly use anything he says?"

"Legally, we can't. This is strictly a fishing expedition. We're looking for information. That's all."

"I don't see how talking to this man is going to prove anything," she said. "If he's upset, he could say anything."

"Maybe not. This guy isn't a criminal. He doesn't have a record, Eli. No history of domestic violence. Not even a goddamn speeding ticket. People don't go off the deep end and murder their entire family without some kind of warning sign."

"Maybe he thought he had a reason. He was depressed, Adam, maybe even desperate. People do unreasonable things when they get into that kind of mind-set."

"All I'm asking is that you keep an open mind." He pulled the Tahoe into the hospital parking lot. "Can you do that?"

Dread congealed in Eli's chest when he parked and shut

down the engine. She felt his eyes on her, but she didn't look at him. She didn't want to do this. Didn't want to talk to this man. Didn't want to know what he'd done or why. Didn't want to bear witness his pain or the pain he had caused.

Without speaking, Adam opened the door and stepped into the driving snow. Eli jumped when he slammed the door. Bracing herself against the cold that seemed to come from within her, she opened the door and stepped into the night.

ELI HAD NEVER HAD AN AVERSION TO HOSPITALS. Hospitals were where babies were born. Where people went for annual checkups and X rays and flu shots. It wasn't the place where she had expected to meet her first mass murderer.

She stood several feet outside the room in the wide, tiled hall while Adam spoke to the uniformed police officer stationed at the door. The floor was eerily silent. Even the nurse's station down the hall was deserted at this ungodly hour.

Adam strode over to her, his face grim. "He's awake. The officer said we can go in."

She looked up at him, surprised to see a glint of concern in his eyes.

"You okay?" he asked.

"I'm fine. Let's just . . . get this over with."

Adam went in first and she followed. The antiseptic smell was stronger in the room. The lights were dimmed, but there was enough light for her to see the man lying in the bed. The first thing she noticed was his short-cropped red hair and the tuft of a beard in the groove of his chin. Then she saw the padded cuffs that manacled both of his wrists, securing him to the bed.

The man watched them approach with ravaged eyes the color of winter smog. A white bandage encompassed the right side of his head, from jaw to crown. He had freckles and looked a lot younger than she'd imagined.

"Scott Milner?"

The man's gaze skittered from Eli to Adam. His eyes were glassy with shock. Bloodshot from crying. His face was swollen and red. "Who're you?"

Removing his badge from an inside jacket pocket, Adam flashed it quickly. "I'm a police detective."

Milner shifted restlessly. "It's three o'clock in the fuckin' morning. I don't want to talk to you guys right now."

"I need to ask you a few questions," Adam said.

The man turned his head away from them to stare out the darkened window. "I don't want to talk to no one."

"It's important," Adam said. "It'll only take a few minutes." Draping his coat over the sled chair next to the bed, he sat. "I want to talk to you about the shooting, Scott."

"I already talked to you guys. I told you everything. Why can't you just leave me alone, for chrissake?"

"The questions I'm going to ask you are different, Scott. I'm here to help you. To do that, I need to understand. I need for you to tell me what happened and why."

The man's eyes were glazed. Listless. He continued to stare at the darkened glass, as if it were a place of escape from the horrors of his mind, as if he could see something in the swirling snow no one else could.

"I want you to help me understand what happened," Adam pressed.

No response.

"Come on," Adam said softly. "Help yourself. Help me understand what happened."

Eli watched him work, fascinated. He was focused and gentle and yet intense enough to demand one's attention and respect. He was good, she realized. Good at getting what he wanted from people. She wondered if he would get what he wanted from Scott Milner. She wondered if it would be enough.

The man in the bed rolled his head and looked over at Adam. "I fuckin' killed her, man. What else is there to say?" His face crumbled. He closed his eyes. Tears streamed down his cheeks. His body shook with sobs. "I can't believe I killed her. I can't believe I killed my kids."

"Why did you do it?"

"I . . . God, I don't know. I want them back. . . ."

"Scott, I know this is hard. I know it hurts. But I want you to tell me what happened. I want you to tell me everything. How you were feeling. What was going through your mind."

Sobs rumbled up from Milner's chest like cries from his soul. It was the sound of the wounded. Of the dying. His entire body shook with each racking sob. "I want to fuckin' die, man. I just want to fuckin' die. I just want it to be fuckin' over."

"Why?"

"I just can't deal with it any more."

"With what?"

"Life, man. Just . . . life. Everyone's always on my fuckin' case. By boss. My mother-in-law. My wife." He closed his eyes again, turned his face to the pillow. "I loved her. I loved my fuckin' kids. Oh, God . . . Oh, my God. They're gone. They're all gone."

"Take it easy, Scott. Don't get yourself worked up. Just tell me what happened," Adam pressed.

"I don't know."

"What do you mean, you don't know?"

"It's like a fuckin' blur."

"What's like a blur?"

"After I got home from work. All I remember is lying down on the couch and going to sleep."

"Is that your regular routine?"

"Well, lately, I guess. The pills I take make me sleepy sometimes."

"What pills?"

"I been having . . . problems."

"What kind of problems?" When he didn't answer, Adam lowered his voice. "We all have problems, Scott. Come on. Talk to me. What kind of problems?"

After a long moment, the man sighed. "I've been . . . down the last few months. The doc I go to through the employee assistance program said I was depressed. He prescribed some of them new pills that's supposed to help with depression." His face screwed up again. "I been so fuckin' down. I just couldn't get myself back up."

Adam nodded. "No one's going to hold that against you, Scott. It happens. People get depressed."

"I didn't tell no one. I didn't want them to know I was taking them kind of pills."

"Did the pills help?"

"I guess so. I mean, things got better. Well, up until the last couple of weeks."

"What happened the last couple of weeks?"

"I don't know, man. I was . . . edgy."

Eli looked over at Adam, saw the leap of interest in his eyes, felt her own interest jump.

"Okay," he said. "You've been on edge the last couple of weeks. How so?"

"I don't know. Yelling at my kids for no reason." A humorless laugh grated out of Milner's throat. "I put my fist through a wall at the plant."

"What set you off?"

"I was late. My boss docked my pay fifteen minutes. It shouldn't have been a big deal. I mean, the guy's an asshole, but everyone knows that. It's the first time I'd ever lost my temper at work."

"What happened when you got home from work?"

Milner closed his eyes for a moment.

"What happened?" Adam pressed.

The other man's eyes clouded, drifted, and Eli knew he was going back. "The TV was on," he began. "I must have fallen asleep." His brows snapped together. "I don't remember waking up. All I remember is . . ." His voice cracked. "Jesus Christ. All I remember is waking up and . . ."

"What happened when you woke up?"

The man sobbed uncontrollably. Eli watched him, her heart pounding, her scientist's brain straining to understand the incomprehensible.

"Tell me what happened, Scott," Adam urged.

The man opened his eyes, blinked back tears, looked at Adam with red-rimmed eyes. His nose ran profusely, but because of the cuffs he couldn't wipe it away, and mucus slicked his upper lip. He didn't seem to notice.

"I was on top of little Kelly. She's so fuckin' small . . ." His voice broke. His body shook. For an instant, he strained against the cuffs, then fell back onto the sheets as if the emotions ripping through him had exhausted him. "I felt the knife in my hand," he said. "God, it was a big fuckin' butcher knife! She was lying on the floor. I was over her. There was blood. Oh, sweet Jesus, it was everywhere. All over me. My hands. The floor. In my eyes. All over her little dress."

Only then did Eli realize he was talking about his child. An innocent little girl. And suddenly she didn't want to be in the room. Didn't want to bear witness to the sins this man had committed.

"Why did you do it, Scott? That's what I'm trying to understand. Why?"

"I don't fuckin' know! I swear, I don't know. It's like I . . . stepped out of my body. I was like an animal. Wild inside. Kelly . . . she was whining before, waking me up. I wanted her to be quiet. I wanted her gone. My little girl . . ." His body convulsed, and he looked up at the ceiling, his face ravaged. "Oh, God, Kelly, I'm sorry. I'm so sorry, baby. Oh, honey, I'm so fuckin' sorry. . . ."

Eli stared at the man. Revulsion and outrage and a profound sadness pounding through her. More than anything she wanted to leave. She wanted to turn around and walk out of that room and never come back, but a twisted sense of responsibility made her stay.

Adam let him cry until his sobs quieted, then asked, "Tell me more about the pills you were taking, Scott. How did they make you feel?"

"I don't know, man. Weird. They fucked me up worse than what I was before."

"How?"

"They made me sleepy."

"What else?"

The police officer knocked twice on the door. Eli turned, saw him poke his head in and tap on his watch. Time to go. Relief swamped her.

"What else?" Adam asked urgently. For the first time

Eli heard desperation in his voice. "Tell me how the pills made you feel."

The man seemed to think about it for a moment. "At first, I didn't feel so down. I think they helped. I hadn't missed any more work since I started taking them."

"What else?"

"I flew off the handle a couple of times," he said. "I don't normally. I mean, maybe at work. You know, if someone was being an asshole. But I never got mad at Tina. Or, Jesus, Kelly or Rodney. They were good kids."

"How many times did you fly off the handle in the last eight weeks?"

"I don't know. I had a lot going on. You know, stress. I figured it was the stress making me crazy. Three, four times maybe."

"And that never happened before?"

"Not till I started taking the pills."

"How did they make you feel?"

"Better. I had good days. Then something would happen, and I'd just . . . go off on someone."

"Like what?"

He thought about it for a moment. "I don't know. Road rage. I'd get really pissed in traffic. And Tina missed the truck payment last month. It was only a few days late. She told me when I got home from work, and I laid into her."

"Physically?"

Tears filled his eyes. "Oh, man, I never hit her. I never did that shit."

"But did you that time?"

"No. I just . . . wigged out for a few minutes. Scared the shit out of her. Scared the shit out of myself. I started yelling and screaming at her." He whimpered. "Oh, man."

Adam was relentless. "How did you feel when you were losing it?"

"Like I was in a movie or something."

"In a movie? What do you mean?"

"Like I was watching myself on TV. Like I was watching someone else. Like it wasn't real, so it didn't matter what I did." He looked at Adam, his face wet, his eyes ravaged. "Like I could do anything I wanted and it wouldn't matter because it wasn't real."

Eli was trembling when they walked out of the hospital. She felt sick as she stood in ankle-deep snow and watched Adam open the passenger door for her. She'd never witnessed anything like Scott Milner's confession. She couldn't imagine the horror of what he'd done, couldn't imagine another human being being capable of such heartless, violent acts.

And for the first time since Adam had walked into her office just over a week ago, she felt a very real fear that didn't have anything to do with her own safety. A fear that had been growing inside her like an insidious cancer since she'd read those articles. A terrible fear that she may have turned a monster loose on an unsuspecting society.

Adam crossed in front of the vehicle and slid behind the wheel. "What do you think?" he asked, starting the engine.

She looked at him, shaken and scared and exhausted. "I'm no psychiatrist, but it sounds as if he lost touch with reality. That for a short period of time he was psychotic."

"Do you think that could be a side effect of Valazine?"

Dread and nausea twisted into a terrible ache. "Oh, Adam, I don't know. It's possible, but I was meticulous during those trials. None of the information I got back from the study participants indicated any symptoms that were even remotely similar to psychosis."

"What if the information was kept from you?"

"It's not likely."

"But not impossible."

"No."

Turning the heat on full blast, he pulled on to the street. "I don't think he's lying."

"Neither do I."

They rode in silence for a moment, then Adam asked, "Did you talk to Peter Roth tonight about the e-mails?"

She nodded. "He was very supportive. Lindquist has already gotten the network backup system."

"He works fast."

"Peter didn't believe a word of it."

Adam looked over at her. "So your position is solid?"

She met his gaze head-on. "I need to get back to Ann Arbor, Adam. I need to decide what I'm going to do about this." For the hundredth time, she wished Walter were there for her to talk to. "I can't let this go on any longer."

"We've got one more stop."

"Where?"

"I need to talk to the primary." He reached for the phone and pressed a few numbers. "Shouldn't take but a minute or two."

She nodded, but the last place she wanted to go was the police department. She was too tired to deal with anything else tonight. She needed to talk to Peter and Kevin, tell them about her suspicions so they could come up with a game plan. If Valazine was, indeed, causing violent behavior, the only answer was to go to the FDA and pull the drug off the market.

Ten minutes later, Adam pulled on to a narrow street lined with snow-covered cars. He parked behind a patrol car and cut the engine. Eli looked out her window at the house where a uniformed police officer stood on the porch, smoking a cigarette. The house was a neat frame with a wide brick porch. A tricycle lay on its side in the front yard. Yellow crime scene tape was wrapped around the front porch like a grotesque bow and fluttered in the breeze. Milner's house, she realized.

The longer she looked, the harder she shook inside. But she couldn't look away. She couldn't stop thinking about what he'd done to his family. She couldn't stop wondering if, perhaps, she'd played a role in it.

"I'll only be a couple of minutes."

She started at the sound of Adam's voice, then looked at him. He stared back at her, his expression inscrutable. She knew he was waiting for her to say she would go inside with him. Part of her needed to, felt somehow it was the least she could do for the people who had died so violently. She wasn't proud of the fact that she didn't have the guts.

Adam slammed the door.

Eli watched him walk up the concrete steps. On the porch, he flashed his badge to a uniformed officer. They spoke briefly. Adam laughed, his breath billowing into the frigid air, then he disappeared inside the house.

Exhaustion pressed down on her like a heavy hand. Leaning back in the seat, she closed her eyes, tried to quiet her brain. But her mind refused to obey. Scott Milner's words echoed inside her head. Her mind's eye saw his ravaged face, his hands straining against the restraints. She heard the wrenching sound of his sobs.

It had been her responsibility to make sure Valazine was safe. Yet more than a dozen of the people who'd taken the drug had committed murder. People who, before taking the drug, had never committed a violent act in their lives.

Suddenly, she felt like a coward for sitting in the truck. Too afraid to walk inside. Too frightened to see firsthand the handiwork of what she'd helped to create.

Throwing open the door, Eli rushed out into the falling snow. She tried not to feel anything as she crossed the sidewalk and started up the concrete steps. But she did, and the emotions inside her jumbled like bees in a hive. On the porch the uniformed officer said something to her, but she didn't understand and she didn't stop. Tugging open the aluminum storm door, she stepped inside.

The blast of heat made her break a sweat beneath her coat. Her eyes swept the room. A long green sofa lined the wall to her left. A staircase dressed in dark wood and old carpet greeted her straight ahead. The storm door closed behind her, and the stench of death embraced her. Knowledge of what had happened here danced inside her brain like a macabre ghost. Vaguely, Eli was aware of voices. Adam, she realized, talking to another man in the kitchen. A tall African-American man in a wrinkled suit.

She started toward them, keeping her eyes on the kitchen. It should have been a comforting room. She saw green cupboards. A lot of windows that would bring in plenty of natural light on a sunny day. Yellow Formica countertops. A white porcelain sink. The row of windows across the back of the room looked out on the backyard. It was a room where a mother could cook dinner and look out the windows so she could see her children playing on the swing set beyond.

Eli had just moved past the sofa when she spotted the blood. It covered one end of the sofa and dripped onto the floor, soaking into the dingy rug like a grotesque oil spill. The cushion and sofa back were soaked with it. Spatters covered the wall behind the sofa. It was on the lampshade. The coffee table. The metallic tang assaulted her senses. Oh, God, it was everywhere. . . .

Eli had seen blood before. In the course of her education, she'd witnessed autopsies. She'd worked with test tubes and vials containing blood samples. But that had been in a clinical setting. This was different. The violence of the scene shook her, reminded her of another time when death had left its mark. In that instant, she was fifteen again, staring into the red bathwater, the smell of blood in her nostrils, the knowledge that her mother was gone forever breaking her young heart to pieces.

Her mind told her to walk away. But her legs refused to obey. She stared at the carnage, felt everything inside her that was human revolt. She smelled death, felt it pressing down on her until she couldn't breathe. She thought about the two children who'd died. She thought about their mother. About the man whose life had been destroyed. The family that was gone forever.

She didn't remember turning. Then she was stumbling toward the door. She needed air. Lots of cold, clean air. She reached the door, twisted the knob, shoved it open. The uniformed police officer turned to her, said something, but she was beyond hearing and she didn't stop running.

Cold slapped her like a rude hand, but she barely felt it for the horror thrashing inside her. Horror for what she had seen. Horror for what she had played a part in. She took the steps at a dangerous speed. At the sidewalk, she fell to her knees and retched violently. Once. Twice. She lost the contents of her stomach, but it wasn't enough to rid her of the sickness in her heart.

Vaguely, she became aware of her surroundings. The sound of sleet hitting the ground. The hiss of traffic from the street down the block. The cold coming through her coat. Wet soaking through her slacks at her knees.

She jolted when strong hands closed around her shoulders. "Eli."

Adam. Eli wasn't sure if she was glad to see him or humiliated that he'd seen her at her weakest. "I'm all right," she said.

"Sure you are." His hands slid beneath her arms and he lifted her. "Easy, I've got you."

"I can do it." But her knees felt like wet newspaper.

Gently, he turned her toward him, his eyes seeking hers. "You okay?"

Only then did she realize she was crying. Wrenching sobs that shook her from the inside out. She closed her eyes against the hot flood of tears.

"Aw, man," he whispered, and pulled her against him. "It's all right. It's going to be all right."

"No, it's not." Eli choked back a sob and let him hold her.

"I'm sorry you had to see that."

"Those poor people." The hard length of his body felt incredibly reassuring against her.

He said nothing, just held her.

"Oh, Adam," she whispered. "What have I done?"

chapter
18

ELI SAT AT HER DESK IN HER OFFICE AND GAZED OUT
the window at the frozen landscape of Roth's parking lot.
A smooth Bach serenade floated from the CD player on
the credenza behind her. The buzz of a ringing phone
sounded from another office down the hall. She could hear
one of the administrative assistants laughing.

It should have been a comfort, sitting in the office she'd
occupied for the last ten years, surrounded by familiarity
and mementos of her achievements. A place where she'd
matured from green college grad to award-winning scientist. A place where she'd laughed with Walter and ar-
gued with her boss and interviewed nervous interns for
summer jobs.

Turning in her chair, she glanced up at the dozen or so
plaques and decrees hung with care on the wall above her
desk. Employee of the year two years running. Research
scientist rookie of the year. Her diplomas from the University of Michigan. She looked at the beautiful Distinguished Woman of Science plaque and a stark wave of
sadness engulfed her. Somewhere along the line, her life's

work had gone horribly wrong. People were dying, and she didn't know why.

She'd worked day and night in the two days since her trip to Dayton, frantically trying to find some shred of proof she and Adam could take to the Food and Drug Administration. Somehow it didn't surprise her that there was no proof to be found.

She hadn't seen Adam since that terrible night in Dayton. The night she'd seen firsthand the horrors her work had spawned. She'd talked with him several times on the phone, but she'd always had an excuse not to see him. The truth of the matter was she just couldn't face him right now. But Eli knew she couldn't avoid him forever. They were going to have to take their concerns public—and soon. The situation couldn't wait much longer. People were dying. Eli couldn't bear having one more death on her conscience.

She'd taken her concerns to Kevin just that morning. Peter Roth would be meeting with them later in the afternoon. Eli was going to recommend that they officially recall Valazine.

A sharp rap on the door startled her. She looked up to see Kevin Chambers, Peter Roth, and Clyde Cummings enter. One look at Kevin's face, and she knew something was wrong.

Kevin held a manila folder in his hand. He wouldn't look directly at her but instead focused his gaze on the window behind her.

"Hi, Kevin, Peter, Clyde." It surprised her that her voice sounded so normal when her heart was beating out of control. "What's this all about?"

Peter Roth stepped ahead of the other two men, his eyes cool and direct. "Eli, this is the hardest thing I've ever had to do in all the years I've run this company," he said.

Uneasiness twisted her stomach into a knot. "I don't understand."

Roth sighed and looked over at Kevin, who opened the manila folder and handed her a sheet of paper.

Eli reached for the sheet and skimmed it, her eyes quickly seeking out the words "termination" and "violating a fully executed confidentiality agreement with individuals outside the company." They were firing her. Disbelief spiraled through her. "You can't do this," she said.

Roth looked over at Kevin Chambers, then back at her. "Don't make this any more difficult than it already is, Eli."

"I didn't breach my confidentiality agreement."

"It was brought to my attention that you did, indeed, violate the agreement. I have proof."

"Peter, I didn't." She heard desperation in her voice, but she couldn't seem to curb it. "Please, you can't fire me."

"Under the circumstances, I think it's best."

"What circumstances?"

"For chrissake, Eli, this is the culmination of a number of things."

"Like what?"

"Aside from sharing confidential information with regard to your research, you were having an affair with a coworker. A seventy-four-year-old man, for crying out loud."

"That's a lie!"

"I didn't want to believe it, but Lindquist showed me the e-mails." He wiped a sheen of sweat off his forehead. "The employee manual clearly states—"

"I don't care what the manual says. I wasn't having an affair with Walter, and I didn't breech my confidentiality agreement."

"For chrissake, Eli, you're involved in a murder case. Roth has enough PR problems without something like that adding to them."

Her brain couldn't seem to absorb the information. "I had absolutely nothing to do with Walter's death. You know that."

Roth looked pained. "We took this to the board. I went to bat for you, but they saw things differently. I'm sorry it worked out this way, but there's nothing I can do."

"Peter—"

"Your severance package is generous. I pushed hard to get it for you."

"I don't care about the severance package." Angry that her life's work had boiled down to a lousy severance package, she looked over at Kevin. "What on earth did you tell him?"

Shoving his hands into his pockets, Kevin stared at his shoes.

Eli's mind whirled, searched frantically for a shred of logic to toss at them. "I didn't break that agreement."

"The board believes otherwise," Roth said. "Legal has been apprised of the situation and concurred with the board. The decision was made last night. I have no choice but to do this. Now, please, get your purse and your coat. Personnel will mail the remainder of your personal belongings. Mr. Cummings will escort you from the building."

Helplessly, she looked at Kevin. His gaze met hers briefly, then skittered away. Roth managed to hold her gaze. Clyde Cummings seemed to be enjoying the show. Bastard.

Knowing she didn't have a choice but to tell Roth everything, she rose and sought his gaze. "I need to speak with you alone, Peter."

"Eli . . ."

"Please," she said. "Give me five minutes of your time."

Grimacing, he nodded at Kevin and Cummings. "Wait for me in the hall, gentlemen." When they'd left, he looked at Eli. "You've got a minute to say what's on your mind."

Eli took a deep breath and plunged. "I have reason to believe my clinical studies on Valazine were flawed. There have been a series of adverse events happening across the country. Serious adverse events, Peter. Several deaths have occurred. I'm in the process of—"

"Deaths?" he interjected. "Those are some very serious allegations."

"So far, I know of seventeen deaths, but I'm looking into the possibility of more. I see a trend, and I'm very concerned. This particular adverse event is hard to track because of the nature—"

Roth cut her off. "Nothing has come through Med-Watch."

"No one has linked the adverse events to Valazine. It's even more difficult because of the nature of the illness for which the medication is prescribed: depression. But I've been working on this for quite some time. I see a link I can no longer deny."

"Why didn't you bring this to me sooner?"

"Because I wanted to make sure I was right first. For God's sake, Peter, I didn't believe it myself. I didn't *want* to believe it."

"So you have no proof?"

"Nothing concrete. But I do have some very compelling circumstantial evidence."

Roth silenced her by raising his hand. "Listen to me, Eli, because I'm only going to tell you this once. If you start making slanderous claims against Roth Pharmaceuticals, I swear to God I'll blackball you. I'll make sure you never work in a research facility again. And if you continue spewing these allegations, I'll sue you for every penny you've got."

"Please, hear me—"

He cut her off. "I have devoted my life to this company, and I will do whatever it takes to protect myself, my company, and my employees."

"People are dying! Don't you even want to look into it?"

Abruptly, he stepped toward her. Alarm swirled inside her when his lips peeled back in a snarl. "You talk to the wrong people about this, and I swear to Christ I'll bury you."

Shock sent her back a step. She wanted to say something more to convince him, but she knew it was too late. No matter what she said, he wouldn't believe her. Any claims she made against Roth Pharmaceuticals now would make her look like a disgruntled ex-employee motivated by revenge.

Eyeing her with unconcealed hostility, Roth reached for

the knob behind him and opened the door. He jerked his head at Cummings. "Get her out of here."

Eli stared at Roth, disbelief and betrayal pounding through her. "Please, don't do this."

"Dr. Barnes, I'll escort you from the building now."

She barely heard Cummings's voice. She couldn't believe her career at Roth had come to this moment. That ten years of hard work would end this way. That the last time she walked out of the building, it would be as a corporate traitor.

"You're making a mistake," she said.

"That's all I've got to say to you." Roth walked away.

Acutely aware that she was being watched, she looked around for her purse, tugged open a drawer, and pulled it out. A profound sense of loss engulfed her when she spotted the photo of Walter on her desk. For a moment, she struggled to hold back tears. Gathering as much dignity as she could, she walked over to where her coat hung on the rack and draped it over her arm.

"I'll need your security access card and ID badge," Cummings said.

Her hands shook uncontrollably as she unclipped the badge from her lapel. She reached into her purse and removed the access card. Squaring her shoulders, she looked over at Cummings to find him smiling.

Meeting his gaze levelly, Eli raised her hand, then dropped the badge and access card onto the floor between them. "Go to hell," she said, and started for the door.

ADAM KNEW ELI WAS AVOIDING HIM. HE UNDER-stood why, but it still pissed him off. The scene in Dayton had been ugly. Worse than ugly, if he wanted to be truthful about it. He was a veteran homicide detective; he'd seen hundreds of crime scenes over the years. The sight of death no longer shocked him. It rarely even disturbed him. He wasn't sure what that said about him as a human being. But the carnage he'd seen in that house had left a mark. It bothered him so much he'd lost sleep. He wasn't sure why. Maybe because there had been children involved. Maybe because it was all so goddamn senseless.

He could only imagine how badly it had affected Eli.
She was a civilian, unaccustomed to the dark side of human nature. While he'd wanted to shock her to ensure her
help, he hadn't intended to devastate her. Only later did
he realize she would blame herself. That she would carry
the images and the guilt with her for the rest of her life.

The last vestiges of a January sunset lit the western sky
when he parked the Tahoe at Eli's curb and got out. He
could hear a snow blower in the distance. The bare trees
shuddered like brittle skeletons in the brisk north wind.
Lights burned both upstairs and downstairs. Satisfied she
was home, he started toward the house.

He rang the bell and waited. He could hear music.
Some classical number he didn't recognize. She was
home. Why wasn't she answering the door?

Impatient, he rapped hard on the door with his knuckles. "Come on," he said under his breath.

He waited another minute, then left the porch, crossed
to the driveway, and peered through the garage door window. The Volkswagen sat safely inside. Annoyed, he went
back to the porch, opened the storm door, and tried the
knob.

Irritation transformed quickly to concern when the door
opened. What the hell was she thinking, keeping her doors
unlocked, for chrissake? Ann Arbor wasn't exactly a high
crime area, but it just so happened that there were a few
unsavory things going on at the moment. Where the hell
was her common sense?

He hesitated only an instant before stepping inside. The
house was warm. The air smelled of incense. A sweet,
exotic scent that was vaguely familiar. "Eli!" he called.
"Hey, it's Adam. Everything okay?"

Growing increasingly uneasy, he crossed through the
foyer and peered into the study to his right. The banker's
lamp cast yellow light over the cherry wood desk. The
computer was on. Papers were scattered on the desk. Eli
was nowhere in sight.

Leaving the foyer, he walked into the living room. The
room was cast in shadows, the only light coming from

two candles flickering merrily on the coffee table. Where the hell was she?

"What are you doing here?"

Adam actually started at the sound of her voice. Cursing under his breath, he fumbled for the wall switch and flicked on the lights. The sight of her curled on the sofa with a colorful afghan thrown over her and a long-stemmed glass in her hand shouldn't have surprised him, but it did. She blinked at him as her eyes adjusted to the light.

"The door was open," he said.

"I had the lights off for a reason," she said quietly. "Do you mind?"

He could tell by the way she was looking at him that she wasn't surprised to see him. He could tell by the way she was holding that glass that it wasn't her first. Judging by the half-empty bottle of wine on the coffee table, it wasn't even her second.

"Why didn't you answer the door?" he asked.

"I didn't want to talk to anyone, including you."

"If that was the case, maybe you should have locked it."

"Guess I forgot." Leaning forward, she reached for the bottle of wine, uncorked it, and topped off her glass. "I'd offer you a glass of wine, Adam, but I don't think I want to share."

She drank from the glass, watching him over the rim. Her eyes were large and dark against her pale complexion. The tip of her nose was pink. She wasn't wearing her glasses; they were on the coffee table next to the candles. He could see that her eyes weren't quite clear and wondered just how much she'd had to drink.

Easing off his trench coat, he crossed the room to her. "That bottle isn't going to help anything."

"Maybe not, but it sure is making me feel better."

"For now, maybe. You're not going to feel so good tomorrow."

"I guess I'll deal with that tomorrow, won't I?"

Draping his coat over the back of the chair, he sat across from her. "Why don't you tell me why you're sitting here in the dark, hard at work on a whole bottle of wine?"

She looked at him for a long time. At that moment,

Adam thought he'd never seen anyone look so . . . despondent. She was wearing a long shirt over a turtleneck and a pair of tight jeans. Her feet were bare. Red toenails peeked out at him from beneath the afghan. That small detail shouldn't have had such a big effect, but it did. He hadn't realized Dr. Elizabeth Barnes painted her toenails red.

"They fired me."

Adam put his elbows on his knees and sighed. He hadn't been expecting her to say that. "Jesus, I'm sorry."

"They took my security access card and my ID badge and escorted me from the building as if I were some kind of common criminal. After ten years, Adam." She took a reckless drink, then set her glass down on the end table a tad too hard. "I can't believe they would do that to me."

"Why did they fire you?" he asked.

"A number of reasons, the main one being that someone told Peter Roth I broke my confidentiality agreement."

"Who would do that?"

"My guess is Kevin Chambers."

"Did he know you were sharing information with me?"

"I'd confided in Kevin and Thomas Bornheimer about your visit to my office that first day when you brought in those articles." She picked up the glass, swirled it, and emptied it in a long gulp. "I trusted him, Adam. I mean, I thought he was my friend. I've been incredibly . . . stupid."

The first real pang of remorse hit him squarely in the chest. He knew all too well how it felt to be betrayed by someone you trusted. "This isn't your fault."

"Of course it is. I should have seen it coming. I should have been prepared." Taking her time, she refilled her glass. "Lindquist told Peter Roth about the e-mails. There's a company policy against office affairs. That my and Walter's alleged affair was documented on the company's network makes it even worse. I should have taken my concerns about Valazine to Peter right away." She took another long, dangerous drink. "Instead, I confided in Kevin. I was naïve enough to believe he would do the right thing."

"That little weaselly son of a bitch."

"Of all the people who would stab me in the back, I

never expected it to be Kevin. Sure, he could be a jerk, but I never thought he was vicious enough to ruin my career."

Adam didn't know what to say, so he remained silent. "You know what hurts the most?"

He didn't want to know, didn't want to risk getting any closer to her or feel any worse about her losing her job than he already did. But he didn't have the heart to turn away when she so obviously needed to get this off her chest. Frowning, he glanced over at her. She was all intensity now. Indignant. Furious. "What?" he asked, feeling something he didn't want to feel in a place he didn't want to acknowledge.

"I thought they were my friends. I mean, I've known them for more than ten years. I trusted them. Kevin. Peter. Thomas. I've been to their homes. I've played with Peter's children, for God's sake. The four of us worked closely together on Valazine. We put in a lot of hours on that project, but there were some good times, too, you know? I just don't understand how they could stab me in the back like this."

If she hadn't been well on her way to getting drunk, he would have pointed out that any of those three men could have an ulterior motive for firing her that didn't have anything to do with friendship or loyalty—and everything to do with her knowing too much about a drug that never should have been put on the market.

Rising, she picked up her glass and crossed the room. Adam watched her, felt his mouth go dry. Her jeans were snug, revealing a nicely rounded ass and long, slender legs. The baggy shirt wasn't buttoned and outlined just enough of the turtleneck beneath for him to see that she wasn't wearing a bra. He could see her nipples through the fabric, and felt a low slice of heat.

Once she reached the foyer, she took another drink of wine and turned to face him. "Not to mention what this will do to our . . . investigation. This is a huge setback." Her eyes were dark and owlish against her pale complexion. Pain shimmered like cut crystal in their depths. Smudges of fatigue and stress darkened the area beneath

her eyes, making her look fragile and fierce at once.
"Damn it. They hurt me."

The way she said it made him think of two people
who'd done much the same to him three years ago. "I'm
sorry they hurt you," he said.

"I can handle the hurt."

"Sure you can."

"That's such a small part of it. It's what they've done
to Walter's memory that really burns me. What they've
done to my career." She approached him. "Roth threatened to blacklist me."

Adam rose, his interest flaring. "Why did he do that?"

"Because I told him I was concerned about some adverse events."

"Eli, I wish you hadn't—"

"He already knew. Kevin had told him. I thought I
could reach him."

"Did you say that in front of anyone else?"

She shook her head. "Just Peter."

"What did he say?"

"He threatened to sue me. Then he said if I talked to
the wrong people, he'd bury me."

"That sounds like a threat." Adam didn't miss the minute shiver that ran the length of her when she turned away.

Gesturing with the hand that held the wine, she sloshed
some over the side and it dripped unceremoniously onto
the carpet. She didn't notice. "If we decide to go public
with our suspicions about Valazine, I will no longer be
seen as credible. I'll seem like a disgruntled ex-employee
out for revenge against the company that fired me."

Adam had already thought of that. Watching her, he
figured now wasn't the time to discuss it. "We can talk
about that when your head is clear," he said.

"My head is clearer than it's been in a long time. In
fact, I feel like I've had my head buried in the sand, and
I've finally come up for air and can see the world around
me clearly for the first time in ten years."

He stared at her, trying not to notice the way those jeans
swept over the curve of her hips. The shirt had parted,
and he could see the pointed nipple of her left breast

through the turtleneck. Lust stirred hotly in his gut, so he
looked away. He reminded himself that she was vulnerable at the moment. Hurting. Drunk. Things were screwed
up enough without his getting stupid and doing something
he would regret later.

"I don't know if you can understand, but my work is
all I've ever had," she said. "I chose my work over marriage. Over family. I devoted my life to developing this
drug. Adam, I don't think I can bear it if we find out my
life's work has been killing people."

"Now probably isn't a good time to get into this."

Ignoring him, she took another long drink. "How many
people have died because of Valazine?" she asked
abruptly. "I wanted to toss some statistics at Roth and
realized I don't even know. I was so deep into denial, I
didn't even ask you."

Adam didn't want to answer the question. Not with her
standing before him shaking with hurt and fury and a
sense of betrayal he knew all too intimately not to recognize. She looked as if she would shatter at the slightest
touch. He didn't want to be the one to cause it. He wasn't
up to picking up the pieces.

"How many?" she repeated.

"I think you've had enough wine." But he didn't move
to take it away from her.

Her hand shook when she took a drink. "How many
people have died, damn it? Tell me. How many? I deserve
to know."

"We don't know for certain—"

"How many!" she shouted.

Adam didn't want to tell her, didn't want to escalate
the situation. But she deserved to know. "Twenty-two fatalities that were either directly or indirectly the result of
someone taking Valazine and reacting violently."

She stared at him, holding the glass out like a shield,
her eyes filling with tears. "Twenty-two people."

He nodded, didn't bother telling her that so far his investigation was limited to the United States. Valazine was
currently on the market in Canada, Europe, and Mexico.
"It's not your fault," he said.

"How can that not be my fault?"

"If someone on your team withheld information from you, then it's his fault, not yours. You did the best you could with the information you had to work with."

She pressed a hand to her stomach as if the thought sickened her. "I've been naïve and stupid."

"No," he said, but it was already too late.

Adam watched the emotional dam break with all the cool of a man standing in the path of a tidal wave. He told himself the tears didn't affect him. That just because he liked her as a person, because he respected her, didn't mean he was going to let her get to him.

But she did get to him. Like a steel spike driven under a fingernail. And he felt every inch of it all the way to his core.

He didn't realize he was going to move until he'd already crossed the short distance between them. She looked up briefly, her expression startled, but she didn't stop him. Didn't say a word as he took the glass from her and set it on the end table next to him. She didn't pull away when he wrapped his arms around her shoulders and held her.

She felt small and fragile in his arms. She was trembling. Adam smoothed his hand down her back, set his other palm against the back of her head where her hair was like silk against his fingers. Her arms went around his neck, and he felt the warmth of her tears on his shoulder. He felt the pain vibrating inside her, and he absorbed it, wanting to take it away because he understood it and knew she didn't deserve to hurt like that.

"It's okay," he heard himself say. But his voice sounded like gravel.

"It's not okay." Her voice was a whisper of warmth in his ear. "People are dying, and it's my fault. That's not okay. It'll never be okay."

The need to protect rose up inside him like a riptide. "We'll fix it," he said. "We'll get to the bottom of it."

"I don't know how to fix it."

"We'll figure something out."

"Adam . . ." She shifted closer, and in that instant

everything changed. One moment he was the unemotional cop comforting a distraught witness, the next he was a man with a man's needs and the unsettling knowledge that those needs were barreling out of control.

Abruptly, he realized just how close they were. Body to body from shoulder to thigh. Her head was against his chest. He could feel the soft swell of her breasts through his shirt, smell the scent of her hair, feel her hands roaming over his shoulders and back.

Turning her head slightly, she whispered something in a low voice. Adam didn't hear the words, but he smelled the richness of wine on her breath, and it intoxicated him, broke down the last of his defenses. When she lifted her face to his, he saw the shimmer of tears in her eyes. He saw pain and vulnerability and a dozen other things he didn't want to see. He should have known what would happen next, but whether he was too involved to notice, or too goddamned weak to stop it, he stood silent and still while she leaned forward and brushed her mouth across his.

The shock of pleasure jolted him. Her mouth was incredibly soft beneath his. He savored the taste of her, reveled in the warmth of her breath against his cheek. Arousal flowed like liquid fire to his groin. A sweet ache that reminded him he was a man and that it had been a long time since he'd been with a woman.

In the three years since the shooting, his physical and mental rehabilitation had been so all consuming Adam hadn't considered a relationship. For weeks after the shooting he hadn't been able to walk or speak or even remember his own name some days. Determined to rebuild his life, he'd devoted every ounce of energy to getting better. There had been little time for anything else—including a woman.

The ache turned electric when she moved tentatively against him. He forgot about all the reasons he shouldn't and kissed her back. Her hands skimmed down his back, then lower to his buttocks. She squeezed his ass. He deepened the kiss, savoring the sweetness of her mouth with his tongue. He ground his erection against her. He felt a ripple of shock go through her, but she didn't stop kissing him. He tasted wine spiced with recklessness. Moving against him, she lowered her hand to his crotch. His vision blurred when she gripped him through his trousers.

"Jesus, Eli," he whispered, and his control broke.

Slipping his hands beneath her shirt, he cupped her breasts. She made a sound—the meaning of which he didn't understand—but he didn't stop. Her breasts were heavy and round in his hands. He molded the flesh with his fingertips, trailed his thumbs over the hardened peaks of her nipples.

Need swiped at him with sharp claws. Hunger dug in to him. He wanted her, he realized. Wanted her more than his next breath. Wanted her wet and open and beneath him . . .

Remembering abruptly that she was drunk, that he had absolutely no business putting his hands all over her when she was vulnerable, Adam set his hands on her shoulders and pushed her away.

She looked up at him, her face flushed, her breasts rising and falling with each breath. "Wh-what are you doing?"

"Leaving." He fought the urge to rearrange himself, and reached down and grabbed his coat instead. "You can thank me tomorrow."

Her expression turned stricken. "I . . . I don't know why I did that."

"It's called booze. Some people can handle it. Some can't. Evidently, you fall into the latter group."

"I didn't mean for that to happen. I'm . . . sorry."

"For God's sake, don't apologize." He wanted to say more, something to let her know it would have been good, but he didn't. Adam had learned about the dangers of playing with fire a long time ago.

He shrugged into his coat. "I have to go," he said, and walked out the door.

chapter
19

ADAM ORDERED A DOUBLE SCOTCH AT THE HOTEL
bar before going to his room. He had hoped it would settle
the restlessness that had been pulsing through him since
he'd left Eli's house an hour earlier. Kissing her had been
a mistake. Touching her had been downright idiotic.
She'd needed a shoulder to cry on, not some loser ex-cop
drooling all over her.

He knew what he was dealing with. A phenomenon that
had nothing to do with the case and everything to do with
the way she wore those jeans. He knew lust when he felt
it, and Eli had brought that unfortunate weakness to the
surface with a vengeance. The affliction had taken down
many a man, and Adam sure as hell wasn't immune. If
the situation had been different, he would have taken her
right there on the living room floor and they'd have gone
at it like a couple of dogs in heat. God knew he wanted
to.

But Adam had been around the block enough times to
know it would have cost him something sooner or later.
Not even lust came without a price. He didn't want things
to get complicated. The case was already complicated

enough without throwing hot sex into the mix. A one-night stand was one thing, but Adam didn't think it would stop at just one night.

He left the bar and took the elevator to his floor. Once inside his room, he switched on an all-news cable network and walked over to the bar. Deciding on bourbon, he took out the small bottle and poured it straight up. He knew he was risking a migraine, but he was feeling edgy and restless as hell. He drank it down in two gulps, then walked over to his briefcase and removed the folder containing all the information he'd amassed on Valazine. Methodically, he spread the papers on the table. He opened his laptop and logged on to the Internet. He did a search on Scott Milner and tried to immerse himself, but concentration eluded him.

He couldn't stop thinking about Eli. He couldn't stop thinking about that kiss. The taste of her mouth. The sound of her sighs. The weight of her breasts in his hands. The slow burn of arousal in his groin . . .

Goddamn it.

Annoyed, he rose and walked over to the phone, snatched it up, held it motionless for a heartbeat. Cursing, he set it back down. No, he wouldn't call her. He wasn't going to go there. Wasn't going to make a fatal mistake that would leave them both sorry for it later.

He walked into the bathroom and stripped off his clothes. A hot shower would help him settle down, let him concentrate. He needed to go over the Valazine summary report again. See if he could find something he'd missed before. Adjusting the spray, he stepped under the jets, closed his eyes, and let the water pound him.

But when he closed his eyes, he saw Eli. The way she'd looked at him the instant before she kissed him. The way her body had molded to his. The hard peaks of her nipples. She'd shivered when he'd caressed her there. He wondered if she'd been wet. . . .

The hot rush of blood to his groin exasperated him. "Goddamn it," he muttered.

Leaning forward, he twisted the hot water faucet until the water ran like ice over his skin. Gooseflesh rose on his arms and legs. He endured the cold, but it didn't help.

Adam wasn't some pimply-faced teenager who got off on his first kiss. He was a man and knew he should go down to the hotel gym and work this off with weights until he was too damn tired to think about sex. But the need was like a fire burning inside him, taunting him, scorching him, driving him to slow insanity.

He thought of Eli, remembered how it had felt when she'd wrapped her fingers around him. Bracing himself against the tile with one hand, he leaned forward, his hand closing around his erection. Because it had been such a very long time, he told himself. Because he needed to know he could.

Because he wanted her in a very bad way, and there was no way in hell he would ever let anything happen between them.

ELI WOKE TO A GRINDING HEADACHE AND A MOUTH-ful of rank cotton. The pain in her head shouldn't have surprised her. That particular year of California merlot had never agreed with her. She looked over at the alarm clock next to her bed and groaned. Eight o'clock. Normally and even though it was Saturday, she would have already been at work by now. Sitting behind her desk in her cozy office with its spindly ficus tree and keyhole window that looked out over the parking lot. Walter would be there and they would be discussing something controversial.

She knew it was silly, but she suddenly felt like pulling the covers over her head and crying. Damn it, she shouldn't be at home lying in bed with a hangover be-cause she'd been fired. She shouldn't be thinking of how to solve Walter's murder. And she sure as hell shouldn't be lying in bed and wondering if a miracle drug she'd spent the last ten years getting on the market was causing people to commit murder.

Closing her eyes, she lay back and tried not to think. The next thought that struck her sent her bolt upright. "Oh, no."

Images of the awkward pass she'd made at Adam flitted

through her mind. A mind-blowing kiss. The feel of his body against hers. A mouth that was amazingly adept and stunningly soft for such a hardened man. She remembered the way he'd looked at her. His expression had been cautious. A little surprised. But he'd definitely been into the kiss. She may not have much experience in the man kissing department, but it didn't take a rocket scientist to know when a man was interested. Adam Boedecker had definitely been interested.

Putting her face in her hands, she groaned. If she hadn't been so mortified, she might have laughed. She couldn't believe she'd made a pass at him. A cop, for God's sake! A man who couldn't be more wrong for her. What on earth had prompted her to do something so out of character?

"Half a bottle of 1997 California merlot," she muttered. "God, Barnes, you're a freaking idiot."

It struck her then that she'd given Adam every chance to sleep with her. She'd practically thrown herself at him! She wasn't quite sure how she felt about the fact that he hadn't taken her up on it. Eli told herself she was relieved things hadn't gone any farther. Surely he understood she'd been distraught over losing her job. That she wasn't accustomed to drinking and the alcohol had affected her judgment. Surely he knew that damn kiss hadn't meant a thing to either of them. Didn't he?

BY DUSK, ELI WAS CLIMBING THE WALLS. SINCE early morning, she had been cruising various Internet sites, compiling adverse event data on Valazine. Events reported to the FDA and other organizations by consumers as well as medical personnel. No matter how much of a stretch—even a consumer reporting that while taking Valazine she had yelled at her children—Eli added it to the database. She spent hours on the phone, trying to connect the dots in a puzzle that refused to come together. She tried several times to log in to Roth's network on the outside chance the techies hadn't yet disabled her account, but evidently they had. How was she supposed to get to the bottom of this when she didn't have access to vital information?

She called Peter Roth four times before noon, but he hadn't returned her calls. He probably thought she was going to beg for her job back, the jerk. She ended up leaving him an urgent message to call her. She even considered calling Kevin, but couldn't bring herself to do it. His betrayal hurt, and she would be feeling the pain for a very long time to come.

She tried not to think of Adam, but he'd been on her mind throughout the day. So what if she'd made a fool of herself? It wasn't the end of the world. A quick apology and they could put it behind them and get on with the business at hand. No big deal.

It was almost six P.M. when the doorbell rang. Eli nearly jumped out of her skin. She knew immediately it was Adam. Resisting the urge to smooth her hair, she walked to the front door and checked the peephole. He stood on the front porch, his expression inscrutable. Eli's mouth went dry. "This is *not* a big deal," she muttered. But the words didn't explain why her heart was pounding. Taking a deep breath, she opened the door.

He wore a long black coat over dark slacks. Everything about him was dark, she realized. Dark eyes beneath thick arches of black brows. Dark hair. For a long moment, he just stood there, expressionless, contemplating her.

Nerves gripped Eli. The need to say something, anything, was strong. She struggled for an instant, felt the words tangle on her tongue. "I'm sorry about last night," she blurted. "I never do that."

"You mean make passes at men?"

"Or drink."

"If it's any consolation, I survived the experience with no lingering ill effects." A glint of what could have been amusement gleamed in his eyes for a second. "I'm not so sure about you."

"I can't believe I did that. I'm . . . mortified."

"Don't be. It happens. You'd had a pretty rough day. Go ahead and let yourself off the hook." He shoved his hands into his pockets. "Can I come in?"

"Oh." Feeling awkward, she opened the door farther and stepped back. "Sorry. It's cold out there, isn't it?"

He glanced at her oddly as he entered, then worked off his coat.

"Let me take that." She reached for his coat. She couldn't look at him. Couldn't look him in the eye. Oh, why had she made that stupid pass at him?"

"This doesn't have to be awkward," he said.

"I'm not. I mean, it's not."

"You're babbling."

"I'm not babbling, damn it."

"Whatever you say."

Turning away from him, she hung his coat in the hall closet, took the moment to regain her composure. What on earth was the matter with her? It was just a stupid kiss. She'd been drinking. Distraught. It was not a big deal. So why the hell were her knees shaking?

By the time she met him in the living room, Eli felt more in control. "We've got to tell someone about what we suspect," she said.

"Who do you have in mind?"

"Peter Roth."

"Didn't you already try to talk to him?"

Eli bit her lip. "Yes, but if I could just get in to see him, I think maybe I could convince him—"

"As far as we know, he could be in on this up to his eyebrows."

The thought made her feel sick.

"We need proof," Adam said.

"How do we get it when I no longer have access to information at Roth?"

"We keep digging."

"I've been beating my brains out all day at various sites on the Internet. I've called the FDA and am waiting for a call back." Frustration billowed through her. "I tried to call Peter Roth several times today, but he isn't returning my calls. This is making me nuts."

"Maybe we could apply some pressure to Roth by threatening to go to the FDA."

Eli hadn't wanted it to come to that, but she knew now

wasn't the time to play nice. People were dying. If Valazine was, indeed, the cause of a number of murder-suicides—and at this point she was almost certain it was—she needed to do everything in her power to get it off the market, no holds barred.

"I tried getting into the Roth network, but the techs have already disabled my account."

"You expected that."

"Yes, but it's made me realize I'm not going to be much help without access to inside information."

"You need something in particular?"

"I need the study files containing the raw data of adverse events. Even the ones that didn't make it to the label. I mean, if someone got a hangnail during the trial, they were supposed to report it. It was up to us—Dr. Bornheimer and me—to translate what we were reading and decide what was relevant to the study."

"Subjective stuff?"

She nodded. "For example, if a study participant reported a hangnail as a side effect, common sense would dictate that I not list it in the study. However, that information would be included in the raw data."

"And that's on disk?"

"Well, actually, it's stored in an on-site storage room."

"Probably safe to say we can't get to it." Reaching into his briefcase, he pulled out a manila folder. "These are the crime stats I've been able to pull together." He handed her several papers. "That includes incidents in which the perps had been prescribed Valazine."

Eli glanced at the data. Names, dates, and cities were neatly typed into columns. The last column heading was titled "Fatalities" and listed the number of people killed during the incident. The total number of fatalities had climbed to forty-six. A number big enough to make her nauseous.

He handed her two more sheets of paper stapled together. "These are the incidents where I was able to get toxicology information from the coroner. All of the perps in this report had levels of Valazine in their blood at the time of the incident."

Eli skimmed the page. At the bottom, he'd highlighted the number of suicides. Twenty-two. God in heaven. She closed her eyes, blew out a slow breath to calm herself.

"I don't think we can count on Roth to help us," he said.

She shook her head. "No."

Leaning forward, he put his elbows on his knees. "Are there any other sources of information you can think of that will help us?"

"The clinic where the trials were administered, but there's no way anyone will share any of that information with me. Especially now that I've been fired."

"What about archive storage?"

"What we could have used was destroyed in the fire."

"There's got to be other sources," he said. "Think outside the box."

"Any chance you could get a warrant?"

He cut her a dark look. "I'm on disability."

"Don't you have a cop friend who could get you a warrant of some type?"

"He's not that good a friend." He scrubbed a hand over his face. "We're on our own. This is going to be a hard sell no matter how you cut it. If we go to the police without bringing them something to back up our story, they're not going to bite. It's not like either of us has much in the way of credibility right now."

The next thought that entered her mind frightened her, but not nearly as much as the alternative. "Do you remember the other day when you told me you didn't do B and Es?"

He scowled at her. "I haven't changed my mind."

"There's a clinic—"

"No."

"The names of the participants are at the clinic."

"Eli . . ." He rubbed his temple, but she could tell she'd gotten his attention.

"That's what you've wanted all along, isn't it?" she asked.

"Yeah, but if it's all the same to you, I'd rather not

spend the next four to six years in prison. Inmates are hard on cops."

"You have a better suggestion?"

"Yeah. I know a computer guy. Maybe I could give him a call and have him hack in to Roth's system. Maybe we could get what we need that way."

"Those names are not on disk. They're nowhere at Roth."

"You mentioned unlisted side effects."

"That's a long shot. The names might be more easily obtained." She blew out a pent-up sigh. "Look, I don't want to do this any more than you do, but we're running out of time."

"Damn it, I'm a cop. I'm not going to break in to some clinic to get possible evidence on a case."

"You're on disability," she pointed out.

He gave her a dirty look. "That kind of evidence wouldn't do us any good in court."

"This isn't for court. It's to convince the police or the FBI or the FDA that there's a dangerous drug on the market. A drug we believe has killed at least forty-six people."

Adam didn't look convinced.

"I know the security code," she added. "If they haven't changed it in the last month or so, I can get us in no problem."

He cursed under his breath. "You give me the code. I'll do it."

"You don't know where anything is. I do."

"Let's think this through—"

"I can be in and out in ten minutes."

"Your getting thrown in jail isn't going to help."

"I don't like the idea of breaking the law any more than you do, but we have to do something." Too restless to sit, she rose and paced to the far side of the room. "People are dying," she said quietly. "I've got that on my conscience, Adam. I can't live with that."

"Don't go there, Eli. Don't take the guilt route. It's counterproductive as hell."

"I have to go there and so do you because we're the only people who can stop this."

Adam rose and paced over to the fireplace. He looked troubled. "This clinic. You really think you can get in and out without any problems?"

Some of the frustration inside her eased. "I've been in that particular lab a dozen times in the last year. It's a small building in an office park off the freeway."

"Security?"

"I think there's a security guard, but he has the entire industrial park to keep an eye on."

"What about an alarm system?"

"The keypad turns it off and opens the door."

"You know the sequence?"

"The receptionist gave it to me because she got tired of getting up and opening the door for me every time I visited."

Adam raked his hand through his hair. He didn't look happy about the situation. Eli figured he didn't have a choice. Neither did she.

"Most companies change their codes every so often," he said. "How do you know they haven't?"

"I don't," she said, aware that her heart was pounding. "I think it's worth a try."

He stared at her long enough to make her want to squirm. As she contemplated him, she found herself thinking about that kiss. . . .

"I'm going to change clothes," she said. "I'll be ready in ten minutes."

AT ELEVEN P.M., ADAM DROVE PAST THE DARKENED building that housed Manicon Laboratories. It was situated in Ypsilanti in an upscale office park just off the interstate.

Beside him, Eli looked out her window and scrutinized the building.

"There's too much light," Adam said. "No place to park."

"There's an industrial complex on the other side of those

trees. You can park there. It's less than a hundred yards from the back of the building. I'll cut through the woods."

Adam had been a cop long enough to know a bad idea when he heard one. Her going into that laboratory to steal files or a disk or whatever the hell she was going in there to do was definitely a bad idea. She was a scientist, not a cat burglar. If she got into trouble, if the security guard happened by when she was inside . . .

He looked over at her. Even in the semidarkness, he could see the anxiety etched into her features. She was scared and damn well should be considering what she was about to do.

He knew this was their best chance to find some hard evidence against Roth Pharmaceuticals. But at some point in the last week, he'd come to care about what happened to her. She was a decent person, and he didn't want to see her get into trouble. He told himself his protective feelings for her had absolutely nothing to do with last night. So what if she turned him on? It had been a long time since he'd been with a woman. Any attractive woman would have tempted him.

But Eli wasn't just any woman. She was soft and warm and more real than anyone he'd ever know, and Adam didn't want her hurt.

"—park it on the street away from the light, okay?"

He jerked his head around, realizing belatedly she'd been speaking to him. She looked lovely with her dark hair tied back from her face. It was an imperfect face. Her eyes were too large. Her lips were a tad too full. But the combination of imperfections made for a perfect package, indeed.

"I'm going in with you," he said.

"We agreed—"

"I don't give a shit what we agreed on. I'm going in with you. Shut up, and get out of the truck." Pulling up to the curb, he shut down the engine and shoved the keys into his pocket.

"Why?" she asked quietly.

For a moment he almost told her the truth. Almost told her he cared about what happened to her. That he couldn't sit in the truck and do nothing while she risked everything. "If things get hairy, I'll get us out."

She thought about it a moment, then nodded. "Okay."

"Like you have a choice," he muttered as he got out of the truck.

She was standing at the edge of the parking lot, studying the woods, when he met up with her. She was wearing snug black jeans and a dark turtleneck beneath a hooded pullover. She looked good enough to eat. "You look like a cat burglar," he said.

She frowned at him over her shoulder. "You really know how to shower a girl with compliments, don't you?"

A hard tug of attraction struck him squarely in the gut. Swell. "Let's go," he said.

The greenbelt separating the residential neighborhood from the office park was so narrow, he could see the sodium-vapor lamps on the other side. "I hope there's a path," he said, starting into the woods.

"Me, too." Eli fell into step beside him, and together they tramped through ankle-deep snow.

Twenty yards later the trees opened to a deserted parking lot. "No security guards in sight," she said, starting for the building.

Adam hooked his finger in the hood of her coat, pulling her back. "Wrong way," he said, and pointed toward the rear.

"Oh," she said. "I knew that."

"Sure you did." He studied the building for a moment. "Does the rear door have a security keypad?"

Eli nodded.

"Let's move." He hadn't intended to take her hand, but he did. They crossed the parking lot at an easy jog, then went up the concrete steps to a deck enclosed by a pipe rail.

Though the parking lot was empty, Adam felt uncomfortably exposed. Next to him, Eli lifted her hand to punch numbers into the keypad. Before she did, Adam grasped her wrist. Even through her coat he could feel her trembling.

He knew touching her was a mistake, and he felt the impact of that mistake all the way to his toes. "You're shaking," he said.

"It's cold."

"It's a good thing to be nervous, Doc. It's the cocky guys who get caught."

She didn't say anything, but Adam saw the myriad thoughts flitting through her brain. She was wondering why he'd stopped her. Why he was touching her. Why he was suddenly standing so close. He was wondering all the same things himself.

He smelled the warm scent of vanilla coming off her. It reminded him of the kiss. His desperate need for release that had come afterward. The intensity of the memory sent a flash of heat through him.

Lowering his head slightly, he cupped the back of her neck, tilted her face to his, and pressed his mouth to hers. The urge to devour was strong, but he didn't. Instead he brushed his lips gently across hers. He heard her quick intake of breath. Felt the shudder that moved through her. He closed his eyes against the pleasure, let it rock him.

He ended the kiss an instant later, but he didn't let her go. Holding her, he looked into her eyes, struggling to control his breathing and willing his blood to cool. "That was for luck," he said.

Eyes wide and searching his, she took a quick step back, opened her mouth, then closed it. "Wow . . . okay."

If he hadn't been high on adrenaline, he might have laughed. Instead, he managed a smile that felt edgy because his nerves were crawling. He jerked his head toward the keypad. "Let's do it."

She turned to the keypad and punched in six digits. A green light blinked twice. A buzz sounded. Adam heard the lock click.

"We're in," she said.

"God help us," he muttered under his breath.

She turned to look at him. "What?"

"I said I'll keep an eye out for the rent-a-cop. You get what you need and be quick about it."

"All right." They jogged down a narrow hallway lined with gray metal doors. "I'm going to try to find the raw data from the study participants first," she said.

"Where would that be?"

"File room, more than likely. The study took place over a year ago, so the files are probably not active."

"Where?"

"Here." She stopped outside a gray door. A signed labeled it ARCHIVE STORAGE ROOM.

He looked at his watch. "I'll meet you back here in five minutes."

She looked over her shoulder and gave him a tremulous smile. A smile that spoke of fear and adrenaline and a dozen other things a woman like her should never have to feel. He knew it was stupid, but for a moment, he just stood there looking at her while that smile shook him inside.

"Be careful," he managed after a time, and handed her his penlight. "Use this sparingly."

Assuring himself she would be fine while he took a look around, he headed down the hall toward the red exit sign in the reception area and peered through the mini-blinds at the parking lot. Piles of dirty snow flanked the entrance. A fire hydrant and a row of sapling trees marked the street. The parking lot was empty. Adam figured if the security guard was going to make rounds, he'd come in through the front first.

Satisfied they were safe for now, he headed back down the hall, familiarizing himself with the office layout, keeping an eye on the windows through the open office doors as he passed. He glanced at his watch. Four minutes had passed. He'd give her another two, then he'd get them the hell out of there whether they had what they needed or not.

He was halfway down the hall when he heard the jingle of keys. At first he thought it was Eli. Then he realized the sound was coming from a side exit he hadn't noticed earlier. He heard footsteps against carpet. The bobbing of a flashlight beam sent him slinking into the ladies' restroom. Silently, Adam eased the door closed and listened. Heavy footsteps sounded outside the door. Male voices. The crackle of a radio.

Adam didn't panic easily, but he felt the hot sting of it rush through his body. Not for himself, he realized, but for Eli—because he was pretty sure she was about to have a close encounter with two security officers.

chapter
20

ELI WAS STILL THINKING ABOUT THE KISS WHEN SHE walked past the rows of beige file cabinets. The pleasure lingered like the sweet remnants of an erotic dream. The tang of his aftershave. The warm pressure of his mouth against hers. The rock solid feel of his body . . .

She knew she should be focused on finding the files she needed, but the kiss was messing with her concentration. If she wasn't so scared at the moment, she'd probably be smiling like an idiot.

Aware that her heart was pounding, not sure if it was from the kiss or the fact that she was in the process of committing a crime, she scanned the darkened interior of the file room. Seven rows of file cabinets labeled alphabetically and lined back to back comprised the room. She had no idea where the study participant information would be filed, but figured "R" for Roth would be a good place to start. Silently, she made her way down the narrow aisle and tugged on the drawer labeled RA — RU. Disappointment quivered through her when it didn't budge. Locked. She should have anticipated that.

"Great," she muttered.

Using the penlight, she looked around for something with which to pry the drawer open. A stack of green hanging folders lay in a haphazard pile on the floor. She reached for one of the folders and tore the metal prong from its sleeve. Shoving the end of the prong into the lock mechanism, she twisted a few times and tried the drawer again. No luck.

"Of course not." Determined not to let such a small thing deter her, Eli slid the metal prong into the space between the drawer and the cabinet and poked around. Still, when she tried the drawer, it didn't budge.

Just a small obstacle, she assured herself. All she had to do was walk out to the receptionist's desk and find the key. No big deal. If the desk was locked, she would find Adam and see if he could get it open. Cops knew how to pick locks, didn't they?

She was halfway down the hall when the jingle of keys spun her around. The beam of a flashlight slashed through the darkness. Adrenaline stuck her like a hammer blow. For an instant, she stood motionless, too horrified to move. Someone was coming down the hall, and it wasn't Adam.

Oh, God! Heart thrumming, she looked wildly around. She couldn't go back to the file room without being seen. She couldn't slip out the rear door without running into whomever had that flashlight. Her only choice was to hide in the reception area.

Realizing she would be cornered there, she fought down a rise of panic and backed into the reception area. A desk and chair sat neatly off to her right. The front of the room was glass, including the door. Maybe she could get the keys out of the receptionist's desk, unlock the front door, and get out before anyone saw her. Maybe she could hide beneath the desk until they left.

The sound of voices reached her a moment later. Security guards. At least two of them. Oh, God. Oh, *God!* Heart raging, she dashed over to the desk and tugged on the pencil drawer. Locked. She was in the process of pulling out the chair to get under the desk when the lights flashed on.

"Hold it right there, lady! Stop! I'm armed, damn it!"

Every muscle in her body froze. Except her heart, which threatened to explode if it beat any harder. Eli looked up, saw a beefy young man with short-cropped hair and a big gun pointed right at her.

"Put your hands up where I can see them! Now!"

Her hands shot up.

"What are you doing here?" he demanded.

Eli had never been very good at lying. But this time lies flew with the fervor of truth. "I—I w-work here. I—I needed some files. T-to work on . . . over the weekend."

"Where's your badge?"

"My badge?"

"Where's your ID badge, ma'am?"

"I didn't bring it because I didn't expect to see anyone here at this hour." Because her knees were shaking violently, she leaned against the desk. "Please don't point that gun at me."

He didn't move the gun. Eyeing her warily, the security guard spoke into his radio. "This is 021. I've got a 10-88. Clear."

Eli wondered what the hell a 10-88 was.

He motioned toward the receptionist's chair. "Have a seat for now, ma'am, until we get this straightened out."

Never taking her eyes off him, she lowered herself into the chair. She felt nauseous, every nerve in her body vibrating with fear. Where was Adam?

"I'll need to see your ID, ma'am."

"I don't have my badge with—"

"Your driver's license will be fine."

Dread gripped her when she realized she wasn't going to be able to talk herself out of this. "I don't have my driver's license with me," she said.

"What's your name?"

For a split second, she considered lying, but knew that would only make things worse. She knew the security officer would call the police and eventually find out who she was.

"My name is Dr. Elizabeth Barnes," she said.

"What are you doing here?"

"Like I told you earlier, I'd forgotten some files I needed to work on over the weekend."

"At midnight?"

"I'm a night bird."

"Uh-huh. Why don't you just sit there while I check that out?"

Another security guard walked into the reception area. He was a burly African-American man with a bald head and direct, intelligent eyes. His badge identified him as Officer Cooper. "The rest of the place is clear," he said and looked over at Eli. "Who's this?"

"She says she works here," the first security guard said.

"I do work here, and I'd appreciate it if you'd let me get my files and go home."

"Where's your car?" the other man asked. "Why isn't it out front in the lot?"

"I . . . my friend dropped me off. I was going to call him when I'm ready to leave."

The two men exchanged looks. "The security director is on his way over," said Officer Cooper. He looked over at Eli. "He IDs you and we can all go home, okay?"

She nodded, trying desperately to think of a way to get out of this. The security director was *not* going to ID her, and she didn't think she was going to be going home tonight.

Ten minutes later, a tall man with mussed gray hair and wire-rimmed glasses unlocked the front door and walked in to the reception area. He looked at the two security officers, then at Eli.

"Who's this?" he demanded.

"She said she works for Manicon."

The gray haired man squinted at her. "Dr. *Barnes*?" he asked incredulously. "Is that you? What on earth are you doing here?"

Eli couldn't think of a valid explanation. There was no way in hell she was going to be able to explain this. She'd already told the two officers that she worked for the company and had needed files. For an instant, she considered telling the security director she'd lost a valuable ring last time she was here, but neither explanation was going to get her out of this.

"I needed some files," she said weakly.

"What files? We haven't worked with Roth in almost a month. For goodness sake, what are you doing here after hours?"

"I needed some files f-from the study we worked on together."

"The Valazine study?"

"Yes."

"Why didn't you just call and ask for them?"

"I . . . couldn't wait until Monday."

"Dr. Barnes . . ." His voice trailed off. "That doesn't make any sense."

Officer Cooper looked at the gray-haired man. "Does she have your permission to be here? Or do you want us to call a city car?"

The gray-haired man shook his head. "She's not supposed to be here. I don't know why she's here, but she's not supposed to be here."

The security officer spoke into his radio, asking for a squad car with a female officer. Panic gripped Eli. The urge to run was strong. But she knew there was no getting away. She was going to be arrested for breaking and entering and then taken to jail. Oh, God, what would her colleagues and friends think? Dr. Elizabeth Barnes caught red-handed breaking into a laboratory and thrown in the slammer. If the situation hadn't been so utterly horrifying, she might have laughed herself into hysterics.

The first squad car arrived ten minutes later. Two police officers, a male and a female, entered through the front door, which had been unlocked by the security director.

Eli sat at the receptionist's desk, watching the entire scene unfold, sick to her soul. When the female officer spoke to her, it took Eli a moment to realize it.

"Ma'am, I need for you to stand up for me."

Heart thrashing in her chest, Eli stood, aware that the security guards and the other officer were watching her intently.

"Raise your arms for me."

Eli did as she was told. "This is a mistake," she said feebly.

"Do you have any weapons or needles or anything like that on you I should know about?"

"Of course not. I'm not a criminal."

The female officer ran her hands quickly and impersonally over her, checking all her pockets and even her socks.

"She's clean," she said to her partner, then focused again on Eli. "I need you to turn around and put your hands behind your back."

Fingers of panic crawled over Eli. The thought of handcuffs and the coming hours at the jail were almost too much to bear. Frantic, she looked from one officer to another. "Please, that's not necessary. I'll come to the police station with no problem."

"Ma'am, it's for your protection and ours." Stepping forward, the female officer removed the cuffs from her belt. "Now turn around and give me your wrists."

Eli turned and offered her wrists. She could hear her own heavy breathing, but it was drowned out by the drumming of her heart. She closed her eyes when she felt the cold steel of the cuffs close around her wrists. Helplessness and humiliation swamped her.

Vaguely, she was aware of the police officers exchanging information with the security guards as the female officer guided her toward the front door. Beyond, two cruisers sat in the parking lot, their emergency lights flashing like strobes.

She couldn't believe she was being arrested. Couldn't believe she'd made such a terrible mistake.

Most of all, she couldn't believe Adam had left her to face this alone.

ADAM USED A BAIL BONDSMAN IN YPSILANTI TO POST bond, then made the ten-minute drive back to the jail just as the sun broke over the horizon. It had been seven hours since Eli's arrest. As a cop, he knew exactly what she'd gone through during the night. The booking process would be hellish for a woman like her. Demoralizing. Dehumanizing. She didn't deserve any of it.

What really bothered him, however, was how this would look to her. Like he'd hightailed it at the first sign of trouble and left her behind to take the heat. He hadn't, of course, but he still felt the hard knot of guilt in his gut. He'd let her talk him into doing something stupid, and she'd paid the price for his lack of judgment.

When the two security guards had appeared out of seemingly nowhere, Adam knew that short of drawing his

Glock and shooting them, there was no way in hell he
could have gotten her out of there. As hard as it was to
leave, he also knew there was no sense in getting both of
them arrested. He'd ended up running out the back door,
sprinting through the trees and driving like a madman
back to the hotel.

Leaving her behind was one of the hardest things he'd
ever had to do. He'd called the jail every hour since, but
each time he was told she needed to be processed and ar-
raigned before bail could be set. Goddamned bureaucrats.

Guilt churned like hot concrete in his gut as he parked
the Tahoe in the lot and settled in to wait. Using his cell
phone, he dialed the number of the jail from memory. This
time, the jailer told him bail had been set and as soon as he
signed on the dotted line, she would be released.

Adam was out of the car and heading toward the facade
of the brick building even before disconnecting. The desk
sergeant directed him to the jail in the basement. The clerk
behind the window produced the form he needed to sign and
told him Eli would be brought up shortly. He took an uncomfortable chair next to the drinking fountain and waited.

Ten minutes later, a female jailer brought Eli to the
secure port and unlocked the door. Adam stood abruptly,
felt his gut clench at the sight of her. She looked rumpled
and exhausted and stressed. Smudges of fatigue shadowed
the area beneath eyes that were large and dark. She still
wore the jeans and turtleneck from the night before. Her
hair had come loose from its ponytail to hang in her face.
She signed her release form without looking at him. Without speaking to him.

Adam had absolutely no idea how to approach her. He
crossed to her as she signed the form claiming her belongings. "Are you all right?" he asked.

She didn't look at him. "I just want to get out of here."

"I don't blame you for being angry."

"What I am right now goes far beyond anger," she said.

"Look, Eli, I'm sorry you had to go through—"

"Don't." Her voice cut neatly, her eyes slashing to his.
"Just . . . take me home."

The window clerk passed Eli her coat and a small

brown envelope containing her things. Without speaking, Eli draped the coat over her arm and started for the door.

Adam followed, not sure what to do or say next. The only thing he knew for certain was that somehow he had to make things right.

The drive to her house was silent and tense. She sat quietly and stared out at the snowy landscape as if he weren't in the car with her. At her house, he parked the Tahoe curbside. By the time he got out, she was already on her way to the front door.

"Your giving me the silent treatment isn't going to help things," he said.

She unlocked the door and swung it open. "I guess I owe you a thank-you for bailing me out of jail." Her eyes met his as she stepped into the foyer and then turned to face him, blocking his way. "I hope it wasn't too much trouble."

"Damn it, Eli, if you'd just let me explain . . ."

"Leave. I want to be alone. I need to . . . I need to call a lawyer. I want to take a shower."

"We need to talk."

She started to close the door, but he stopped her by placing his hand on it. "I'm not leaving you like this."

"I don't want you here."

Adam pushed the door open, sending her back a step. "I don't care. I've got something to say and you're damn well going to listen."

Her hand shot out. He caught her wrist just in time to avoid a black eye, but her other hand grazed his left cheekbone. Cursing, he grasped both her wrists and backed her deeper into the foyer. "Cut it out," he growled.

"Damn you. Don't," she said, trying to twist away.

"Don't what? Try to explain what happened? Care about you?"

"If you cared, you wouldn't have left me to be caught by the police!" she shouted.

"I didn't have a choice."

"You left me alone in a situation I had no idea how to handle. I didn't know what to tell the police. I didn't know where you were." Her voice broke. "Damn you."

Adam relaxed his grip on her arms and she turned away. He stood there for a moment, watching her, but she didn't make a sound. Her shoulders were square, her back ramrod straight. He closed the door behind him. "I'm sorry," he said.

"You put me in an untenable situation."

"There were two security officers, Eli. They were between you and me, and there was no way I could get to you."

"So you left me."

"Do you think it would have improved our situation if both of us had been arrested?"

"Of course not, but maybe we could have explained——"

"I'm a cop, Eli. You know as well as I do that no amount of explaining would have prevented arrest. Cops are bound by the law. They don't get to pick and choose who they arrest."

She looked up at him with large, wet eyes. "I'm in serious legal trouble, Adam. I'm facing jail time. I need a lawyer. For God's sake, there's going to be a trial."

He knew better than to go to her, but the need to touch her overrode caution. She jolted when he put his hands on her shoulders and squeezed gently. "When we blow this thing wide open, you'll be exonerated, Eli. The lawyers call it extenuating circumstances. I'm willing to bet all charges against you will be dropped."

"Not without proof." Her expressioned turned ravaged. "What happened last night took away what little credibility I had left. Without credibility, there is absolutely nothing I can do to stop this."

"We'll stop it," he said. "I promise."

"Don't make promises you can't keep."

The urge to pull her into his arms was strong, but Adam resisted. He didn't want to get any more involved with her than he already was. She didn't know it, but he'd been going slowly out of his mind since last night, worrying about her.

"That's one promise I won't break," he said, and meant it.

chapter
21

THE WATER POUNDED DOWN ON HER IN A HOT, cleansing stream. Eli had been in jail a little over eight hours, but the place had left her feeling indescribably dirty. She soaped her body twice and was washing her hair for the second time when the water started to get cold. Shutting off the faucets, she quickly sloshed on some moisturizer, blow-dried her hair, and slipped into a pair of comfortable jeans and her favorite sweatshirt. A ponytail for her hair and she felt halfway human again.

At the base of the stairs, the smell of food gave her pause. Breakfast, if she wasn't mistaken. Adam must be feeling guilty, she thought. He didn't seem like a cooking kind of guy, yet he was braving her kitchen. She wasn't sure how she felt about that; she needed some time to mull it over.

Her stomach wasn't quite as discriminating and growled when she entered the kitchen. The sight of Adam standing at the stove in a pair of snug jeans and a faded flannel shirt stopped her dead in her tracks. Her heart did a weird little ping, then all the blood seemed to rush from her head and settle in her feet. Eli wasn't the kind of woman to go weak in the knees over a man no matter how good he looked. She was a mature, even-tempered creature. A scientist. A woman who prided herself on her analytical mind and logical thinking.

There wasn't anything analytical or logical about the thoughts running through her mind at the moment.

As if sensing her presence, he turned from the stove and gave her one of his almost smiles. "I was getting ready to send out the troops," he said. "I made coffee."

"I hope you don't think food is going to make everything all right."

"Of course not."

She held her ground a moment longer, then glanced over at the coffeemaker, desperate for caffeine. Snagging a cup from the bar, she padded to the stove. "What are you making?"

"Omelet." He used the spatula to fold the egg mixture. "The mushrooms are out of a jar." That not-quite smile again. "It's all you had."

"I'm not what you'd call much of a cook. I'm a Chinese-takeout kind of girl."

"Well, then, you're in luck."

She arched a brow. "You cook?"

Rolling his shoulder, he shot her a sheepish look. "Self-taught. Nothing too complicated. And only when I'm in deep shit."

"I guess this qualifies." She poured coffee into her cup. "I never had you pegged as the cooking type."

"It's the disability thing. I watched a lot of the cooking programs on cable." He shrugged. "A man has too much time on his hands, and he's got to make use of it."

She reached into the skillet and sampled some of the omelet. A little tingle of surprise went through her when she glanced over at the dining room table to find it perfectly set and two taper candles flickering.

"I figured I owe you after what happened," he said.

She didn't know what to say, wasn't even sure what she felt. He was making it difficult to stay angry, even if the last hours had destroyed a career she'd devoted the last ten years of her life to.

"I hated doing that to you, Eli." He shoveled omelets onto plates and carried them over to the table. "If it makes you feel any better, I was going out of my mind with worry."

"I'm going to have a record," she said quietly. "I'm ruined."

He stopped what he was doing and gave her a long, lingering look. "No, you're not."

She stared back. "Everything I've ever worked for is gone."

"This isn't over. Not by a long shot, so don't throw in the towel now."

The reality of everything that had happened in the last hours struck her like a wrecking ball. Hating it that she had to blink back tears, she turned away, hoping he didn't come to her because she suddenly needed him. She didn't want to need him, and she wasn't sure what that meant in terms of just how emotionally involved she had become.

Adam held his ground at the counter for several long moments, then said quietly, "You want to grab the toast?"

Taking a calming breath, she popped toast from the toaster and began to butter the bread. "I hope you know you're impressing me."

"I'm trying really hard. Have a seat."

Eli wasn't sure where all this was coming from, but it felt good. Being here with him. Doing ordinary things. Even with the arrest and the dark mystery surrounding Valazine hanging over her, she felt oddly comforted by the normalcy of the moment. Her legs were a little jittery when she walked over to the table and sat down.

He joined her a minute later. She watched as he tugged off her apron, draped it over the back of the chair next to him, and sat down. "Are you okay?" he asked.

"Better." She sipped some of the coffee, felt its warm embrace ease into her system. "The coffee is good."

Grimacing, he looked down at his plate. "Eli, I'm sorry about last night. I swear, if there had been another way—"

"You've already apologized, Adam. Let's just . . . not talk about it. Okay?"

He nodded.

She ate some of the omelet, realized after several bites that she was famished. When she looked up from her food, he was gazing steadily at her with dark, unsettling eyes. "What? Do I have jelly on my chin?" she asked.

"I'm just . . . not very good at this."

"Not good at what?"

He didn't answer for such a long time that for a moment Eli thought he wasn't going to. Then he said, "Being with you. Like this. It's . . . nice."

It wasn't poetry, but she knew the words hadn't come easily for him. And she knew he didn't speak words like that often. She wasn't sure what either of those things meant, but she was glad he'd said the words nonetheless.

"I wish the circumstances were different," he said.

Feeling awkward, she reached for her juice. "Me, too."

After a few minutes, Adam asked, "When you decided to go into research, why did you choose depression?"

She looked up from her food, met his gaze. "I've spent half of my life studying depression in one form or another. The causes. The treatments. The debilitating effects of it. How it affects people and their families and relationships. It's an insidious disease that's every bit as terrible and devastating as cancer. It eats people from the inside out and takes away every emotion except for hopelessness and despair. I've looked at it through the perspective of a doctor. But I know what it's like to see it from the inside, too. And that's a very different perspective."

"Personal experience?"

She should have expected a question like that from him. He was a cop, after all. But the question jolted her. It always jolted her to think of her mother. Even now, almost seventeen years after her death, the memory had the power to make her hands shake. "My mother struggled with bipolar disorder her entire adult life."

"That must have been tough."

"It was. She tried to hide it from me, but children are amazingly intuitive. I didn't understand, but I knew there was something wrong. She committed suicide when I was fifteen."

"I'm sorry."

"It's okay. I mean, it happened a long time ago. I'm okay now."

"Life makes an indelible impression of our minds when we're young."

"Death does, too."

"Yes, it does." He contemplated her for a moment. "What happened?"

Eli looked at him, trying to gauge his curiosity. She didn't usually talk about her mother; most people didn't ask. But then Adam wasn't most people. He didn't mind asking the hard questions.

She'd told herself a hundred times the pain could no longer touch her, could no longer twist her heart into knots. But it still did sometimes. No matter how far she ran from that little farmhouse in Indiana, the pain could still find her.

"If you don't want to talk about it, you don't have to," he said. "I probably shouldn't have asked."

"It's okay." She toyed with the egg on her plate. "I was fifteen years old when my mother slit her wrists. I found her like that. In the bathtub."

He stopped eating. "I'm sorry. I didn't mean to—"

"You didn't. Really. I mean, it happened a long time ago. I've come to terms." She took a sip of coffee, then met his gaze. "My mother was also an alcoholic. After having me, she suffered from severe postpartum depression and decided not to have any more children. She struggled with alcoholism. She was fine when she wasn't drinking. But when she was . . ."

Feeling her chest getting tight, took a breath, let it out slowly. "When she drank, things were bad. I mean, she was never abusive. Not in a physical sense, anyway. She just . . . hurt, and that pain radiated out to the people who loved her. By the time I started junior high school, she was out of control. She sought help toward the end, but by then she was seriously depressed. A few months after she began medication, she committed suicide. She was thirty-five years old."

"I'm sorry."

"So am I. So was everyone. But she's gone. I . . . healed. Life goes on. We've all moved on."

"What about your dad?"

"He still lives on the farm in Indiana. I drive down to see him every couple of months."

"Farm, huh?"

"Soybeans. Corn. Wheat fields." She smiled. "I led an exciting life growing up."

"You're very dedicated. You've made a difference. That's admirable, Eli."

Emotion rose unexpectedly. Because he was watching her, she shoved it aside, tried hard not to let it show. "I think Valazine could have been a good drug, Adam. I was so sure we'd finally broken through. Instead, I feel as if I've created a monster."

"What happened with Valazine isn't your fault. You didn't do anything wrong."

"It was my responsibility." Eli hated it that she had to blink back tears. She knew it was the fatigue nipping at her emotions, the stress of the last few days tearing her down. She didn't cry at the drop of a hat. But in the last days she felt as if she'd been turned inside out and scraped raw.

Rising, he came around behind her and pulled out her chair. "Come here."

"I'm okay."

"I know you are." Still, he eased her to her feet, then turned her so that she was facing him. When she didn't meet his gaze, he lifted her chin with his fingers. "Let me tell you something," he began. "You don't know where your research on Valazine will take the pharmaceutical industry in the future. You've had a setback. Maybe with some additional research, the next generation of drug—"

"ROT-535," she put in.

"Maybe ROT-535 will be the drug that eradicates depression . . . at least as we know it."

"I can't hang my hopes on that, Adam. For Valazine to cause that kind of violent behavior . . . there has to be an inherent flaw in the chemical structure. Something I missed during the trials."

"Information someone withheld from you."

"Whatever the case, I won't know how to fix it until I can narrow down the specific chemical or chemical combination that's causing the behavior. That could take years." She searched his face. "In the interim, we've got to get it off the market. We can't let this go on."

"I know."

"I've got to stop it. I just . . . oh, God, Adam, I don't know how to stop it. I don't know if I can. I feel so damn helpless, and I hate it."

Gently, he pressed his index finger to her lips. "Easy. We'll get to the bottom of it."

She turned her head, dislodging his finger. "People are dying. We're running out of time—"

"You haven't slept in over twenty-four hours, Eli. You need to rest. This isn't going to be a quick thing. Roth isn't going to voluntarily pull Valazine off the shelves."

"Then I'll force them. I'll find a way. Damn it, I'll talk to Peter if I have to drive over to his house. If he refuses to listen, then I'll go to the FDA. If they don't act, I'll take it to the media." Her head swam with all the things she needed to do. "Adam, I can't wait until we have proof. We've got to act now."

When she started to turn, he reached for her and stopped her. "You're not going to be any good to anyone if you drive yourself to exhaustion."

"How in God's name can I rest when I know people are dying? We haven't even begun to research other countries that might be involved. What about Europe, Mexico, and Canada?"

"Eat your breakfast. Get a few hours' sleep. When we're rested, we'll think this through and decide how to do this."

Eli knew he was right. She couldn't function much longer without food and sleep. She wasn't going to do their cause justice without having a solid plan in place. Rushing out and confronting Peter Roth or going to the FDA without proof wouldn't accomplish anything except, perhaps, discrediting her further.

"Okay. Damn it. Okay." She lowered herself back into her chair. Even though she was no longer hungry, she picked up her fork and forced herself to eat. Adam went back to his chair and sat.

"I want to meet with Peter Roth," she said after a minute.

"We need to keep in mind that he could be involved."

"I still need to talk to him. It's worth a shot."

"All right. What about the FDA?"

"I can start by filing a post-marketing adverse experience report. To do that I need an identifiable patient, an identifiable reporter, a suspect drug or biological product—in this case Valazine—and an adverse event or fatal outcome." She looked at him. "I want to use the cases you brought to me."

"I did the research. It's there. I think it's compelling. How long will it take to get these reports together?"

"We should be able to finish in a few hours. I can get the forms on-line. You've got most of the other information. If I could just get Peter Roth or Kevin to cooperate, I think it would help us tremendously."

"I don't think that will happen," he said. "They've got too much at stake."

"You're probably right, but I've got to try."

Adam smiled at her. "I think we just came up with a plan."

ADAM SAT AT THE DINING ROOM TABLE AND watched the digital clock on the stove change to midnight. He could hear computer keys clicking in the study where Eli was entering data and printing the forms she'd completed and would be filing with the FDA. He looked up when she entered and tried not to notice the quick jump of pleasure at the sight of her.

"I finished entering all the data," she said. "The reports look good."

She looked tired, he thought. Circles of fatigue ringed her eyes. She'd been at it all day without sleep. They hadn't eaten since early morning, but she hadn't wanted to stop working.

"Tomorrow I'll send the reports via overnight delivery." She pulled out the chair opposite him. "I've got a contact at the FDA. I'll give her a call, see if she will expedite things. Unfortunately, the FDA isn't known for its speediness."

Several times throughout the day, Adam had found himself watching her as she worked. She was single-minded, focused, and driven as hell. Not only did she have a quick, logical mind that demanded his respect, but a genuine passion for her work. Dr. Elizabeth Barnes was the most fascinating woman he'd ever met.

"I need coffee," she said.

He watched her walk to the kitchen and pour a cup of coffee, liking the way the denim stretched taut over her hips. He wondered what it would feel like to run his hands over some of those curves. He thought about the other night when she'd kissed him, felt his sex grow heavy.

Realizing he was staring at her—and that she'd noticed—he looked down at the papers in front of him aware of his heart beating rapidly in his chest. Abruptly, the house seemed too warm. The dining room too small. Adam had never been claustrophobic, but he suddenly felt as if the dining room walls were closing in on him.

"I need to get some air," he said, rising.

Eli looked up; her expression surprised and a little puzzled. He didn't give her a chance to say anything. Leaving the kitchen, he stalked to the hall closet, pulled out his coat, then opened the front door. The night embraced him with icy fingers as he made his way down the sidewalk to the Tahoe. What the hell was he thinking, lusting after a main player in what could conceivably become the biggest case of his life? He was in no position to be thinking of her in sexual terms. After the fiasco with Shelly and Chad, Adam had no desire to take on a relationship. He didn't need the headache. He sure as hell didn't need the complication.

What he needed was sex. Hot, sweaty sex with one stipulation: no expectations. Only he didn't think Eli was the kind of woman to partake in sex for the sake of sex. While a roll in the hay with her might scratch an itch that had been driving him nuts for days now, it would also jeopardize his goal. Thinking of Michael, he realized screwing up the investigation was the one thing he wasn't willing to do no matter how bad he had it for the good doctor.

Cursing beneath his breath, he started toward the house. On the porch, he stomped the snow from his shoes, then opened the door. He hung his coat, then walked into the living room. The sight of Eli curled on the sofa fast asleep stopped him cold. Her lashes were dark against her pale cheek. Her ponytail had come loose and her hair spread out over the arm of the sofa. She lay propped against a pile of throw pillows with her knees drawn up to her chest. From where he stood, he had a perfect view of her ass, the soft curve of her hip.

For an instant, he didn't know what to do. Walk away. Wake her. But Adam knew if he went to her, if he touched her, he wouldn't be strong enough to walk away. He didn't want to screw this up. Not the case. Not the tentative partnership he'd found with Eli. But the draw to her was powerful, stronger than him, and for the first time in three long years he felt like maybe he was willing to take a chance.

"Eli."

She jerked awake instantly, sat up and looked at him through wide, sleepy eyes. "Oh. Jeez, I . . . conked out for a minute."

"You okay?" His voice sounded like a rusty hinge.

"Fine." She grappled for her glasses, shoved them onto her nose. "I was waiting for you to come back in so we could—"

"I think we ought to call it a night."

Yawning, she rose. "I'm sorry I fell asleep. I could make some coffee—"

"No. I've got to go. I'll be back in the morning."

"Oh, well. Okay." Her brows went together. "It's late, Adam. Do you want to stay here tonight?"

Something must have registered in his expression because an instant later, she clarified. "I mean, you could sack out in the guestroom."

"No. I'd better go."

But Adam didn't move, and neither did she. His intellect told him to turn around and get the hell out of there. Something inside him that wielded a hell of a lot more clout told him to stay put. Vaguely, he was aware of his heart beating hard in his chest. Of the hot rush of blood to his groin. A little voice in the back of his head telling him he was about to make a very bad mistake.

He didn't realize he was going to move until he'd already taken a step toward her. Her eyes widened, but she didn't retreat, and Adam didn't stop. He didn't stop when he reached her. And he didn't stop with touching her.

He gripped her shoulders, ran his hands down her arms and back up again. The contact went through him like a lightning strike. She shivered, but he knew instinctively it wasn't from the cold. Then his hands were on her face, cradling her lovely face. He stared down into her eyes, seeking something elusive. Something he would be a fool for finding.

"If you want to run, Dr. Barnes, now is the time to do it." His voice was rough as gravel, low as the rumble of thunder.

"I'm not afraid of you," she whispered.

"You should be," he said, and lowered his mouth to hers.

chapter
22

ELI HAD BEEN KISSED BY MEN BEFORE. THE JOINING of male-female lips was not a new thing to her. She'd been kissed plenty of times in her thirty-one years. But no kiss had ever kicked the air from her lungs and turned her legs to water in two seconds flat. No kiss had ever made her heart pound so hard that she thought he might have to pick her up off the floor if she didn't get a grip.

Adam Boedecker's kisses were an all-out assault on her senses, and if she wasn't careful she was going to lose her head and let this get out of hand.

She felt his hands rake through her hair. Warm fingers brushing her scalp, then skimming down her nape, touching her shoulders, and moving lower. All the while his mouth plundered. He wasn't a shy kisser. He was bold and sexual and wasn't the least bit hesitant about letting her know what he wanted. In the back of her mind she knew that was a problem. For the life of her she couldn't remember why.

She gasped when his hands slipped under her sweatshirt and cupped her breasts. Logic told her to pull away and put a stop to this before things went too far, but the sudden explosion of pleasure was so intense, her protest came out as a moan. She arched against him. He was like granite against her. She could feel his arousal, a steel rod against her belly. Feel his hot breath against her cheek.

She accepted his tongue, tasted male frustration and lust. Her hands roamed over the solid span of rock-hard shoulders where his muscles quivered with tension. Within her, pleasure warred a bloody battle with control. Eli didn't want to relinquish her control, but she could feel it slipping, feel the mindless draw of passion overwhelming her.

She assured herself she could handle this, that she wasn't out of her element. She was a mature woman; she could handle a simple kiss. But Eli knew there wasn't anything simple about this moment. About what she was feeling. About the man who now held her in his arms.

His mouth wreaked havoc on her willpower. Her body melted beneath the onslaught of pleasure. She went wet between her legs. Need turned to desperation. And for the first time in her life she didn't care about logic or intellect or right and wrong.

A sound tore from her throat when he trapped her nipples between his thumbs and forefingers. The rush of blood from her head made her dizzy. The throb of heat between her legs ached with every beat of her heart.

Abruptly, she felt her sweatshirt lifted over her head. She raised her arms, let him slip it from her body. Out of the corner of her eye, she saw him toss the shirt onto the back of a chair a few feet away. Then his mouth found her breast. Eli jerked hard at the initial shock of pleasure. He suckled her hard, nipping with his teeth. She arched, giving him better access. Her hands went to the back of his head and pressed him closer. She threw her head back, felt her body begin to contract.

His tongue flicked over the sensitized tip of her breast. Eli grappled for control, felt it slip and tumble. She writhed in his arms, wanting him closer, desperate for him to be inside her. She heard a mewling sound, realized it had come from her.

His fingers fumbled with the button of her jeans. His hands were trembling, she realized, and felt a surge of feminine power that she could make a man like Adam Boedecker shake. Impatient, she helped him, unfastening the button, then lowering the zipper. She closed her eyes when his hand moved over her mound. Powerful waves built low in her belly. Her panties were wet against her. The contractions were building again. The need for release tormented her.

Wanting to give him the same pleasure he was giving her, she reached for him, wrapped her fingers around his shaft through his trousers. He jerked once against her, then began to move.

The blood rushed like a white-water rapid in her ears. She squeezed her eyes tightly shut when his fingers separated her. She clung to control by a thread, knowing it was a battle she would lose. And she knew the loss would be devastating and irrevocable when it came.

She cried out when his finger slicked over her and found her center. She tried to breathe, but her lungs refused oxygen. The waves built relentlessly. High waves that washed over her, tumbling her, so that she didn't know up from down. Her breaths rushed between clenched teeth. The pleasure was so intense, she had to withhold a scream as the waves crested and broke.

"Not . . . here," he ground out.

His words registered slowly in a brain overloaded with sensation. She wasn't sure how she managed it, but Eli opened her eyes and looked at him.

He stared back at her, his expression tense. "I want you in bed," he said. "Right now."

"Adam, I—"

Her words died in her throat when he stroked her. Deeply and with the kind of precision that sent an electrical shock through her body. Eli opened to him, clung to him, silently begged him to finish what he'd begun.

"You . . . don't play . . . fair," she whispered.

His eyes burned into hers as he stroked her. "Not when I want something as badly as I want you right now."

The beleaguered remnants of her logical mind surfaced, then were lost again in a churning sea of sensation when he slipped two fingers inside her. Eli saw stars, then he retreated like a cruel army drawing out the final battle.

"Let's finish this upstairs," he said.

Eli knew sleeping with him would be a mistake. A bad mistake that could cause problems she couldn't fathom at the moment. But she also knew that buried beneath the hard words and brooding demeanor lay a decent man who'd seen more than his share of pain. A man determined to do the right thing even if it meant giving up his own career to do it.

In answer, she took his mouth in a kiss and he swept her into his arms.

ADAM WASN'T SURE HOW HE MADE IT UP THE STEPS with Eli in his arms and her mouth fastened to his, but he did. Dully, he was aware of the roar of blood in his ears. The hot jet of lust in his veins. The taste of her on his tongue. The wetness from her body on his fingers.

He'd known lust before. Different degrees of it with different women for an array of reasons, some purely physical, some not. Yet he'd never experienced anything like this. The violent churn of need in his gut every time she looked at him. He told himself the chemistry between them was so powerful because he'd been celibate for three years. But Adam knew that wasn't the only reason. And he knew better than to ponder the explanation too closely at a time like this.

Once upstairs, he stumbled into the hall, used his foot to open the first door.

"Wrong room," Eli said.

"I don't care." He started into the room.

"Bigger bed in my room."

That stopped him, changed his mind.

Eli smiled. "Last door on the right."

Moving quickly now, he carried her down the hall and shoved open the door with his hip. Light filtered into the room through the two windows facing the street. He saw frilly curtains. An armoire and mirrored dresser that were shadows in his peripheral vision. A big poster bed piled with fussy pillows. He carried her to the bed. Eli slid to her feet and faced him.

Adam was breathing hard, blood pounding like a drum

in his veins. The lust was like a beast inside him, caged and ranting and frantic to be free. He gazed down at her breasts. They were large and rounded with tiny, pointed nipples. Her waist was small enough to span with his hands. Lower, her belly was flat where her jeans were unzipped and open.

He wanted to devour her. Wanted to throw her onto the bed, plunge into her, and finish it. Instead, he looked into her eyes. In the instant before she dropped her gaze, he saw the spike of nerves. Adam had never considered himself intuitive when it came to women, but he knew discomfort when he saw it and it was suddenly very important to him to know she wanted this as badly as he did.

Reaching out, he cupped her cheek. "You're nervous."

"I . . . never do this," she said.

"Neither do I."

"I'm not very good at it."

If she hadn't been so serious, he might have laughed. But because she looked so vulnerable, because there were butterflies in his own stomach, he didn't. "If you make love half as good as you kiss, I'd say we're in for some mind-blowing sex."

She laughed self-consciously, and the sound was musical in the silence of the room. "I don't think I've ever had that before."

"I think we're in for quite a treat."

She was beautiful in the semidarkness. Her eyes revealed an odd mix of desire and uncertainty. He drank in the sight of her, felt her beauty touch him in a place he'd always thought was untouchable.

Lowering his hand, he brushed the side of her breast with the tops of his fingers, watched the dark tip pucker. Adam stared at her, awed that such a lovely creature would have him.

"You're beautiful," he said.

She smiled. It was such an open smile. Trusting. Sincere. For a moment, he considered telling her this could never mean anything to either of them, that this was just sex, a man and a woman reaching out during a time of high stress. But he didn't.

Not wanting to deal with repercussions, he leaned forward and took her breast into his mouth, laving the hardened peak with his tongue. He heard her gasp, felt her shudder. His hands shook as he worked her jeans down her hips. Her panties were plain. But he'd never been more aroused by the sight of practical white cotton in his life.

When she was naked, he stepped back, wanting to look at her, wanting to remember her. He could tell his perusal embarrassed her, but he couldn't look away. Hesitant, she reached for the snap of his slacks. Adam allowed her to undress him. He shivered when she ran her hands over his chest and down his belly to his penis. He growled low in his throat when she cupped him. He grasped her wrist when she closed her hand around him.

"It's been a long time for me," he ground out.

She looked into his eyes, and he knew she was trying to understand.

"Me, too," she said.

"I haven't been with anyone since . . . I was shot." He wasn't sure why he told her that. Maybe because he wanted an excuse if things didn't work out the way he'd planned. Maybe because suddenly he was ridiculously, excruciatingly nervous.

"Come to bed." She turned and slipped under the covers. Adam followed. The sheets were cool against his skin. Her leg brushed against his as she leaned over to light the candle on the night table. Her flesh was like satin against him. He smelled vanilla on her flesh. The lemon scent of her shampoo. His every sense seemed sharpened, heightened to a fever pitch.

He moved against her, his penis sliding against warm, soft skin. Urgency burned him, and he felt his control falter. He kissed her, drove his tongue deep into her. She accepted him, making a small sound of pleasure in her throat. He plundered her mouth, her throat, her breasts. When he moved lower, she raised her arms above her head and closed her eyes. He kissed her belly, dipped his tongue into her navel, moved lower, leaving a wet trail all the way to the dark vee of her curls.

"Adam . . . wait." She started to sit up, but he moved quickly between her thighs.

"I want all of you," he said.

Her small sound of protest barely reached him as he spread her knees. Opening her, he dipped two fingers into the hot center of her. She tensed, but he didn't stop. She cried out when he put his mouth on her. He flicked once with his tongue, and she jolted hard against him. He kissed her there, deeply, exploring her soft wetness in the most intimate way a man could touch a woman. As if from a distance, he heard her cry out his name. Once. Twice. She rose up to meet him. He felt her contract, her body going rigid. She crested an instant later. He feasted on her, suckling and nipping and tonguing until she writhed beneath him, mindless with pleasure.

She was still trembling when he moved over her. She opened to him. He kissed her hard on the mouth, then pulled back to look at her, felt something primal and possessive stir deep in his gut. "You're mine." He didn't know why he said it, barely recognized his own voice.

She stared up at him, her face flushed. Perspiration beaded on her forehead. Her eyes were glazed with pleasure. His heart did a weird little dip when she smiled.

"This time we go together." Never taking his eyes from hers, he pushed into her.

Adam thought he'd been prepared for the assault on his senses. He thought he remembered just how intense lovemaking could be between a man and a woman. But the tight heat gripping him tested his control. Shook his resolve to take it slow, make it last. Dizziness swooped down on him as the blood rushed from his head. He closed his eyes against the intensity and moved within her, into the deepest reaches of her with long, steady strokes. He felt the climax building, knew it was too soon, but he couldn't stop, couldn't slow.

Vaguely, he heard her cry out. He felt her rising up to meet him. Flesh slapping against flesh. Hard against soft. Grinding his teeth, he pumped into her. He heard his own voice, realized he'd cried out her name. Not once, but twice and then too many times to count.

An instant later, he reached the precipice, and free-fell into oblivion.

chapter
23

ELI DREAMED OF ADAM. SENSUAL DREAMS THAT made her thrash and sweat and tremble for his touch. Dreams that made her breasts ache and sent hot pangs of longing to her womb . . .

She jerked awake abruptly, unsettled by the intensity of the dream, keenly aware that she was aroused. Stretching languidly, she reached for him only to find the bed empty. Confused, she sat up and shoved the hair from her eyes. Dim light from the streetlamp slanted in through the windows, casting the room in shadows. A look at the clock beside the bed told her it was three A.M.

She could hear the wind outside ripping around the house. The sound of the furnace pumping heat through the vents. Another sound caused her to cock her head and listen. The shower, she realized. Not the one adjoining her bedroom, but off the guest room down the hall.

Puzzled, she got up and slipped into her terry robe, knotting it at her waist as she left the room. Down the hall, light seeped through the open door of the guest bedroom. Why on earth hadn't he used the shower in her room? Why take a shower at three o'clock in the morning in the first place?

Wondering if, perhaps, he hadn't been able to sleep— and didn't want to wake her—she stepped into the guest bedroom. The bathroom door was ajar and dim light bled through the opening. She hesitated an instant before knocking. "Adam?"

No answer.

She knocked again. "Adam? Is everything all right?"

That was when she heard the sound. The kind of sound that made the hair at the back of her neck stand on end. Not quite a moan. Quieter than a cry. Concerned, she pushed open the door. The shower was running. The lighting was somehow wrong. Eli looked over at the vanity lights above the sink. Three of the four bulbs were dark, as if someone had unscrewed the bulbs. Puzzled, she glanced over toward the glassed in shower. "Adam?"

"Get out."

The words were barely audible. Frightened now, she stepped into the room and started toward the shower. "Adam? What's wrong?"

She reached the stand-up shower, expecting to see his silhouette through the glass block. When she didn't, she opened the door and gasped. Adam was lying on the floor with his knees drawn up to his chest, nakcd. Cold water rained down on him, but he didn't even seem to notice. He raised his head at the sound of her voice and looked at her with ravaged eyes.

"What happened?" she asked.

"Get the fuck out."

"Adam, my God . . ." Eli turned off the shower, then knelt beside him. "Are you sick?"

He didn't answer. Just lay there with his head in his hands, breathing hard, like a wounded animal waiting to die.

Shaken, Eli reached for a bath towel and laid it over his hips. "Please, Adam, tell me what happened."

"Migraine . . ."

Understanding dawned, followed by a stir of compassion so strong it brought tears to her eyes. One of her college roommates had suffered with migraines. Eli remembered clearly how debilitating they'd been. "What can I do? Is there medication? What?"

At some point, he'd been sick and vomited. She could smell it, see the spill on the floor next to the commode. Pity stirred inside her. She hated seeing him like this. Hated seeing such a strong man helpless and laid out on the floor by pain so terrible it paralyzed him.

"Turn out the goddamn light," he growled.

Realizing the single burning bulb was making his pain worse, she rose and hurried to turn the light off. When her back was to him, she heard him retch, and a wave of pity washed over her. She grabbed a washcloth out of the cabinet and wet it with cool water. Kneeling next to him, she lifted his head and wiped his mouth.

"What can I do?" she asked.

"My briefcase . . . downstairs."

Even in the dim light she could see that his face was contorted with pain. He was trembling. She didn't know if it was from pain or cold. She grabbed another towel from the rack and covered his torso with it. "I'll be right back."

He stopped her by grabbing her wrist. "I didn't . . . want this to happen. Not tonight."

Only then did she see the humiliation etched into his features. And suddenly it was very important to her to let him know this didn't make her think any less of him.

"It's okay," she said, feeling helpless and inept. "You're soaking wet. Let me help you into the bedroom."

"Just . . . let me lie here for a moment. Get my briefcase," he ground out. "Bring it."

"Are you sure you'll be all right?"

She looked down at him, saw misery on his face. His eyes closed tightly against the agony. His jaws were clenched. His hands bunched into fists. "Just . . . go," he said.

Knowing there was nothing more she could do for him, she rose and strode into the hall. She took the steps two at a time, and rushed into the dining room. His briefcase sat on the kitchen table where he'd left it. Eli grabbed it and carried it back up the steps. In the bathroom, she plugged in the night-light so she could see, then set the briefcase on the counter.

"What do you need?" she asked.

"Syringe."

Quickly, she rummaged through papers and file folders, finally finding the packaged prefilled syringe in a small pocket. She read the wrapper and frowned. *Sumatriptan. Six milligrams.* A powerful migraine abortive.

Unwrapping it, she took it over to him. "You didn't tell me you suffered from serious migraines."

"You never asked."

"Sit up."

He didn't move. "Give me the goddamn thing."

She handed him the syringe. "Can you manage?"

Slowly, he eased himself to an upright position, then jabbed the needle into his thigh and depressed the plunger.

"How long does it take to work?" she asked.

"Too long."

Though neurological medicine was not her specialty, she knew enough about migraines to know he would sleep once the medication kicked in. "Let me put you in bed."

He didn't answer. Just leaned against the tile with his eyes closed.

"I'll get you some ice. Please, Adam, you're wet. Let me get you dry and into bed."

For a full minute he didn't move, didn't speak. Then, holding his head perfectly still, he got to his knees, then slowly to his feet. His face was pale and drawn. She rose with him, ready to move quickly if he showed signs of collapsing.

"It's stupid not to ask for help when you need it." Grabbing one of the towels, she dried as much of him as she could. Starkly aware that he was naked, she wrapped a dry towel around his waist and secured it.

"No one ever accused me of being smart." When he swayed, Eli put her arm around his waist. Even weak with pain, his body was as hard and unyielding as granite.

He didn't lean on her, but she took on as much of his weight as she could. Slowly, she helped him to her bed-

room, then into bed. Once he was lying down, she toweled
his hair, then left the room and went downstairs. She had
a gel pack in the freezer left over from when she'd pulled
a muscle at her aerobics class. Removing the pack, she
wrapped it in a towel and returned to the bedroom upstairs.

He was lying on his back with his eyes closed when
she walked in. "I've got a cold pack," she said.

"Won't help." But he didn't protest when she set it high
on his forehead.

The grandfather clock in the living room clanged four
times. The wind clawed at the bedroom window. Her
heart went out to Adam when he groaned and shoved the
ice pack aside.

Eli sat beside the bed and watched him for a long time.
She saw his body slowly relax as the pain medication
flowed into his bloodstream and began to work. His
breathing returned to normal. The tight clench of his jaw
eased. The lines between his brows smoothed out.

She was about to rise and go downstairs when he whispered her name and reached for her hand. The gesture
shouldn't have meant so much to her, but because of the
kind of man he was, the humanness of it brought tears to
her eyes. He'd touched her in so many ways in the last
hours. Intimately. Emotionally. She'd opened up and let
him inside. Her mind. Her body. Her heart. She didn't
know where that would lead or what it would mean in
terms of their relationship.

All she knew was that she'd come to care for him more
than she'd ever imagined possible. More than she wanted
to. And a lot more than was wise.

She held his hand for a long time after he'd gone to
sleep.

ADAM WOKE TO DARKNESS AND THE MEMORY OF
vivid pain. His temples throbbed, but the lingering pain
was manageable. If he'd learned anything in the aftermath
of the shooting, it was that pain was a relative thing and
could always get worse.

He lay still for a moment, careful not to move too quickly, orienting himself. He remembered the sex next. The intensity of the physical pleasure. The way she'd looked at him when she'd come. He remembered the sweetness of her mouth. The taste of her body. The feel of soft flesh beneath his hands.

If some jerk hadn't been inside his head with a jackhammer, he might have smiled. Yes, he thought, sex with Eli after three years of celibacy had definitely been worth the wait.

Cautiously, he eased to a sitting position and looked over at the alarm clock on the night table. Seven o'clock. He stared at the clock, wondering if it were morning or evening. He couldn't count the number of times he'd wakened in a migraine-induced stupor in the last three years not knowing if it was night or day.

Goddamn migraines.

Feeling slightly better knowing he could move without his head exploding, he eased his legs over the side of the bed and stood. A moment of dizziness, then the room leveled. He found some oral medication in his briefcase and swallowed two pills. He brushed his teeth, then showered by the dim light of a seashell night-light, letting warm water pound down on him.

He wasn't sure how he felt about what had happened between them. The sex had been good. Better than good, if he wanted to be truthful about it. Maybe even one of the most erotic experiences of his life.

But he couldn't let a night of hot sex interfere with the case. Hopefully, she felt the same and wouldn't let what had happened between them affect their working together. But Adam didn't put a whole lot of weight in that hope. Women got weird when it came to sex. They liked to analyze and inject all sorts of complex emotions into it. Adam preferred to keep things simple; he didn't want to get sidetracked and could only hope Eli was logical enough to see things the same way.

Twenty minutes later, he found her in the living room, hunched over her laptop. She looked up when he entered and smiled. "Hi."

She looked happy to see him. That should have pleased him, but it didn't. He wasn't sure why having a pretty woman smile at him bothered him, but it did. Maybe because he was a twisted son of a bitch. He wished he was in a better mood, but he wasn't, so he said nothing.

"Did you get some sleep?" she asked.

"I guess that depends on if it's seven A.M. or seven P.M."

"P.M.," she said.

"Well, in that case I got about sixteen hours of sleep."

She was wearing a gray pullover and matching drawstring pants. Her hair was pulled into a ponytail, but strands of it fell forward to frame her face. Her glasses sat on the end of her nose. Next to her, a stack of manila folders sat atop a TV tray. She shouldn't have looked sexy, but she did.

Looking at him the way a mother would look at a sick child, she unfolded her legs and stood. "How are you feeling?"

Embarrassed. Humiliated. A little mean. "Better," he said.

"You look better."

He entered the living room, annoyed because he was feeling awkward. "Sorry I threw up all over your bathroom floor."

"It wasn't a problem."

"But it can sure as hell put a damper on a night of sex, can't it?"

"It's not a big deal."

"Yeah, well, you weren't the one throwing up." He strolled over to the TV tray and picked up one of the manila folders, barely looked at it, then set it down. "I guess cleaning it up wasn't that much fun, either, though, was it?"

Her expression turned cautious. "I wish you'd drop it."

"Consider it dropped."

"You're angry," she said. "I don't know why."

"Migraines put me in a pissy mood."

"Thanks for the warning."

He turned to face her. "Don't expect anything from me."

She watched him warily. Prey watching a predator about to strike. "I don't know what you mean."

"I'm not relationship material," he said flatly.

One thin, dark brow arched. "Well, I appreciate your pointing that out to me. Not that I hadn't already figured it out on my own—after all, I *am* a scientist. But, for your information, I wasn't going to ask you to marry me this week. Probably not next week either. So rest assured that you haven't crushed my hopes."

Adam didn't appreciate the smart-assed response. He wasn't in the mood, and his temper stirred. "Just so we can both consider it a closed subject."

"You know what? I'm not going to let you push my buttons."

"Buttons aside, I want you to know where I stand."

"I don't think you even know where you stand."

"I stand alone. That's all you need to know."

"Why are you so angry?" she asked.

"Because I'm a son of a bitch. Because that's who I am. It's what I do."

"Really? Well, I hate to break this to you, but that isn't who you were last night."

The response knocked him off-kilter, but only for an instant. "Last night was about sex. Don't get it mixed up with something else. I'm not a touchy-feely kind of guy."

She deflected the blow by rolling her eyes, but he knew he'd scored a direct hit and hurt her. He wanted to believe that was satisfying, but it wasn't. "I'm not someone you want to get involved with," he said. "I'm doing you a favor by telling you this now."

"I can do without your granting me favors."

"At the very least I owe you honesty."

"You don't owe me a damn thing."

"Look, Eli . . . things happen. People get caught up in them. I don't want that to happen with us. I'm being honest. Take my word for it; I hurt the people I care about."

"You cared about your brother. Now I see you risking everything to clear his name. I see you risking your life to get a dangerous drug off the market. If that makes you a son of a bitch, then I'd say your definition is skewed."

That she would argue the point stopped him cold. He felt his hands clench into fists at his sides. He wanted to strike out at her, he realized. He wanted to hurt her, drive her away. He didn't want her getting too close. For God's sake, he didn't want to have to deal with his own feelings for her. It was easier to be alone where he didn't have to deal with anyone's feelings but his own. These days, that was a full-time job.

"I don't want to hurt you," he ground out.

"Don't insult me by thinking you have that kind of power," she snapped.

The statement struck an unexpected blow. Adam stared at her, disconcerted and speechless and ruthlessly angry. She stared back, smaller but every bit as fierce.

"You don't know what you're getting into," he said.

"I'm a big girl. I'll figure it out."

For a moment he considered telling her about the shooting. About the traumatic brain injury and ensuing rehabilitation that had turned his life upside down and changed him forever. About the lingering aftereffects he would have to deal with for the rest of his life.

But for whatever reason, he didn't want to discuss it with her. Didn't want to bring it into the conversation. It would only excuse what he was. Would only give her a reason to forgive him. He didn't want her forgiveness.

But after what had happened between them the night before, he figured she deserved the truth. If she was half as smart as he thought she was, she'd walk away from him and not look back.

For her sake, he hoped she did exactly that.

ELI SHOULD HAVE KNOWN HE WOULD BE RAW. THAT he would be like a wounded animal, snarling in pain and ready to tear to shreds any hand that tried to help, including hers. She could only imagine how hard it had been for him to be helpless and vulnerable. Part of her understood his anger, his need to strike out. But his words hurt.

She could tell by his body language that he was still in pain. She'd taken a crash course on migraines on the Internet while he'd slept and had a pretty good idea of the kind of agony they caused, the kind of havoc they could wreak on someone's life.

Refusing to look at him, she concentrated on ladling soup into bowls. At the table, Adam brooded over the papers he'd dragged out of his briefcase. She poured soft drinks, then carried the food to him. He shoved the papers into folders, then set them in his briefcase and closed it. For several minutes they ate in silence.

"How long have you suffered from migraines?" she asked.

He shot her an annoyed look. Sympathy cooled what little anger remained when she saw that he was still pale. His dark eyes and five o'clock shadow were a stark contrast to his complexion. She saw tension in the tight set of his jaw and felt another stir of compassion.

"Three years," he said. "Since I got shot."

"A head injury?"

He sighed, looked resigned for a moment. "Traumatic brain injury." He touched the area behind his ear on the left side. "A fifteen-year-old kid put a Saturday night special against my head and pulled the trigger."

"I didn't know." She looked down at her food, felt her appetite wane. "I'm sorry."

"Bullet went in behind and below my left ear. Slug penetrated my skull and lodged near the left temporal lobe. The frontal lobes control memory, speech, and comprehension. The parietal lobes located at the back of the head and above the ear control the ability to read, write, and understand. Well, the son of a bitch got lucky and damaged both, including the area in between the two lobes that regulate movement and sensation."

Even though she wasn't a medical doctor; Eli knew how the brain worked, knew fully how devastating a traumatic brain injury could be. "How bad was the damage?"

The only indication of tension he gave her was the flexing of his jaw. "I was in a coma for five weeks. I lost some of my memory. Short-term stuff, mostly. I don't remember anything that happened in the six months preceding the shooting."

"I'm sorry. That must have been terrible."

"After I woke up and they got me off the respirator, I spent the next few weeks in diapers slobbering all over myself and anyone else who got close enough. There were times when I thought death would have been more humane."

The slash of pain came brutal and swift, like someone putting a bayonet through her chest. "Don't say that."

He shrugged. "A lot of people thought it. Cops. Guys I'd worked with most of my adult life. My friends and family. I could see it in their eyes when they came to see me. They just didn't have the guts to say it."

"Did you lose motor functions?"

He looked away from her then to stare out the French door off the patio at the snowy landscape beyond. "I had to relearn almost everything. How to walk. How to talk. How to feed myself. How to dress." He sighed heavily, and Eli thought she heard a tinge of emotion in the rush of breath through his teeth. "The neurologists didn't think I'd ever walk again. They sure as hell didn't think I'd be a cop." He laughed, but it was a dark, humorless sound. "I guess the jury's still out on that, though, isn't it?"

"What about your family? I mean, did you have someone to help you through this?"

"I was married."

She tried to hide her shock. "You're not still . . ."

"I may be a lot of things, but an adulterer isn't one of them." He shot her a wan smile. "I'm divorced."

She looked down at her hands, fought back the slow burn of tears. She hurt for him. A deep pain that throbbed like a wound in her chest. She wanted to let him know that his past injury didn't make any difference to her, but didn't know how.

Rising abruptly to hide the tears that had broken free, she gathered the bowl and silverware and carried them to the sink. "What you did . . . what you overcame. That's incredibly admirable," she said when her back was to him.

"Depends on your point of view. Nurses thought I was a pain in the ass."

A pent-up laugh choked out of her. "Somehow I can see that." Then she sobered again. "I don't know how you can make light of something like that."

"Lots of practice. Something like that happens in your life and you take stock. You decide what's important. You learn to let the little things go."

She jolted when he walked up behind her and put his hands on her shoulders. "Turn around," he said.

Eli knew what would happen if she turned around, if she looked into those dark, troubled eyes. While she longed to do just that, another part of her feared it. Never in her life had she lost control the way she had last night. This man had taken her apart piece by piece, atom by atom, and she could only pray that she would be able put all the pieces back together when he walked out of her life.

He didn't wait for her to turn, and he didn't ask again. He simply turned her to face him. She sought his gaze, felt the power of it all the way down to her toes. "I'm sorry you had to go through that," she said. "It must have terribly difficult."

"I'm okay now," he said simply. "The migraines are bad, but they don't come often like they used to. Maybe two or three a month. I can live with that."

"What brings them on? Stress? Tension?"

"Mind-numbing sex, mostly," he said, deadpan.

It took her a moment to realize he was joking. "Oh. *Oh.*" She laughed outright.

"I like it when you laugh," he said. "Come here."

She stepped into his embrace and let herself be held. He was solid against her and smelled of a subtle mix of pine and the out-of-doors. He stroked the back of her head with hands that were incredibly gentle.

"Thanks for helping me out last night," he said after a moment.

"You mean with the migraine?"

He smiled down at her, and her heart pinged hard against her ribs. "And the sex." He brushed his mouth across hers. "I haven't been with a woman since before the shooting. I was feeling a little out of practice."

"You did fine."

"Fine, huh?"

"Well, for a man who was out of practice."

"Ouch." He kissed her neck. "Maybe I need some more practice."

Logic told her to pull away, but every nerve ending in her body jumped when his hands closed over her breasts. Sensation coursed through her with each beat of her heart. She kissed him back, felt a wave of dizziness engulf her as blood rushed to erogenous zones she hadn't know existed before last night. Heat blossomed low in her belly and spread downward like a fire burning hot and out of control.

He made love to her mouth with his tongue, and Eli melted beneath the onslaught of pleasure. The voice of reason cried out for her to stop this before things careened out of control. But she knew they already had. His kisses tore down her defenses and wreaked havoc on her common sense. She moaned when he brushed his thumbs over her sensitized nipples. Wet heat throbbed between her legs. Never in her life had her body responded so powerfully. The intensity of the need pounding through her shocked her, made her long for something indefinable and elusive. Made her wish for things that could never be.

Adam had made it clear he wasn't interested in a relationship. The harsh honesty of that hurt. And the startling truth of what was happening shattered her. She was falling in love with him. The realization terrified her. Vaguely, she wondered how she'd gotten herself into such an impossible situation, wondered how her heart and her body and her intellect could be so completely at odds.

When he kissed her again, she no longer thought at all.

chapter
24

THE NEXT DAY DAWNED COLD AND GRAY. ADAM rose early and built a fire while Eli made breakfast. They ate together, then spent the rest of the morning going over every aspect of the case with a fine-tooth comb. At noon, he took the package she'd prepared for the FDA to the FedEx drop. Eli seemed hopeful the administration's reaction would be proactive. Adam wasn't quite so optimistic. By afternoon, the frustration was starting to get to him.

He went through his list of suspects for what seemed like the hundredth time. Walter Sanchez. Peter Roth. Thomas Bornheimer. Kevin Chambers. He couldn't prove it, but he knew one or more of them had manipulated drug trial data and withheld vital information from the Food and Drug Administration.

Across from him, curled in the easy chair, Eli cradled her laptop against a pillow, tapping the occasional key. Her brows were knit, her eyes focused on the screen with absolute concentration. He'd caught himself watching her a dozen times throughout the afternoon. He knew better than to indulge himself in such things, but he couldn't seem to stop. The same way he couldn't seem to stop thinking about what had happened between them the night before . . .

Unable to concentrate, frustrated because the case seemed to be going nowhere, Adam rose and stretched.

She looked up at him over the top of her glasses. "You okay?"

"This is driving me nuts." When she only continued to stare at him, he added, "The case."

"Oh."

He didn't want to get into what else was driving him nuts. "There's something we're missing. Something we're not seeing."

"Like what?"

"I don't know. But somebody can't hide this kind of information without leaving *something* behind. Some kind of clue. A mistake. Something he overlooked." He paused. "Is there any piece of information I haven't seen?"

She tapped her pen against her temple, shook her head. "I don't think so."

"What about the tape?"

She uncurled her legs and stood. "You want to watch it again?"

"Maybe we'll notice something we missed before." He watched her cross to the entertainment center, trying not to notice the way her jeans stretched taut across her rear as she bent and slipped the video into the VCR.

Picking up the remote, she padded back to the sofa and sat next to him, her eyes on the TV. Adam was keenly aware of her proximity, but he didn't acknowledge her, didn't touch her, and he didn't take his eyes off the television. She hit the PLAY button and the video began to roll. The camera work was jittery and amateurish. The lighting was bad, but he could see lab jars on stainless-steel shelving. The camera panned and he noticed the desk and chair in the background. . . .

"Freeze it," he said.

Raising the remote, Eli hit the button. "What?"

"Back it up."

She hit another button.

"Pause."

The video stopped. Rising, Adam went to the TV and knelt, adrenaline kicking swiftly through him. "There's a jacket on the back of the desk chair. I think there's a logo sewn into the fabric, but I can't make it out."

Eli approached the television and opened a small panel on the front of the TV. "Let me see if I can fine-tune it."

"Let me do it." He edged her aside, watching the screen fade and darken and sharpen.

"I see it," she said. "It's familiar."

"How so?"

"The colors. Red and blue. I've seen it before."

Never taking his eyes from the screen, he struggled to get a better picture. "Damn it."

"Oh, my God."

He stopped tuning and turned to her. "What is it?"

"The logo. It's from Trinity Laboratories."

"Do you think that's where this video was taken?"

"Oh, no." Eli paled, pressed her hand to her stomach. "I was right. Oh, God."

"Right about what?"

She looked at him with wide, frightened eyes. "Trinity did the animal trials on Valazine."

THE DRIVE NORTH FROM ANN ARBOR TO DETROIT took more than an hour because of rush-hour traffic. It was after six o'clock when Adam parked the Tahoe across the street from Trinity Laboratories. The two-story, brick building was located in a seedy section of town on the south side of Detroit.

"Who runs this place?" he asked, cutting the engine.

"Graham Porter. He and his staff do contract work for larger labs and pharmaceutical firms. Roth uses them every so often for small contracts." She motioned toward the CLOSED sign on the front door. "Looks like they're closed."

"Shit," Adam muttered. "We're here. We may as well knock. Someone may still be inside."

Cold sunlight glinted off the facade of the building as they crossed the street. The wind coming off Lake St. Clair to the east chilled Eli to the bone. Huddled in her coat, she tried the front door, found it locked.

"Got your lock-picking kit on you?" she asked.

He tapped on the glass with his keys. "If I decide to take the law into my own hands, I'll do it alone."

"I appreciate that more than you know."

A moment later an Asian woman approached from the inside and pointed at the sign, mouthing the words "We're closed."

"Yeah, honey, I can read." Adam slapped his badge against the glass. "Open the goddamn door."

The woman's eyes widened, then she turned and scurried off.

"That was real smooth police work," Eli said.

"Damn it," he growled. "Shit."

"Maybe she's going to get someone to let us in."

"Maybe someone's running out the back."

Leaning forward, Eli cupped her hands and peered through the glass. A cheap metal desk and ugly-as-sin sofa comprised the reception area. Adjacent to the sofa, a coffee table was stacked with an array of trade publications and popular magazines.

"Real classy place," Adam said.

"If you like retro."

He'd just raised his fist to knock again when a man in a white lab coat entered the reception area. Eli recognized him immediately. "That's Graham Porter," she said.

"Charm him."

She cut him a sideways glance. "You mean I get to be the good cop?"

"That's exactly what I mean."

Keys jangled as Graham twisted the key and opened the door a couple of inches. "I'm sorry, but we're closed."

"Dr. Graham. Hi. It's Elizabeth Barnes from Roth Pharmaceuticals in Ann Arbor. I'm sorry to bother you without calling first, but can we come in to talk to you for a few minutes?"

"Dr. *Barnes*?" he said, clearly surprised to see her.

Forcing a smile she hoped looked real, she slipped her hand through the narrow opening and offered up a handshake. "Call me Eli. We met briefly when you worked with Dr. Sanchez on the early Valazine trials."

"Ah, yes, I remember you." Graham shook her hand halfheartedly, his eyes skittering to Adam. "What's this about?"

"I'm Detective Boedecker." Flashing his badge, Adam pushed open the door, sending the other man back several steps. "I need to ask you a few questions."

"What kind of questions?" Graham's eyes darted from Eli to Adam, then back to narrow on Eli. "We're closed. I was just on my way home for the day."

"I'm sorry, Dr. Graham." Eli forced another smile and stepped into the reception area. "We got tied up in traffic."

Adam closed the door behind them and locked it. "We appreciate your cooperation."

Graham's eyes flicked to the lock. "I don't know what you think you're doing, but I don't appreciate your barging in like this."

"I'm working on a case in conjunction with the Ann Arbor police department," Adam said. "This will just take a few minutes."

Graham didn't look appeased. "Does this have something to do with what happened to Dr. Sanchez?"

"All I can tell you is that the investigation is ongoing and may involve one or more employees of Trinity Laboratories."

"*Trinity?*" Graham laughed, but it was an incredulous sound that held no humor. "All of our employees are carefully screened."

Adam cut to the chase. "I understand Trinity did the animal testing on Valazine for Roth Pharmaceuticals."

Graham's Adam's apple bobbed. "Yes, we did the preliminary testing, but I don't see—"

"I need to see your records," Adam said. "All of them."

Graham made a sound of incredulity. "Do you have a warrant or something?"

"Look, we can do this one of two ways," Adam began. "Either I can go to the Wayne County prosecuting attorney and get a search warrant for the premises and have a few sheriff's deputies tear this place apart, or you can be a good citizen and give me access to your records."

"I—I can't make that kind of decision without first checking with the managing director, Mr. Layton."

Adam gestured to the phone on the desk. "Call him. I don't mind waiting."

"Mr. Layton is at a conference in Atlanta until Tuesday."

"I can have a court order in two hours," Adam countered. "If we do it your way, Mr. Layton won't have a say in the matter." He looked around. "I can promise you, your comfy little office won't be quite so comfy when we're through."

"You can't come in here and threaten me. This is a private business. I have rights."

Eli nudged Adam aside. "There is no threat, Dr. Graham. Please, we're merely asking for your cooperation."

Shaking his head in indignation, Graham started toward the phone, then stopped and turned back to her, his eyes narrowing. "I recall hearing you're no longer with Roth, Dr. Barnes. Is that true?"

She searched her mind for a lie, but nothing came. "Not exactly . . . It was a misunderstanding."

He looked from Eli to Adam. "I don't know what's going on here, but I'm not going to open my files to you people. I'm afraid you're going to have to go ahead and get the court order."

"All we're asking is to see the reports from the initial testing of Valazine," Eli said.

"You should have that information at Roth." Graham shook his head. "What the bloody hell is going on here?"

"We believe the data was altered," Eli said. "Please, we need to compare the two to make sure the data we forwarded to the FDA matches your raw data."

She could tell by his expression that he didn't believe her. "I'd like to see your badge again," he said to Adam.

When Adam didn't produce it, Graham walked over to the desk and picked up the phone. "I don't know who you people think you are, but I don't appreciate your coming in here and trying to intimidate me into giving out confidential information on a client we did contract work for. I won't stand for it."

He punched three numbers on the dial pad. Eli's heart began to pound, then jumped into a staccato when Adam crossed to the desk and pressed the down on the plunger. "I wouldn't do that if I were you," he said.

"Get the bloody hell away from me," Graham snarled.

"What do you have in those records you don't want us to see?" Adam asked.

"I'm calling the police." He tried to dislodge Adam's hand to no avail.

"Please, Dr. Graham, we just need a little cooperation," Eli tried.

"What are you hiding?" Adam asked.

"Nothing!"

"What are you afraid of?"

"Get out! Both of you. I know my rights. I don't have to talk to you." Graham slapped Adam's hand, trying to dislodge it from the phone.

Adam's face darkened. Eli saw anger in his eyes and knew he wasn't going to let it go. Moving quickly to avoid a disaster, she grabbed his arm, tried to pull him away. "Adam, take it easy."

Ignoring her, Adam grabbed the other man's collar. "You just assaulted a cop, asshole."

"Get your hands off me."

"Not a chance." Using his forearm, Adam muscled him toward the wall. But Graham was heavier and a lot faster than he looked. Breaking Adam's grip, he drew back and landed a punch just below Adam's ribs. Cursing, Adam went down on one knee.

Eli saw Graham line up to kick him. "Look out!" she cried.

Adam lunged sideways just in time to avoid getting kicked in the face. He scrambled to his feet as Graham charged. Eli watched the two men in stunned amazement, unable to believe that what had started out as a peaceful information-seeking mission had turned into something closer to a barroom brawl.

Snarling a profanity, Adam grabbed the larger man's lab coat and slammed him against the wall. "You're lucky I'm in a good mood today," he said.

Graham sputtered something about his rights, but he didn't move. Eli stood frozen, trembling, acutely aware of the snap of violence in the air. She watched Adam stride over to the phone and jerk the cord from the wall. "Damn shame I tripped over the cord. Send the bill to the Ann Arbor police department."

"You going to pay for this," Graham said. But he didn't leave his place at the other side of the room.

"Tell that to the nice sheriff's deputies when they come out and turn this dump upside down." He turned to Eli. "Let's get the hell out of here."

chapter
25

THE RIDE BACK TO ANN ARBOR WAS TENSE. ADAM drove too fast, his temper still pumping, weaving through the remnants of rush-hour traffic like a NASCAR driver with a death wish. He knew better than to lose his temper. He couldn't afford to start making stupid mistakes. But he was tired of getting the runaround. Tired of people lying and evading. Tired of smug sons of bitches like Graham Porter stonewalling him.

They'd hit yet another dead end. This case was quickly becoming dead ends piled on top of dead ends. He needed a break. They were running out of time. *He* was running out of time. The thousands of people taking Valazine were running out of time with every minute that passed.

"You're going to find yourself in hot water if Graham decides to press assault charges against you," Eli said.

Adam glanced over at her. "Graham's not going to do shit."

"How can you be so sure?"

"Because he's got a dirty little secret and doesn't want a bunch of cops sniffing around his lair."

"What are we going to do now?"

"I don't know," he snapped. Then, furious, he rapped his palm against the steering wheel. "*Damn* it!"

Eli didn't say anything else. Adam didn't want her to. He wasn't feeling particularly reasonable. He figured they both knew he'd bite her head off if she started spewing logic.

He didn't even look at her as they sped south and then west toward Ann Arbor. He needed his anger. Needed to hold on to it because at the moment it was the only emotion he was sure of.

He knew he was treading on thin ice. With the case. With Eli and his growing feelings for her. He knew that ice was going to shatter beneath him. The question was when—and whether or not he would survive the plunge.

Once at Eli's house, Adam headed toward the kitchen for his briefcase, opened it on the dining room table, and began to assemble everything he had on the case. Not much considering the time and effort he'd put into it. He had a solid theory. Some circumstantial evidence that wouldn't hold up for shit in court. In a nutshell, he didn't have squat.

He could hear Eli in the kitchen, making a pot of coffee. In spite of everything that had happened, the lack of progress, the migraine, the very real threat of a promising drug gone horribly wrong, he still couldn't keep his eyes off her. He was having a hard time focusing on the case at all whenever she was around. Sleeping with her had been a mistake. He'd noticed the way she was looking at him. As if he meant something to her. He knew that would cause complications at some point down the road. Complications he had absolutely no desire to deal with.

Vaguely, he wondered why he was still here, why he was still with her. Why didn't he just pack up his briefcase and hit the road? But Adam knew why, and he despised himself for falling victim to something as predictable as lust. Somehow, in the last few days, she'd gotten to him. She'd gotten under his skin. Into his head. Like a parasite that caused temporary madness. He told himself it was just the sex. After a three-year hiatus he'd been more than ready to test the waters. He just hadn't expected those waters to suck him down like a whirlpool.

He watched her cross to the dining room and set a cup of coffee in front of him. He felt the sexual tug of her closeness like a physical touch. He felt that odd stirring in his gut when she looked at him and gave him that little smile he'd come to cherish. He didn't let himself smile back at her, didn't let himself react at all. He didn't want to do that to her. He didn't want to do it to himself.

"We need to talk," he said.

She shot a wary look at him over the rim of her cup.

"About the case."

"Okay." She pulled out a chair and sat across from him.

"I think someone at Trinity doctored the preliminary testing data. I think someone at Roth paid them to do it."

"That's a logical assumption. Who?"

"I don't know." He picked up his cup and drank, barely tasting the coffee. "The only person who we know for sure knew about that tape was Walter Sanchez."

Denial rose swiftly in her eyes. He saw the walls go up. "Walter wouldn't be involved in something like this."

"We have to consider everyone at this point, Eli. You have to keep an open mind."

"I knew Walter. He would never put thousands of people at risk. He would never do something so heinous."

Knowing he wasn't going to convince her otherwise in the next five minutes, he steered the conversation in a different direction. "All right. Let's work on the crime scenario. What would it take to pull this off?"

Eli set down her coffee. "If Walter sent that tape to me, then this was in motion even during the early stages of testing."

"Okay. That's plausible. Who else would have to be involved?"

"Someone at Roth who dealt with the trials at all stages. Someone who has access to both the raw data and control over what is ultimately sent to the FDA."

"Who?"

"Me," she said. "Walter. Thomas Bornheimer. But again, it would have had to have been a concerted effort."

"Why?"

"Because there are too many people looking at the data."

"How so?"

"For example, I could drop by the clinic and pick up the data personally." She stopped speaking abruptly, her eyes widening. "Someone at the clinic could have changed the data before it ever reached Roth. It's diabolical, but brilliant. If that's the way it was done, then the real information never went to Roth at all."

"So someone at Roth paid off a tech at one or more of the clinics." A theory snapped into place in Adam's mind. "This is a concerted effort, Eli. A lot of people are involved. There are billions of dollars at stake. Enough to go around for everyone."

"Right under my nose."

"They kept you in the dark because they knew you couldn't be bought."

She lowered her head and rubbed at her temple. "I hate this, Adam."

The urge to go to her was strong, but he knew it would only make things worse, so he didn't. Instead, he rose and walked over to the French doors and stared out at the snow. He was aware of her eyes on him, of the need to touch her snapping through him. He didn't want to need her, damn it. The last time he'd needed a woman, she'd ripped his heart out and left him bleeding in the street.

The logical side of his mind told him Eli wasn't anything like Shelly. The two women were as different as night and day. He reminded himself he didn't have an emotional investment in his relationship with Eli. He wasn't vulnerable to her. They'd had a few hours of hot sex. They'd been working together under stressful conditions.

But Adam knew his feelings for her went deeper than the flesh. He knew that if he gave in to those needs again, he'd end up getting tangled up with her. He didn't want to do that to himself. Certainly not to her. He respected her too much to let her get involved with a man like him.

Not liking the direction his thoughts had taken, he

moved away from the door, picked up his cup, and took it to the sink.

"We have to go to the police or the FDA," she said. "Now. There's no other way."

Adam didn't look at her, knew if he did he would fuck this up the same way he'd fucked up just about everything else in his life. "The question is: Do we have enough proof to convince someone at the FDA? Are the reports we sent them enough to get this drug off the market? I don't think so."

She began to pace. "I should have seen this coming."

The note of panic in her voice turned him around. "They were careful."

"I've been blind and incredibly naïve," she said.

Because he couldn't bear to stand there and do nothing while she trembled and fought a fear she should have never had to feel, he crossed to her and reached out. "Eli . . ."

She shook him off and headed toward the hall.

Adam followed. "Calm down."

She didn't stop until she'd reached the living room. When she ran out of space, she turned to face him. In the pale frame of her face he saw fear and panic and a sense of betrayal he knew all too well not to recognize.

"Adam, I'm scared."

That he'd failed to protect her—not only as a cop, but as a man—hurt more than any physical blow. "It may not seem like it now, but the case will come together," he said. "Something will break. We may not have physical evidence, but we've got a hell of a lot of circumstantial. A solid theory. We've got a dead body. The fire at the warehouse. That's attempted murder."

"Is there any way you can get a search warrant for Trinity or Manicon?"

Adam wished he could say yes. But he couldn't, and it made him feel useless as hell. "I'll make some calls. Call in some favors. My ex-partner owes me."

She jolted when the phone jangled. She started toward it, but Adam stopped her. "Let the machine pick it up," he said.

He heard the greeting, then Detective Lindquist's deep voice. "Dr. Barnes, this Detective Lindquist. I want to speak with you as soon as possible. It's urgent. Please call the station or my cell phone." He rattled off several numbers, then disconnected.

Eli stared at Adam, wide-eyed and trembling, then punched the PLAY button on the recorder. There were two earlier messages from Lindquist, asking her to call him.

"He thinks I killed Walter," she said.

"Lindquist isn't stupid, Eli." He didn't like seeing her so rattled. Up until now, she'd kept her head and stayed cool. But her hands were shaking. Her eyes had the look of a wild animal faced with perishing in a raging forest fire or jumping off a cliff. He wanted to tell her everything would be all right, but he didn't know if it would.

For the first time, he considered the very real possibility that she would be arrested for murder and that even with his police connections—tenuous connections that they were—he wouldn't be able to help her.

She picked up the phone, but Adam took it from her and set it back down. "Lindquist is going to come for me if I don't call him," she said.

"He's going to come for you if you do."

Her hand visibly shook when she shoved a strand of hair out of her eyes. "I don't want to go to jail," she whispered.

Adam wished he could reassure her. He wished even more he could hold her. Because he couldn't do either of those things and keep his head, he turned away. "Pack a bag," he said. "You're staying at the hotel with me tonight."

"Adam—"

"Don't argue. I'm going to see if I can get us some help."

She managed a shaky smile, but he saw clearly that she was scared. For the first time in a long time, so was he.

ELI FOLLOWED ADAM TO THE HOTEL AND PARKED her Volkswagen in the rear lot, which was out of sight from the street. Adam parked in the front lot and carried her overnight bag to his room.

The hotel room smelled faintly of Adam. A button-down oxford shirt had been tossed haphazardly over the back of a chair. His shaving supplies were lined up neatly on the bathroom counter. Even though he'd been there only a few days, the room spoke of him.

Her nerves were strung tight as she crossed to the round table near the window and opened her laptop. She tried to keep her mind on the case, working out the details of who might have done what and why. But she felt shaky inside, her thoughts scattered. She felt as if her life was spiraling out of control.

To make things worse, she could no longer think logically when it came to Adam. Since making love with him, she couldn't look at him without wanting him. Without wondering where this was going to lead. Without wanting to be held and loved and cherished by a man who didn't give any of those things easily.

Adam Boedecker was a difficult man to understand and more emotionally isolated than anyone she'd ever known. It was as if he'd surrounded his emotions with a fortress designed solely to keep people out. Eli wanted inside those walls. She knew it was insane for her to be thinking at a time like this of their having a relationship. She needed to stay focused on finding the person responsible for putting a dangerous drug on the market. On staying out of jail. On defending the career she'd devoted her life to building.

Realizing she was staring blindly at her laptop screen, she sighed. "I'm going to take a shower," she said. "I need to clear my head."

"I'll order some food."

She didn't look at him as she started toward the bathroom, but she felt his eyes on her, burning into her, making her want things she knew she could never have. Once safely inside, she locked the door, stripped, and stepped beneath the spray.

Eli had always considered herself an intelligent woman. She was logical and methodical and she never did anything without thinking it through first. She was much too smart to get tangled up with a man like Adam. He would hurt her if she allowed it. He would destroy her if she wasn't careful. She didn't *want* to have feelings for him. She didn't want to be attracted to him.

But her heart didn't necessarily give a damn about any of those things and, evidently, neither did her body. Both seemed determined to betray her intellect, and Eli knew she was going to have to deal with her feelings for him sooner or later. She was going to have to figure out what was real and how much of what she felt was a result of adrenaline and hormones. Then she was going to have to decide what to do about it.

Closing her eyes against the fist of emotion clenching in her chest, she shut off the water and stepped out of the shower. She didn't look at herself in the mirror as she toweled her body and applied a bit of lotion. She didn't want to see what she knew her eyes would tell her. That she was in over her head—and that she'd already lost her heart.

She wrapped herself in the hotel's robe, then stepped into the room. The TV was tuned to the cable news channel. A tray containing two sandwiches and two iced teas sat on the table. From his place on the edge of the bed, Adam looked up from his reading when she walked out.

"Feel better?" he asked.

"Lots," she lied, ignoring the jump of nerves when his eyes traversed the length of her.

"I ordered club sandwiches."

She walked over to the tray and began unwrapping one of the sandwiches. She was keenly aware of Adam across the room. He hadn't come over to eat, but she could feel his eyes on her. And the burn on her back was like a hot laser.

"Why are you trembling?" he asked quietly.

Eli stopped what she was doing, but she didn't turn to face him. She didn't know what her face would reveal to him, and she certainly didn't know how to explain something she didn't understand herself. She wanted to think she was shaking because she was scared, but she knew the emotions stabbing at her heart were much more complex.

"Why won't you look at me?" he asked.

She closed her eyes against the question, against the answer, afraid that if she turned around and looked at him, he would see the truth.

Her heart began to pound when she heard him rise. A moment later, he came up behind her. She jumped when he put his hands on her shoulders.

"Everything's going to be all right." Gently, he turned her to him. When she didn't look at him, he put his fingers under her chin and forced the issue.

She stared up into his dark eyes, felt the earth tilt beneath her feet. "I don't think everything is going to be all right," she said hoarsely.

His eyes narrowed, and she knew he was trying to figure out what was going on inside her head. If only he knew . . .

"What is it, Eli? What's wrong?"

She choked out a laugh. It was either that, or cry. God knew she didn't want to start crying. She might not ever stop.

"I didn't realize that was a funny question," he said.

"It's not," she replied. "I'm just . . . losing it."

"You're in good company."

It took some effort but she smiled. "You, too, huh?"

"Oh, yeah." He ran his finger over her lower lip. "I like it when you smile."

"Same goes, but you don't do it much."

"No sense of humor."

"I don't believe that."

He was standing so close she could smell the intoxicating scent of his aftershave. It swirled in her brain like drugging smoke. In the back of her mind, Eli knew that if she stepped forward and laid her head on his shoulder, he would wrap his arms around her. She knew how that would feel, and she longed for his embrace. She knew that for a short time he would make everything all right. The temptation was powerful, tugging at her like the summer solstice pulling the tides of an unruly ocean.

She was keenly aware of his hands on her shoulders, his dark, troubled eyes burning into hers. Eyes that had seen untold pain. And a heart that had been betrayed.

"I think you've been hurt," she said after a minute. "I think that's why you don't smile."

A frisson of tension ran the length of him. His expression changed. His gaze hardened. An impenetrable shield rising to protect his inner sanctum against a marauding enemy. "My battle scars are showing, huh?"

"Sometimes." She set her hand against his face, felt him wince. "Who was it, Adam? Who hurt you?"

"Come on, Eli. The last three years haven't exactly been a picnic."

"There's more to it than that. You mentioned your ex-wife before. Did she divorce you before or after the shooting?"

He stared hard at her, and she knew he was trying to get inside her head, trying to figure out where she was going with this. It was disconcerting because he was so damn good at reading her. "I don't want to get into that with you."

"I'm asking because I want to know you."

"Maybe it's best if you don't."

"I want to understand. Please don't shut me out."

He shook his head. "You don't want to get tangled up with me, Eli."

"You don't have the slightest clue what I want."

His jaw flexed like steel under great pressure as he regarded her with those hard eyes. "My wife and my partner," he said. "They're . . . together. He was my best friend."

"They betrayed you," she said.

He nodded.

"I'm sorry."

He stared at her unflinchingly. "It happened—they happened—after I'd been shot. While I was in the hospital."

Her heart gave a single, hard jerk. As if someone had prodded it with a sharp instrument. For the first time, she wasn't sure opening up this old wound was the best way to heal it. "Oh, Adam."

"It was a long time ago," he said.

"But it still hurts. I see it in your eyes sometimes."

"I'm probably just thinking you're a pain in the ass." She smiled. "How long were you in the hospital?"

"Four months," he said. "Shelly and Chad were there with me the entire time. They showered and ate and slept at the hospital. Day and night for weeks on end they were together. They stayed until I was released to a convalescent home. By then, it was too late."

"That must have been incredibly difficult."

"I got through it." Pulling away from her, he walked to the window and stared out at the cold beyond. "As bizarre as it sounds, they were there for me when I needed them most. Shelly stayed by my side. So did Chad. I was in bad shape, Eli. I couldn't speak. I couldn't go to the bathroom by myself. It was a tough time for everyone."

"When did you find out they were together?"

"I was in the convalescent home for six months. When I got out of rehab and finally went home, things were . . . different. I mean, between Shelly and me. I'd been away from the house for ten months. I was different. Shelly was different. I was a goddamn mess, not only physically but in other ways, too. My balance was off. I had a hard time remembering things. My vision was weird for a while. My emotions were skewed. I couldn't . . . I couldn't . . . Ah, Christ." He scrubbed a hand over his face. "I couldn't function sexually."

Hurting for him, Eli came up behind him and put her hand on his shoulder. "You overcame tremendous odds," she said.

"She put up with me for six months, then moved out."

"Did she tell you why?"

"Chad came over one night and told me."

"That must have been devastating."

Adam shrugged. "It was, at the time. I mean, here's my best friend, coming into my house to tell me he's in love with my wife, that they'd been carrying on the entire six months I'd been in rehab pissing all over myself. I mean, Christ, he just walked in and blurted out that he's in love with her."

Eli couldn't imagine what that must have done to him. The pain and betrayal he must have felt. It explained something about him, she realized. And for the first time, she felt as if she truly understood him.

"I was using a cane at the time. I went after him with it and put a gash in his chin. He still has the scar. But in the end, it was him picking me up off the floor and calling my sister to stay with me."

"You had every right to be angry."

"It took me a long time to get a handle on my emotions. I still fly off the handle, Eli. That and the migraines are the two main reasons I haven't gone in for my psychiatric exam."

She thought of the times she'd seen him lose his temper. "I've seen you angry, Adam. You haven't been terribly unreasonable. I mean, I thought you were just losing your temper."

"A cop can't lose control like that."

She nodded. "Will it get better?"

He shrugged. "I don't know. Not even the doctors know."

"I think going back to work would be good for you."

"Chicago PD wants me back, but they won't put me on the street. I've put it off because I don't have the guts to see the company shrink."

"You have more guts than anyone I've ever met. And you have every reason in the world to be apprehensive about taking a test that could conceivably end your career."

His eyes softened. "That sounds good in concept, but this is more of an ego thing for me."

"How so?"

"I'm a street cop, Eli. If I can't work on the street and do what I do best, I'm not sure I want to go back."

"Adam, you've overcome so much. There's no doubt in my mind that you can do whatever you put your mind to."

A smile tugged at one side of his mouth. "Ah, you're a real balm for the burned-out cop's soul, you know that?"

"I'll send you a bill later."

Settling one hand on her shoulder, he used the other to lift a strand of hair that had fallen into her eyes, swept it back. "That's why I am who I am. That's why smart women stay away from me." He tilted his head, his eyes seeking hers and turning serious. "You're a smart woman, Eli."

The words went through her like tiny arrows, piercing her, making her bleed. "It sounds like you're trying to warn me off."

"I am."

"You think you know what's in my mind. You think you know what's in my heart. You don't know either of those things."

"Look, the last couple of weeks have been . . . intense," he said. "Adrenaline has a way of messing with people's perceptions. I care about you. I like being with you. But that doesn't make me relationship material. I'm not, Eli. Not even close. I walk around feeling wounded and mean. I strike out at people I care about. You won't be any different. When this is over, I'll walk away. If I don't, I'll hurt you. I'll hurt you badly, and I won't even feel guilty. For the first time in a long time, I care enough not to want that to happen."

Words and emotions tangled like inside her like thorny branches. She wanted to tell him what was in her heart but knew he didn't want to hear it. "I'm not looking for a relationship," she said.

Pulling back slightly, he looked down at her, searched her face. "What are you looking for?"

"I don't know," she said truthfully. "I don't know where this will lead."

Need coiled dangerously inside her. It took all of her courage, but she bridged the short, treacherous space between them. He stiffened when she put her arms around him. The breath rushed from his lungs when her body came against his. She could feel the steel ridge of his arousal against her pelvis.

"I'm not a strong enough man to walk away from this." His arms went around her. Her head fell against his chest, and she could hear the strong beat of his heart. Tilting his head, he sought her mouth, brushed his lips against hers. "Not from this."

"Then don't walk away."

"I'm getting too goddamn close to you. You deserve better."

She absorbed the kiss. He used his tongue like a weapon, his breath quickening against her cheek. Arousal hummed through her body. She was already wet, could feel the slick moisture between her legs where she throbbed. She closed her eyes against the intensity, told herself she was in control. Logic mocked her, called her a liar and a fool.

"Don't count on me to do the right thing when this is over." He tore his mouth from hers, trailed his tongue down her throat, leaving a wet path in its wake. Pulling away slightly, he opened her robe, looked at her with dangerous eyes. "I'll disappoint you."

Eli shivered when his gaze raked down her body. Her swollen breasts ached. The heat between her legs was unbearable, a fire burning out of control.

She jolted when he cupped her breasts, flicked his thumbs over her nipples. "I won't let you," she whispered, and closed her eyes.

chapter
26

ELI DIDN'T WANT TO THINK. FOR THE FIRST TIME IN forever, she only wanted to feel. She wanted to feel Adam against her. Wanted to hear the drum of his heart. Hear him whisper her name, feel the pulse of him as he moved within her.

He kissed her hard on the mouth without the finesse he'd shown her before. There was a desperation in the way he kissed her. Something dark and primal had been released inside him. A side of him that frightened her as much as it thrilled.

Only Eli had never been a thrill seeker. She was responsible. Conservative. Logical. None of those things seemed to matter when Adam Boedecker kissed her.

"I'm not going to apologize for this later," he said.

"I don't expect you to."

Without warning, he lifted her, carried her to the bed a few feet away. He dropped her onto the mattress, then reached for the robe, worked her arms from it, and tossed it aside.

Need pulsed like a living thing inside her, wild and out of control. The insides of her thighs were wet. She resisted the urge to writhe, but the need was tortuous and dark and all consuming. She watched Adam take off his shirt. He was breathing hard, his lips pulled back into a snarl. He unfastened his belt, jerked the zipper down. Raw lust speared through her when he stepped out of his slacks and boxers and his erection sprang free.

He didn't ask for what he wanted. Crawling onto the bed, he grasped her knees, lifted them and spread her wide. Embarrassment tortured her. She tried to close her legs, but he held her open and vulnerable.

"Adam, please . . ."

"This is how I want you."

Leaning forward, he kissed her mouth, his tongue plunging into her. Simultaneously, he thrust into her. Eli cried out, her spine arching at the combination of pleasure and pain. The muscles in her thighs flexed. Her hips rose to meet him, taking him deeply inside her. The contractions followed, as swift and powerful as anything she'd ever experienced.

Vaguely, the sound of her own voice registered. The cry of his name on her lips. But she barely heard it over the jet engine that was her heart.

He moved within her. Long, sure strokes. Too hard. Too fast. Too . . . everything. Sensation pummeled her, violent waves rushing over her, overwhelming her senses until she felt as if she would explode if it didn't stop.

He didn't stop.

The pleasure built to a crescendo. She accepted him into the deepest reaches of her body. He took what she offered, made it his own.

The orgasm wrenched a scream from her. Somewhere in the back of her mind, she felt herself coming apart. Piece by carefully constructed piece. Cell by cell. Atom by atom. All the controls she'd so diligently put into place over the years scattered and ceased to exist.

The only thing that mattered was Adam. Holding her. Moving within her. And the pleasure crashing down all around her.

*   *   *

ADAM TOLD HIMSELF IT WAS ONLY SEX. MIND-bending, earth-shattering sex. He refused to consider anything else, refused to acknowledge the emotions banging around inside him. All he cared about was the moment. The pleasure pounding through him. The feel of her flesh beneath his hands. The taste of her mouth. The wet heat wrapping around him and driving him toward a final release.

He kissed her deeply, but didn't look at her. He couldn't look into those soft brown eyes knowing what he did. He closed his ears to the sounds of her cries. He concentrated on his own pleasure. On the orgasm building in his groin.

"Adam. Oh, God, Adam!"

He heard her but didn't stop moving within her. He didn't want words or tenderness or emotions. He knew that at a time like this words were as dangerous as any gun. He hooked his arms around her legs and pounded into her, driving himself higher. He felt her contracting, gripping him, and he ground his teeth against the intensity of pleasure streaking through him.

"I love you!" she cried. "I love you."

Adam had never been an emotional man. He had never been an emotional lover. But when he looked down into her eyes and saw tears, he felt the touch of their gazes like a punch. He never stopped moving within her. He didn't want to think about what she'd just said, didn't want her to mean it. He sure as hell didn't want to consider what it meant in terms of their relationship. In terms of what came next.

He let go of his control, closed his eyes against the hot rush of semen, felt his body tremble as he emptied his seed deep inside her.

For a full minute neither of them moved. The only sound came from their labored breathing and the quiet din of the heating vent by the window. Slowly, the world came back into focus. The soft warmth of her body against his. The smell of sex mingling with the sweet vanilla scent of her. The heat of where she still held him within her body.

The realization of what had happened gave him the strength he needed to move. He disconnected from her, then rolled onto his back and stared up at the ceiling. He sensed more than felt her hurt. It welled up around her like swollen flesh around a broken bone. He knew she wanted him to touch her. To put his arms around her. To look into her eyes and tell her he loved her. Adam couldn't do any of those things. Couldn't live with himself if he did.

He rose without looking at her. Crossing the room naked, he searched for his slacks, stepped into them, and yanked them up. "You didn't mean to say that," he said.

She sat up, pressed the sheet to her breasts. Her hair was mussed. Her cheeks were flushed. Her mouth was kiss-bruised and wet. He'd never seen a woman look more beautiful. He was still breathing hard, only partially erect, and already he wanted her again.

"Do you want me to lie to you or tell you the truth?" she asked.

"I want you to get a hold of yourself."

Angry now, she rose, jerked her arms into the robe. "I know what I feel."

"You have no idea!" he shouted. "You have good, raunchy sex for the first time in your repressed life and you go off the deep end and start blubbering about love. This is not some fucking fantasy."

Shock and hurt clouded her eyes. For a moment, he wanted to take the words back. She hadn't deserved that. But he didn't. Adam knew what was at stake, knew he couldn't let things stand the way they were.

"You're a coward," she said.

"Don't push me, Eli. I'm not in the mood."

"And the world revolves around Adam Boedecker's moods, doesn't it?"

He did his best to ignore her, but his temper was lit up like a fuse, burning short and hot.

"You don't even have the guts to look at me," she said.

Something inside him broke. Adam was across the room before he realized he was going to move. He had her against the wall before realizing he was going to touch her. Her back hit the wall hard. She gasped, her head snapping back. He held her flat against the wall, the lapel of her robe in his fist at her chest. Pressing against her, he kissed her hard, felt a hot flare of lust, then released her abruptly.

Shock and fear and a pinpoint of anger scrolled across the window of her eyes, but she didn't fight him. "Don't ever do that again."

The shame of what he'd done shook him. Adam had never raised his hand to a woman in his life. Stepping away from her, he shook his head as if awakening from a bad dream. He backed away from her. "That's what kind of man I am," he said.

Her knuckles were white at the collar of her robe. She stared at him, her eyes dark and shimmering. "I don't believe that. Neither do you."

He wanted to apologize but couldn't make himself do it. He wanted to go to her but couldn't make himself take that first step. He wasn't sure what he would do if he touched her. Kiss her or maybe get down on his knees and beg her to forgive him. But Adam didn't want to be exonerated. There was no exoneration for that kind of behavior. He'd be doing both of them a favor if he just got the hell out of there and never came back.

"I'm a lot of things." His voice actually shook. "But I'm not a coward."

She was breathing hard. Pale as death. Visibly trembling. Still, he couldn't go to her. What kind of a man did that make him? Why the hell couldn't he do the right thing for once in his lousy life?

Turning abruptly, he stalked to the table, stared down at the papers spread across it. He scooped up handfuls at a time and flung them into his open briefcase. He was aware of her watching him as he crossed to the bathroom and snapped open his shave kit. He dragged his forearm over the counter, dumping his toiletries into the bag. He had to get out of there. Before he made everything worse.

Before he did something irrevocable.

He left the bathroom, stalked to the closet, and retrieved his coat and garment bag.

"Where are you going?" she asked.

He looked at her. She hadn't left her place against the wall. He felt sick when he saw a red mark on her throat. *I did that to her,* he thought with self-loathing. He wondered if it would be enough to keep her away.

"I'm going back to Chicago." He slung the garment bag over his shoulder.

"Chicago?"

"I'll work the case from there."

"Adam, you can't leave like this."

"There's nothing more I can do here."

"You can finish this."

He glared at her, felt something tremble inside him. Something unfamiliar and terrifying. "You mean the case or did you want some more sex?" he asked nastily. "Give me a couple of minutes and I can probably accommodate you."

She stared at him, her eyes stricken and angry. Forcing a smile he didn't feel, he started for the door. She said something, but he didn't stop. He heard his name when he stepped into the hall. He prayed she didn't come after him, because if she did he knew he'd never make it out of there.

She walked to the threshold but didn't cross the line. "You bastard," she said.

He slammed the door in her face.

ELI HAD BEEN HIT IN THE SOLAR PLEXUS BY A schoolyard bully in a scuffle over a baseball game when she was nine years old. The punch had sent her to her knees, and it had taken her several minutes to catch her breath.

She felt much the same now as she stared at the door. Pain vibrated through her with every beat of her heart. She couldn't believe he'd walked out on her, that he'd walked out on the case, or that he'd hurt her so cruelly. She'd known what kind of man Adam Boedecker was. Volatile. Unpredictable. She knew he'd been hurt and betrayed. Just as she knew he was the kind of man who would strike a vicious blow at anyone who threatened to do either of those things to him again.

By telling him she loved him, she'd done exactly that.

Eli knew crying wasn't going to help, but it was the only thing she seemed capable of at the moment. The tears came in a flood. Lowering her face into her hands, she sank down onto the bed and wept. How could she have been so stupid? Why had she ruined everything by telling him she loved him?

A tremor moved through her when the full impact of what she'd said struck her. Oh, dear God, did she love him? Had she fallen in love with a man who could never love her back? A man who would never admit it even if he did?

She could still feel the wetness of their lovemaking between her legs. She could still feel him inside her, the warm press of his body against hers. Eli hadn't been with very many men in her life, but she knew there was no way a man could make love to her the way Adam had and not feel something profound.

Wiping useless tears from her cheeks, she stood and looked around the room. Her clothes were scattered on the floor. Her briefcase lay on its side on the table. She could still smell Adam's aftershave.

The reality of his departure pressed down on her like a cold hand. She was going to have to finish the case without him, she realized. Once she ascertained who at Roth had withheld data from the FDA, she would also find Walter's murderer. In the process she would exonerate herself. Hopefully, she wouldn't get arrested before she could get the job done.

She was dressing when her cell phone chirped. Her voice was breathless when she uttered his name. "Adam?"

"It's Thomas."

Surprise rippled through her. She hadn't talked to anyone at Roth since the day she'd been fired. She wondered why Thomas would call her now. "I wasn't expecting to hear from you."

"Hey, are you okay? You sound upset."

"I'm okay," she said. "It's just . . . been a tough week."

"Eli, I need to see you. It's important."

Something in his voice made the hairs at her nape stand on end. "What's this about, Thomas?"

"I can't say over the phone."

"Why not? What's going on?"

"Eli, I hate to lay this on you . . ." His voice trailed off. "This is going to sound crazy, but I think you're in danger."

"Danger?" A month ago, Eli would have laughed. Today, the word echoed in her ears like a shotgun blast. "What kind of danger?"

"It's about Valazine. I think there's something going on at Roth."

Eli shivered with a sudden chill. "What happened?"

"Not on the phone. Look, I think someone at Roth didn't disclose adverse events. After you gave me those articles, I looked into a few things. I mean, I wasn't even looking hard, you know? More like keeping my eyes open. Well, Jesus, I found some shit."

"What did you find?"

"Eli, I've got some documents I want you to look at."

She gripped the phone tighter. "What do you have, Thomas?"

"Can you meet me up at the corporate cabin?"

Peter Roth owned a beachfront cabin on Lake Huron one hundred miles to the north. It was a place where she and Walter and the rest of the executive team had spent countless weekends working on Valazine in the early stages. It was in a quiet summer community. A pretty town where Roth sequestered his staff of scientists for working retreats. Aside from the local ice fisherman, she knew it would be deserted this time of year.

"Why don't I just drive over to your house, Thomas? We can talk there."

"I guess you haven't heard the news."

"What news?"

"Oh, Eli . . . Jeez. There's been a warrant issued for your arrest."

"What?" She was already turning to the television and tuning in to a local news station.

"The cops think you had something to do with . . . what happened to Walter."

"Oh, God, Thomas." Pressing her hand against her stomach, she sank down onto the bed. "What am I going to do?"

"Look, I know this is going to sound paranoid as hell, but I think someone's been following me. I don't know if it's the cops or . . . if there's something else going on. Whatever the case, I don't think it's a good idea for us to meet here."

Stealthy fingers of fear walked up her spine. "Okay," she said. "What can I do?"

"Is your cop friend still there?"

Eli closed her eyes, put her hand over the phone so Thomas couldn't hear the quick intake of breath. "No."

"Damn. I thought maybe he could help. I think we're in this over our heads."

"He went back to Chicago. Do you want me to call him?"

"Let's you and I talk first. I have some documents I want you to look at. If we decide we need him, we'll call."

"Okay. Why don't I meet you up at the cabin? You bring whatever documentation you have. I'll bring what I've got." She took a deep breath. "We'll call Detective Boedecker when I get there. Sound fair enough?"

"Eli, be careful. If anything happens, just drive directly to the police station in Ann Arbor. Tell Lindquist everything."

"Nothing's going to hap—"

"Eli, listen to me. I know this sounds paranoid, but if anything happens to me, if I'm not at the cabin when you get there, call the police."

"Thomas, you're frightening me."

"I'm leaving copies of everything at my house, hidden beneath my stereo."

A chill raced through her. "Please, Thomas, just . . . be careful."

"I will. And, Eli . . . one more thing."

"What?"

"I just want to tell you . . . I know you didn't have anything to do with what happened to Walter. I never believed it."

Fresh tears threatened, but she forced them back. "Thanks."

"See you in a couple of hours," he said, and disconnected.

Eli sat on the bed, her head spinning with everything Thomas had told her. This could be the break they were looking for. Adam needed to know about it. She looked down at her cell phone, wondered if he would talk to her if she called him. If he cared enough to come back.

Shoving aside the hurt, she snatched up the phone and punched in his cell phone number, waited while the phone rang once. Twice . . .

You have good, raunchy sex for the first time in your repressed life and you go off the deep end and start blubbering about love. This is not some fucking fantasy.

His words rang cruelly in her ears. Hurt and humiliation burned inside her. Closing her eyes against the pain, Eli punched the OFF button and disconnected the call. Tears squeezed between her lashes, but she didn't give in to the need to cry.

She couldn't call him, she realized. After what he'd said to her, there was no way she could ask him to come back. If Thomas had information for her, she would contact Adam then, but not before.

chapter
27

ADAM WAS STILL SHAKING WHEN HE PULLED THE Tahoe into a dreary rest area just east of Battle Creek. It had started with his hands, then spread to his arms and legs. Sweat pooled at the back of his neck. His chest was so tight he could barely draw a breath. He could feel the fingers of a headache gripping his brain like a vise. Nausea seesawed in his gut. If he didn't know better, he'd think he was in the midst of some kind of a goddamn anxiety attack.

He'd put almost sixty miles between him and Eli in the last hour, but he knew it wasn't enough. He could put all the miles in the world between them and it wasn't going to help.

Locking the truck behind him, he made his way to the men's room. In the stall, he bent over the toilet and spat several times, waiting until he was certain he wouldn't be sick. At the sink, he turned on the tap and splashed water on his face, then jerked a paper towel from the dispenser and dried off.

He leaned against the sink and took several deep breaths. "Get a hold of yourself, goddamn it."

When he looked into the mirror, he saw a stranger staring back at him. A stranger with tortured eyes and a grim expression. A man whose face was fraught with pain and the knowledge that he'd made a very big mistake.

I love you.

He'd been inside her when she'd said those words. As close as a man and a woman could be. She'd been inside him, too, he realized. Inside his head. In his heart—a place he swore he would never share again. How the hell was he supposed to deal with this?

Adam had thought he could handle loving her. Thought he could handle loving her and being without her because he knew it was best for both of them. Whether that was to protect himself—or her—he figured he could live with it. He'd learned to live with a lot of things in the last three years. He'd learned to live with the reality that he would never be the same man he was before a fifteen-year-old crack addict put a bullet in his head. He'd had to accept the loss of his wife to his best friend. Adam had let Shelly go, not because he hadn't loved her, but because he had. He hadn't fought for her. He hadn't fought Deaton, either, though he had made it a point to make the other man's life a living hell whenever he could.

Adam had learned to choose his battles. Walking. Speaking. Getting his life back. Those had been the battles he'd chosen. Battles he'd fought with everything he had because he hadn't been able to live with the alternative.

It had killed him to hurt Eli. He could still see the shock and pain on her face when he'd slammed her against the wall. When he'd bruised her like the son of a bitch he was. Only now did he understand why he'd reacted so violently. He'd wanted to believe he'd driven her away to protect her. From him. From herself. Only now did he realize he'd done it because he was in love with her and the thought of relinquishing his heart terrified him.

The realization sent a greasy wave of nausea through him. Fear mixed with bile and tasted bitter on his tongue. Fear that he wasn't good enough for her because he wasn't the man he'd once been. Fear that he would hurt her. Fear that she would hurt him.

Maybe she'd been right when she'd called him a coward.

Adam felt steadier by the time he climbed into the Tahoe. He could feel the headache building behind his eyes. Not a bell ringer yet, but something was on the way and he could tell by the nausea it was going to be bad. Hopefully, he'd reach Ann Arbor before it rendered him useless.

He wasn't sure what he was going to say to her when he saw her, but he couldn't let things stand the way they were. Putting the truck in gear, he turned around and headed back in the direction from which he'd come.

INTERMITTENT SNOWFLAKES SWIRLED IN THE BEAMS of her headlights when Eli turned off of Highway 25 and onto the county road. Flanked by the naked branches of winter-dead trees, the road was unpaved and bumpy but she didn't have far to go. A half a mile in, she turned onto the gravel lane that would take her to the cabin.

The drive north from Ann Arbor had taken almost two hours. The clock on her dash told her it was nearly midnight. Before leaving, she'd gathered everything she had acquired on Valazine, made copies, and stuffed the thick manila folder into her briefcase. She'd stopped to pick up coffee and a few groceries. More than likely, she and Thomas would be working through the night.

She'd tried not to think of Adam, but her efforts were in vain. She'd seen him walk out that door a hundred times in the last two hours. The pain twisted like a dull knife in her heart every time. No matter how hard she tried, Eli couldn't get him out of her mind. The way he'd looked at her when he'd made love to her. The fury in his eyes when he'd shoved her against the wall. He had killer instincts when it came to knowing where to strike, and he'd landed a blow directly to her heart.

The cabin loomed into view then, forcing her thoughts back to the present. She slowed the Volkswagen, taking in the neat white siding against the black expanse of Lake Huron beyond. The cabin was quaint but large enough to comfortably house four or five adults for a weekend. The place was surrounded on three sides by trees. Lake Huron flanked the rear.

She spotted Thomas's tan Camry and parked the Volkswagen next to it. The brisk wind cut through her coat when she got out of the car. It was always windy here, she thought. In the summer, the cool breezes were welcome. In the winter, they cut like a knife.

Shivering, Eli slung her purse and briefcase strap over her shoulder and gathered the bag of groceries. She shut the door with her foot and started for the cabin.

Yellow light shone merrily through the windows. She hoped Thomas had started a fire. Coming up the sidewalk, she noticed the music. The alternative rock Thomas preferred. It was a haunting sound in the dead silence.

She took the front steps carefully because they hadn't yet been salted. Crossing the porch, she knocked once, then tried the knob, found it unlocked. She pushed open the door.

"Thomas? Hey, it's Eli."

Closing the door with her foot, she carried the groceries to the small, galley-style kitchen and set them on the counter. The cabin was cold and smelled as if it had been shut up for a long period of time.

For a moment, she considered making coffee, then realized the need to find Thomas was more immediate. Turning, she peered into the living room. "Thomas? Hey, are you around? I brought food."

A large picture window looked out over the lake. In the foreground, a wooden deck huddled beneath a foot of snow. It was a breathtaking sight in the summer. She couldn't count the number of times she and Walter and some of the other scientists from Roth had sat out there until the wee hours of morning, drinking coffee or beer or soda and talking about all the things they were going to achieve.

Shoving the memories aside, she walked back into the kitchen to make coffee. She was halfway to the grinder when she noticed that the back door was open. Cold air wrapped around her legs like icy hands. The first tinges of uneasiness crept over her.

"Thomas?" she said, hating the tremor in her voice.

A noise from behind her spun her around. Thomas stood a couple of feet away, looking at her with an odd expression. "You startled me," she managed to say.

"I didn't mean to."

He was holding something in his hand. She looked at it, then at him. "What on earth is that?"

He looked down at the object. "A stun gun."

Eli's heart began to pound. "Thomas . . ."

He lunged at her. She'd barely turned to run when electricity crackled. Pain jolted her body. She tried to keep moving, but her muscles seized. Vaguely, she heard another *crack!* It was like being hit by a truck. Pain exploded through her body. Her bladder let go. A scream hovered in her throat, but all she managed was a mewling sound. The room spun. She saw lights. The floor rushed toward her. She tried to break her fall, but her arms refused to move. She struck the ground hard on her left shoulder, and then everything was still.

Confusion clouded her mind. She knew she should get up and run, but her limbs refused to move. She felt hands on her body, dragging her across the floor. She heard Thomas's voice, but couldn't tell if he was really speaking or if she was imagining it.

As if from a great distance, she heard a high-pitched noise. Slowly, it dawned on her that someone was whistling.

ADAM STOOD ON THE PORCH OF ELI'S HOUSE AND dialed her number from memory. Twice, he got the answering machine. Twice, he left the same message: Call me, damn it. Cursing, he crossed to the garage and looked through the window. The Volkswagen was gone.

Where the hell had she gone at midnight?

Back on the porch, he dialed Detective Lindquist and got voice mail. He punched zero and finally got back to the desk sergeant. Adam identified himself as a police officer, then asked, "Has Elizabeth Barnes been detained or arrested in the last several hours?"

The sergeant put him on hold. Snarling and pacing, Adam waited. Two minutes later, the sergeant came back on the line and told Adam she had not been arrested or detained. Adam thanked him and hung up.

Crossing the porch, he cupped his hand and looked in the living room window. A dim light shone from the tidy kitchen. The rest of the house was dark. "Where the hell are you?" he whispered.

He couldn't believe he'd hurt her the way he had. He would never forget the way she'd looked at him, as if he'd slashed her with a knife. He knew she was better off without him, but that was no excuse for what he'd done. He'd had no right. He wanted to apologize. He wanted to make sure she was all right. He wanted her to forgive him.

Elizabeth Barnes was the best thing that ever happened to him and he'd fucked it up just like he'd fucked up everything else in his life.

Frustrated and on edge, he left the porch and walked around to the rear of the house. He peered through the French door. The light above the stove burned. No sign of Eli. He told himself he wasn't worried. That he was probably more of a threat to her than anyone at Roth. Still, the hairs on his neck stood on end at the sight of her empty kitchen.

Adam had been a cop long enough to know when something wasn't right. He wanted to believe his emotions were getting in the way of logic. But for the first time in a long time, he trusted his instincts. Something was wrong.

He tried the door. Locked, as he had expected. Not letting himself consider the consequences, he walked over to a winter flower bed, brushed away the snow, and picked up a good-size rock that had been part of a decorative border. He carried it back to the French door and smashed the pane closest to the knob. The sound of breaking glass was thunderous in the quiet neighborhood.

Somewhere in the distance a dog started to bark. Adam didn't care.

He reached through the broken pane and unlocked the door. If Eli pressed charges against him later, he figured he deserved it. He'd deal with it when and if it came up.

Inside, the first thing he noticed was her scent. The house held her essence. The pang of longing hit him so hard that for a moment he could only stand there and absorb it and try not to shake. The need to see her, to touch her, to know she was all right ate at him like a voracious beast.

Determined to keep a handle on his emotions, he strode to her study and flipped on the banker's lamp on her desk. Normally, her briefcase sat neatly next to the chair, but it was gone. The thick file they'd amassed on the Valazine clinical trials was missing as well. The laptop wasn't plugged in to the docking station. She'd taken everything with her. But where had she gone?

Picking up the phone, he dialed her cell phone number. He'd already left two messages. Maybe if she saw her home number, she'd pick up just to yell at him. The phone rang six times. Seven. Adam cursed. "Come on, damn it."

Just when he was certain she wouldn't answer, the line clicked. "Eli?" he said.

He could hear the hiss of an open line. The blare of rock music in the background. "Goddamn it, Eli. Is that you?"

The sound that met him made gooseflesh rise on his arms. It was nothing more than a soft puff of air. A sigh or a moan. The kind of noise a dying animal would make.

Cold, hard fear crawled over him, a marauding army stealing his thoughts, his logic. He knew it was her. And he knew she was in trouble.

"Eli! Where are you?"

The line went dead.

Adam stared down at the phone in his hand, felt ice spread through him. He tried to keep his head, to think. He tried to think like the cop he'd once been, but fear jumbled his thoughts. He tried to recall details about the call, any detail that might tell him something, but panic crushed his concentration.

Heart pounding, he walked over to the desk and looked around wildly. She was neat. Organized. Reference books were stacked tidily on the right. A Rolodex sat next to the phone. He paged through the Rolodex, found Kevin Chambers's number, and punched it in.

Chambers answered on the eighth ring, his voice groggy with sleep.

"This is Detective Boedecker."

"What the . . . what the hell are you doing calling me? It's after midnight, for chrissake."

"Is Eli with you?"

"What?"

"Is she with you?"

"No . . . Why the hell would she be with me? What's this all about?"

"I think she's in trouble." Adam took a deep breath. "She's missing."

"Missing?" The concern in the other man's voice surprised him. "What do you mean, missing?"

"I can't find her."

"She's probably home."

"She's not."

"Oh. Well . . ."

"Any idea where she might be? Any girlfriends? Boyfriends? What about her father's place in Indiana?"

"Aw, man. She doesn't go to the farm. Probably because of what happened to her mom there. She used to hang out with Walter on occasion, but . . . he's gone. I don't know."

"Come on, Chambers, think. Where would she go if something was bothering her and she wanted to mull things over? Would she go to see Peter Roth? Would they meet at the office? What do you think?"

"I don't know. I don't think so. Roth was pretty pissed at her. Besides, he's out of town. A conference in Cincinnati."

"What about Bornheimer?"

"I don't know. They're friends. Not too close, but . . .

everyone liked Eli. If she wanted to see Thomas, I'm sure he'd agree to see her."

Adam rubbed at his temple where the pain thumped nastily. He prayed it didn't turn into a full-fledged migraine. Please, God, not now. "Will you do me a favor and find Bornheimer? Call him at home. Find out where he is. I want to talk to him."

"Why? What the hell's going on? Is Eli in some kind of trouble?"

"I think she maybe in danger."

"What the hell do you mean by that?"

"What I mean is I'm fucking worried about her!"

Chambers shut up for a moment. "You're worried about her physical safety?"

Quickly, Adam described the call he'd made to her cell phone. "I think someone may want to hurt her."

"Maybe you should call the cops."

"I'll call Lindquist. You find Bornheimer and tell him to call me ASAP." He recited his cell phone number, then disconnected.

Adam dialed Eli's cell phone number again. Her greeting came on without ringing this time. Someone had turned off her phone. He listened to her voice, felt worry augment into something closer to fear. He left another message, then dialed the police department.

chapter
28

ELI REGAINED HER SENSES SLOWLY. SHE WAS LYING on her back, partially reclined. The ceiling was a white blur above her. She swallowed, but her mouth was parched. Her limbs felt shaky and weak. She was aware of someone moving about. Her crotch was wet, and she realized with dismay that she'd peed her pants when Thomas Bornheimer had hit her with the stun gun.

Thomas. Oh, dear God.

Blinking to clear her vision, she turned her head and tried to get her bearings. She was on the recliner in the living room. She could see the sliding door leading out to the deck and the black expanse of the lake beyond. She tried to move, realized her arms were bound tightly with something. Cocking her head, she looked down at her body. Panic swirled when she saw the straitjacket.

Oh, God in heaven, what was going on?

Aware that her breathing had gone ragged, she struggled against her binds, against the terror bubbling inside her. She could hear Thomas in the kitchen, moving around, clanging dishes as if he hadn't a care in the world.

Her only thought was that she was helpless and alone and at the complete mercy of a madman.

Don't panic.

Closing her eyes, Eli ordered herself to calm down. She forced her muscles to relax. Her hands, her arms, her shoulders. She laid her head back against the recliner and took inventory of her physical condition. She felt shaken and weak, but there wasn't any pain. He hadn't hurt her. At least not seriously.

She shifted in the chair, tested the strength in her legs. He hadn't tied her feet. That meant she could run. Or kick. Abruptly, she remembered her cell phone. It had been in her purse. Vaguely, she remembered it ringing, using the last of her strength to reach for it. Adam's voice . . . Raising her head, she looked around for it.

"Looking for something?"

She jolted at the sound of Thomas's voice. Adrenaline spiked in her muscles when she turned and saw him approach. He stood several feet away, looking small and unthreatening in his faded jeans and cashmere sweater, watching her. Eli had never imagined a madman could look so . . . benign. Thomas had fixed himself a sandwich with the groceries she'd bought. She could smell coffee brewing in the kitchen. She could hear the wind off the lake hammering against the patio doors. Everything seemed absurdly normal.

Except that she'd been immobilized and had the sinking suspicion that a man she'd thought was her friend was going to kill her.

Setting the plate down on the coffee table, Thomas walked over to her with his sandwich in hand. "I only hit you with three hundred thousand volts. You didn't go down the first time, so I increased it to 500,000 volts and hit you again." He took a bite of the sandwich. "You pissed all over yourself. I'd offer you a towel, but . . ." Shrugging, he let his voice trail off. "This is going to sound weird, but I really hated doing that to you."

"I don't understand." Her throat was thick and raw. "Why are you doing this?"

"You're kidding, right?"

She stared at him, aware of the fear writhing inside her like a snake in the throes of death.

"For crying out loud, Eli! Valazine. It's a fucking gold mine. How could you not get that?"

"Thomas, we could . . . we could fix it," she said quickly.

"I already thought of that. I looked at it. The chemical makeup. There's no way."

"But what about ROT-535?"

"Same flaw."

The words registered like a scream in her brain. "Thomas, you can't let this continue. You can't let another drug go to market. It's turning people into animals. Worse than animals. God, Thomas, people are dying. We could stop it. I'll help you."

"Roth is getting ready to take the company public, Eli. Do you have any idea how much money is at stake?"

"Thomas, we'll tell everyone it was an honest mistake. I mean, it was, wasn't it? We'll isolate the flaw and correct it. You and I. We'll work as a team. Just like before."

"Working out something like that could take a lifetime, Eli. I'm not willing to wait. Think about it. The Nobel Prize nominees are being considered right now. This isn't exactly a good time for us to go public with news that the drug we've spent the last ten years researching and developing is turning people into mass murderers."

"We couldn't have foreseen—"

"I concealed information from the FDA, Eli. I can't let you take this public. I thought you would have figured that out by now. I mean, shit, that's why you're here." He shook his head. "I didn't want it to come to this."

Eli swallowed the bile that had risen into her throat. "Come to what? What are you going to do?"

Without speaking, he reached out and touched her cheek. "I always liked you, Eli. This isn't going to be pleasant. In fact, I hate the idea. But I can't let you destroy what I've worked so hard to achieve." He dropped his hand. "I'm committed now. All of us are. We've already crossed the point of no return."

"Who?" she asked. "Who else is involved?"

Thomas walked over to the sofa. "Peter Roth. Walter Sanchez. The tech over at Trinity Labs. A couple of doctors at Manicon Labs."

Walter Sanchez. The name swirled in her head, cutting her like shrapnel. "I don't believe you. Walter wouldn't—"

"Of course he would, Eli. For God's sake, don't be naïve."

"I'm not. I knew Walter. He wouldn't get involved in something like that."

"It doesn't matter, Eli." He shook his head. "It's over."

"You won't hurt me." But she knew Thomas had already taken this too far to turn back now. "I know you, Thomas. You're not cold-blooded. You don't have that inside you."

"That's what Sanchez thought," he said. "He had an attack of conscience, the old fool. He threatened to blow the whole thing. We couldn't let that happen. Then we found out about the videotape. Turns out he'd given his lawyer instructions to mail it to you upon his death. Walter thought that would somehow protect him. It didn't, did it? This would have set him up for the rest of his life." He shrugged. "He was as naïve as you are."

"What about the e-mails?" she asked. "How did—"

"It was a team effort, actually. You kept your purse in the lower right-hand drawer of your desk. While you were in Peter's office playing Miss Distinguished Woman of Science, I made an imprint of your house key. When you were working late one night, I simply walked into your house, changed the date on your computer and compiled some very damning e-mails."

Terror and disbelief seesawed in her gut. She stared at the man she'd known most of her professional life. A man she'd worked side by side with. A man she'd trusted and cared for.

A cold-blooded murderer.

"And Kevin?" Keeping her voice level, she measured the distance to the door. She wanted her cell phone but didn't know what he'd done with it. If she could get to the door and then to her car, maybe she could get away.

"Kevin's an idiot. He couldn't think his way out of a box without being told how to do it." Thomas finished the last of the sandwich and used the napkin to wipe his mouth. "Don't even think about running. You can't run in a straitjacket."

"Let me go, Thomas. Please. I won't tell anyone."

He sighed. "Eli, please. You don't expect me to believe you'll let this go, do you? Come on, you insult my intelligence."

"Please. Thomas. I swear . . ."

"Oh, for chrissake, don't beg." He bent to pick up the plate. "I can't stand—"

Abruptly, Eli rolled over the side of the chair, got her feet under her, and ran. She heard Thomas curse. Then she was sprinting down the hall. Toward the front door. Less than ten feet away. The straitjacket hampered her balance, but she ran at a reckless speed. She heard him behind her, but she didn't stop. She was halfway down the hall when strong fingers bit into her shoulders.

"Damn it, Eli!"

She tried not to think about the stun gun. She had to get away, or he was going to kill her. "Let go of me!" she screamed.

Strong hands shoved her to the floor. She fell hard, her head snapping against the planks so forcefully she saw stars. She tasted blood, realized she'd bitten her lip. Turning her head, she saw Thomas, the stun gun extended.

"No!" she screamed.

A loud *crack!* sounded. Pain exploded through her body, then the world faded to gray.

"THIS HAD BETTER BE FUCKING GOOD." LINDQUIST'S voice was rough with sleep. "It's one o'clock in the morning."

Adam didn't bother with niceties. "Eli Barnes is missing."

There was a thoughtful silence on the other end of the line. "What makes you think that?"

"I'm at her house. She's not here."

"Maybe she went to the goddamn grocery."

Shoving aside his own annoyance, Adam quickly told him about what he'd heard when he called her cell phone. "I think she's in trouble."

"And I think I'm getting only half the story. I've been getting that impression since the first time I talked to Dr. Barnes. You going to fill me in?"

Praying he wasn't making a mistake that would cost him his credibility, Adam quickly summarized the Valazine situation.

"You got any proof?" the detective asked.

"Some. Nothing rock solid."

"Dr. Barnes was helping you with it?"

"Yeah." Adam looked around the empty kitchen, felt the panic tighten like a noose around his throat. "I need your help."

"Let me make some calls."

"I need to find her."

"You two are . . . involved?"

Of all the questions Lindquist had asked, that was the most difficult. "Yeah."

"Where do you think she is?"

"I don't know. Maybe with someone from Roth. Thomas Bornheimer or Peter Roth." He thought about Chambers, added his name as well. "Maybe with someone from one of the clinics that administered the drug trials." He began to pace as the list of possibilities grew.

"How long has she been missing?"

Adam looked at his watch. "Almost three hours."

Now it was Lindquist's turn to sigh. "You know I can't officially put out a missing persons report for twenty-four hours. Dr. Barnes is an adult. As far as we know, she's out driving around."

"She's not. Goddamn it, I know she's in trouble. And I know it has to do with the case. With Walter Sanchez's murder."

"You know she's a suspect, don't you, Detective?"

"Yeah, but we both know she didn't do it."

"Look, I'll put out an APB. If she gets stopped by the MHP or if they spot her car, we'll get her. First thing in the morning, I'll put a couple of officers on it."

"I need officers now," Adam snapped.

"An APB is the best I can do."

Adam's hands were shaking when he disconnected. He stood in her kitchen, feeling as if the world had just come down on his shoulders. "Where the hell are you, Eli?" he whispered.

He started when his cell phone chirped. "Yeah?"

"This is Kevin Chambers. I just tried to reach Thomas Bornheimer at home, but there's no answer."

"What's the address? I'm going over there."

Chambers hesitated.

"Give me the address or I'm going to come over there and beat it out of you."

"It's 6999 Gettysburg."

"Where is that?" Adam grabbed his coat, putting the directions to memory as he went through the front door and into the night.

HE'D TIED HER FEET THIS TIME. THE THOUGHT CAME to her in a flurry. Eli opened her eyes, watched the light ebb and flow as her senses slowly returned. She remembered running. The sickening crack of the stun gun as it discharged 500,000 volts of electricity into her body.

She ached everywhere. She could feel the pain of a split lip. Turning her head, she saw movement and struggled to focus her eyes.

"Eli, I wish you hadn't run." Thomas Bornheimer stood over her, looking down at her as if she were a sick dog that needed to be euthanized.

"Let me go," she croaked.

"I wish you hadn't busted your lip. That'll make it harder for me to make this look like a suicide."

Suicide.

"Thomas . . . no."

He reached down and picked up something off the table. For an instant, Eli thought it was the stun gun and braced for pain. Then she saw the pastel-colored plastic and recognized an oral medication syringe. It was jury-

rigged with a four-inch flexible tube. Medical professionals used oral syringes for administering medication to
difficult patients. Alzheimer's patients. The mentally ill.

Panic rose like a tidal wave inside her when she realized what he was going to do. She struggled against her
binds, but the straitjacket held tight. For the first time she
considered the very real possibility that she was going to
die. That she would never see Adam again. She would
never know if he loved her.

"I'm going to put this tube down your throat."

Her heart stuttered and began to hammer hard against
her ribs. "Thomas, please, no."

His hand shook when he raised the oral syringe and
looked at it against the light. Eli could see that the syringe
was full—sixty milliliters of fluid. She wondered what it
contained. If he planned to force poison down her throat.
"Don't do this, Thomas. Please."

For the first time, he looked agitated. "Nobody wanted
to do this, damn it! I mean, we're scientists, for chrissake.
We don't fucking kill people."

"Don't kill me, Thomas. I won't tell anyone. I won't—"

"Peter Roth knew about your mother, so we decided it
would be best if you committed suicide. You know, like
mother like daughter. It won't be bad for you. I can promise you that. Peter was adamant about that. He likes you,
Eli. All of us like you. This was an extremely difficult
decision for us. We don't want you to suffer needlessly.
We just want you gone."

Cold terror gripped her at the insanity behind the
words. She looked at the syringe in his hand, felt the terror
squeeze the breath from her lungs. "You're insane."

He held up the syringe. "Don't you want to know
what's in here? Don't you want to know how you're going to die?"

"You won't get away with this. Adam Boedecker
knows everything. I've left copies of everything behind.
Lindquist knows. Everyone involved will be in jail by the
end of the day tomorrow."

"Shut up."

"There's enough proof against you to get an investigation started," she said.

"I'm sure the investigation will take a very interesting turn when they find proof that you withheld adverse event data from the FDA," Thomas said. "Of course, it will never be prosecuted because, overcome with guilt, you decided you would rather take your own life than face professional ruin and prison time. There's a certain romance to it, isn't there?"

He looked at the syringe he held. "Considering that the drug you spent ten years developing will be the instrument of your death makes it even more so."

Eli stared at him, cold terror paralyzing her.

"It's a cocktail I devised. It should be relatively painless. I dissolved twenty ten-milligram Valazine tablets in sixty milliliters of vodka. Top shelf, of course." He glanced at her. "That was your mother's drink of choice, wasn't it?"

"You sick bastard." Her voice shook with fury and the utter horror that he would think of something so diabolical.

"Within the hour you'll begin to suffer the effects of serotonin syndrome resulting from excessive stimulation of central and peripheral serotonergic receptors. It is characterized by changes in mental status and motor and autonomic function. You'll develop tremors. Your blood pressure will elevate. You'll run a fever. Tachycardia will set in. You might have seizures. Finally, you'll succumb to a coma. With the dose I'm giving you, you'll die of a massive stroke in two or three hours."

Eli shuddered. Her heart thrashed like a wild animal trapped inside her chest. Her breaths came in short gasps. She tried to calm herself, ordered herself to think.

Only she knew she'd run out of time.

chapter
29

ADAM RAPPED HARD ON THE FRONT DOOR OF THO-
mas Bornheimer's house. He leaned on the bell for a full
minute. He paced the porch. Either Bornheimer slept like
the dead, or he wasn't home.

Betting on the latter, Adam headed around to the back
door. He broke in the same way he'd broken into Eli's
house and entered through the kitchen. One look in the
garage told him the other man wasn't home.

The pain in his head had grown steadily worse. He
knew stress could exacerbate a migraine. He didn't have
time for a migraine. Not now, for God's sake.

He roamed the house like an angry bull, looking for
anything that might tell him where Bornheimer had gone.
He found the study, a paneled room filled with books and
wall plaques, a desk, a high-dollar color copier, and a
computer.

Bornheimer was a neat freak, he realized quickly. In
the top drawer of the desk, he found a leather appointment
book and paged through it, realized it was for last year.
Adam flung it across the room. Feeling on the verge of
panic, he strode into the hall. A leather briefcase sat next

to the door. Picking it up, he carried it to the kitchen and dumped it on the table. Files and papers and a Palm Pilot spilled out, followed by a leather appointment book. Quickly, he flipped it open, paged to today's date. Several appointments were listed. No mention of Eli. Cursing, Adam slammed it shut.

He went through the other papers, finding nothing. Desperation pressed down on him. He would never forgive himself if something happened to her. Frustrated and angry, his head pounding like a drum, he reached for his cell phone and punched in Kevin Chambers's number.

"You locate Bornheimer yet?" Adam asked.

"I was hoping you were calling to tell me you'd found him."

"He's not here." Adam paced the length of the kitchen. "I need to find her. You've got to think. Is there anywhere else he might be? Someplace where he might have met her? A favorite restaurant? A meeting place?"

"The corporate cabin. I can't believe I didn't think of that sooner."

Adam stopped pacing. "Where?"

"Port Sanilac. It's about a hundred miles northeast of here. A waterfront cabin. Roth keeps it for retreats and meetings. It's pretty isolated this time of year."

"You got a phone number?"

"We use our cells when we're there."

"Damn it."

"You don't think Thomas took her there, do you?"

Adam didn't want to think about that. Not when he was already hanging on to control by a frayed thread. "What's the fastest way to get there?"

ELI COULDN'T BELIEVE IT HAD COME TO THIS. THAT her life would end this way on this cold and terrible night. That it would be done at the hands of a man she'd once called friend and a drug she'd devoted her life to developing.

"Stay the hell away from me," she warned.

"Don't make it any more difficult than it already is,"

Thomas said. "Don't fight me. You can't possibly win."

Horror slithered through her when he moved toward her with the syringe in hand. She spotted the pistol on the coffee table a few feet away, but knew she wouldn't be able to reach it. "I won't let you give me that."

"You know I can force you. I'll hit you with the gun again if I have to."

Eli screamed and struggled against her binds. "Get away from me! Help me! *Please!*" In the back of her mind, she knew no one could hear her. The cabin was set away from the road. There were no neighbors for miles. She was alone. On her own. Trapped with a madman who wanted her dead.

Coming up behind her, Thomas clamped his arm around her head so that her chin was at the crook of his elbow. Eli jerked her head from side to side, fighting him with all her might, but he held her prone.

"Open your mouth," he snarled.

Squeezing her eyes shut, she breathed through her nose, refusing.

"I'll hit you with the gun again, you little bitch! Do it!"

Oh, God. Oh, God! She didn't want to die. Not like this. *Please, God, help me. Help me!*

Panic exploded inside her when his fingers closed over her nostrils. Eli opened her eyes, found herself staring into pale blue eyes fringed with insanity. For a full minute, she held her breath. Held it so long her vision blurred and the room spun wildly around her. Finally, the need for air overwhelmed her. She opened her mouth to suck in oxygen. At the same time, Thomas thrust a dental surgical speculum between her teeth. She bit down, but it was too late. She saw his hand move, then felt the tube at the back of her throat, gagging her. He depressed the plunger. She felt the fluid rush down her esophagus. She tasted vodka and the bitterness of the dissolved pills.

And the countdown to her death began.

ADAM PUSHED THE TAHOE TO 105 MILES AN HOUR and held it steady. The pain in his head billowed with every beat of his heart. Oncoming headlights cut into his brain like scalpels. He saw halos around lights and streaming tails that ran across his vision like shooting stars. Nausea taunted his stomach, ebbing and flowing with the pain and filling his mouth with the bitter tang of bile.

Just north of Port Huron, he pulled over at a rest area, threw open his door, and vomited. For a full minute he rested his head against the steering wheel, unable to move, letting the cold air rush over him to clear his head.

But when he closed his eyes, he saw Eli. He saw the way she'd been the first time he'd made love to her. The sweetness of her smile. The heat of her kisses. The tight grip of her around him when he'd made love to her . . .

He loved her. Loved her more than his own life. He would never be able to live with himself if something happened to her. *Dear God, please let her be all right. I'll do anything. . . .*

Panic and terror coiled and sprang inside him. Turning in his seat, he dug the syringe out of his briefcase, ripped off the wrapper, and jammed the needle into his thigh. He knew the drug would affect his clarity, but he also knew if he didn't do something, the pain would paralyze him and he would be useless.

He sat in the cool darkness of the cab with his eyes closed and waited for the medication to kick in. He prayed it would be enough to get him up to the cabin. He prayed once he got there he would find her and she would be fine . . .

ELI COULD STILL TASTE THE BITTER PILLS AND vodka at the back of her throat. She stared at Thomas, horror and dread crawling inside her like maggots.

"It shouldn't be long now," he said. "Have you eaten anything? That will slow down absorption." He looked at his watch. "The tremors will probably come first. I'd give them twenty minutes or so."

"How could you do this?" she whispered.

Thomas looked away. "Don't make this any harder than it has to be. I'm not going to enjoy watching you die."

"Thomas, please. Don't do this," she said.

Rising, he picked up the bottle of vodka and a brown vial of pills. Eli watched as he wiped both clean, then walked over to her. "I need for your prints to be on these bottles."

"Go to hell."

"I'm going to cut one of your hands free. Don't try anything stupid, or I'll hit you with the stun gun again."

"Untie me," she said. "I'm uncomfortable. Please. I won't try anything."

Never taking his eyes from hers, he pulled a pocket knife from his pants pocket and began cutting the strait-jacket from her right hand. "I don't want to risk your moving and my cutting you by accident. This has got to look like a suicide." He frowned at her. "That cut on your lip is bad enough. But I suppose the police will think you drank the vodka and fell."

"Please, untie me. I'm . . . not feeling well. I won't try to get away."

"You don't think I'm stupid, do you?"

She hadn't even noticed that her right hand was free. He held it for a moment, looked down at it, then smiled cruelly at her. "Your muscles are beginning to spasm."

The fear was a dull roar inside her now. Her head felt fuzzy, as if she were watching the scene from inside a plastic bag. She remembered that there was something she'd wanted to do, but couldn't remember what it was. Then she realized Thomas was holding her hand, caressing it. Inwardly, she cringed. Her mind wandered, and she thought about Adam. She wondered where he was. If he was looking for her. She wondered if he was sorry for the things he'd said to her. If he would mourn her death . . .

The cool glass of the vodka bottle against her palm jerked her thoughts back to the present. Thomas wrapped her fingers around the bottle. She knew she should pull her hand away, but her muscles refused to obey.

When he tilted the bottle and splashed the alcohol over her mouth, she barely felt the burn against her cut lip. Then he laid her hand across her abdomen. Eli watched her fingers twitch. Intellectually, she knew it was her hand, but for the life of her she couldn't make it stop.

"Adam . . ." She hadn't even realized she was going to speak his name until she heard it. Every time she closed her eyes she saw him. The smile she'd come to cherish. The way he looked at her. The feel of his kiss.

Thomas knelt at her side and pressed the plastic bottle of pills to her palm. "You miss your cop, huh?"

She'd almost forgotten he was in the room with her. She looked over at him, felt the muscles in her neck seize. There was no real pain, but for an instant she couldn't move.

"I've got Valium for you, Eli." Thomas sighed, looking shaken and upset. "You're beginning to suffer muscle rigidity. Jesus Christ, I don't want to see you like that. Valium will make you more comfortable."

"I don't want any more drugs," she said, feeling oddly detached. "I feel hot." The fear was still there, but it was no longer razor sharp. She could feel it galloping through her, but her mind had accepted it.

A cool cloth against her forehead surprised her. She looked up and saw Thomas standing next to her.

"Fever," he said. "Your body temperature is climbing. Eli, I'm sorry. Try to relax. It'll be over soon."

She closed her eyes and thought of Adam. All the things they'd shared, good and bad. She longed for him. Grief cut like a blade when she thought of their last moments together, the things they'd said to each other.

Heat burned her from the inside out. Perspiration broke out all over her body. She could feel the heavy pound of her heart in her chest, racing out of control. She was dying. She felt death creeping up on her.

Oh, Adam, where are you?

ADAM TURNED OFF OF HIGHWAY 25 AND PUNCHED off the headlights. Tall, naked trees lined both sides of the road. Occasionally, he caught a glimpse of Lake Huron to his right.

The pain in his head exploded with every beat of his heart, bad enough to make his eyes water. Bursts of light blinded him. He leaned forward, squinting through the darkness, barely able to see as he checked the names on the mailboxes. A half mile down the road, he spotted one that said "Roth" and turned down the narrow drive.

It was darker under the cover of trees. Adam struggled to see in the darkness, praying he'd been wrong, that he would find Eli safe and alive. That she would be annoyed to discover he'd followed her all the way to the corporate cabin to check up on her. He prayed to God she was all right.

He stopped the Tahoe out of sight from the cabin and shut down the engine. Pulling the Glock from the glove box, he tucked it into the waistband of his jeans and got out of the truck.

The moon moved out from behind a cloud. The moonlight was so bright he could see his shadow on the snow as he ran toward the cabin. Twice he had to stop and wait for the pain in his head to subside. He knew he wasn't in any condition to do too much if he ran into trouble. He couldn't hit the broad side of a barn when he was seeing double from the pain. He hoped he wouldn't run into trouble.

His heart thumped hard when he spotted Eli's car parked directly in front of the cabin. She was here. Christ. A tan Toyota Camry was parked next to the Volkswagen. Thomas Bornheimer's car. He remembered it from the information Chad had given him.

Adam jogged past the front door and headed toward the rear, keeping low. Holding the Glock at his side, he stepped onto the porch. The back door stood open; the storm door was closed. Squinting against the light, he peered through the glass but didn't see any movement. Silently, he reached for the knob and eased open the storm door.

He stepped into the galley-style kitchen. Steel guitar screamed from a CD player on the counter. The light hurt his eyes, but Adam didn't let himself think about the pain. He crept across the room, then pressed his back flat against the wall and peered around the corner. The living room stood in semidarkness. No movement. No sign of

Eli or Bornheimer. Adam moved into the room, every muscle tensed.

Then he saw her, and his heart stopped dead in his chest.

She was lying on the recliner. Bound with some type of straitjacket. Her eyes were closed. Her face as pale as death. God in heaven, she looked dead.

Cold, hard fear gripped him. A vise around his throat that wouldn't let him speak or breathe or think. He darted across the room without considering his own safety. "Eli. Christ. Are you all right?"

He touched her, found her flesh slicked with perspiration and hot. When she looked at him, there was no spark of recognition. Just the glazed look of the dead.

"What happened?" Looking quickly around the room, he worked on getting her free of the straitjacket.

She made an unintelligible sound.

He leaned closer. "Where's Bornheimer?"

"Adam . . . you came. Thomas . . ."

"I'm here. I'm sorry. Just . . . hang on, okay?" Emotion squeezed cruelly at his throat. "What did he do to you?"

"Drugs . . ."

"Bornheimer?" Fear whipped through him. "Overdose?"

She nodded. ". . . kill you . . ."

"Where is he?"

"He's here . . . be careful."

Another wave of fear encroached. Fighting panic, Adam worked his cell phone from his coat pocket and hit zero. "What did he give you?"

He saw movement out of the corner of his eye an instant before he heard the *crack!* He dodged but wasn't fast enough. The jolt of electricity hit him like a freight train, sent him sprawling to the floor, his phone sliding out of reach. Pain zinged through his body. He looked up, saw Thomas Bornheimer standing over Eli, a stun gun in his hand.

"Five hundred thousand volts will take down even the most determined criminals," he said. "That's what the training manual said, anyway. How are you, Detective Boedecker?"

Adam lay very still, willing his thoughts back to order, giving his body time to regroup.

"It looks like our Eli is well on her way into serotonin syndrome." Bornheimer glanced at his watch. "It shouldn't be long now." He smiled. "I'm going to hit you with the gun once more while you're down. Don't want you back up to speed too quickly. I'm sure you'd be much harder to handle than she was."

Bornheimer scooped a .380 semi-auto pistol off the coffee table and started toward Adam. "I never bargained on you showing up, but I've always known the value of having a Plan B. I don't have time for you to die of an overdose, so once I've got you tied nice and tight I'm going to drag you outside and put a bullet in your head."

He looked down at the stun gun and pistol in his hands. "With the advances in forensic science, I can't risk traces of DNA in the cabin. But if you try anything stupid, I'll blow your fucking head off where you lay." He sighed. "Once the dirty deed is done, a trip out to the lake on the snowmobile, a few weights securely tied to your body, and no one will ever know what happened to Adam Boedecker. Pretty brilliant, don't you think?"

Adam lay on the floor, watching him, and waited until the other man was close. When little more than a foot separated them, he jerked out the gun that had wedged under his body. But the jolt of electricity had slowed his reflexes and he fumbled with the gun as he brought it up. Bornheimer's eyes widened. He lunged forward, the gun in his hand coming up. The blast fractured the air.

Adam braced for pain that didn't come. Scooting back, he gripped his pistol with both hands and fired three times in quick succession. The first shot went wide and hit the ceiling. The second tore a tiny round hole in Bornheimer's left cheekbone. The third hit him in the temple, snapping his head back. The gun clattered to the floor. Bornheimer looked utterly surprised for a moment. Then his eyes glazed. His knees buckled. And he fell forward like dead weight.

Knowing Eli didn't have much time, Adam grabbed his cell phone off the floor and punched zero.

"Put me through to the sheriff's office! I'm a police officer! I've got a medical emergency at the Roth cabin on Highway 25 south of Port Sanilac. I need an airlift chopper. *Now!*"

He barely heard the voice on the other end of the line. Kneeling beside the recliner where Eli lay, he unbuckled the last of the straps on the straitjacket and removed it.

"Eli. Honey, it's me, Adam. Talk to me. Tell me what they gave you."

"Serotonin . . ." Her voice trailed off.

"What did he give you?"

"Val . . . zine."

"Honey, stay with me. Help's on the way. You're a doctor. Damn it, tell me what to do." He shook her gently, but she didn't respond.

Horror ripped through him when she began to seize. Her head snapped back. Her body went rigid. Adam had known helplessness before, but never like this. Never had he had to stand back and watch someone he cared for, someone he loved, die.

Struggling to keep his head, he held her until her muscles relaxed. Using his cell phone, he called Kevin Chambers. The other man answered on the first ring.

"Bornheimer shot her up with Valazine. She's . . ." Adam's voice broke. He looked down at her, watched her eyes roll back. "Jesus. She's convulsing. Damn it. Tell me what to do!"

"Call Careflite."

"Done. What do I tell them when they get here?"

"I'll stay on the line. She's going to need an IV of chlorpromazine, 12.5 milligrams, intubation, and a bunch of other stuff. Is her airway open?"

"She's breathing, but it's labored. Jesus Christ! Stay on the line." He turned back to Eli. Her face was deathly pale and slicked with sweat. Brushing the hair back from her face, he kissed her softly on the forehead. "Hang on, Eli. Just . . . for God's sake, hang on."

"Adam?" she whispered.

"I'm here. You're going to be fine. Careflite is en route."

"I knew you'd come," she said. "I know you don't want to hear this . . ."

"I just want to hear your voice," he said softly. "Keep talking."

"Talk about . . . what?"

"Anything but the weather."

"I . . . love you." Her muscles went rigid again. Her eyes rolled back. Another seizure shook her body.

"Eli . . . Honey, hang on." Adam felt something give way inside him. Something hot and painful that ripped through him like a bomb. Closing his eyes against the hot rush of tears, he rested his forehead against hers.

"I love you, too," he whispered, and began to pray.

chapter
30

Three days later

ADAM DIDN'T LIKE HOSPITALS ON PRINCIPLE. HE'D spent too much time in them in the last three years to hold anything but loathing for the antiseptic smells, clinical atmosphere, and smug-faced doctors.

It wasn't enough to keep him out of St. Francis.

After three days of worry and four hellish nights—and a lot of soul searching in between—he'd realized the alternative was infinitely worse. He needed to see Eli. Needed to touch her. Talk to her. Look into her eyes and see her smile. He needed to make sure she was all right.

The last three days had been a whirlwind of lawyers and prosecuting attorneys and internal affairs inquiries. The good news was that he hadn't been charged with any crimes. There would, of course, be a grand jury investigation into the death of Dr. Thomas Bornheimer. Adam figured he could live with that. There was no jury in the United States that would hold him responsible after what Bornheimer had done to Eli. After what the corporate team at Roth Pharmaceuticals had done to thousands of innocent people who'd put their trust in a breakthrough drug.

Peter Roth and several medical doctors involved with the clinical drug trials of Valazine and ROT-535 had been questioned in connection with the case now unfolding thanks to an aggressive media. An emergency recall of Valazine had been issued by the Food and Drug Administration just that morning. Lawsuits were expected to start coming in before the end of the week. Losses incurred by Roth were predicted to be in the billions.

Adam should have drawn some satisfaction in that he'd accomplished his mission, that he'd gotten a dangerous drug off the market and shut down a pharmaceutical company that had caused untold suffering. He should have felt good knowing he'd stopped the people who'd cost his brother his life. That Michael's death had not been in vain, that his reputation had been cleared.

Adam could finally get on with his life. The commander of the Chicago Police Department had even offered him a position on the new homicide task force, thanks to some fast talking by Lieutenant Stuart Henderson and his ex-partner Chad Deaton. Adam wasn't sure why the two men he'd given so much grief in the last weeks had gone to bat for him, but they had. Adam should have been walking on air. Everything he'd ever wanted was finally within reach. Justice for Michael. A new career within the department. A chance for a new start.

For some reason he couldn't bring himself to give a rat's ass about any of it.

All he'd been able to think of in the last three days was the young woman lying alone in a hospital bed. A woman who'd risked everything to help him. A woman who'd put her own life in jeopardy to do the right thing. A woman who'd broken down walls, made him feel like a human being—like a man—and touched him in ways he'd never imagined possible.

He took the elevator to the third floor, then made his way down the wide, bright hall and started watching for the room number. He knew he should have come sooner, but he'd had some sorting out to do. He'd thought three days would be enough time for him to figure out what he wanted. How he was going to handle this.

But he didn't have a clue what he was going to say to her.

He stopped outside her door, telling himself he wasn't nervous about seeing her. That his heart wasn't pounding, his palms weren't wet. It wasn't like he was some insecure teenager, for chrissake.

Taking a deep breath, Adam stepped into the room. He barely noticed the dozen or so bouquets of flowers lining the windowsill and taking up most of the space on the dinner cart. He hadn't sent flowers. Damn it, he should have sent flowers.

The television volume was on low. Eli was sitting up in bed, watching him with dark, wary eyes. Adam approached her, wondering why she didn't smile. Not that he deserved it after the way he'd treated her that day in the hotel. Hell, maybe he'd been wrong about this. Maybe he shouldn't have come. Maybe she didn't want to see him at all.

"Hi," he said.

"Hi back."

"Nice flowers."

"Thanks."

"You look really good."

She did smile then, just a little, but it dazzled him.

"You're a really bad liar," she said.

Shoving his hands in his pockets, he looked down at his shoes, then back at her. "How are you feeling?"

"Pretty good. I get to go home tomorrow if all the tests come back okay."

"I'll keep my fingers crossed for you. I'm not a big fan of hospitals."

"No, you wouldn't be. It's that personal experience thing, huh?"

Grimacing, he nodded.

She fiddled with the plastic hospital band on her wrist, then glanced out the window.

"I'm really bad at this," he admitted.

"Bad at what?"

"Apologizing. Doing the right thing. I don't know." Uncomfortable, he looked around the room. "Mind if I sit down?"

"Sure."

He moved a wrapped package from the chair next to the bed, wishing he'd thought to bring a gift, and set it next to a vase of fresh-cut flowers. Their eyes met, held. She looked away first by glancing at the television, then out the window. Adam saw her discomfort, wished he could do something to make this easier for her.

Do it, hotshot, an inner voice said. *Tell her. Get it over with.* "The department offered me a desk job," he blurted when he could no longer stand the tension. "They want me to head up a task force. In homicide." He watched her carefully, starkly aware of the steady thrum of his heart, the electric zing of nerves.

"Oh, well . . . that's . . . wonderful news. Congratulations."

"Wonderful might be pushing it a little." He scrubbed a hand over his jaw. "It's a desk job. I can probably live with that. I'm thinking about taking it."

"It sounds like a good opportunity." She dazzled him with a smile that was warm and sincere and filled with all the things he'd come to love about her. "Adam, I'm happy for you. And proud. This is what you wanted."

Incredulous because his nerves were jumping, he wiped his palms on his slacks and leaned forward, putting his elbows on his knees. "When I walked in here, I thought I would know what to say. I thought the words would come, Eli. I thought I would know that walking away is the right thing to do." He sighed. "I didn't think my feelings would get in the way."

Her expression turned wary. "In the way of what?"

"Of doing the right thing."

"Adam . . . don't. You don't have to—"

"Yeah, I do. I have to do this. I have a few things to get off my chest."

"This may not be a good time for either of us to make any decisions. The last few weeks have been . . . intense."

She looked down to where her hands were gripping the sheets, relaxed them.

"I couldn't stay away. Eli, I was worried out of my mind about you."

"I'm fine."

"I can see that. But . . . that's not the only reason I'm here."

She blinked at him. "Why are you?"

"This is where things get . . . complicated." When she only continued to stare at him, he trudged on, telling himself whatever the outcome, he could handle it. With her or without her, he'd be all right. "I'm going back to Chicago," he said.

"I'm okay with that. I mean, that's what you want, and I'm happy for you."

"Eli, for God's sake . . ."

"I'll be fine." She smiled, but this time it didn't reach her eyes.

"I want you to come with me," he said.

THE WORDS POURED OVER HER LIKE A WARM BATH on frostbitten skin. Eli felt the solid impact of them, as soft as a breath, as powerful as a blast, warming her from the inside out. For an instant she couldn't speak, couldn't do anything but stare at him and wonder if it was possible to love someone so much it hurt.

"If you were smart, you'd tell me to take a hike," he added. "God knows I deserve it."

"Adam, I—"

"I'm not an easy man to live with," he said. "I have a bad temper. Mood swings. The migraines are unpredictable. With any traumatic brain injury, there's always the threat of seizures. A year from now. Five years from now. Tomorrow. There are no guarantees. But that's part of who I am now. And it comes with the territory."

Eli had seen him handle some intense situations in the last week or so, but she didn't think she'd ever seen him this shaken. She watched him, her heart knocking hard against her ribs. "What are you saying?"

"I'm telling you this because you deserve better than what I can give you. I'm telling you because I think you're better off without me." He laughed, but it was an unnatural sound. "But, Christ, that doesn't make me want you any less. I couldn't stop thinking about you. I couldn't stay away. And I think it's selfish as hell of me to ask you to take a chance on someone like me."

Her head was spinning, but she was laughing inside. Laughing with joy. At the knowledge that she hadn't been wrong about him. That her own heart had been right on the money. "Perhaps if you made about a hundred concessions, we could negotiate something we could both live with."

He went perfectly still.

Eli smiled.

"I'm good at concessions," he said, deadpan.

"What about negotiation?"

"I'm an excellent negotiator." He took her hand. "And I don't give up easily."

"Good. Neither do I."

Standing, he crossed the small distance between them. His hand was large and warm as it encompassed hers. "You were right that day in the hotel—"

"Adam, we don't have to—"

"Yes, Eli, we do. I do. I need to say this. Just . . . let me say what I need to say, okay?"

"Okay."

"You were right on the money when you called me a coward."

"I didn't mean—"

"Yes, you did. And you were right. I *was* a coward because I didn't have the guts to tell you I love you." His gaze searched hers with an almost desperate intensity. "I do. I love you more than anything in the world. I want to spend the rest of my life loving you."

Eli saw the raw truth of the words in his eyes. Such a strong man. An uncompromising man willing to face the one thing in this world that terrified him. Willing to risk the one thing that was truly his. His heart.

"I love you, too," she whispered. "That hasn't changed."

"I hurt you." Reaching up, he thumbed a tear from her cheek. "I'm sorry for that."

"Love doesn't have to hurt."

"I know that now," he said.

"I'll never hurt you." She touched his face with her hand. "I'll never betray you."

He turned his face into her palm, closed his eyes, and brushed a kiss over the flesh. "I want you in my life," he whispered. "Right or wrong, I want you with me."

"I'm here."

"I don't know where this will lead, Eli. Maybe to no-where, but you make me happy." His voice broke. "I want to make you happy. I want to try."

Happiness shimmered inside her, like the sun glinting off a frozen lake on a crystal morning, bright and new and pristine. She looked into his eyes and saw his heart, felt it beating in time with hers.

"I'd like to try, too," she whispered.

Leaning close to her, he cupped her face with his hands and sealed the words between them with a kiss.

Turn the page for a preview of
Linda Castillo's new novel.

FADE TO RED

Coming soon from Berkley Sensation

DEATH TERRIFIED HER. SOMEHOW, SHE'D ALWAYS known hers would be violent. That it would come early in life. That it would be terrible and grueling, and in the end she would beg for it.

This was worse than terrible. Worse than anything she'd ever imagined even in her nightmares. Not even the lavender haze of the drug could dull the sharp bite of the knife. She felt every injury to her flesh with a thousand screaming nerve endings. Every second ticked by like a death knell.

They were going to kill her.

She struggled against her binds, twisting and straining until the steel cuffs clanked against the exposed ulna causing agonizing pain in her wrists. But she knew it was useless. They had been as careful as she had been careless. Now she was going to pay the ultimate price.

The realization sent a surge of hopelessness through her, followed by a sickening rise of panic that pooled inside her like vomit.

She was dying.

The reality that fate could be so merciless filled her

with outrage. After everything she'd been through, everything she'd overcome, everything she had endured in a
life that had been far from easy, the last thing she would
ever see was this dank warehouse and her own blood under the bright glare of the lights.

Goddamn them all.

She didn't care. Hadn't cared for a long time. About
life. About death. She just wanted it to be over. Quickly.
Without all the humiliations of dying. As far as she was
concerned she had died a long time ago. Her body just
had to catch up.

She drifted toward the darkness, reaching and straining
for it with her mind, wishing desperately for it to swallow
her whole like a giant, ravenous beast that would devour
her so she would simply cease to exist.

Another vivid flash of pain wrenched a scream from
her, long and shrill and animalistic. She bit down on the
gag and screamed a second time in outrage and fury, cursing them with every cell in her body. She rode the agony,
felt it tear through her like a thousand tiny blades wak-
ening every nerve with a ferocity that left her breathless.
She tried to deny the horror of what was happening. Tried
to convince herself that the God she'd always known
would never be so unmerciful. But the pain was hellish
and relentless and a thousand times worse than death.

She looked up at her tormentor, through the hair that
hung wetly in her face, and hatred welled inside her. The
mask he wore should have terrified her, but it didn't. She
understood all too well why he wore the mask, and she
hated it. Hated him. Hated all of them.

She tried to speak through the ball gag, but it was impossible. With her last dying breath, she wanted to tell
him she had betrayed him. That she'd left evidence behind
that would destroy him. She wanted him to know she'd
won one last, tiny battle if only for a fleeting instant of
satisfaction before he killed her. That was all she had left,
but it wasn't enough to save her life.

I'll see you in hell, she thought, and a maniacal sound
bubbled up from her throat.

The eyes within the mask darted to hers. Even through
the small slits, she saw the light of his exhilaration. And

in that moment, she accepted her death. Accepted that it would happen here and now and there wasn't a damn thing she could do about it.

Except die.

Oh, but she didn't know how. Didn't know how to take her last breath. Didn't know when to close her eyes. When to let her muscles go slack. She didn't know how to stop living.

Dear God, she hadn't wanted to die alone.

She thought of her sister and grief stabbed through her with the same hot vengeance as the knife. Regret stung her brain, but she knew there would be no reckoning, no righting of wrongs, no last good-byes.

Don't cry for me, she thought.

And when she closed her eyes, the world faded to red.

"TWO HUNDRED CAPER-AND-SALMON CANAPÉS COMing up!"

Lindsey Metcalf glanced up from the flour-dusted counter where she'd been working to see her partner, Carissa Ross, push through the swinging doors, a round tray heavily laden with canapés hefted onto her shoulder.

"We need two hundred more," Lindsey said.

"And I need a tummy tuck and collagen injections." Carissa set the tray on the stainless-steel counter and slapped her hands against her apron-covered thighs. "That doesn't mean I'm going to get them. Besides, we're out of time."

Ignoring her friend's snappish tone, Lindsey stared at the delicate swan-shaped canapés in admiration. Tiny works of art. A sliver of baby carrot for the beak. Shiny black caviar for the eyes. A short stalk of shredded celery for the tail. Flaky butter crust for the belly that was filled with fresh Canadian Salmon and imported Greek capers.

I did that, she thought, slightly shocked that the melding of food and art could be so beautiful—and so totally satisfying.

"And it's snowing like the dickens out there," Carissa added peevishly.

"People eat, even when it snows," Lindsey put in.

"They'll never notice a few missing canapés."

"Mrs. Basehart will notice if two hundred of these babies are missing."

"I'm glad she's only got one daughter. One more wedding like this and I quit. I can't believe people get married in January, for chrissake. Whatever happened to June? It's sacrilege."

Lindsey touched one of the tiny swans with her index finger, almost expecting the tiny wings to spread. "This is the best work we've ever done."

Carissa sighed. "They're almost too beautiful to eat."

"Almost." Lindsey scooped up the tiny bird and popped it into her mouth, closing her eyes against the slow melt of pleasure. Delicate salmon. The bold flavor of capers. Crisp vegetables. Buttery crust. Caviar. A hint of horseradish. "God, we're good."

Carissa chuckled. "Now we're two hundred and one short."

"I'll bake up some more of those wonderful little crusts." Lindsey turned to the dual ovens behind her and switched both to the correct temperature. "You whip up some more of the filling."

"We've got to have all of this to the Basehart estate in less than two hours, Lindsey. You're pushing it."

"Plenty of time." Ignoring her partner's good-natured grumbling, she opened a tin of pre-sifted flour, measured out ten cups and dumped it into the stainless-steel bowl of the pastry mixer, followed by softened, unsalted butter and salt.

She'd been up to her elbows in flour since three-thirty that morning. Not her usual arrival time, but she'd always found solace in her work. That she needed solace now disturbed her. Almost as much as the dreams that had been invading her sleep recently.

Lindsey didn't usually have nightmares. Not even as a child, back when she'd had plenty to be afraid of. In fact, she normally didn't dream at all. With a fledgling business that kept her busy seven days a week, she usually collapsed into bed and fell into swift unconsciousness and didn't stir until five o'clock the following morning. At least until two nights ago, anyway.

For the second time in as many nights, the unsettling dream had wrenched her from sleep. She'd wakened with a scream in her throat, her heart pounding and her body bathed in cold sweat. It was bad enough waking up terrified, but what disturbed her even more was the fact that she couldn't remember what the nightmare had been about. All she could recall was a man in a red mask and the utter certainty that something unspeakable was about to happen. At two o'clock that morning she'd been so shaken she hadn't been able to get back to sleep. And because she could always find comfort in her work, in baking and creating, Lindsey had showered and driven to Spice of Life and started her day early.

It was a good thing she had. Carissa had arrived at just before seven and both women had worked like mad to finish everything that needed to be done. In just a few hours they had managed to produce enough food for two hundred guests, including two hundred salmon-and-caper canapés, twenty merlot-braised tenderloins, sixteen pounds of angel hair pasta with alfredo sauce, waldorf salad with a cider vinaigrette, two-hundred raspberry mousse tarts, and a wedding cake that rivaled the size of her apartment.

And they still needed two-hundred more canapés.

Lindsey didn't mind the pressure. In fact, she thrived on it. After six years of barely eking by—and several scrapes with closing down shop because of financial problems—Spice of Life Catering was finally profitable. Success, she believed, was right around the corner.

If they managed to pull off this wedding party, she thought.

The cell phone clipped to her belt chirped once. Frowning, Lindsey used her apron to wipe the flour from her right hand and snatched it up. "Spice of Life, this is Lindsey."

"Linds, this is Murph."

"Hi Murph."

Carissa stopped piping filling into the still-warm crusts

and sent her a killing look. Lindsey waved her off and returned her attention to the call. "Are you on your way?"

"That's why I'm calling. Uh, I'm not going to be able to make it in this morning."

Lindsey glanced over at Carissa and shook her head, resisting the urge to snap. "That's too bad. We were counting on you to help us deliver to the Basehart wedding party. We were going to use your van, remember?"

"I'm sorry," he said. "I forgot about that."

Knowing the value of guilt, she let the silence work for a moment.

"I can probably be there in an hour or so," he said reluctantly.

Lindsey sighed in resignation. Dean Murphy was their delivery driver . . . when he decided to show up. She'd hired him two months earlier after meeting his parents at an event she had catered. She'd liked his parents. They were repeat clients and threw hellacious parties. Murph was a good kid, but had proven himself irresponsible. He'd left Lindsey in some tight spots by either being late or calling in sick. In the last few weeks Lindsey and Carissa had fallen to calling him Murphy's Law because every time he was involved something invariably went wrong. This was one of those times.

"That's not going to help us, Murph." Lindsey frowned into the phone and tried to ignore Carissa's silent ranting. "Look, we'll talk about it later. Right now, Carissa and I have to get this food delivered."

"I'm sorry, Linds."

"Yeah, me, too." She disconnected before he could say anything more and frowned down at the two hundred half-formed canapés staring back at her with their impertinent swan faces.

"You're going to have to fire him," Carissa said.

"After I kill him." She looked down at her phone and checked the incoming numbers. "Keep piping."

Carissa hefted the icing dispenser and squeezed salmon-and-caper filling into the tiny crusts. "How we doing on caviar?"

"Got plenty. Filling?"

"Going to be close. What time is it?"

"Eleven fifteen."

"You like to live dangerously, don't you?"

Distracted because she was going to have to figure out how to get all this food across town to the Basehart estate in her Mustang in forty-five minutes, she only gave her phone messages half of her attention as she browsed through her incoming calls. Mrs. Basehart had called twice. No surprise there; the woman was psychotic about details. Her CPA had called, probably about taxes. Her landlord, probably because her lease was up and he wanted to raise her rent. Like she was going to call *him* back. Vaguely annoyed, Lindsey deleted the number. Her finger stilled on the next number. Traci, her younger sister had called from Seattle. Not once, but twice. Lindsey felt a prickle at the back of her neck. Traci rarely called. If not for Lindsey's determination to stay in touch with her sister, they would have fallen out of contact years ago. She wondered what had prompted Traci to break protocol.

Out of nowhere a flash of the nightmare jolted her like a high voltage electrical shock. The man in the mask. The vivid white of exposed flesh. The flittering light of a blade . . .

"Hey, are you okay?"

Lindsey glanced up from her phone to see Carissa staring at her with a concerned expression on her face, and gave herself a hard mental shake. "Yeah, I just . . . zoned out for a second."

"Jeepers, Lindsey, you went sheet white."

"I always do that when Murph calls in sick and we have food for two hundred people to deliver."

Carissa cut her a sharp look. "If I didn't know you so well, I might actually buy that."

Lindsey looked down at the canapé she was working on and inserted the carrot beak, hoping her friend didn't pursue it, knowing she would.

"What's really going on, Linds? You've been preoccupied for two days now. You show up here at three o'clock in the morning looking like you've been up all night. Come on. Spill it."

She shook her head. "Not now."

"Did you have the nightmare again last night?"

Lindsey had mentioned the nightmares to her friend the day before and now wished she hadn't. She didn't want to talk about it. Especially this morning when they didn't have time. Lindsey was a firm believer in the out-of-sight-out-of-mind philosophy. There were a lot of things she didn't talk about. Carissa, on the other hand, liked to analyze things until they died a slow death.

"I'll take that as a yes," Carissa said.

Because she knew she was busted, Lindsey nodded.

"Same thing?"

Lindsey rubbed at her temple and sighed. "It's really weird. I wake up scared. I mean, like really terrified. But for the life of me, I can't remember what the dream was about. It's freaking me out a little."

"You *have* been working pretty hard. You're not getting much sleep. Maybe you're stressed out."

"I'm doing what I love." She shrugged. "I don't feel stressed."

"You look tired."

"That's my I'm-going-to-kill-Murph look."

Carissa snickered. "You know, if the dreams continue, you might want to talk to someone about it. Maybe your subconscious is trying to tell you something."

Putting her hands on her hips, Lindsey frowned at her over the two hundred canapés they had yet to package and deliver. "Right now my subconscious is wondering how the heck we're going to get all this food over to the Basehart's."

"I'm confident you have a plan B."

"It's called scrambling." Lindsey looked at the clock, decided returning her sister's call would have to wait just a little bit longer.

"Oh brother." Carissa shook her head. "Your car or mine?"

"Both," she replied and clipped her phone back onto her belt.

*   *   *

IT WAS NEARLY FOUR P.M. WHEN LINDSEY unlocked the door to her apartment and let herself inside.
Somehow, she and Carissa had managed to pull off mission impossible. They'd prepared and delivered food for
two hundred people in the midst of a snowstorm without
wrecking either of their cars or losing a single canapé.

By God, next year she was going to buy a van and hire
a decent driver.

Kicking off her shoes, she dropped her bag on the console table in the foyer and was working on the hook of
her bra when she spotted the message light on her phone
blinking wildly. Groaning, she tugged her shirt over her
head, stripped off her bra and walked into the bathroom
to start a hot bath. Her back ached. Her feet felt as if
they'd been trampled by a herd of wild elephants. To top
things off, some mean little bastard with a baseball bat
had been hammering at the base of her skull for the last
two hours.

Stepping out of her slacks, she grabbed her terry-cloth
robe off the door and slipped it on. Back in the living
room, she punched the "play" button on her answering
machine and walked into the kitchen for a glass of wine.
From the answering machine, her landlord's voice blared
annoyingly, asking her to return his call. Feeling practical,
Lindsey chose a tall water glass over stemmed crystal and
filled it to the top with a crisp 1994 California sauvignon
blanc.

She'd just taken the first sip when her sister's voice
came over the answering machine. "Lindsey, this is Traci.
Call me. It's important." Click.

Lindsey looked over her shoulder at the answering machine and felt that prickle at the back of her neck again.
Something in her sister's tone wasn't right, she thought.
Puzzled, she put the bottle of wine into the refrigerator,
only half listening as a computerized voice tried to sell
her carpet and upholstery cleaning. Glass in hand, she
padded down the hall to the bathroom, dribbled some es-
sential oils into the water, and turned off the faucet. When
she got back out into the living room, a second message
from Traci was just starting.

"Lindsey, it's Traci. If you're there, pick up. Please. I think I'm . . . in trouble. I need to talk to you." A muttered curse and then an abrupt *click* as the line disconnected.

Lindsey stared down at the answering machine, aware that her heart was pounding. In all the years Traci had been in Seattle—even when she'd first run away at the age of fourteen—Lindsey had never heard her voice quiver like that. The only time she'd ever heard Traci scared was when they'd been children. Back then, they'd both had very good reason to be frightened.

Shoving the thoughts of her childhood to the back of her mind, she snatched up the phone and dialed her sister's number from memory. Four rings and Traci's answering machine picked up. "Hi guys. It's Traci. You know what to do if you want me to call you back." Beep.

Lindsey hesitated an instant before speaking. "Traci, it's Lindsey. If you're there pick up the phone." She paused a moment, aware that her heart was still beating too hard and that it was suddenly vastly important that her sister be there. "I'm at home, Traci. I'll be home all evening. Give me a call, okay, sweetie?"

Lindsey tried to shake off the uneasiness pressing down on her. She told herself it was silly to get herself worked up over a couple of cryptic messages. If anyone knew how to take care of herself, it was Traci. She was self-reliant and independent to a fault. Lindsey supposed it ran in the family, though there were plenty of days when she didn't feel as if she were either of those things.

Realizing she was gripping the phone so hard her knuckles hurt, she replaced the receiver. Knowing Traci, she'd probably get a good laugh out of her overprotective older sister getting worried over nothing. "Give it a rest, Metcalf," she muttered and headed toward the bathroom.

Half a glass of wine and a long soak in a tub full of bubbles, and Lindsey's nerves began to unwind. She was stepping out of the tepid water when the phone trilled. Belting her robe, she bolted out of the bathroom, into the living room and snatched up the phone. "Traci?"

"It's Carissa." Her partner hesitated. "Is everything okay?"

"Oh . . . well . . ." Lindsey sighed. "I'm not sure."

"You sound rattled. What gives?"

She told her about the messages from Traci. "Including the calls she made to my cell phone, that's four calls in one day. It usually takes her a year to call me that many times."

"Maybe she has good news she wants to share with you."

"I don't know, Carissa. She sounded . . . upset. I haven't been able to reach her."

"It's still early in Seattle," Carissa offered. "Maybe she'll call later."

"I hope so."

"Hey, you're really worried, aren't you?"

For the first time, Lindsey realized just how worried she had become. "It's not like her to call four times in one day and leave messages like that. I mean, we may have drifted apart a little bit in the last few years, but I hear something in her voice."

"Maybe she's out with some hunky new boyfriend. Maybe they're holed up in a motel somewhere having mind-blowing sex. Maybe they're—"

"Okay, I get the picture," Lindsey cut in.

"Like you have any idea what it's like to have mind-blowing sex."

"The kind of sex I have is none of your business."

Carissa snickered. "That's because you don't *have* sex, dearie. You give a whole new meaning to the word celibate."

"Maybe I like it that way."

"Maybe that's because you don't remember what an orgasm feels like."

Lindsey sighed, wishing she could dispute her friend's assessment. Not wanting to deal with her lack of a social life, she steered the conversation back to the subject at hand. "You're getting off topic."

"Sorry. Hmmm. Have you tried the restaurant where she works? Do you have phone numbers for any of her neighbors?"

"I'll try the restaurant."

"I'm sure she's all right, Lindsey. You're a mother hen when it comes to your sister. Try not to worry too much, okay? I'm sure she'll call you when she gets in." Carissa hesitated. "You got anything to help you sleep?"

Lindsey thought about the dreams and felt an unusual moment of anxiety. "I've got some Tylenol P.M."

"Not my first choice, but it'll do in a pinch. Take two with a glass of milk and find something boring to read. No slasher movies tonight, kiddo."

Lindsey jolted when images of the nightmare flashed in her mind's eye. She saw emotionless eyes within a red mask. The flicker of something cruel in those eyes. The smell of fear mingling with the stench of blood . . .

A chill rippled through her with such force that she had to set her glass on the counter. The wine turned to acid in her stomach. Jesus. Maybe she was coming down with something.

"If you want to find out why you're dreaming," Carissa said, "I know a good dream interpreter."

"I think I'll stick with the Tylenol."

Carissa huffed. "You're such a skeptic."

"Pragmatist." Lindsey rubbed at her temple. Carissa might believe in all that New Age mumbo jumbo, but Lindsey was far too grounded in reality to put any faith in hocus pocus. "Thanks for checking on me."

"Oh, I almost forgot. The reason I called. Mrs. Basehart was thrilled with the food. Loved the canapé art. Said her guests raved. We may have picked up a couple more clients. Says she's sending a bonus with the check."

Lindsey smiled, but the good news did little to untie the knot in her stomach. "Thanks for the good news. If all goes well, I'm going to buy a van next year."

"And fire Murph."

"After I kill him."

Carissa chuckled. "I'll believe it when I see it. See you tomorrow."

Lindsey disconnected, then glanced down at her answering machine and frowned. She pressed the "play" button and listened to Traci's messages again. By the time she'd listened a third time there was no doubt in her mind that Traci was at the very least upset. At the very worst frightened. The question was why? And why hadn't she called back?